Sanguinity Point

Peter Palmieri

Sanguinity Point

ISBN: 9781973537236

Sanguinity Point

Dedication:

For Emma

This book is a work of fiction. Any perceived similarity to actual people or events is completely coincidental.

Midway upon the journey of our life

I found myself within a forest dark,

For the straightforward pathway had been lost

Dante Alighieri, Inferno Canto I

1

For a brief moment, just twelve minutes before he'd become an accessory to murder, Dr. Benjamin Snow had nearly persuaded himself that he was no longer an outsider. In the neon haze of the nurses' station of the Pediatric Intensive Care Unit, he thought he had at long last found, not just a refuge, but the place where he belonged.

Sitting next to him, Pork Chop Malloy peeled the paper wrapper off of a tongue depressor, split the wooden blade in half to create jagged edges, and used one of the splintered ends to dig under the nails of his stubby fingers.

"No kidding?" Malloy said. "That was your first one?"

"First one by myself," Benjamin said. "I've assisted on a couple."

"Well blow me down Olive Oil!" Malloy said. "I just helped deflower the enigmatic Dr. Snow White. Know what that means?" Benjamin shook his head. "It means you're the only Peds Resident in the hallowed halls of Houston Children's that can slip a sub-clavian line in a kid without bleeding it half to death."

That was as close to a compliment the second-year Critical Care Fellow had ever bestowed on a Resident and it was enough to make Benjamin blush. Comradeship can be an acceptable substitute for friendship when one has no friends, even more so in times of war. And for Benjamin this residency had certainly been a war — a war of attrition he had managed to survive on his own terms. The other residents, that band of grovelling sycophants, young men and women bereft of substance, with their snazzy clothes and dippy minds, whose depth of medical knowledge was as shallow as the abstract section of the journal articles they scanned, skated their way through the various rotations by cozying up to their attending physicians, somehow always managing to pluck a suitable comment from their boiler plate arsenal of cliches, always flashing the correct expression to alternately feign interest or compassion, as the situation demanded. As a rule, Benjamin struggled to find the right words. His usual facial expression, lips pressed together, eyes vacant as he focused on the problem at hand, was easy to misinterpret as aloofness, disinterest or something more sinister. Benjamin knew he put most of his attendings on edge, not because he challenged them or defied their authority, but perhaps because they sensed there was something deep and dark lurking under the still surface of his reticence, an idea that Benjamin found both frustrating and amusing.

He told himself he didn't care. His objectives were not those of his peers. And he had long become accustomed to being an outcast. But he found himself enjoying this moment with Pork Chop Malloy, a fellow warrior he'd somehow stumbled upon in the smoky haze of the battlefield. He could almost smell the acrid smoke now, feel the glowing warmth of an imaginary campfire where the two sat triumphantly — Benjamin having survived his baptism of fire; Pork Chop, his gruff lieutenant, branding him a warrior with a mark of blood.

The moment was fleeting. A nurse in pale blue scrubs, "Donna Hill, R.N." embroidered in pink thread over her breast pocket, trudged into the nurses' station, her shoulders sagging. She leaned with one hand onto the counter, pressed her eyes shut and kneaded her temple with her thumb. Pork Chop craned his neck to ogle her cleavage, then glanced at Benjamin, gave a quick jerk of his head in Donna's direction and stretched his lips in a smirk.

"Malloy," Donna said, her eyes wide open now, "you gotta do something about the father in six-oh-two."

Malloy tilted his head and said, "What seems to be the problem, toots?" pulling off a surprisingly good Humphrey Bogart impersonation.

"Okay, so all week I put up with the crucifixes, the prayer beads, the postcards of Mary and Joseph and the apostles plastered all over the place. But now he's rubbing his son in some kind of embalming oil."

"You mean, anointing oil," Malloy said.

"Same difference," the nurse said. She curled her lower lip. "The man is so damn creepy. For the last hour he's been standing bed-side, rocking back and forth, mumbling all this mumbo-jumbo in his strange language."

"Spanish?" Malloy said.

"Not the kind of Spanish *I'm* used to hearing," she said. "And now, the oil rub-down. Are you kidding me?"

Malloy turned to Benjamin. "What's the story with six-oh-two? You know him?"

Benjamin said, "Yeah, I'm following him." He cleared his throat as he always did when he was about to present a case history and Malloy must have picked up on the mannerism because he interrupted Benjamin before the first word came out.

"The Cliff Note version, ace. Don't give me War and Peace."

Benjamin was caught off stride. He tried to gather his thoughts while Donna flashed him a get-on-with-it look. "Three-year-old Hispanic male," Benjamin started, "traumatic brain injury, cerebral blood flow studies show-"

"Wait, let me guess," Malloy said. "The kid's brain-dead." Benjamin nodded. "A Mitchell patient?"

"How'd you know?" Benjamin said.

"What's the legal angle?" Malloy asked.

"Legal angle?" Benjamin said. "I'm not sure what you mean."

"When the chief starts tilling the vegetable garden, there's always a legal angle. Dad's not in jail, so how'd the kid get jelly-for-brains?"

"Mom's boyfriend beat him up," Benjamin said. "The parents are separated."

"Well, ain't life a bowl of alphabet soup," Malloy said. He studied the tongue depressor he'd been cleaning his fingernails with, brought it to his nose and gave it a whiff before tossing it in a trash bin. "So, who called the full-court press?"

Benjamin furrowed his brow. "Mom is pretty distraught. She doesn't want to withdraw support. Said she'd get a court-order to keep life-support going."

"She won't need no court order," Malloy said. "Mitchell will keep the kid plugged in. He'll also fold her laundry and wash her windows if that's what it takes to avoid a media blitz. This thing has circus written all over it."

Donna placed her arms akimbo and thrust out her chest. She said, "So what are you going to do about this dad, Malloy?"

"Nothing. Absolutely nothing. The poor bastard is saying good-bye to his kid," Malloy said.

"In some cultures, family members anoint their loved ones as an act of purification," Benjamin said.

The nurse ignored him.

"Exactly. That's it," Malloy said. "It's all about the purification, baby."

"It smells," Donna said.

"Everything here smells, my dear," Malloy said, switching back to his Bogey voice. "The urine, the stool, the blood, the people. It all smells to high heaven I tell ya."

"He was going to light a prayer candle," Donna said.

"Well, don't let him do that, toots. What with all the oxygen we're pumping in there, it's liable to blow us all to the day-after-tomorrow," Malloy said. "Tell you what, if something *medical* happens to the kid, just whistle. You do know how to whistle, don't you? You just put your lips together and blow." He turned to Benjamin. "*Como se dice* 'blow' *en Espanol*?"

The nurse glared at Malloy. She removed her hands from her hips, loosened the bow of her scrub pants, tightened the cord in a snug new knot and slogged out of the nurses' station without uttering another word.

Malloy curled his lips and said, "Of all the gin joints, in all the towns, in all the world…"

Benjamin managed a weak smile before turning his gaze to the floor and shifting in his seat.

"Look, Snow, if you can't stomach a few kids dying from time to time, you're just not cut out for this line of work," Malloy said. "You're better off getting out now. Join a practice in the 'burbs. Treat the odd diaper rash, tell cute neurotic moms when they should introduce solid foods, and still find time to shoot the back nine at the country club Wednesday afternoons."

"No way, man," Benjamin said. "I'm going critical care all the way."

"Then indulge me a moment, if you don't mind me asking," Malloy said. "What the hell's your major malfunction?"

"What?" Benjamin chuckled but felt himself blushing again. "What do you mean?"

"Don't get me wrong. We all have a major malfunction. Hell, I have at least a dozen. What I mean is, here you are, you got brains, you got skills — Christ, you even got some heart by the sound of it. And your looks are utterly unfair for the rest of us mortal slobs. Hell, if I was queer I'd do you in a heart-beat." Benjamin laughed. "Which I'm not," Malloy continued. "So don't come sneaking in my call room tonight. The thing is, you got the whole package, you know what I mean? You should be the golden boy of this program. So why didn't Mitchell pick you for Chief Resident?"

"I don't want to be Chief Resident," Benjamin said. "I'm starting my critical care fellowship in July."

"That's not what I asked," Malloy said. "Why the hell didn't he *pick* you? Are you some kind of ax-murderer? Or did he catch you in his grand-daughter's knickers? You tell *me*. I can't figure it out."

Benjamin felt a trickle of perspiration forming just below his hair line. He was relieved to see nurse Donna storm back into the nurses' station.

"Now he wants to talk to the doctor in charge," she said.

Malloy turned to Benjamin and said, "Did you hear that, Dr. Snow? The father of your patient in six-oh-two would like to have a word with you."

"I'm not the doctor in charge," Benjamin said.

"Why, how true. As the critical care fellow, I outrank you. But as it so happens, it's T-minus-fifteen minutes to Adult Swim on Cartoon Network and I have to stop by to see Mildred first."

"What? Who's Mildred?" Benjamin said.

"Mildred," Malloy said in an incredulous tone. "The brisket lady at the cafeteria. How do you even stay alive?"

"Guys!" Donna said, cranking her thumb like a hitch-hiker, pumping it in the direction of room six-oh-two. "Tonight!" She rounded the curve of the counter and plopped down in front of a computer terminal, tapping her password on the keyboard with more force than necessary.

"Look, I don't know what to tell this father," Benjamin said in a hushed voice.

Malloy slowly rose, and reached up to adjust the collar of his white coat. Benjamin shot to his feet in reflexive deference. The Fellow frowned and took a step back.

"Listen, Snow," Malloy said. I don't talk to family members when I'm on call, okay? That's *your* job. But since I'm in a charitable mood, I'll give you the best advice you ever heard." Malloy stepped in closer now. "For starters, when it comes to talking to parents, be sure to never say anything concrete. You know what I mean? Don't ever paint yourself in a corner. And never,

ever forget Malloy's golden rule of communication."

"Which is?"

"Platitude..." Pork Chop Malloy waved his right hand through the air like a birthday party magician, "is the attitude."

"Platitude is the attitude?" Benjamin said.

"That's right. Platitude *is* the attitude. Let me give you some examples: God works in mysterious ways, okay? The kid's off to a better place. Haven't you ever watched Oprah? You gotta tap into the cultural kitsch. The key is to use phrases — cliches are always good — that don't actually communicate any information. Jesus! and the last thing you want to do is to try to educate. So don't give them anything that will make them think. Family members don't want that. They never remember anything of substance anyway, or nine times out of ten they get it all wrong. But they sure as hell remember the tone of your voice, so watch out for that. What they really want, what they expect of you, is to fulfill a social function, like saying, 'Good morning', 'Have a nice day', 'How about this weather we're having?' So later they can tell everyone that will listen to them that they talked to the doctor, don't you know, and the doctor said Johnny's off to a better place. Boy, the Lord sure works in mysterious ways!"

"Platitude is the attitude," Benjamin repeated.

Malloy gave Benjamin a slap on the cheek, meant to be playful, no doubt, but the force was poorly measured and Benjamin felt more than just a sting. "You got it, ace," Malloy said. "Say anything you can come up with that is so blatantly false yet so cliche' that it carries the ring of truth. And remember, platitudes are like bit Bitcoins: they're the new currency of communication." Malloy cocked his head in mock surprise. "Boy that sounded good. I better write that one down."

Benjamin rubbed his sweaty palms together. Something wasn't right. He was trying to listen to Malloy while in his mind he played back Donna Hill's words — words which now seemed to carry a solemn heaviness, words that resonated in Benjamin's ears like the muffled thud of a falling boulder.

Benjamin did not believe in intuition but he was sure getting a queasy feeling. Something wasn't right. In high school he had been able to look at an algebraic equation and sense that it was unsolvable even before going through the required steps. There was something unsolvable about this situation. Benjamin considered the possibilities: unaccounted variables everyone was ignoring, undefined numbers in the denominator…

Malloy said, "You're in charge, Snow. This is your moment. You want to do critical care? Do it right now. Just don't put any babies in body bags while I'm gone. *Comprende*?"

Benjamin nodded. "No problem, I can do this."

"That's right. Just relax, walk out there like you own the place and do a Fred Flintstone."

"A Fred Flintsone?" Benjamin said.

Malloy smiled. "Just Yabba-dabba-do-it, baby." He headed toward the exit, turned to do an imitation of Fred Flintsone driving away in his floor-less car, and left the unit.

Benjamin stood there a moment, shaking his head. He ambled next to Donna, hoping something she might say would bring clarity, or at least a sense of reassurance that his misgivings were out of place. He waited stiffly as she ignored him, and finally asked her, "What is it with Pork Chop and cartoons?"

The nurse shrugged. "He's an asshole."

The intensive care unit reminded Benjamin of a corny museum exhibit from his youth where, in an alcove behind a glass barrier, a group of wild-eyed Neanderthals made of wax remained frozen in time, spears in hand, eternally hunting a very pissed off woolly mammoth, while off in another corner, a group of decidedly more domestic early humans sat around a campfire and fashioned stone tools to their own utter amazement. Each room of the PICU had a glass partition you could peer through to spy inside, each room depicting a scene for Benjamin to study, to learn from, to categorize with a diagnosis, prognosis and treatment plan. But unlike that old museum, the scenes here would change from day to day, the characters switched out with stunning regularity. Proof that there was an infinite supply of pain and suffering in the outside world.

Benjamin looked through the glass showcase of six-oh-two. The lights inside were dimmed but he could make out the silhouette of a slight man standing by the bedside. He wondered what lesson this exhibit had in store for him. He pushed on the sliding glass door and stepped inside.

The man turned with a jerk, startled by Benjamin's entrance. "You the doctor in charge?" he asked.

He had large dark eyes that jutted out. The rest of his facial features appeared to have been lifted straight out of Mayan petroglyphs. His shiny black hair was braided into a ropy pony-tail that reached down to just above his waist. Droplets of perspiration covered the cinnamon complexion of his stony brow, and that alone should have alerted Benjamin that something was amiss. That and the fact that the guy was wearing one of those tan, duck-bomber jackets construction workers and cowboys favor during North Texas winters. This was Houston, oppressively hot and muggy in early June.

But Benjamin was too preoccupied with remembering his hastily rigged script to bother with what was happening around him. "Poor situational awareness," the report commissioned by the hospital's ad hoc investigative body would later read, "was a significant contributing factor to the events of June the eleventh."

Benjamin stood tall, flashed the empathetic smile a medical school classmate had recommended he practice in front of the bathroom mirror and said, "I'm Dr. Snow."

"You in charge?" the man said.

"I'm the senior doctor here," Benjamin said. It wasn't really a lie. Since Malloy had slipped out, Benjamin was also the only doctor in the unit.

"No more," the man in the pony tail said. He had a thick guttural accent and spoke in a timbre that was hard to perceive in the din of monitors and alarms.

"I'm sorry?" Benjamin said.

"*No mas.* Please, no more."

No more what? Benjamin wondered, and continued repeating the question to himself even as the man reached into his jacket, fumbled for a moment, and pulled out a stubby pistol which he lifted nonchalantly and pointed at Benjamin's chest. For a few seconds, Benjamin's brain was numbed by puzzlement, his neural circuits scrambling to try to make sense of what was happening. Then the gush of adrenaline hit him.

Fears may germinate at any age, but the seeds of raw terror are sown in childhood. And the sight of the gun hovering near his chest roused dark specters from a sooty corner of Benjamin's memory. A familiar heaviness swelled in his chest, spread to his arms and legs, pinning him to the patch of linoleum on which he was standing.

"*No mas,*" the man repeated.

"*No mas,* what?" Benjamin asked. He struggled to get the words out.

"What you're doing to my boy," the man said. "Please, no more. Everything off. Enough."

"Oh, I can't do that."

"You're in charge," the man said.

"I'm just the doctor in charge right here-" Benjamin's voice cracked. He swallowed hard. "Just in charge right now. I would need to call-" He froze, unable to get another word out. The man had pressed the tip of the gun's barrel on his chest. Benjamin felt an electric charge spreading from the point of contact on his sternum, around his torso and up the back of his neck where the hairs stiffened and stood up. Benjamin slowly raised his hands above his head and felt utter self-contempt for doing so. If there were any lingering doubts, he had just proved to himself that he was just as weak, just as cowardly as he had been on that torrid afternoon, so many years ago.

Like that child, that former self he thought he had outgrown and shed like molten skin, he wanted it all to just stop, to go away. He wondered what he could say to make the man put the gun away, to walk out of the unit as though nothing had happened. His mind was a void. Which was just as well, for even if had had come up with the appropriate words, he was, by now, far too breathless to mutter anything coherent.

Donna Hill marched into the room, turned on the overhead light and was striding to the bedside when she did a double-take. The plastic IV-bag she was carrying flew out of her hands like a wet fish as her whole body recoiled.

"Oh, shit," she said, but as soon as the words were out, she seemed to regain her composure, if not her nervy attitude.

The father turned his attention to her but kept the gun pointed at Benjamin's chest. "Lady, you help," he said.

Benjamin lowered his hands slowly and let them settle by his thighs, embarrassed by the fact that Donna seemed far less affected by the sight of the handgun than he was. He half expected the man to wave the pistol at him to keep his hands up, the way bad guys are apt to do in the movies. That didn't happen.

"What the hell is going on here?" Donna asked.

The father gave Benjamin a nod.

Benjamin said, "Uhm, we're taking Anselmo here off of life-support, it seems." Benjamin said.

Donna's eyes narrowed. She shook her head. "The hell we are!"

"You do it," the man said, "or I shoot the doctor."

"Come on, man…" Benjamin said.

"Shoot him!" Donna said. "What do I care? I'm not losing my job over this."

The man took the gun off Benjamin's chest. Benjamin exhaled slowly, let his eyes close. His relief was short-lived. The next moment he felt the cold metal press against his forehead. Somehow, it brought on a ringing in the ears.

"I kill him," the man said. "I kill him right now." His voice was steady, dispassionate, eerily resolute.

Someone outside the room shrieked. Another voice said, "Oh my god!"

Donna said, "OK, fine. You win. Let's do this. Just put the damn gun down already."

Benjamin could have kissed her. "Yeah, let's do this," he whimpered.

It's surprising how quickly a central line, an endotracheal tube and a Foley catheter can be removed from a child's body when someone's got a gun pointed at you — even when your fingers are trembling. The operation hit a snag when the boy's father insisted Benjamin remove the bolt that measured intra-cranial pressure from the boy's head. Benjamin confessed, with unabashed candor, that he didn't have an inkling as to how to do that, the pretense of acting like the doctor in charge having fully dissipated by now. He was still trying to explain to the father that the instrument did nothing to keep the child alive when Donna leaned in with over-sized shears and clipped the connecting cables snaking out from the heavy dressing on the child's head.

"There!" she said.

By now, a small crowd had gathered on the other side of glass partition, nurses and unit secretaries, partly shielded on either side of the room's border, a head or two bobbing into view every so often. Benjamin caught a glimpse of a very pale Pork Chop Malloy standing several feet behind the sliding glass door, his jowls slackened, his unbuttoned white smock drooping on his frame like a wrinkled shroud. Behind Malloy, a hospital security guard was prancing his way toward the sliding door, one hand unbuckling the black leather holster on his belt.

Benjamin's muscles tightened. He yelled at the guard, "Stop right there! Get the hell out of the unit. I mean it."

The last thing he needed was to be caught in the crossfire of a shootout between two men who didn't seem to have particular aptitude in the use of firearms. The security guard froze in mid-step in a floundering half-crouch, then straightened, stiffly took a couple of backward steps, his facial expression flitting between perplexity and disappointment, before settling into a grimace of indignation. The guard finally turned and headed for the exit of the Intensive Care Unit, cocking his head to talk into his shoulder-mounted radio on the way out.

The boy's father nodded his head, a gesture that made Benjamin feel that he might have crossed a fateful line: that he was now no longer a hostage but a willing accomplice.

With some haste in his movements now, the boy's father took a seat on a plastic-lined recliner, gun still in hand. Benjamin approached the padded hospital bed, slipped his arms under its tiny occupant and lifted the body of the child straight up, but the boy's midsection folded and drooped between Benjamin's arms, sliding back onto the mattress. He adjusted his grasp, clasping the bruised swollen flesh, palpating it with his fingertips, at once getting a better grip while searching for a quiver of life. He lifted the tiny body again, brought it up high, secured it at the level of his breast, then turned, stooped down and carefully placed it on the lap of the father. The man cradled his son and nonchalantly pointed the barrel of the gun in the direction of a chair across from him. It came off as an inviting gesture, as if he were lifting a glass of wine for a toast. He said, "You sit there." Then he glanced at Donna and, with a nerve-jarring wave of the pistol, said, "You go."

Donna walked towards the open doorway, stopped, turned, and folded her arms as she squared her body into an open foot stance. "No. I stay. Anselmo is my patient."

The father seemed to consider this for a

moment. He looked down at his son as if he were seeking the boy's counsel. He nodded. "*Esta bien.* You stay there." The coarse features of the man's face softened, the corners of his mouth tugged down on his lips as he scanned the boy's still form, as if searching for a sign: the slightest movement, even an agonal gasp of breath. There was nothing. He whispered something unintelligible, then cleared his throat.

"I know his soul want to go," the man said. "It is waiting to go on the long voyage, farther than the stars." The man set his gun on a cluttered bedside table and began to comb the boy's hair with his slender, calloused fingers. "No man must to see his little boy die." His voice caught on the last syllable. He pressed his full lips together as if trying to hold something from gushing out. And then he began to sing what sounded like a lullaby, and as he sang his eyes drooped heavily as though he were entering some kind of a trance.

Benjamin looked at the pistol lying on the table just a few short feet away from him. Maybe it wasn't too late. With a lunge he'd be able to grab the gun and turn the tables on the father. There might still be time to intubate the kid, get him back on life-support before the electrical activity of his little heart extinguished — still time to save the life of a brain-dead child.

Benjamin's head began to throb. Deep in his ears he heard the pounding of his own heart growing louder with each beat, the sounds around him muffled by the steady, rippling cadence of his pulse. He glanced at Donna. Her body was swaying to the rhythm of the lullaby. Tears trickled down her cheeks.

For some reason, this steeped in Benjamin an odd sense of relief, as though she too had sanctioned a kind of tacit acquiescence. There was nothing to do now but wait. Hadn't that been his only option all along?

By now, what seemed like an eternity had passed since the boy's last mechanically generated breath. The boy's chest was stubbornly still, his skin the color of unpolished marble. The father stopped singing. He gave the boy a flit. A more forceful shudder. He raised his blood-shot eyes to look at Benjamin.

Quietly, Benjamin got to his feet, slipped his stethoscope on and stooped to listen to the boy's chest. He moved the diaphragm of the stethoscope over the areas of the tiny chest that corresponded to the mitral valve, the aortic valve, the pulmonic, in the disciplined routine he had employed since his second year of medical school, knowing there was nothing to listen to.

He removed the eartips of the stethoscope from his ears, looked at the father and shook his head, hoping the gesture didn't come off as too corny. The father nodded. The man lifted and turned the tiny corpse so that the boy's head was on his shoulder. He said to Benjamin, "Please, sit."

Benjamin shuffled and settled heavily in the chair. The father waited for Benjamin to be seated, then shifted his weight in the recliner. Benjamin got the sense that he was getting ready to get up and leave and take the boy's body with him. He thought, *oh no, you can't do that,* but said nothing. The father reached for the gun and Benjamin opened his mouth to reason with the man, but before he could utter a syllable the father spoke.

"*Jach Dyos b'o'otik.*"

"I'm sorry?" Benjamin said.

The father's eyes gleamed. A smooth coolness spread over his face. Benjamin was utterly spooked.

"I… I didn't get what you said," Benjamin said.

The man smiled. "*Jach Dyos b'o'otik,*" he repeated. He raised the gun, sealed his lips around its greasy muzzle as if he were trying to suckle from an over-sized straw. A second later, a starburst of blood and tissue splattered on the wall behind him.

Benjamin flinched at the sound of the gunshot. He stared at the crimson blotch oozing down the wall and the oddest memory flickered to life for the first time in many years: the vision of a frazzled Mr. McNulty, his grandparents' next door neighbor, plodding up the walkway of his best friend's house with a roll of wallpaper under his arm.

2

"I brought you some coffee."

The man entered the narrow room where Benjamin had been sitting for the better part of two hours, a paper cup in each hand, a bulky manila envelope tucked in one armpit, the faint smile appearing out of place on his hardened face, as if painted on in pale watercolors. Everything about the man, the stocky forearms, the closely-cropped gray hair, the crisp white shirt and thin black tie, screamed former military.

Benjamin said, "Are you supposed to be the *good* cop?"

The man chuckled. "Detective Glenn Krikorian, Houston PD, Investigative First Responder Division." He set the cups on an end table and extended his broad hand, waiting patiently until Benjamin grasped it half-heartedly, then sat on the sofa opposite to him, dropping the manila envelope on his lap. "I added cream and sugar. Couldn't find a stirrer but a nurse gave me a tongue depressor of all things."

"Look, I already answered a bunch of questions," Benjamin said.

"Sargent Hirsch said you were very cooperative."

"And now I need to get back to work."

"Looks like they've got that covered. We finish up here and you can go home, get some rest."

"Damn it!" Benjamin whispered. He had never asked for help in covering a shift, never once called in sick in three years. Even made rounds pushing his own IV pole with a bag of normal saline as a second-year resident (to the utter horror of the head of the infection control department) when he picked up a stomach bug and spent most of the early morning hours kneeling in front of the toilet, still dry-heaving well after his stomach had been reduced to the size of a dried prune.

"It's been a hell of a night for you," Krikorian said. Benjamin didn't respond. The detective shook his head, exhaled through his nose. He placed a hand on the manila envelope, hesitated a moment, then lifted it and let it plop on the center of the end table. It landed with a surprisingly loud thud. "Cops and doctors… Cops and doctors, we have a lot in common, we do. The long hours, what the public expects of us. You might say we're made of the same cloth."

"But I don't see a tongue depressor in your cup," Benjamin said.

"Sorry?"

"Would you have put cream and sugar in a cop's coffee?"

This time Krikorian's smile flashed bright, complete with crow feet that deepened around the detective's eyes.

"I'm not here to bullshit you, Dr. Snow. Just need to clear up a couple of points so we can put this sordid matter to rest."

"That easy," Benjamin said with unveiled sarcasm in his tone. "We chit chat and go home. Forget about the whole damn thing."

"From a criminal point of view, yes."

That one word was so crisp and clear that it reverberated in Benjamin's ears for a few moments. Krikorian seemed to relish the ensuing silence. The detective was staring him down as if to see if he had made his point. He had. *Good cop my ass!*

Benjamin suddenly had an urge to take a sip of that damn coffee, see if it might dampen the echo of that word still bouncing around inside his skull, but he wasn't sure whether his hand would be steady enough to grasp the cup without spilling. He brought his hands together between his knees and interlocked his fingers. "Like I said, I answered all the… what is it you want to know exactly?"

"I hate to burden you with this after what you've been through, but some of the witnesses reported that, well, in their estimation, you might have done more to avert the outcome. They wondered aloud, speculated the point, you might say — and I want to stress this is their opinion, not mine — why it was you offered so little resistance."

"I had a gun pointed to my head," Benjamin said.

"And therein lies the problem, I think. You see, not everyone saw the whole event as it unfolded, so we're getting conflicting accounts. But the nurse, Donna Hill, she was able to corroborate that part of your story."

"*My* story?"

"Some witnesses report that you ordered the armed security guard to leave the unit when Mr. Tepal, the deceased, was distracted and vulnerable to a counteroffensive."

"Counteroffensive? Seriously? Did you get a good luck at that security guard?" Benjamin asked.

Krikorian nodded. "Reminded me of Barney Fife on the old Andy Griffith show. Oh, you're probably too young."

"You think I was some kind of a silent accomplice?"

"Not at all," the cop said. He paused, furrowed his brow. "You ever hear of the Stockholm syndrome?"

"Give me a break."

"What a question! You're a medical doctor. You probably learned about it at some point in your training. Anyway, my personal opinion? The phenomenon is rare. Extremely rare, if it even exists at all. But maybe… is it possible that you empathized with Mr. Tepal on some level? I mean, the poor man after all, his kid is on life support, no chance of a recovery, kept in limbo by a callous medical establishment."

"Dr. Mitchell wants a full-court press? Hell, I'll do everything I can to keep the kid alive," Benjamin said.

"Really."

Benjamin reached for the coffee. He was pissed now. The questions were venturing into the ridiculous. He took a sip and put the cup back down.

"I guess you had no choice but submit to authority," Krikorian said. There was a lofty, knowing tone to the detective's voice, vague and probing in the same breath. "When Mr. Tepal set the gun down on the table, and his arms were occupied with the body of his son, did you feel that you had an opportunity to disarm him?"

"No," Benjamin said flatly.

"Not a chance at all?"

"I was too far."

"Look," Krikorian opened the manila envelope, reached in and pulled out a hand gun, a stubby little piece with a deep gash in the metal above its grip. "If you're wondering, yeah this is the gun. And no, it's not loaded." Krikorian placed the gun on the table, next to Benjamin's cup of coffee. Benjamin sat still, staring at it, wondering if the cop could see how his arms were quaking. "Pretend you're the father. You're holding a child in your arms, now reach down and pick up the gun as fast as you can."

"You want to get my fingerprints on the gun," Benjamin said. He raised his eyes just to avoid having to look at the pistol.

Krikorian looked confused. "Gun's already been dusted and processed. Anyway, now it has *my* fingerprints all over it. If it makes you feel better we can wipe it clean when we're done."

"What are you trying to prove?"

"Just pick up the gun. Reach over, pick it up."

"Why should I?"

"I want to see something. Satisfy my curiosity."

"Too bad."

"Come on, Dr. Snow. Pick it up."

"Won't happen."

"Benjamin, grab it! Now!"

"I don't want to," Benjamin shouted. He hardly recognized his own voice, the peal of vulnerability ringing out, a childlike frailness coming through which made his own ears perk up.

Krikorian straightened his back. "It's not that you don't want to." He paused, pressed his thin lips together. "It's that you can't. You simply can't do it."

"What do you want from me?"

"I've seen it before," Krikorian said. "Some people call it hoplophobia. You heard of it?"

"What?"

"Hoplophobia. A morbid fear of firearms. It's not a real medical diagnosis. But I can see the sweat beading on your forehead just as I mention the word. It's nothing to be ashamed of. What you have is a paralyzing fear of guns along with a near-pathologic impulse to submit to authority."

"Are you my shrink now?"

"Dr. Snow, before tonight, had you ever witnessed a violent crime?"

"No," Benjamin said.

"A murder, a suicide, perhaps a violent accident that resulted in the loss of life?"

"No."

"Never?" Krikorian said,eyebrows raised.

"Never."

"Huh. What about Toby McNulty?" Benjamin felt the blood drain from his face. Krikorian puckered his lips. "What do you know, Dr. Snow? I *am* a good cop after all, in case you're still wondering, and not because I fetched you coffee. I do my homework, look things up. I make no assumptions and I don' jump to conclusions until I've done my due diligence. That behavior pattern sound familiar? The wife says I'm obsessive-compulsive. I guess guys like us are misunderstood. See, the thing about kids your age, you grew up in the electronic era. It's not that hard to look up your past. The good folks at Naperville P.D. were pretty accommodating in responding to my query — downright congenial in fact." Krikorian took a sip of his coffee with a loud slurp, swallowed with an expression bordering on pain, took one more sip and set the cup down. "That's right outside of Chicago, Naperville, isn't it?"

"I didn't witness anything," Benjamin said. "That was your question."

"But you're the one who called 911. How'd you know to call?"

"I heard the gun shot."

"And you were at his house that day."

"I left before it happened."

"That's what I find odd. Usually in these situations a kid pulls out his father's gun to impress a friend. Strange that it happened when he was home alone, don't you think?" Krikorian reached back and rubbed the nape of his neck. "Were you close?"

"We lived next doors to each other. That's how I heard the gunshot."

"I mean, as friends."

Benjamin tried to steady his voice. "We played soccer." Krikorian looked on impassively. He was biding his time. Giving Benjamin the time to be straight with him. "He was my best friend."

Krikorian nodded solemnly. Benjamin couldn't deny that there was a guileless sincerity glistening in the cop's pale eyes.

"Well, I spoke to the deputy who was first on the scene. Still on the force after all these years, can you believe it? Anyway, he's still convinced you were there when it happened. You got scared maybe, didn't know what to do, didn't want to get in trouble, so you slipped home, thought about it a little, then called 911 from your kitchen phone."

"I was cleared, never even investigated."

"And that was a good call," Krikorian said. "I mean, what would have been the point? One young life lost, why ruin another?"

"It was an accident. Everyone said so."

"No doubt."

"So why the hell did you bring it up? What does it have to do with anything?"

Krikorian frowned. "You see," he said, after a moment's hesitation, "Every case I investigate, there's always one essential question that just begs to be answered. If I can nail down that question then, well, I get the feeling I'm looking at things from the right angle." He narrowed his eyes as though he were considering something, then shrugged. "I just had to satisfy myself," Krikorian said. He reached for the gun lying on the table, slipped it back in the manila envelope and said, "Need a ride home?"

3

Ten days had gone by since the incident. Ten days Benjamin passed at home, the curtains of his apartment windows drawn to avoid the sight of the news van parked across the street. Ten days of not answering phone calls from unknown numbers, of deleting unsolicited e-mails from media outlets throughout the country, of avoiding the social media onslaught that swelled like a tsunami. When on the third day, a local news reporter with a salacious shade of red lipstick had referred to him as, "Young Doctor Death" he unplugged his television set and spent the rest of the evening sitting in the dark, his eyes fiery from the lack of sleep.

At the age of ten, Benjamin Snow attended the funeral of Toby McNulty. Since that day, the smell of fresh-cut flowers instantly evoked in him thoughts of impending doom. And on this eleventh day, on the morning he was summoned to Dr. Joel Shapiro's office, what jarred him was not the Channel 5 reporter in high heels and tight skirt tailing him clumsily across the hospital's parking lot, camera-man in tow, not the doe-eyed stares of doctors and nurses in the polished marble lobby, but the soft fragrance of a bouquet of daisies wrapped in cellophane tucked in the plump, hairy hands of an oblivious delivery man. By the time he reached the bank of elevators off a side hallway, Benjamin's hands trembled so fiercely, he had trouble pressing the call button.

Joel Shapiro's office was unusually tidy for an academic physician. The only exception being a mess of finger-paint art adorning a single wall — far too many drawings to tack side-by-side on the over-sized cork-board.

"How are you holding up?" Dr. Shapiro asked Benjamin as he guided him to an armchair.

"Feels like I'm under house arrest," Benjamin said.

"You're not being punished. You were absolved of any criminal wrong-doing."

The word "criminal" seemed to resonate again, its sound loitering annoyingly in Benjamin's auditory cortex.

"So when can I come back to work?" Benjamin said.

"What's wrong with a little time off? Your call slots have been filled for the rest of the month and you still get full credit for the rotation. Relax. We'll see you in a couple of weeks at graduation," Shapiro said.

"It's my ICU elective," Benjamin said. "I need to get all the experience I can before I start my fellowship July first."

Dr. Shapiro scratched his chin with the back of his fingertips, his face scrunched up in an awkward grimace. "Do you really think that's a good idea?"

"I'm ready to come back," Benjamin said.

"I wasn't talking about finishing your rotation," Shapiro said. "I meant the fellowship."

"Are you kidding?" Benjamin said. "This fellowship is what I've always wanted."

"But after what's happened…"

"There's no way I'm backing out now," Benjamin said. "Nothing's changed as far as I'm concerned."

Dr. Shapiro brought his palms together as if in prayer and exhaled slowly. He straightened in his chair. "Benjamin, I've been at this institution for nearly a quarter of a century. I've lost track of how many residents I've served as an academic advisor, how many fires I've had to put out over that time. But this…" He drummed his fingers on his desk. "This is the single hardest thing I've ever had to do."

Benjamin fluttered his eyes. "What's going on?"

"You don't have to back out of your fellowship," Shapiro said.

"I don't intend to."

"Dr. Mitchell already gave your spot to another candidate."

Benjamin stared at Dr. Shapiro, half-expecting some sort of negation, even a punchline, as though Dr. Shapiro had suddenly become the worst kind of practical joker. Shapiro looked back at him with a numb expression.

Benjamin cleared his throat and hoarsely said, "Bullshit! He can't do that." Shapiro averted his eyes. "But why?"

"I'm afraid this whole media circus has been an embarrassment to him and he doesn't take kindly to being embarrassed."

"But I did nothing wrong," Benjamin said.

"No one is suggesting that you did," Shapiro

said.

Benjamin said, "Then I'll sue the bastard!"

"Oh, that would be a very bad idea, indeed," Shapiro said. "Dr. Mitchell's influence reaches far beyond Houston. Far beyond the state for that matter."

"OK, so I'll find a damn fellowship somewhere else," Benjamin said.

"Benjamin," Dr. Shapiro picked up a metal pen and moved it three inches to the right on his desk, "I took the liberty of making some phone calls on your behalf. I have an old buddy from residency. He runs the critical care fellowship in Dallas. We had a little chat."

"And?"

"He told me their slots were filled for the year," Shapiro said.

"There are tons of other programs," Benjamin said.

"And he told me that even if he had a spot, he wouldn't have offered it to you. No place in the country will. With all the scrutiny on physician training these days, program directors are skittish. No one wants to attract undue attention. My friend said you were… well, he used the word, radioactive".

"Well, he's an asshole," Benjamin said.

"No, he's a good guy. A decent man, and he was not only very impressed with your academic record, as he should be; he was sympathetic to your situation. So he offered some advice. He suggests you lay low for a while, let the news cycle run its course, let the whole thing blow over. People have short memories. In a year, once the dust settles, he might be able to offer you a spot."

"A year?" Benjamin said. "And what am I supposed to do for a year? I have over a hundred grand in student loans to pay back.

"I told you I made some phone calls on your behalf," Shapiro said. "I responded to some classified ads placed by general pediatric practices throughout the state. One of them may be interested in hiring you."

"One of them? How many did you call?" Benjamin said.

"That's not important." Shapiro gave a lopsided smile. "You don't want to know."

Benjamin tapped his lips with the knuckle of his index finger. "General pediatrics?"

Shapiro shrugged. "You're a pediatrician, after all."

"I'm a pediatric intensivist," Benjamin said. "I mean, that's what I'm meant to be."

"Benjamin, this may be hard for you to appreciate right now, but one of the secrets to finding contentment and fulfillment in one's work is to allow for a certain degree of flexibility. You've invested so much of your identity in the idea of being an intensivist, I wonder if that's healthy."

"You're saying I should give up the one thing, the *only* thing I care about in life," Benjamin said.

"Oh dear," Shapiro said, "if that's the only thing you care about in life, this is far worse than I thought." Benjamin stared at the floor and said nothing. "A year of general peds under your belt will do you good no matter what you end up pursuing."

"Where is it?" Benjamin asked.

"Purgatory." Benjamin squinted. Shapiro laughed. "Purgatory, Texas."

"Where the hell is that?" Benjamin said.

"Down south on the Rio Grande. Smack on the border with Mexico," Shapiro said.

"Never heard of it."

"That makes two of us," Shapiro said. "Thank God for Google maps."

Shapiro slid open a drawer, pulled out a manila file and pushed it across his desk. Benjamin flipped it open. A small square glossy cutout was taped inside the folder. It read, "*General Pediatrician needed to fill immediate need. Thrive in a casual tropical setting. Low cost of living. Excellent compensation package. Spanish proficiency a plus.*"

Benjamin said, "For starters, I don't speak Spanish."

"Pablo Medina, the doctor who runs the clinic, says that's OK. On the phone he sounded very gracious, a real affable character."

"And he knows about what happened?"

"Like I said, he seems like a very gracious man," Shapiro said. "He wants you to call him this evening, sometime after five. The phone number's at the bottom of the ad."

Benjamin shut the file and got to his feet. Shapiro walked him to the door, put a hand on his shoulder.

"Don't forget, Benjamin, there's more to life than one's professional career," Shapiro said.

"Not for me," Benjamin said and shuffled out

the doorway.

He made his way down the hallway and waited for the elevator, stepped on the down-going car with a muscular asian man in tan scrubs who was pushing a bulky linen cart. He rolled the file folder Shapiro had given him into a tight cylinder and started bouncing it on his open palm. The pediatric critical care fellowship had been his sole objective since his senior year of medical school. The thought of letting it slip away felt like a betrayal of the self. But it's not like he was letting go of it; it was being torn away from him. He was the chosen scapegoat — the sacrificial lamb offered up by a crass administrator to quiet the tides of public indignation.

The elevator slowed to a stop and the doors opened. Benjamin followed the man with the linen cart out of the elevator, even giving the cart a helpful push when the back wheels caught on the gap of the threshold, and was so lost in thought it took him a few moments to realize he had exited on the wrong floor — the basement, of all places. He jogged back towards the elevator but got there just as the metal doors clanged shut.

He cursed under his breath and slapped the call button with the heel of his hand. Seeing his fingers quiver, he squeezed his hand into a fist to make them stop. He was disgusted with himself, shaking like a little girl.

Behind him, a whirring sound was growing louder. A squat latino, a towel rolled inside his shirt collar, gray stubble in the shape of a goatee encircling fleshy brown lips, was pushing a floor buffer, occasionally squirting a sprinkle of solution from an atomizer he wore slung on his worn leather belt. There was something exotic, almost indigenous in the man's countenance which captured Benjamin's attention.

Benjamin hesitated, thought about it for a moment, then stepped in front of the man's machine as he was about to pass by him. He waved to get the man's attention. "Excuse me!" he shouted out, his voice drowned out by the buzz of the machine. "Excuse me," he repeated until the man flicked a toggle switch on the handle of the machine and the whirring wound down. "Can I ask you something?"

The man nodded, pulled a red bandana handkerchief from a hip pocket and wiped his brow.

"I wonder if you can help me with a little translation," Benjamin said.

The man's gaze settled on the file in Benjamin's hand. He shook his head and said, "I no read too good, Mister."

"Oh, no. There's nothing to read. Just a phrase. What does *Jach Dyos b'o'otik* mean?"

The man shrugged. "What language is that?"

"Maybe I'm saying it wrong. *Jack Dos bootich*?"

"Dos mean two," the man said. He smiled exposing a mouthful of crooked teeth held together by a metal bridge.

"Is it a curse maybe?" Benjamin said. "You know, like…" Benjamin whispered, "Fuck you, or something like that?"

"Oh, like bad words?" The man wiped his fleshy

lips before stuffing the handkerchief back in his hip pocket.

"Right."

"I no think so, Mister."

The muffled tone of a bell signaled the arrival of the elevator car. Ben nodded, waved at the man and ambled towards the opening doors.

"You want to learn bad words, I know lots," the janitor said, chuckling, the laugh growing louder until it seemed as though something had sprung loose from the man's voice, a gear had slipped in his larynx triggering a burst of wheezy cough.

"That's OK. Thanks," Benjamin said. He stepped inside the elevator car and pressed the button for the first floor.

As the elevator doors started gliding shut, a final cackle of laughter erupted from the hallway.

"*Puta madre! La chingada, pendejo!* I teach you bad words, Mister!"

Benjamin jabbed at the elevator control board with his knuckles lighting up a half dozen buttons. Kept punching until the doors slammed together.

4

Benjamin turned into the street leading to his apartment complex cautiously, the wheels of his beat up Nissan Xterra hugging the right curb to give himself plenty of room in case he needed to make a quick U-turn. When he saw that the news van was gone, his grip on the steering wheel relaxed. He pulled into an open parking spot, sprung out of the vehicle, house keys in hand, and in mere seconds was past the threshold and into the air-conditioned safety of his home.

He tossed the file Dr. Shapiro had given him onto the kitchen table. It glided across the polished surface, slipped off the opposite edge and landed on the floor. Benjamin stooped to pick it up and read the ad once more. He stepped over to his desk, flipped his laptop open and typed "Purgatory Texas" in the internet search box. The first three results all read, "Local officials warn of looming humanitarian crisis."

Benjamin scrolled down until he came across the caption, "Hospital's bold business model reaps profits, delivers healthier outcomes." He clicked on the link. It opened an article posted in an online newspaper called The Purgatory Sentinel. The article was one of those small news outfit puff pieces that laud local enterprises, inevitably inflating their merits. He scanned the text, his eyes pausing on the words, "state-of-the-art robotic surgery", kept skimming until he reached a quote by the hospital's medical director.

"No way," Benjamin muttered.

He read the sentence a second time. "According to medical director, Dr. Fermin Soto-Prinz, by the end of the current calendar year, El Dorado Hospital will surpass the Mayo Clinic in number of cardiac catheterization procedures performed annually."

"How is that even possible?" he mumbled, scratching his jaw.

He scrolled down to the bottom of the article where a photograph showed a burly man with black bushy eye-brows and a chevron mustache standing arms folded in front of a silver Rolls Royce. In the background stood a steel and tinted-glass building with a sign that read, "El Dorado Hospital" in boxy, gilded letters. The caption under the photograph read, "The Midas Touch: El Dorado Hospital's profits have soared under the helm of its medical director and Chief Financial Officer, Fermin Soto-Prinz, M.D."

Benjamin studied the photograph more closely. There was something peculiar about the picture: the man's complexion was ashen, sallow, like that of a wax statue. The photograph reminded Benjamin of an old, poorly colorized black-and-white snapshot from his high school history textbook of the embalmed corpse of Josef Stalin lying in state, the only difference being that here it appeared as though the corpse had been propped up in an erect position, the eyelids glued open to complete the prank.

"Where the hell is Purgatory?" Benjamin asked himself.

He cracked his knuckles and clicked on the maps option.

He waited until 5:15, then stared at his cell-phone for another half-minute. It was just a phone call, he told himself. He wasn't committing to anything. He'd talk to this guy Medina, then tell Shapiro that he had made the call but as far as the job went, well, it just wasn't for me.

He wiped his palms on his pant legs and dialed the phone number. The voice on the other end answered after two dial tones.

"Bueno."

Benjamin had prepared somewhat of a loose script to follow but the unexpected greeting immediately threw him off stride.

"Oh, hello? I'm sorry, I think I might have dialed… My name is Benjamin Snow?"

"Yes, yes, yes. How are you, Benjamin? This is Pablo Medina."

"Oh, okay, I'm-"

"I'm so glad you called. Dr. Shapiro said only great things about you and, *no pues*, we would love to have you."

Benjamin paused. "To have me for an interview?"

"No. I mean, yes, yes, yes, an interview. Listen Benjamin… Dr. Snow, can I call you Benjamin?"

"Sure, of course."

"Listen, one thing you need to know, down here we have our own ways. Our own culture, you might say, not so formal like up North." It was the first time Benjamin had heard anyone refer to Houston as up

North. "Dr. Shapiro says you're a hard-worker and very, very smart. That's all I need to know. So, you tell me. What do *you* need to know?"

Benjamin was befuddled. Was the guy ready to hire him already? Just like that? He searched his mind for one of his scripted questions. "Maybe you can tell me a little about the practice," Benjamin said. Always a diplomatic question. Doctors loved to talk about their practices as if they were entirely unique, which they never were.

"Two-hundred thousand base salary. With bonuses you could make over two and a quarter, easy," Medina said.

"I was referring to, you know, the practice."

"Look Benjamin, when it comes to brass tacks, the one thing every candidate wants to know is the pay. But they all treat it like it's the pregnant bride. You know what I mean? Everyone's so darn discreet, don't want to broach the subject, but through the entire church service all they do is sneak peeks at that big round belly and try to guess just how far along things are. So I wanted to put it out there plain as day. I'll be open with you. All I ask is that you're open with me."

"OK," Benjamin said. "Was there something you wanted to ask me?"

"Benjamin, no one here in Purgatory knows anything about what happened, and the ones who do don't care." This was spoken in a lower timbre, with careful enunciation of each syllable — the sort of voice doctors use when they clutch a patient's hand to assure them that everything will be all right. After an uncomfortable pause he added, "Actually, yes, there is something I need to ask you. That interview, how about the day-after-tomorrow? Are you free?"

Just an interview, Benjamin told himself. No commitment. "Yeah, sure," he said, even as he wondered if he'd be able to get a flight on such short notice. If there even *were* flights to Purgatory from Houston.

"Good, good, good. Listen, Wednesday morning, go to the Corporate Airport in Sugar Land. Walk in, ask for the El Dorado Hospital jet. Ten o'clock. No, make it nine-thirty."

"Nine-thirty. OK," Benjamin said.

"And Benjamin?" Medina said. "Don't worry about a thing."

5

Wednesday morning Benjamin was out of the shower by seven a.m. With a towel wrapped around his waist, he stuffed a dress shirt, T-shirt, jeans, a change of socks and underwear into a duffel bag. He wasn't told how long his visit to Purgatory would last but, with only one dress suit to his name - the one it took him months of saving up to purchase for his medical school interviews - there wasn't much of a business wardrobe to pack in any case.

He buttoned the collar of the white shirt he had ironed the night before, looped his solid-black silk necktie into a Half Windsor and slipped on his suit jacket. It was a tight fit in the shoulders. He buttoned the jacket, tried raising his arms and felt the seam in the right armpit rip.

Great. Just great. He probed the tear with his index finger. It wasn't large enough to warrant searching for needle and thread. He undid the jacket buttons and swiveled his arms haltingly. No one would notice, he told himself.

Traffic was heavy as usual on U.S. 59 all the way to the Sam Houston Parkway. Though he had given himself a generous time cushion, by the time he reached the exit off the Southwest Freeway he started to worry he might not make it to his destination on time.

A patch of moisture began to form on his back. He cranked up the fan setting of the air-conditioner.

The air blew out of the vents barely cooler than room temperature. He leaned forward hoping the forced air would somehow circulate between his back and the seat. After a mile of one red light after another, he gave up on the forced posture and leaned back in his seat again. He could always freshen up with some wet paper towels in the plane's lavatory after all, add an extra splash of cologne and be as good as new.

The terminal of the private airport looked like the lobby of a luxury hotel, complete with a marble counter atop which an engraved brass plaque read, "Concierge". A man with wavy sandy hair wearing a blazer with a double row of gold buttons greeted Benjamin with a high pitched, "Good morning."

"El Dorado Hospital?" Benjamin said.

"Of course." The man opened a ledger and pulled a Mont Blanc pen out of his breast pocket. "Would you mind signing our guest book?"

Benjamin grasped the pen. As he wrote his name in the ledger, the man walked out from behind the counter with a hand-held metal detector. He waited for Benjamin to return the pen to him in what was certainly a practiced pose, and with a pained smile said, "If you'd be so kind…"

"Huh?"

"I am truly mortified. Please separate your feet and raise your arms."

"Oh," Benjamin said. He widened his stance and lifted his arms until he could feel the tightness in his sleeves. The concierge waved the paddle up one pant leg, across Benjamin's crotch and down the other leg.

He then swept up one side of his chest and paused.

"I know this is really too much to ask," the man said. "But I wonder if you could raise your arms above your head."

"I don't think I can do that. You want me to take my coat off?"

The concierge studied him and smiled a crooked smile. "No need, sir. I'll manage." He passed the paddle past Benjamin's arms with surreptitious strokes. Finally, he lay the metal detector on the marble counter and asked Benjamin to open the duffel bag. He quickly zipped it shut again after the most cursory of inspections, as though toxic fumes might emanate from its interior. The concierge pointed to a glass door to Benjamin's left. "Out that door," he said. "Follow the path to the tarmac, then go right. El Dorado is the second Gulf Stream on the right."

Benjamin had no idea what a Gulf Stream looked like but the apprehension over finding the right craft evaporated when he saw a sleek jet with "El Dorado Hospital" stenciled in large gold letters across the fuselage. He paused, looked at the plane, then down at his watch. It was 9:20. He couldn't decide if he had somehow arrived too early and he wondered how many other passengers might be on the plane. They wouldn't have sent a private jet just to pick him up, would they have? As he was considering this, a petite Hispanic woman in a navy blue skirt-suit, chiffon white blouse, and a red silk scarf around her neck came stepping down the plane's gangway ladder. She seemed very young, and though her outfit was impeccably stylish there was something naive in her poise and movements that reminded Benjamin of a college co-ed dressed up for career day.

"Dr. Benjamin Snow?" she said.

Benjamin nodded. "Yes, good morning."

"Welcome, Dr. Snow. I'm Giselle, Dr. Soto-Prinz's administrative assistant." She clicked her heels together, thrust out her perky chest and offered her hand in a stiff, exceedingly cute gesture. Benjamin shook her hand with graceless formality. She let out a suppressed giggle which rang out, not as a lack of self-restraint, but as a sort of acknowledgment of the awkwardness of the moment — a tender absolution for Benjamin's gawkiness, as though she had become accustomed to flustering young men with her beauty but was nonetheless flattered by it. Her chestnut brown eyes widened in what Benjamin took to be a hint of surprise, perhaps at Benjamin's own youth or appearance, eyes that gleamed a thinly veiled coquettishness that made Benjamin's face grow flush.

"Please make yourself at home, doctor." She waved a hand towards the jet's gangway in an airline stewardess sort of way. "I need to take care of some formalities at the terminal before take-off. Can I get you a coffee? Cappuccino? Latte?"

"I'm fine," Benjamin said, stupidly patting his belly.

Giselle giggled again, in a polite way, as if Benjamin had intended to be funny. She winked at him and marched towards the terminal. Benjamin waited a moment, then bent his neck down and took in a whiff of each of his armpits. He frowned, turned and slowly stepped up the gangway.

There were no other passengers on the plane, which again made him think he had arrived too soon. They wouldn't have sent such a plane just for him. Every surface of the interior of the craft, except for the floor, was finished in hand-stitched taupe leather or polished mahogany. From the main galley, an arched doorway opened onto what appeared to be a private cabin at the aft of the plane.

Benjamin dropped his luggage onto the cream colored plush carpet and plopped onto the only forward facing couch next to a window. The seat was firmer than he expected — not quite as comfortable as it looked. He considered moving to a built-in sofa across the aisle and imagined Giselle joining him there during the flight, cozying up to him, stretching out her short shapely legs, asking him if there was anything she could do to make his trip more comfortable, really, anything at all. He shook his head. He wasn't about to let himself be seduced into a job he didn't want, not by luxury jets with stiff leather seats and not by well-trained nubile girls dressed in silk. He lay back into the seat, pushed it into a reclined position, and let out a roar of a yawn.

"Do you intend to join me, Dr. Snow?" a voice called out.

Benjamin jerked up in his seat. He craned his neck to look in the direction of the private cabin which seemed to be source of the baritone voice. "Please do join me if it's not too much trouble. I should be delighted to have the honor of your company." The words were spoken in that sing-song cadence patronizing salespeople find amusing. Even worse, it had an English accent that seemed strained, unnatural, almost contrived. It reminded Benjamin of Rory Quinn, his former college roommate, a performing arts major, who persisted in using an off-pitch Shakespearean inflection for months after appearing in a disastrous production of The Merchant of Venice.

Benjamin got to his feet, grabbed hold of the handles of his duffel bag and stooped through the arched doorway. The compartment he entered was even more lavish than the main cabin. A pale Persian rug adorned the floor. A half-moon shaped walnut desk, broad at one end, gradually narrowing along its arc to reach a rounded point, emerged from the plane's paneling, making it look as though the fuselage had been punctured by the blade of a giant scythe. Behind the desk, in a red suede captain's chair, sat a man with jet-black bushy eyebrows a half-shade darker than the sparse hair combed across his crown, a painstakingly groomed mustache the same hue as the eyebrows, and a sallow gray complexion that was even more startling in person than on that photograph that reminded Benjamin of a defunct Josef Stalin.

"I'm Dr. Soto-Prinz," the man said, rolling the "r" of his last name. He dipped his shoulders forward and extended his arm just barely above the desk. Benjamin clumsily shifted his grip on the duffel bag and reached to shake the doctor's hand when he realized that Soto-Prinz was reaching for the ornate handle of a tea-cup resting on a silver platter on the desk. Soto-

Prinz lifted the cup slowly with a sort of ceremonial reverence, puckered his ashen lips and blew over the cup's contents. He took the tiniest of sips, set the cup down and dabbed his mouth with a monogrammed cloth napkin. Benjamin shifted his weight onto his heels and rubbed his hand on his thigh, feeling foolish.

"Sit," Soto-Prinz said.

Benjamin lowered himself in a leather-lined couch that felt even firmer than the one in the main galley. He glanced at the tea cup resting on its silver platter and thought it looked too fragile to be practical on an airplane. Next to it was a dish of fine china, covered by a cloth napkin folded in the shape of a triangle, and just beyond lay a larger platter garnished with carved ham, thin red sausages, slices of hard cheese, and olives stuffed with chunks of red pepper. A small basket of fruit sat off to the side, with pears, tangerines and grapefruit all glowing in a column of light streaming from a porthole at Soto-Prinz's back. Benjamin's eyes settled back on the platter, if only to avoid making eye contact with Soto-Prinz. He said, "Thank you," in a hollow tone, the sound of his voice immediately muffled, as if sucked up by the softer surfaces of the small cabin.

"*Jamon Serrano*?" Soto-Prinz said. "Some *Chistorra* sausage, perhaps? I'll have Giselle bring you a dish."

"Oh no, thank you," Benjamin said.

"It's quite delicious." Soto-Prinz's mouth stretched into a slanted smile.

"I'm sure it is," Benjamin said. "Thank you. I'll

pass."

Soto-Prinz narrowed his eyes. "I must insist," he said. He slid open a desk drawer, pulled out a dagger set in a silver scabbard with inlaid green onyx, unsheathed the blade and stabbed a slice of ham. He lifted it and brought it forward so that the the cold-cut hovered no more than a foot in front of Benjamin's face. "Grab it with your fingers. Put it in your mouth."

Benjamin remained frozen in place and stared at the blade. Its gleaming steel was intricately engraved along its entire length. He wondered if there were any human fetish more hideous than that of adorning weapons in an attempt to transform them into objects of beauty.

"Put it in your mouth!" The smile had vanished from Soto-Prinz's face. This was not a request but an order.

Benjamin grasped the slice of ham, placed it in his mouth and chewed slowly. It had a pungent, smoky savoriness.

Soto-Prinz sat back again, wiping the dagger's blade on the back of his monogrammed napkin, a gleam of satisfaction sparkling in his watery eyes, still keeping watch over Benjamin the way his grandfather would keep watch over him at the supper table, scrutinizing his strained chewing motion until he gulped down the entire mouthful of food. For a moment, Benjamin felt that Soto-Prinz half expected him to open his mouth and stick out his tongue like a good boy, to show that the ham was all gone.

"Dr. Medina sent me your curriculum," he

finally said, the "r" rolling like crazy. He moved a brown, leather-bound notebook aside, lifted a manila file off his desk, waved it in the air. "I must say, you look good on paper."

It was only then that Benjamin noticed the one-week old copy of the Houston Chronicle, folded in half, laying askew on the patch of desk where the file had lain. Benjamin knew it was one week old, knew the exact date of the issue, because it was the one festooned with a picture of him under the caption, "Doctor Death".

Soto-Prinz chuckled and lowered the file back on top of the newspaper with a deliberate languidness.

"Dr. Medina is an esteemed colleague, a pillar of our medical community. So, when he sponsors a new physician for accreditation to the medical staff, El Dorado is obliged to pay heed," Soto-Prinz said.

"I wasn't aware that he… I mean, it's not like I signed a contract yet or anything," Benjamin said.

"Oh? Do you have other job offers that you're considering? Please edify me, Dr. Snow, are disgraced physicians in high demand these days in the haute suburban practices of Houston?" Soto-Prinz speared a piece of sausage with his fork and slipped it in his mouth. He nodded. "You will come to Purgatory, Dr. Snow. You'd be a complete fool not to, and you don't strike me as a complete fool. But understand, as medical director, I require certain assurances."

"What type of assurances are we talking about?" This was going to be a damn long flight.

Soto-Prinz said, "You were already kind enough

to offer me one." That crooked smile again. He grabbed a large grapefruit from the basket, brought it up just under his nose, turned it in his hand then plunged the dagger into it with unnecessary force. He cut it into halves with stabbing motions, red juice trickling off the blade. "This is a Ruby Red picked from one of the many orchards a stone's throw from the Rio Grande. The locals say the pulp gets its color from the blood of the innocents that has seeped into the soil over the centuries."

He lifted the dagger at an angle, let drops of red juice drip onto his plate. "I see you have an eye for fine objects," Soto-Prinz said.

"The knife?" Benjamin said.

"Not a knife. It's a Spanish conquistador dagger."

"It's unique, I guess."

"No, not unique," Soto-Prinz said with a chuckle. "This is a replica. The original is far too precious to use for cutting grape-fruit." He paused as if he were waiting for Benjamin to provide a retort. When none came he said, "I keep the original in a climate-controlled glass case in my home. I'm a bit of a collector, you see."

"Of knives?"

"Of Spanish relics of that era," Soto-Prinz said. "Do you know what the mission of the conquistadores was?"

"To plunder for gold?"

"Not plunder, no. It was to do the work of God. And to grow rich in the process. Are you a man of God, Dr. Snow?"

Benjamin hesitated. It bothered him that his medical training had instilled in him a reflexive impulse to submit to men of authority, to underscore their power over him by peddling himself as a mindless flunky. "I was raised Methodist," Benjamin said.

"Then you should have no problem with the idea that God rewards with a rich harvest those who do His work," Soto-Prinz said. "That is the mission of our hospital. To help the infirm, the decrepit, the destitute, the wretched hoards that swarm our community, and for this…" he waved his forearm to display the luxury of the airplane, "we are compensated quite handsomely. Wouldn't you say?"

"How does that work?" Benjamin asked.

"What do you mean?"

"I mean, if that region is so poor, how does the hospital make so much money?"

Soto-Prinz chuckled. "There's a lot of money in poverty these days. You will learn of our business model in due time. What I need to know now is, do you have a problem with money?"

"Why would I?"

"Some people do," Soto-Prinz said. "They find wealth disagreeable, dirty."

"I owe a hundred and twenty-thousand in student loans," Benjamin said.

Soto-Prinz guffawed. He leaned forward, narrowed his eyes. "That little boy, it was the right thing to do, after all, don't you know?"

"What little boy?" Benjamin asked. For a

moment he had almost forgotten. Now he regretted asking such a dumb question.

Soto-Prinz tilted his head and studied Benjamin. "What little boy? What little boy, indeed! The truth is the world needs people like us, who are willing to execute those bold acts which others find too tawdry for their fragile sensibilities. I think you'll fit in just fine at El Dorado, Dr. Snow. Just fine."

Benjamin said nothing. Could think of nothing to say.

"Dr. Soto-Prinz?" Giselle was standing in the doorway. "The pilot just informed me we'll be ready for take-off in five minutes."

Soto-Prinz glanced at his heavy wrist-watch. A Rolex, no doubt. He said, "Excellent. Then we are done with our *petit dejeuner*." He reached for the brown, leather-bound notebook, stashed it away under the newspaper with a defensive gesture when Benjamin happened to glance at it.

Giselle walked to the desk, stood close enough to Benjamin that he could smell her perfume. She cleared the desk of the various dishes with a tranquil grace, giving no indication of being annoyed if this was a duty below her pay grade. With the dishes balanced in her hands, she pivoted on her heels, looked back to flash him a coy smile, and strode out of the cabin with confident steps. Benjamin followed her with his gaze, perhaps for a moment too long.

"Quite charming, isn't she?" Soto-Prinz said.

"She seems very efficient," Benjamin said.

"Efficient? Ha!" Soto-Prinz slapped the surface

of his desk and let out a chest-rattling laugh. "Efficient indeed. And on that merry note, our meeting comes to a lamentable conclusion. Any questions?"

Benjamin shook his head. "Did you want me to go sit out in the front?"

"Out in the front?" Soto-Prinz said. "Heavens, no. I'd say this is a rather opportune time for you to deplane." He waved a hooked finger in front of his nose. "And I do hope you packed lightly."

By the time Benjamin reached the Galleria area, it was nearly noon. He wasn't particularly hungry but thought this would be a good time to grab a sandwich at Eatzi's before the lunch-time rush, then take refuge in his apartment the rest of the afternoon.

The girl at the counter barely looked at him as she rung him up, but from the corner of his eye, Benjamin caught sight of two middle-aged women in skin-tight yoga pants leaning their heads together in a conspiratorial whisper before turning nonchalantly to spy on him. He stared back at them and they quickly looked the other way. Benjamin snatched the plastic bag with his sandwich off the counter and headed for the exit.

Don't get too paranoid, he told himself. Still, as he crossed the parking lot, he couldn't shake the eerie feeling that he was being watched. He pulled the key fob for his SUV out of the front pocket of his pants and quickened his step. When he reached the Xterra he stopped in his tracks. Two words in craggy block letters were etched into the faded yellow paint of the driver's door: *Baby Killer.*

Benjamin cursed under his breath. He bit his lower lip as he ran his thumb across the inscription, felt the jagged sharpness of the gashes extending down to the metal. A steel shaving dug into his thumb. He brushed it off on his trousers but opened a tiny gash where a droplet of blood bloomed and clung to his skin like crimson dew. Benjamin leaped in the truck, cranked on the engine pushing the gas pedal as far as it would go, jerked the gear shifter into reverse and gunned out of the parking spot. He tore out of the lot, tires squealing and drove the next two blocks cursing out loud.

Up ahead, a line of cars had formed at a traffic light. He pumped the brakes and swerved into the parking lot of a laundromat. He brought the SUV to a stop, still in second gear, forgetting to engage the clutch. The engine heaved and stalled with a bone-jarring shudder.

Benjamin sat breathless, clutching the steering wheel tight enough to keep his hands from shaking. He wiped away the stupid tears that had welled up in his eyes, then glanced at his open hands to study how the tears had diluted the blood on his thumb. Once more he cursed and punched the dashboard. The ringer of his cell phone froze him before he could punch the dashboard a second time. He let the ring tone continue its merry chime for a few more seconds before picking up the phone to answer it.

"Benjamin. This is Pablo Medina. Did I catch you at a good time?"

Benjamin turned his head to clear his throat, to release the rawness from his voice, then pressed the phone to his ear again. "I can talk."

"Good, good, good. Well, so how did the interview go?"

"I thought I was flying down to interview with *you*," Benjamin said.

"Oh, I don't need to ask you anything else. But El Dorado Hospital, well, they support our practice. And to be on staff there you have to go through *El Jefe*. By the way, he really liked you."

"Dr. Soto-Prinz?" Benjamin said.

"I know, he's a real son-of-a-bitch. But you must have done something to impress him."

"Like what?"

"Like not being Mexican." Medina laughed. "I don't know. Anyway, he rubber-stamped your application," Medina said.

"I didn't even fill out an application." Benjamin opened the car door and stepped out on the blacktop.

"Oh, we did that for you already. Hope you don't mind. We just updated the Texas standardized application you filled out in residency. We take care of everything here. All you do is see patients and relax."

"This is all going so fast. I need time to think things through. I mean, I haven't even seen a contract yet."

"Yes, yes, yes, of course. I understand." There was a pause during which no one spoke, then Medina said. "If I e-mail you the contract this afternoon, you think you can start on Monday?"

Benjamin kneaded his temple with his free hand, started pacing in the parking lot. A potbellied woman in a pink tank top and denim cut-off shorts stepped out of the laundromat. She lit a cigarette, took a deep drag and blew out a plume of gray smoke from her nostrils.

"I don't want to be rude or anything," Benjamin said, "it's just-"

"It's very standard. No scary clauses. To tell you the truth, I'd be fine with just a handshake if it were just up to me."

Who else would it be up to? Benjamin asked himself.

The lady from the laundromat was staring at him. She squinted her eyes. Maybe it was from the smoke of her cigarette, or the fact that she had just walked out into the brightness of the parking lot, but she continued to follow Benjamin with her gaze even as he turned and stepped back towards his truck.

"I really need someone in a hurry," Medina said.

Benjamin inspected the graffiti freshly etched in the door of his truck. The familiar feeling of being out of place pressed down on him.

6

Rick Harvey, the manager of the Las Colinas apartment complex, didn't make a fuss about breaking the one-year lease Benjamin had renewed just a month ago. In fact, he even went so far as to help Benjamin load a full size bed and a tan sofa with sagging arm rests onto the trailer Benjamin had rented for the move. A thoughtful gesture on the part of Mr. Harvey, who managed to mention what a nuisance the television vans parked on his street had been only a couple of times

His shabby furniture wedged onto the trailer, a few cardboard boxes and clothes strewn in the back of his truck, Benjamin attended to a final detail. He cut two strips of gray duct-tape and pressed them over the words "Baby Killer" on the driver-side door of his vehicle. Just minutes later, he turned the key in the ignition and eased out of the parking spot feeling the strain on the engine from the added weight of the trailer. He headed south-west.

He'd been driving on highway 59 for the better part of 4 hours, passed through Edna and Victoria and Goliad — towns whose somber plantation homes and beaux-arts courthouses stood as stubborn memorials of more prosperous times. He stopped in Beeville where a guy with black nail polish and purple bangs manned the White House Burger drive-thru.

"Honestly, I thought you said *two* large fries," the guy said in a reedy voice that was all cream and honey.

"It's OK. I'll take the extra fries," Benjamin said, collecting his change.

"Oh my God, I'm mortified."

"Really, it's no big deal."

The guy slipped something in the paper bag and winked. "Cherry pie, on the house. You'll thank me later. You'll see. You'll say, 'Thank you, Ramon.' That's my name, by the way, Ramon." Another wink.

It was on the outskirts of Beeville that Benjamin felt as though he had crossed an unmarked boundary and entered into a foreign land: a land of squat road-side buildings painted in canary yellows and pale purples, of scorched pastures where aloof cattle huddled in the flimsy shade of live oaks, of dirt roads branching off the highway at odd angles only to lose themselves in overgrown brush. As the sun began to sink from its zenith, Benjamin felt as though the horizon were closing in on him.

He kept driving even as he ate, the paper bag from the burger place propped between his thighs. The burger wasn't half bad, but the fries clung together in soggy lumps. Benjamin picked at them for a while until he realized there were just too many to ingest. He rolled the paper bag shut and tossed it on the passenger seat. *Thanks a lot, Ramon!*

At the town of Freer he turned south on Highway 16. It was a straight shot to Hebronville now, then a slight jog up the Rio Grande to Purgatory. The road curved through a grove of dogwoods and opened up onto an unexpected spectacle: a sprawling meadow of fully-bloomed sunflowers, straight and tall. Benjamin was not one to become distracted by shows of nature, but he couldn't help looking off to his side. He had to admit he had never seen anything nearly as beautiful in all his years living in Houston. Not that it mattered.

When he looked back at the road ahead of him he noticed a hazy orange cloud about the size of a delivery van, hovering just over the blacktop. It expanded and contracted, changing its shape as he approached it.

"What the hell?"

Benjamin had grossly misjudged the distance of the cloud. In fact, just as he took his foot off the gas pedal the cloud was upon him and the windshield of his SUV was pelted by a briny rain which was over after a just a short pattering. Frail orange wings with black rims fluttered in the metal grooves of the wiper arms, while yellow blotches surrounded by a fine white and orange powder dappled the glass, each blot marking the spot where a Monarch butterfly disintegrated on impact.

"Thousands of miles of migration and you had to cross the path of Doctor Death," Benjamin said. "Sorry, guys."

He pulled the lever on the right of the steering column and a feeble mist sputtered onto the windshield. A moment later the wipers came to life and spread a fine goop throughout the span of the worn blades. Now the entire windshield became a soupy blur. Benjamin eased his right foot onto the brake and slowly brought the vehicle to a stop onto the gravel shoulder of the highway, near a patch of thick brush of mesquite. He grabbed a bottle of drinking water and a paper napkin from White House Burger and exited the vehicle.

He splashed water over the driver's side of the windshield and used the napkin to rub the glass clean. It was hotter than he expected for that hour and the water seemed to evaporate just as soon as it made contact with the windshield. He rounded the front of the vehicle to work on the passenger side when he heard a hissing sound coming from the brush. He heard it again.

"Psst! *Ehi, señor!*"

Benjamin squinted to look into the shadows of the foliage. He almost recoiled when he saw, staring back at him, two large brown eyes framed in a dirt-streaked cherubic face. A boy, no more than eight or nine years old, sat on his haunches under the crooked branch of a mesquite. The boy began to talk in a melodic inflection which was both reserved and compelling — the cogent voice of one who has a pressing need. Of the entire soliloquy, Benjamin only made out the words *agua, señor,* and *por favor.*

"*Agua*, yes. Here, have some water. What are you doing out in this heat, anyway?"

Benjamin approached the brush. A scrawny arm reached out and snatched the bottle clean out of his hands.

"*Gracias.*" The boy didn't take a sip. He clutched the bottle and started to waddle away in the bush.

"Hey, wait! You hungry? Shoot! How do you say, hungry? Food? How about some food?" Benjamin snapped his fingers. "*Comer!* You want *comer*?"

The boy stopped. Benjamin opened the passenger door, grabbed the paper sack sitting on the seat. He walked back to the bush and gave the sack a shake.

"French fries and cherry pie. Mmm, *muy bueno*!"

The kid stared at him impassively. This time he trudged towards Benjamin, reached slowly and grasped the top of the sack with his free hand.

"*Muchas gracias,señor.*"

The boy slipped back into the darkness of the bush.

Benjamin stood there, searching the brush. He muttered under his breath, "Thank you, Ramon."

He got back in the car, disengaged the parking brake and craned his head to look at the brush, just in time to see three, no, four boys, scampering out of the foliage. Two of them had tattered rucksacks on their shoulders. The one with the big eyes was the smallest of the four, trailing his companions, still clutching the bottle of water.

A few miles down the road, a green and white Border Patrol SUV was parked on the shoulder, emergency lights flashing. Benjamin eased his foot off the gas. As he coasted by, he saw a stocky officer in an olive uniform and a cowboy hat who was talking into a shoulder-mounted radio, standing in a field off the highway. At the officer's feet a half-dozen dark-skinned children, maybe one or two teen-agers in the whole mix, sat huddled together.

Two hours later he was still thinking about the kid with the big eyes. He could have kicked himself for not giving him an extra bottle of water which was still sealed and wedged in the car's cup-holder. Wished he had known to order a few extra burgers from Ramon. He had heard of unaccompanied children coming across the border, making their treks all the way from Guatemala, Honduras, Nicaragua, even before it became national news. He just never expected to run into them. Not on his first day in South Texas. Not like this.

The highway widened and a grassy median appeared. A metal road sign read, Purgatory, population 74,000. Just past it, on the cinder block wall of a warehouse, someone had spray painted, "Welcome to Borderlandia".

7

The Medina Pediatric Clinic occupied a center suite in the Royal Palms Medical Plaza, saddled between the Royal Palms Pharmacy and the office of Dr. Efrain Gutierrez, M.D., Psychiatrist. The stucco facade was painted a sensible tan with maroon trim which nearly matched the clay tiles of the porticos built around each of the glass doorways.

Pablo Medina had asked Benjamin to come a little early on his first day. "I need to show you, you know, how the ropes work," he had told him on the phone the night before. "Heck! I want to meet you in the flesh before you start seeing my kids."

Benjamin parked in the row farthest from the office (don't want to take away the best spots from the patients), slipped on a clean white coat he had laid out on the back seat of his Xterra, and crossed the parking lot, his usual small duffel bag in hand. A bell chimed as he opened the front door. The waiting room was empty. He looked around, walked to the front desk. There was no receptionist in sight. The only sound was the hum of the blower for the air conditioner.

"Hello?" he called out.

As if on cue, a door leading to the back swung open with a blaring of trumpets. In single file, a mariachi band paraded into the waiting room: first the trumpeters, then the fiddlers, finally two guitarists and a cross-eyed *guitarron* player, the strap of his sombrero riding high under his jowls, snug as a bridle's throat-latch. They positioned themselves in a semi-circle near the center of the room, the trumpets playing a tinny staccato, the violinists rapt in a frenzied bowing while one of the guitar players let out a *grito* in a high-pitched falsetto. "*Aaayiiii ah ha haaaa!*"

Now a dozen men and women wearing matching fuchsia scrubs poured into the waiting room, some clapping their hands, others waving them in the air, all bouncing with delight, giddy as school children. Lastly, a round-faced man in a white lab coat walked out, laughing heartily. He appeared to be in his late forties yet managed to radiate a boyish mien, due in no small part to his circa 1964 Paul McCartney hairdo. Now, they all clapped in unison; a few let out screams of their own. They circled around Benjamin, still clapping. One young man with a stiletto mustache took the hand of a plump, middle-aged woman and the couple broke out in a rabid foot-stomping jig. With amazing synchrony they all suddenly erupted in song, "*Guadalajara, Guadalajara!*"

Benjamin didn't quite know how to react. Once the initial surprise had subsided he felt flattered, almost indebted to be given such a reception. But as the song continued, the usual diffidence set in, and with it, a swelling tide of cynicism. This was not an induction; it was a manifestation: a way for Pablo Medina to communicate in no uncertain terms that Benjamin was no longer ensconced in the ivory towers of academia, that things would be done differently here — specifically, they'd be done Medina's way, perhaps with more flair, almost certainly without the hard-boiled adherence to rote discipline practiced "up north", and it would be Benjamin, the interloper, the perpetual outsider, who would have to adapt.

Benjamin had grown accustomed to being an outsider. He wouldn't let that bother him. But watching the spontaneous choreography unfolding around him, he became aware of a prickling sense of envy. These goofy people in their zany rapture had something palpable that held them together: the soft mortar of tradition, of shared culture, of practiced ritual. He had nothing like that. Using varying criteria, it was possible to file Dr. Benjamin Snow, based on all his demographic information, and the degrees and diplomas he had collected over roughly a quarter of a century, into multiple categories, under dozens of subheadings, if one used the same cold objectivity one might employ to classify a biological specimen. But Benjamin Snow, the person, was not a member of any group. Hadn't been for a long time. That was not entirely his fault, he told himself.

Midway through the song, Benjamin began to feel increasingly ill at ease. He was reminded of how, without fail, every year he attended college, his grandmother would call him on the phone to sing Happy Birthday from 700 miles away, and he'd just stand there holding the phone away from his ear, waiting for it to end.

When the mariachi number ended with the requisite trumpet stab-note finale, there were applause and hoots and hollers to go around. The man in the white coat approached him, his smile so broad that his eyes were reduced to slits. He grabbed Benjamin's hand with both of his and said, "Welcome Benjamin! I'm Pablo Medina. What do you think of the mariachis?"

"Oh, they're terrific," Benjamin said.

"Really? You like them?"

"Absolutely."

Medina turned to his staff. "You see! I told you he'd love the mariachis." He put his hand on Benjamin's shoulder. "Let's go in the back. We have *cafe de olla* and breakfast tacos. You like tacos?"

"I love tacos," Benjamin said.

Medina shouted out to no one in particular, "*Nombre!* What did I tell y'all? Benjamin is *puro Mexicano*!"

"*Sin sombrero y sin bigotes!*" one of the male staff members added.

Everyone laughed. Medina gave Benjamin a slap on the back and directed him towards the back of the clinic. The mariachi band struck up another number.

"You have the mariachi band here every day?" Benjamin asked.

Pablo Medina erupted in laughter. "*Nombre!* Today's a special occasion." He shook his head, mumbled, "Do we have mariachis every day! I like your sense of humor. Maybe we should, eh?"

They walked up a hallway, Medina motioned with an outstretched arm. "We have eight exam rooms. See the plastic flags on the doorways? Blue means its my patient, white they're for you. Don't worry about the other colors. Things move fast here. You'll get the hang of it. It's easy. You do almost no charting. Nothing to slow you down. You're here to see patients, not to be a secretary."

They arrived to a large nursing station in the back of the clinic. Platters of tacos, stacks of paper plates and Styrofoam cups were arranged on the counter atop a plastic red and white checkered tablecloth.

"What about documentation?" Benjamin asked.

"We have medical scribes. They follow us into an exam room with a tablet, write the notes as we see the patients. We use lots of templates, you know, so it's super-fast. Best of all, they all speak Spanish so they're also going to be your interpreters. All you have to do is write the prescriptions — electronically of course, from a touch-screen menu — and cosign the notes at the end of the day. Piece of cake?"

"Sounds easy enough," Benjamin said.

"I mean, you want a piece of cake? The nurses brought it in. *Tres leches*."

"A taco would be great," Benjamin said.

Medina didn't seem to be listening. He looked over Benjamin's shoulder. "Ivan!"

A tall guy, late twenties, with a pencil mustache and v-shaped sideburns that tapered into a fine point turned to face them with a questioning look. The guy looked to one side, then the other and finally pointed at his chest.

"Yes you, *cabròn*," Medina said. "Come here. Benjamin, this is Ivan Montero. Ivan the terrible we call him. But don't let his looks fool you, he's our most experienced scribe. He'll be working with you all this week. You have any questions, you just ask him. If he doesn't know the answer, then you ask me."

"Nice to meet you, Ivan," Benjamin said. He reached over to shake his hand, but it was a misfire. Their palms came together awkwardly and Benjamin ended up holding the shafts of the man's slender fingers. As Benjamin released his grasp, Ivan spun his hand around and grabbed Benjamin's thumb. Their hands came together in a stiff homey handshake.

"It's all good," Ivan said, his chin raised, head tilted to one side, staring at Benjamin with droopy, defiant eyes.

"Grab a taco, Benjamin," Medina said. "I'll show you our office."

On cue, a squat nurse with wiry hair and over-sized prescription glasses scooted in, holding a paper plate with a taco wrapped in foil, raised it up to Benjamin's chest as an offering. "Is *chorizo*, egg and potato OK?"

"Sure, thanks," Benjamin said.

"Aah Cristela, now we're playing favorites. Where's *my* taco?" Medina said.

"Your cholesterol is too high," the nurse retorted.

"How do you know Dr. Snow's cholesterol isn't too high?" Medina said.

"Impossible," Cristela said, raising her chin. "He's too cute to have cholesterol." She turned and walked away, but not quickly enough to hide the rosy glow that swept across her cheeks.

"*Nombre*, Benjamin. You're going to cause trouble here already."

The doctor's private office was a sparsely furnished square room off the nurse's station. A built-in pine bookshelf with two narrow desks, each equipped with a desktop computer, spanned one wall. The bookshelf was nearly empty with just a Physician's Desk Reference, an Atlas of Pediatric Dermatology, and a short stack of journals covered by a fine layer of dust occupying the two lower shelves. A round table sat in the center of the room and a brown felt recliner was tucked in a corner. From inside the room, Benjamin could see that the mirror he had noticed on the outside of the office was actually a darkly-tinted window that spied onto the nurse's station.

"One-way mirror," Medina said. "I love it. I can sit here at the table and still see what's going on out there. And even when I'm not looking, they think I am. We've got our computer terminals here," he pointed int the direction of a door, "our own private toilet, and if you need a little after-lunch *siesta…* " Medina sat on the recliner, pulled a wooden lever sticking out of its side and went nearly horizontal. "*Nombre* Benjamin, you have to try this."

"Looks comfortable," Benjamin said.

"What am I doing, showing you the dumb recliner?" Medina said. "Eat your taco, I have something for you."

Benjamin sat at the table and began peeling the foil off the taco. Medina crossed the room, slid open a drawer of the built-in bookshelf and pulled something out. He set it on the table next to Benjamin's plate.

"I know I didn't give you a signing bonus," Medina said, "but you might appreciate this."

Benjamin picked up the slip of paper. It was a check for $8,500.

"It's for moving expenses," Medina said.

"Dr. Medina, I—"

"Please, call me Pablo."

"Pablo, I didn't come anywhere close to spending this much on my move."

"Don't worry about it."

"Do you need receipts or anything?"

"Receipts? Benjamin, this isn't Houston. We do things more… relaxed here in South Texas. So relax. Buy yourself something nice."

Benjamin stared at the check. At the top left it simply read, "EDPG" and the address underneath the company heading was not the clinic's address. The stub attached to the check had an accounting column that read, "For moving expenses - $10,000. EDPG PAC - $1,500. Net remittance - $8,500."

"What does EDPG PAC mean?" Benjamin asked.

"I told you not to worry about it." The words came out with a barbed edge. Medina slipped his hands in his coat pockets. His lips spread in a conciliatory smile that was not endorsed by his eyes. "You have student loans?"

Benjamin nodded as he bit into his taco.

"How much?"

"Quite a bit," Benjamin said. He wasn't quite

ready for all this openness.

"More than a hundred grand?"

"In that neighborhood."

"I'll look into getting you some help for that," Medina said. "Some loan-repayment program or something. This is an under-served area after all. I don't want you owing money."

Benjamin shrugged. "Why not?"

"You have to trust me."

There was an uncomfortable lull in the conversation. It seemed that Medina was waiting for Benjamin to give some form of confirmation of his trust. Benjamin couldn't think of anything diplomatic to say. Finally he said, "Pablo, I really appreciate everything you're doing for me."

But Medina's attention had been pulled away by some movement outside the office. He seemed to be peering through the one-way mirror, resting a hand on the backrest of a chair as if to brace himself and murmured, "Oh shit," just before the door to the office swung open.

Benjamin turned in his seat. Framed in the doorway stood a woman in her late twenties with dark smooth hair and pale brown eyes that gleamed with a frightening determination. She had one hand resting on her hip, the other still holding the doorknob. She paused there, not out of hesitation, but to hold a deliberate poise, as if to show she was in control. In steady, feline steps, she sauntered in the room and slammed the door shut behind her back. Benjamin felt an electric charge move through the air. He swallowed hard and put his taco down on the plate.

"Good morning, Claire," Medina said.

A chillingly ironic smile spread across the woman's face. "Why, good morning, Pablo."

She moved confidently about the room, pacing around the table where Benjamin sat. She was wearing a sleeveless, pale beige knit blouse which hung loosely over her hips and a burgundy tiered skirt which flowed to just above her ankles and moved back and forth with every step she took. The movement reminded Benjamin of the movement of water on a rocky beach, at once receding before springing forth again in ever-repeating cycles. Benjamin couldn't make up his mind whether she reminded him more of a gypsy fortune-teller or some 1960's era flower-child gone rogue.

Medina said, "Care for a breakfast taco? You got here just in time."

"No thanks," she said, a chilling serenity in her voice. She reached into a cloth tote bag with large round wooden handles that was slung on her shoulder and pulled out a creased sheet of paper which she slapped atop the table. Her smile had vanished. Benjamin could see the muscles of her jaw tightening. "Do you care to explain this?"

"Well," Medina said, "it looks like a bill." The woman's silence urged him on. "For medical services rendered."

"You know what this is?" she said.

"I just told you."

"This is a sham. A complete fraud. No, it's worse than that. It's an outrage, that's what it is."

Medina settled heavily in the chair he had been propping himself onto, crossed his arms and his legs. "Really, Pablo? A hundred and sixty-five bucks for an ear ache?"

Medina glanced at the invoice. "We did a strep test, a flu test, a CBC."

"Why?" The woman threw her hands in the air as if she might catch the answer if only it would fall from the sky.

"I don't like the tone of this conversation," Medina said. "I don't feel the need to justify to you, you know, how I care for my patients." As he kept talking, it seemed Medina's speech acquired more and more of an accent.

"*Your* patient? No, no, no. *Our* patient, Pablo. This is *our* patient."

"Someone walks in my office," Medina said, nodding in the general direction of the front door, "they're my patient."

"He had an ear infection, for crying out loud," the woman said.

"And a fever…"

"You look in the ear and there's your diagnosis. No lab tests needed."

"That's quite a bad habit you have," Medina said.

"Which one? I have many."

"Telling doctors how to practice medicine. You're not in New Orleans anymore."

The woman smirked. This drew Benjamin's focus to the shape of her lips: the firm tubercle of the superior lip, the fullness of the curves arcing down to the commissures on each side where, on the right, he thought he spotted the faintest of scars. Then, as if triggered by his gaze, her lips twitched. Benjamin looked away for a moment, feeling as though he had been shooed away, then redirected his gaze to her eyes, feeling a bit foolish.

"I grew up here," she said in an even tone. "This is my home as much as yours."

She glanced at Benjamin. It was the first time their eyes had met and it made him feel even worse than a pestering insect: he was a petty voyeur. He half-expected a verbal rebuke, or at least some sort of and-what-are-you-looking-at glare. Or perhaps she would just dismiss him, look away with just the mildest of annoyance, the way attractive women do when confronted with a gawker. What he got was far worse. There was a subtle softening of her eyes that spilled out a glint of unveiled pity.

"What do you want from me, Claire?" Medina said. "I'm trying to run a business here."

"A business?" Claire said. "Well, that's the crux of the problem, isn't it?"

"You want me to take a vow of poverty?"

"I don't think your ex-wife would allow that, now would she?"

"She has nothing to do with anything," Medina said, a strain building in his voice.

"Is that a new Lexus I saw her driving last weekend?" Claire said. "Business must be booming."

"What do you want from me?"

"This family has no money." The sarcasm had evaporated from her tone.

"Look, I didn't know he was one of yours," Medina said. He uncrossed his arms, skimmed his finger tips in gentle loops on the table top. "I'll make sure it doesn't happen again."

"That's not good enough," Claire said.

Medina's hand motion came to an abrupt stop. He shook his head. "No way."

"Not a full refund," Claire said. "I figure forty-five dollars is a reasonable and customary charge for a simple office visit. They paid a hundred and sixty-five. Give me one-twenty and I'm on my way."

"Eighty," Medina murmured

"One-twenty."

"How do I know you won't keep the money yourself?" Medina said.

Claire cocked her head ever so slightly. She narrowed her eyes and slowly crossed her arms. She had no need to utter any more words and she knew it. Her poise declared unequivocally that she knew she had just won.

Medina knew it too. He got up, crossed the room and picked up a phone receiver. "Sonia? I need you to draft a check for one-hundred and twenty dollars to Miss Claire.

Benjamin looked at her left hand. Her fingers were exposed over her crossed arms. A jade ring fit snugly on her thumb. Her ring finger was bare. As if it mattered…

"I'll take cash," Claire said.

"Make that cash, Sonya," Medina said in the receiver. A pause. "I don't know, take it out of the petty cash box. Mark it, patient refund."

After Medina replaced the receiver on its cradle, Claire said, "See. That wasn't so hard." She turned on her heels and swaggered toward the door.

"How about that breakfast taco?" Medina said, a faint smile returning to his lips.

"You're in a generous mood today, Pablo. What's the occasion?" She shot a glance at Benjamin as if to answer her own question.

"Only five dollars," Medina said. "I need to recoup my losses. I'll throw in a slice of *tres-leches* for seven."

Claire chuckled. And just like that, there was no perceptible trace of enmity left in her manner. Benjamin wondered how much of her fury had been just a well rehearsed act.

"The offer is enticing but…" she said, "I make it a habit not to eat with wolves."

"Did you hear that?" Medina said, sounding surprisingly cheerful for a man who had just been whooped. He gave Benjamin a jab in the shoulder. "She just called you a wolf."

"I've been called worse," Benjamin said. He had been quiet for so long his voice came out hoarse.

"That's too bad," Claire said. Again that painful softness in her eyes. "Love the Mariachis, by the way," she said before walking out the door.

Benjamin stood up to spy her through the one-way mirror. She strode down the corridor, a rhythmic swing to her hips, no doubt aware she was being watched.

"Don't even think about it," Medina said. "That..." he wagged his finger in her direction, "They say there are are demons in Purgatory, and that, my friend... that is the chief devil."

8

By mid-morning Benjamin had seen a couple of infants with diaper rashes, a teenager who needed a sports physical, and a half-dozen toddlers with snotty noses. Medina's system of using scribes shuttled patients through the clinic with remarkable efficiency but Ivan the Terrible was starting to fray Benjamin's nerves.

For starters, he would get into back and forth conversations with parents in Spanish without interpreting what was said verbatim, making Benjamin wonder how much of his own medical advice Ivan was dispensing. And if that weren't enough, he volunteered unsolicited guidance almost incessantly to Benjamin, from which laboratory tests to order to which medications to prescribe.

"Might want to get a strep test on this one," Ivan said as they stepped out of the room where Benjamin had seen a two year old with obvious symptoms of a cold.

"Why?" Benjamin asked.

"His mom said he had an achy throat."

"That's because he's been coughing. Cough and snot don't go with strep. Did you know that?"

"I already documented throat pain," Ivan said.

"So what?"

"So, we can do a strep," Ivan said.

"It'll be negative," Benjamin said.

Ivan shrugged. "We get paid for negative tests

too. Did you know that?"

Just past eleven o'clock the next patient on Benjamin's docket was a fourteen year old girl who swung her legs in an infantile way as she sat perched on the edge of the exam table. The only makeup on her plain face was lip gloss and eye-liner that stretched past the lateral canthi of the eyes to give her a mock ancient Egyptian look: a puerile Cleopatra in cut-off jeans. Far too voluptuous for her own good, her breasts surged from the cleavage of her blouse, squeezed together in the mid-line by a bra whose size she had outgrown some time ago.

She spoke English with a lilting Tex-Mex accent, every answer to Benjamin's question prefaced by an "I don't know." Her older sister, who had introduced herself as the girl's guardian, was of little help. With considerable effort, Benjamin was able to learn that the patient had not passed a bowel movement in nearly a week, and that the last bowel movement was hard and painful, which was not surprising since her diet excluded all forms of plant matter with the exception of French fries. Benjamin ordered a stool softener and gave her some dietary counseling, burst her bubble when he informed her that puffed cheese snacks are not a good source of dietary fiber.

He headed back to the nurse's station, Ivan sauntering several feet behind him.

"You want a pregnancy test, doc?" Ivan asked.

"What for?"

"Abdominal complaints in a fourteen year old girl…"

"She's constipated."

"She's high risk," Ivan said.

Benjamin turned on his heels. "What makes her high risk?"

"Look at her name," Ivan said.

"Kia Romero. So what?"

"She got a luxury car name. That's high risk."

"The hell you talking about?" Benjamin said.

"You didn't know that? Girls with names like Lexus, Mercedes, Porsche, they're all high risk for STD and teenage pregnancy. We had this one girl, Infinity, she couldn't stop getting pregnant."

Benjamin rolled his eyes. "You're kidding me, right?"

"Luxury car name," Ivan shook his head, "Man, that's an automatic pregnancy test," Ivan said.

"And what would the physiologic mechanism behind this phenomenon be?"

"I don't know about no physiologic mechanism," Ivan said. "but a mother who names her daughter after a car might not be such a good role model, you know?"

"A Kia isn't even a luxury car," Benjamin said.

"Maybe not where you're from."

"We're not ordering a pregnancy test based on someone's name."

Benjamin felt a tug at the sleeve of his lab coat. A medical assistant with black framed prescription glasses looked at him imploringly.

"I'm sorry doctor. Your pregnancy test result is back," she said.

"I didn't order a pregnancy test," Benjamin said.

"Kia Romero?" She stretched on her tip-toes, cupped a hand around her mouth and whispered, "It's positive."

Benjamin glanced at Ivan. The scribe shot him a smirk. "I'll refer her to OB," Ivan said. Benjamin stood there speechless trying to make sense of what had just happened. "You gonna go tell her?"

"Yeah," Benjamin said. "Yeah, I guess I better." He began to pace back toward the exam room.

"Hey doc," Ivan said, not taking his eyes off the screen of his tablet. "Told ya so."

Benjamin rapped tentatively on the door to the exam room and stepped inside. Kia was sitting in a chair, perched over her sister's shoulder to look at a video playing on her sister's cell phone.

Benjamin sat in his stool. You have to sit to give this kind of news, he remembered being told repeatedly in residency.

"I'm sorry, doctor," the older sister said. She turned the phone off and dropped it in her purse. Kia tried to fish it back out. Her sister gave her a well-measured slap on the back of the hand and said, "Stop! The doctor's here."

"Ms. Romero," Benjamin started, "I wonder if I might have a word alone with Kia. At her age there may be things she might be uncomfortable talking about in the presence of others."

The sister's eyes widened. "What, is she pregnant?"

"I'm pregnant?" Kia echoed.

Benjamin cleared his throat. "I'd like to be able to speak to Kia alone if you don't mind."

"Oh, she don't mind I'm here. Do you, Kia? She tells me everything"

"Kia, it's up to you," Benjamin said. "Would it be okay if I discuss personal issues about your health in the presence of your sister?"

"Uh-huh," Kia said. "Am I pregnant?

"Yes," Benjamin said. "Yes, you're pregnant."

"Kia!" the sister squawked as she jabbed the girl in the shoulder. "Didn't I tell you to be careful?"

"I didn't do nothing," Kia said.

"Oh come here, baby sis," the sister said and wrapped her arms around the girl.

There were no more white plastic flags turned out when Benjamin stepped back in the hallway. At the nurse's station, Ivan was tapping away at a computer keyboard.

"Looks like we're done for the morning," Ivan said. "The boss is looking for you."

Ivan nudged his head in the direction of the one-way mirror. Benjamin couldn't help but wonder if he was being watched.

When Benjamin entered the office, Medina was sitting at a computer terminal. He spun around in his chair when Benjamin shut the door.

"Hey, Benjamin," Medina said, a wide grin on his face. "So what did you think? You're not ready to quit yet?"

"Not yet."

Medina chuckled. "That's the spirit. I hear you did a good job. A real good job."

"It was interesting, that's for sure."

"Great pick-up on the pregnant teen-ager."

"I had good help," Benjamin said.

"I know, I know. Ivan's a real pain in the ass. But he knows the system. I think he likes working with you."

"Oh, it shows."

Medina laughed. "I really like your sense of humor, man. Oh, listen, before I forget." Medina straightened. "Good news. Purgatory Regional approved your application. You just need to meet the Chief of Pediatrics to have him sign off."

"What's Purgatory Regional?"

Medina laughed. "Man, I *love* your sense of humor! Purgatory is the other hospital. It's just two blocks away from here.

"How many hospitals do we go to?" Benjamin asked.

"Practically speaking? None."

"I don't get it."

"Look Benjamin, technically speaking, El Dorado is our place. That's where we refer our patients. And if you want to admit someone and manage them on your own, hey, you're welcome to do it. But I stopped doing in-patient work years ago; been there, done that. I let the hospitalists take care of my kids now. The only reason I go to the hospital these days is for the buffet in the doctor's lounge."

"What about Purgatory Regional?"

"Purgatory Regional is what I call PR. As in, public relations. We keep privileges there so no one can say we're favoring one hospital over the other. Makes us look balanced."

"But we do favor one hospital?" Benjamin said.

"Of course, not. Not technically. But in truth? Yes. We're part of EDPG, El Dorado Physician Group, though we have no contractual obligations with the hospital per se. It's complicated, but you don't have to worry. Everything is taken care of for you." Medina looked at his wrist-watch. "You better get going. Your meeting is in fifteen minutes. Head east, two blocks, the hospital will be on your right. There's a sign for the doctor's parking lot. Go through the ER entrance and ask for Dr. Rizzo. Dr. Joe Rizzo."

"He's the Chief of Pediatrics?"

"No. The chief is Dr. Bolaños, but he's in Hawaii." Medina frowned. "Rizzo is an ER doc, head of the Credentials Committee. Hey, while you're at it, grab a bite at the doctor's lounge. Try to meet people, mingle and make friends. But go!"

Benjamin removed his lab coat, draped it over the seat back of a chair and grabbed his car keys from a side pocket of his duffel bag.

"One thing, Benjamin." Medina said. "Just a little warning. That Joe Rizzo? He's one crazy son-of-a-bitch."

Benjamin nodded. *Unlike everyone else I've met here so far.*

9

Purgatory Regional was an eight story building of pale yellow brick. A newer two-story stucco wing, a neon sign reading, *Emergency Room* plastered on its facade, extended from the main structure at a disproportionate length, producing the appearance of an amputated stump. There were surprisingly few cars parked on the baking tarmac of the doctor's lot, particularly considering it was the middle of the day. Benjamin parked his XTerra a safe distance from a gleaming Mercedes and climbed out onto the black top. The heat rolled off the asphalt in churning swells making it hard to breathe.

He had hardly taken a step when a crayon-yellow Dodge Viper with a license plate that read, "KRIPP" pulled into the parking spot next to him, forcing Benjamin to lean back against his SUV. The sound of Lynyrd Skynyrd blaring from the car's stereo was silenced in synchrony with the cutting off of the engine. A man, the size and approximate shape of a wardrobe closet, somehow managed to squeeze out of the sports car. He had beefy lips framed by an orange walrus mustache. His ruddy nose was a bulbous lump, pocked with dark over-sized pores which gave it the appearance of a giant grimy strawberry. The man pulled up on his belt buckle and strode toward Benjamin with urgency in his step.

"Hey, buddy," he said. "This here's the doctor's lot. Move your trap or be towed."

"I *am* a doctor," Benjamin said. The man's jaw slackened, his bottom lip drooping. He glared at Benjamin's truck in disbelief. "I'm new here. I just joined Dr. Medina."

"Is that duct tape?" A sneer surfaced on the man's face. "Oh man, I'm sorry." He started laughing. "I'm really sorry!" he repeated and kept laughing as he walked away.

Benjamin stood there, sweat beginning to gather on his forehead. He wanted to stay back, let the guy get a good head start to grow the distance between them even though he felt like the soles of his shoes were about to melt on the black top. As he waited, an odd sense of relief began to materialize. Clearly, the man had not recognized him. Perhaps it was true: news did not percolate from the concrete arteries of Houston down to the hinterland of the Rio Grande Valley. Maybe, just maybe, he had regained his anonymity.

He was still considering this when a military green Land Rover — the kind you'd expect to see motoring down a rutted trail of the African savannah, complete with wheel wells caked in dry mud — pulled into a spot just across from him. A tall man, in his mid-sixties, judging from his rumpled salt and pepper beard, stepped out of the vehicle. He wore a burgundy Hawaiian shirt hanging loosely over baggy khaki pants, his feet clad in leather-bottomed flip-flops which slapped the black-top with every breezy step he took.

He waved at Benjamin. "That your car?" he said.

Here we go again, Benjamin told himself.

"Yeah. I'm a doctor."

The man chuckled. "That's just swell. So am I." The man winked. "Just in case you were wondering." He looked in the direction of the Dodge Viper and pursed his lips, glanced back at Benjamin with a knowing look. For a moment Benjamin got the feeling that the man must have witnessed the incident that had just played out, but that seemed unlikely. Perhaps sensing Benjamin's befuddlement, the man spoke again. "I don't think we met." He leaned and extended his hand. "Virgil Thibodeaux at your service."

"Benjamin Snow."

"Snow! I heard about you. You're over there with Pablo." Benjamin wondered how the man could have possibly known about him working with Pablo Medina when his move had been on such short notice. "Well, it's my honor and pleasure to make your acquaintance. Lord knows, Purgatory can always use a good pediatrician." The man's velvety voice, the glimmer of his cobalt eyes, the firm grasp of his surprisingly slender fingers conveyed a cool sincerity.

"It's nice to meet you, Dr. Thibodeaux," Benjamin said.

"That a four-wheel drive?" Thibodeaux said, pointing a finger at Benjamin's SUV.

"Yeah. A crappy one."

"You kidding? She's a beauty. The way I see it, every ding, every scrape, every dent is a mark of honor."

"I'll trade you for your Land Rover," Benjamin said.

The man let out a guffaw, gave Benjamin a slap

on the back and left his hand resting on Benjamin's shoulder. Benjamin caught a whiff of his after-shave: a mix of sandalwood and cinnamon.

"I'll never get rid of that old lady. Glad I got her when I could still afford her." He shook his head wistfully. "You coming or going?"

"Just got here," Benjamin said.

"Well, let's get out of this sun before you wilt."

In the lobby of the Emergency Room Dr. Thibodeaux gave Benjamin directions to Dr. Rizzo's office. After what seemed like a very long handshake, Thibodeaux stepped onto an elevator and waved at Benjamin as the doors closed. Benjamin couldn't help but feel that all-too-familiar feeling that someone he had just met seemed to know him far too well.

He found Dr. Rizzo's office down a beige corridor that zig-zagged into the bowels of the hospital. The door to the office was open and Benjamin could see a man in teal scrubs with very short sleeves riding high over huge deltoids, sitting at a computer terminal, his back to the door. Benjamin cleared his throat and rapped on the door jamb. The man swiveled around in his chair and peered over metal-framed reading glasses perched near the tip of his nose. A sour scowl was etched on his features in sharp, deep furrows — furrows so well chiseled as to generate the impression that this was the man's habitual, if not his perpetual, facial expression.

"What's the matter with you?" he said. "Didn't you read the e-mail?"

Benjamin stood there, open-mouthed. "I'm

sorry, what e-mail?"

"The conference room is down the hall."

"Oh, you wanted to meet in the conference room?" Benjamin asked.

The man squeezed his eyes shut and shook his head, as though some stoic level of patience had been completely exhausted. "What's your name?" he said in a feeble voice.

"Snow. Benjamin Snow."

The man blinked his eyes. His face softened into a dumbfounded expression. He jumped to his feet, reached out with his right hand. "Joe Rizzo. Christ! I thought you were one of the new family practice interns. Why didn't you say anything?"

Joe Rizzo was in his early thirties, handsome in a clean-cut, rugged way, maybe just a hair below average height for a man, but the girth of his shoulders, the breadth of his arms, the way he puffed out his chest, made Benjamin think that he was overcompensating for a perceived inadequacy.

"You're Medina's new hotshot," Rizzo said.

"I don't know about the hotshot part."

"I saw your CV. Rutgers undergrad, Tufts medical school, you're a hotshot all right. What the hell are you doing in Purgatory?"

"Long story," Benjamin said, wondering if Rizzo knew more about his past than what was printed on his CV.

Rizzo glanced at a clock on the wall. "I wasn't expecting you here so early. I have to give this orientation talk for the new interns starting their ER rotation."

"I can come back," Benjamin said.

"Nah. Tag along. It won't take a minute. Heck, I'll orient *you* too."

Rizzo grabbed a stiffly creased white coat off of a hook behind the door and the two walked down a narrow corridor.

"Rutgers, huh?" Rizzo said. "You know, I'm from Jersey."

"I would have never guessed," Benjamin said.

Rizzo smiled. "I don't care how long I live here, I'll never sound like a Texan. You from the garden state?"

"Illinois."

"Yeah, I didn't think you were. How'd you end up at Rutgers?"

"Seemed like a good idea at the time," Benjamin said.

"What are you a joker? Of all the colleges you could have attended, with a few choice ones right there in the Midwest, you ended up at Rutgers? How come?"

Benjamin shrugged his shoulders and gave a dopey smile. "Long story."

Rizzo raised his eyebrows. "Every thing's a long story with you," he said as he opened the door to a conference room.

Three women and two men sat at the long table of the narrow room. Their expressions were a mix of confusion, eager anticipation and trepidation. Interns in July: a pitiful, dangerous lot.

Rizzo marched to the front of the room.

"Should have brought my Ray Bans," he said. "Your coats are so white I think I'll go snow-blind." There was subdued laughter. Rizzo's facial features stiffened, "Listen up, clowns. I'm Dr. Rizzo, and this is my Emergency Room. Not a bird falls to the linoleum that I don't know about it, *capish*?"

Benjamin remained on his feet, leaned his back against a wall and crossed his arms. He looked over the interns. They were already squirming in their seats.

"This here is Dr. Benjamin Snow," Rizzo continued. "He…" Rizzo pointed at Benjamin, then did a gesture with both hands as if he'd produced a white dove out of thin air, "…is a doctor. You know what you guys are?"

"Interns?" a guy with a pencil neck said in a half-whisper. More nervous laughter.

"You guys are sponges. Promiscuous sponges. Nothing but a bunch of mindless bottom-feeders in a murky sea of unfiltered information. The only thing you know how to do is suck up facts and regurgitate them on command, unchewed and undigested. You've never had to use your virgin brains. Those lumps near your ears, those quivering flaps of gray matter, might as well be gills because no one's ever taught you how to think, how to analyze, how to make inferences. To make things worse, you're equipped with vestigial sense organs. Few of you can feel, most of you are deaf, and all of you are blind. You know what that makes you?"

"Interns?" pencil neck repeated a little louder. No one laughed.

"It makes you deadly," Rizzo said. "A thousand

times deadlier than a great white shark. So, rule number one in my ER, try not to kill anybody. Rule number two, ask for help. Rule three, look out for each other."

Rizzo paused, let that hang in the air for a while.

"Now, I need one of you clowns to be lead intern for July," Rizzo said. "That means you have the privilege of reporting directly to me, any gripes, complaints, grievances, and even the odd useful observation. You will also lead your fellow 'terns by providing an example of efficiency, hard work and dedication. So, who's going to be my lead 'tern?"

A woman with intense eyes and shiny red hair raised her hand.

"What's your name?" Rizzo said.

"Abigail Morton."

"Why the hell should I pick you?"

"I'm organized, I'm motivated-"

"So what?"

"I was in the top third of my class at-"

"Now, get one thing straight, all of yous. I don't give a rat's rump where any of you clowns went to medical school. Don't matter to me if you went to Harvard, Yale or Tufts." Benjamin's ears perked up. Of all the schools he could could have picked, he had to bring up his own alma mater. Not a coincidence. Rizzo must have really meant it when he said he was going to orient him too. "That kind of stuff don't impress me at all. What I really want to know, Dr. Morton, you ever worked as a waitress?"

She shook her head, said "God, no," as if the mere suggestion was offensive.

"Any of yous here work as a restaurant server?" Rizzo asked. A plump man with a receding hairline raised his hand just to the level of his shoulder. "What's your name?"

"Osvaldo Campos."

"All right, Ozzie, what kind of restaurant was it?"

"It was, you know, Italian."

"Family-owned?" Rizzo asked.

"Yeah."

"So, let's see if I get this right, see if I can surmise your job description, so to speak, what your work-flow was like, cause I'm into work-flows as you'll soon find out. So the customers walk in. They get seated. You bring them menus and take their drink orders. So far so good?"

Osvaldo nodded.

"Then they order their entrees. And that's the longest time you'll spend at their table, the time taking their order, wouldn't you say?"

"Sounds about right," Osvaldo said.

"Now, the entrees, they come with soup or salad?" Rizzo asked.

"Soup *and* salad."

"Soup *and* salad. What a deal. So, do you push your ticket to the kitchen right away after taking the order?"

"Depends," said Osvaldo. "If they order the chicken *Cacciatore* or the *braciole* I do."

"And why is that?" Rizzo said.

"'Cause that takes a while to cook. But if they

order a pasta dish, you better hold onto the ticket for a while. Otherwise the entree comes out half-way through their salad."

"And that's not good."

"No. The customers get upset like you're rushing them."

"Got it." Rizzo said. "And what's the key to making a killing on tips?"

"Well, be nice, smile, don't screw up the order…"

"And what else?"

"Well, keep turning over the tables so you get more tickets."

"How many tables in your station, Ozzie?" Rizzo said

"Anywhere from eight to ten."

"What happens if you don't turn those tables over?"

"Man, everything gets backed up. Everyone gets pissed."

Rizzo clapped his hands. "Ozzie, congratulations. You're my lead 'tern. The rest of you listen and learn."

"I don't get it," Abigail Morton said.

"You don't *get* it?" Rizzo said. "Weren't you paying attention? Didn't you hear what he just said?"

"About soup and salad? I heard every word. I still don't get it."

"Listen up, scouts. This ER is like Ozzie's Italian restaurant. Instead of tables, here we got sick bays. The customers are known as patients. Our reservation method is called triage. When the patients get seated they don't need a menu: they know their symptoms by heart, and many of them are repeat customers — they already know what they want. We don't serve any drinks, but a pillow and a warm blanket go a long way to keeping the customer happy till you get around to taking their order. The order? That's your history and physical exam, that's where I want you to spend the most time with your customer. The key to not screwing this up is to listen, touch the patient, and keep your eyes open. We don't do soup or salad here but we have things like vital signs, pain medication and IV fluids. Try to get those things out *pronto.* Our main courses are blood tests, EKGs and x-rays but everyone is really waiting for the dessert — our house specialty: the diagnosis. Once you've got the right diagnosis, the treatment plan is a cinch. You either stabilize and admit, or you treat and street. To keep those beds turning over, learn which entrees come out quick and which ones take forever. Just so you know, our CAT scans take longer to cook than Ozzie's chicken *Cacciatore.* That department works on geologic time, so try not to order one unless you really need it. Same goes for admissions to the floor. If you got an admission, push that ticket to the kitchen right away. Now get to work."

"And that's it?" the pencil neck guy said.

"No, one more thing," Rizzo said. "Don't forget to smile and be polite."

Rizzo nodded at Benjamin and headed for the door. Benjamin followed him out.

Walking back down the corridor, Rizzo asked,

"So, hotshot, what d'ya think?"

Benjamin said, "I think if medicine doesn't work out for me I know enough to be a waiter now."

They reached Rizzo's office. Rizzo stopped at the doorway and said, "It'll work out for you." He grabbed Benjamin by the arm and led him into his office.

Rizzo sat behind his desk, legs crossed and rubbed a thumb just under his jaw line. He said, "So how does a boy from Illinois end up at Rutgers?"

"I had a soccer scholarship," Benjamin said.

"No kidding. What position?"

"Center forward," Benjamin said.

Rizzo nodded his head, his lips in a grimace to demonstrate he was properly impressed. "My baby brother played a little college soccer. I guess we can say he was a star in high school but guess what? He didn't score a single goal in four years of college. How about you?"

"I scored a few."

"You played all four years?"

"Only three. Didn't play my senior year."

"Injury?" Rizzo asked.

Benjamin shook his head. He wasn't ready for this conversation. Hadn't talked to anyone about it in ages. "It's a long story."

"Another long story."

"Let's say I had different priorities my senior year."

"Fair enough." Rizzo nodded. "Right. Well, I don't have a problem with your application for privileges here."

"Seems like nobody in Purgatory does," Benjamin said, an unintended edge in his voice.

"I guess you already met Soto-Prinz," Rizzo said. "Did he slip you the ham?" Benjamin must have had a puzzled look on his face. "The *prosciutto*. Did he feed you the ham?"

"Yeah. Yeah, as a matter of fact, he did."

"That old pompous goat. You know what that's all about, don't you?"

Benjamin shook his head. "It was weird, though. Practically shoved it in my face with a knife."

"Old Spanish custom from centuries past. You see, there were a good many Jews living in Spain back in the day, and there was a good amount of anti-Semitism to boot. So they were forced to live in hiding, the Jews, that is — took Christian names and all to avoid persecution. Except some Spaniards got tricky. To avoid having their fine Christian homes sullied by the presence of a Jew, they came up with a sort of litmus test. They'd serve up a little ham and pork as an offering of welcome. If you refused to eat, it outed you as a Jew. Nobody does that anymore, except for the esteemed Dr. Fermin Soto-Prinz."

"I thought he was British," Benjamin said. "You know, the way he talks."

"Studied at Oxford, but he's a Spaniard," Rizzo said. "He's lived in Texas way longer than England, you'd think he'd have dropped that phony British accent by now."

"You don't seem to like him very much,"

Benjamin said.

Rizzo uncrossed his legs and leaned forward. "You go by Ben?"

"Benjamin."

"Listen Benjamin, I work some shifts over at El Dorado. Have little choice over that, but I go in, I go out, mind my own business and keep my mouth shut." He paused, as if waiting for a response from Benjamin.

"OK."

"The same I did when I bussed tables at this restaurant in Newark where all the good fellas came for a bite. I'm a Jersey boy, after all. Got a sixth sense when it comes to these things."

"A sixth sense about what?" Benjamin said.

"Just take a look at the doctor's parking lot over at El Dorado. See all those luxury cars? And don't forget the fancy homes, the personal jets. Those bonuses and dividends the partners get, how does that happen in a backwater town no one's ever heard of deep down in South Texas?"

"A great business model, I guess," Benjamin said.

"Right. Now tell me, what business is that?"

10

Benjamin entered the Medina clinic from the rear access door after parking in the covered car-port. When the heavy metal door clanged shut behind him, the air-conditioning unit shuddered to life and settled into a low-pitched hum. There was no one in the hallways. The sound of muffled voices were just perceptible above the whirring of the fan's motor. They grew more distinct as Benjamin approached the nursing station.

Ivan was sitting, leaning forward resting his elbows on the counter, his head slightly tilted, listening intently. He put his finger to his lips when Benjamin said, "Hey, Ivan."

Benjamin glanced at the only exam room door that was shut. Behind it, the muffled voices grew louder, more animated.

"Wait for it…" Ivan murmured. He straightened in his chair and pretended to be busy on a computer keyboard. "Here it comes."

The exam room door swung open. A flushed Pablo Medina walked out. He slapped the blue plastic door flag flat against the wall and pulled out the white flag.

"Oh, Benjamin," Pablo said when he turned and saw Benjamin standing there. A meek smile formed on his lips. "This one's for you."

"Is everything okay?" Benjamin said.

Medina's smile vanished. "I just can't take him anymore. I'm getting too old for this crap, okay? He's all yours."

Medina trudged toward the private office, wiping his brow with the back of his hand.

Benjamin waited until he was gone before asking Ivan, "What's the story?"

"Jesus Tamez. High school drop-out. No good punk."

"What's he here for?"

"Hell if I know," Ivan said.

"What's the chief complaint?"

"None listed." Ivan pushed back in his chair and rose to his feet. "You ready to roll?"

When they stepped in the room, the patient was sitting on the wheeled doctor stool, spinning in dizzying pirouettes.

"That's the doctor's chair," Ivan said.

The boy stopped spinning. He regarded Ivan with an expression of feigned contemplation, then snorted and rubbed the side of his nose with his out-stretched middle finger.

"Hi Jesus. I'm doctor-"

"Man, my name ain't *Hay-soos.* It's *Jee-zus.* Get it straight. And that home-boy," he pointed to Ivan, "can get the hell out right now."

"It doesn't work that way," Ivan said.

"You wanna bet, princess?" the boy said lifting his chin. He had shiny black hair that settled over his crown in waves, and a mustache that seemed to have been painted with the lightest of brush strokes.

"You want a piece of me?" Ivan said.

"Ivan," Benjamin said. "I got this."

"You hear that, home-boy? He got this," the boy said, a contemptuous smile stretching across his lips.

"It doesn't work that way," Ivan said.

"I got it," Benjamin said.

Ivan paused. He nodded, walked to the door, opened it, then turned on his heels and said, "You think you're tough, but you're just a punk," before exiting and shutting the door behind him with a thud.

"Yeah *vato*, get out and stay out. And don't go pressing your ear on the door like you always do," the boy shouted.

Benjamin waited a moment, let out a soft sigh, then stretched out his hand and said, "Jesus, I'm Dr. Snow."

The boy pulled his finger tips across Benjamin's palm and laughed. "Man, the name ain't *Jee-zus*. It's *Hay-soos*. I was just fooling."

"All right, Jesus."

"You want your chair back?"

"No, it's okay." Benjamin leaned against the exam table. "So, why are you here today?"

"I got *el chorrito*."

"You'll have to help me," Benjamin said. "I don't speak Spanish."

The boy sighed. He cleared his voice and said, "Leaky pipes."

"Say again?"

"Well, it's like… you know, I got the leaky pipes."

Jesus was looking up at him beseechingly. Benjamin crossed his arms and shook his head.

The boy's Adam's apple lurched. In a near whisper he said, "I got custard in my boxers."

Benjamin leaned forward, trying to make sense of the boy's unintelligible speech, his mind still a blank.

Jesus hesitated for a moment. Finally he blurted out, "You know what I'm saying, man? I'm pissing needles."

"Oh. You have a penile discharge."

"That's what I been saying the whole time."

"OK, let's take a look then," Benjamin said.

Jesus got to his feet and started unbuttoning the fly of his jeans.

"Man, are you going to stick that Q-tip up my snake?"

"You've had this before?" Benjamin said as he washed his hands.

"What can I say? I'm a player." Jesus pulled down his pants and boxers in a single motion. His exposed genitalia were shaved and smooth but for the short stubble that was just starting to sprout from the dark, goose-pimpled skin over the pubic promontory, making his penis look like the head and neck of a scraggy, plucked bird. A tiny drop of watery yellow discharge clung guiltily to the urethral opening.

"We can just get a urine test," Benjamin said. "No swab needed."

"No shit?" Jesus said.

"We'll need to get a blood test though."

"What for?"

"HIV. Syphilis."

"Aww, man. What the hell?"

"You said you're a player," Benjamin said.

"Why you gotta go there? I don't have no AIDS. My girls be clean."

Benjamin looked at him impassively. "You can pull up your shorts now."

Jesus pulled his pants back up and buttoned them. He smiled, "I got it. You trying to scare me, right?"

"You should be scared."

"Don't worry, doc. I don't got no AIDS. Go ahead, do the blood test. You'll see."

"You can't keep doing this," Benjamin said.

"I know, man." The boy's expression turned solemn in an overdone way. "Deep down, I know you're right."

"You have to use protection."

"What can I say? When you're right, you're right."

Jesus patted Benjamin on the shoulder, as if to console him. The boy had gleaming onyx eyes. The sneaky smile that was just dawning on his lips was disarming. Benjamin couldn't help but like the kid.

"You go to school?" Benjamin asked.

"I'm all done with school already."

"Really."

"Yeah. I'm in the body work business. You know, cars, trucks, all that." The boy was all bluster. In a softer voice he added, "My uncle's shop."

"Did you graduate?"

"It don't matter," Jesus said.

"I know that at your age you might not

appreciate the value of an education," Benjamin said.

Jesus laughed. "Man, how long you been down here?"

"Just a couple of days."

"A couple of days? Hell, you don't know nothing then. Look here, an education won't do nothing for someone like me. Not in Borderlandia."

"Borderlandia?"

"Yeah, man. Borderlandia, the place of the in-betweens, where nothing is as it seems," Jesus said in a dreamy voice, his eyes narrowed, his shoulders moving side to side to an unheard rhythm.

"You don't have to live here your whole life. You can always leave if you want."

"Hardly anyone ever leaves Purgatory, not alive, anyway. And that's the truth."

The boys words grated on Benjamin's nerves. He tried to change the conversation. "You plan to work for your uncle all your life?"

"All my life is today. If tomorrow comes, then we'll see. Maybe one day I'll go work for *El Chacal*."

"Who?" Benjamin said.

"Oh man, you really don't know nothing. Now I'm worried about you."

"You're worried about *me*," Benjamin said with a sardonic smile.

"*El Chacal* owns Borderlandia, don't you know? They say he has the blood of the devil in his veins, that he can kill a man just by looking him in the eyes." Jesus raised his forearm to show Benjamin the gooseflesh that was sprouting. He laughed and rubbed his arm: a boy who believed his own ghost stories. "What's your name again?"

"Snow. Dr. Snow."

"Like snowflake? Hell, there ain't never been a snowflake in Purgatory before. You're the first. Man, you're going to melt here."

Benjamin took a step toward the door. "I'll go print out your prescription. See you back in two weeks?"

"So you going to be my doctor from now on?"

"That's up to you."

Jesus nodded. "Yeah. I like you, Snowflake. And don't worry, I got your back."

"Condoms, *Hay-soos*. And your girlfriend…"

"Yeah, I know. I'll get her checked."

"Back in two weeks." Benjamin opened the door.

"Hey Snowflake," Jesus called out. "Welcome to Borderlandia."

11

It was a couple of days later when, late in the morning, Benjamin was called to the nursing station of the Medina clinic to receive a phone call. "A doctor," the medical assistant said. "He said it was an emergency or something like that."

"This is Dr. Snow," Benjamin said, pressing the horn against his ear.

"Dr. Snow, Joe Rizzo over at Purgatory Regional. Look, I got a kid here, a real piece of work, says you're his personal doctor. Came to the ER wheezing pretty badly. Apparently ran out of his asthma meds."

"Really? I don't have any personal… I mean, I don't think I can be his personal doctor."

"Name is Jesus Tamez," Rizzo said. "Ring a bell?"

"Oh. Oh yeah. I didn't know he had asthma," Benjamin said.

There was a pause.

"That might be a good thing to know about your patients."

"Right, right. What should I… I mean, you want me to come right over?" Benjamin said.

"We got his airways opened up pretty well now. But he insists on seeing you before we discharge him. I was thinking, what the heck? Why don't you make a cameo appearance in the ER when you finish up your morning patients, give the kid your blessing, and you and me grab some lunch at the doctor's lounge?"

Half-an-hour later, Benjamin walked into the Emergency room, stethoscope dangling around his neck. He asked a nurse who was busy charting on a computer terminal where he might find the patient by the name, Jesus Tamez. She looked him over and said, "And who are you?"

Just then, Joe Rizzo walked out of an exam room. He said, "There you are."

The nurse quickly lost interest in Benjamin and went back to charting.

"I tell you, that kid's a piece of work," Rizzo said. "Let's get him out of here before he drives my entire staff nuts."

Benjamin followed Rizzo up a corridor that smelled like cleaning solution and buffed linoleum. Rizzo slid open the glass door to an ER bay and stood back to let Benjamin enter first.

Jesus Tamez was sipping orange juice through a straw from a round plastic container. He looked up and grinned. Set the empty juice container on the table that was extending over the bed.

"Hey doc," Jesus said. "I knew you'd come."

"Dr. Rizzo tells me you were pretty sick," Benjamin said.

Jesus glanced at Rizzo who was was standing in the doorway with his hands in the pockets of his lab coat.

"Ah, what does he know? *You're* my doctor. I don't trust nobody else," Jesus said.

"You didn't tell me you had asthma," Benjamin

said.

"You didn't ask," said Jesus. "Anyway, this ain't like real asthma. It only happens when they burn the sugar cane."

Benjamin shot Rizzo a quizzical look.

"They burn the sugar cane fields south of the border this time of year," Rizzo said. "Makes it easier to harvest. Not so good for the lungs but we do get a hell of a sunset."

"I could have refilled your medications," Benjamin said. "Save you a trip to the ER."

Jesus said, "It's all good. No need to beat yourself up about it, Snowflake."

"What did he just call you?" Rizzo said.

"It's okay, Joe," Benjamin said.

"Wait a minute," Jesus said. He cackled with laughter until he coughed. "Wait a minute, wait a minute, wait a minute. Your first name is Joe?"

"Yeah, so?" Rizzo said.

"Joe Rizzo?" Tears were welling up in the boy's eyes as he convulsed with laughter.

Benjamin looked at Rizzo and shrugged his shoulders, unable to conceal a grin of his own.

The boy was able to regain some sense of composure and managed to say, "Hey *Chorizo! Chorizo*, listen here, what's your wife's name? *Jamon* and eggs?" He erupted in laughter again.

Rizzo tapped Benjamin on the shoulder. "Get him the hell out of my ER," he said, and stormed out of the room.

Joe Rizzo appeared to be one of those guys who can't hold a grudge for more than a few minutes. "Piece of work, that kid," he muttered as he led Benjamin to the doctor's lounge, the usual scowl on his face.

The doctor's lounge at Purgatory Regional had five or six mismatched tables. Along one wall was a buffet table with a fogged-up glass sneeze-guard. A flat screen TV locked on a news channel with stock prices streaming along its bottom was bolted to the opposite wall. There was a small group of younger physicians huddled morosely at one table. At the other end of the room a familiar figure sat alone: Virgil Thibodeaux, wearing a deep blue Hawaiian shirt featuring giant white Hibiscus blooms.

"How's the chicken, Virgil?" Rizzo asked as he approached the table.

"Rubbery," Thibodeaux replied, "but still less lethal than the Tilapia."

"Benjamin," Rizzo said, grabbing Benjamin by the arm, "let me introduce you to Dr. Virgil Thibodeaux, physician, philosopher, philanthropist, and most importantly, the last true gentleman in this town of rogues."

"Joe, as much as I appreciate your hyperbole, you're a tad late," Thibodeaux said. "I already had the pleasure of meeting Dr. Snow. So why don't you stop the jabbing and put your masseters to better use."

Rizzo and Benjamin went to the buffet table, scooped up pale chicken breasts and wet green beans and gritty mashed potatoes and sat down with Thibodeaux.

"So what's the good news?" Rizzo asked.

"*Les haricots ne sont pas sales,*" Thibodeaux said.

"What's that mean?" Benjamin asked.

"That's Cajun talk," Rizzo said.

"It means, the green beans are not salty," Thibodeaux said. "And I'm not referring to the green mush on your plates. It's a way of saying, I've got nothing spicy to report. They gave me the usual song and dance upstairs."

"Those bastards," Rizzo said.

"No need to be so harsh," Thibodeaux said.

"What is it with these people? Don't they get it?" Rizzo said.

"It's hard to apply judgment when you're immersed in fear," Thibodeaux said matter-of-factly. "How's your chicken, Dr. Snow?"

"It sure is chewy," Benjamin said.

"Amazingly rubbery," Thibodeaux said. "The lengths they must go through to produce this effect! But it you can ignore the texture, it's really quite tasty."

The door to the lounge swung open. The oaf of the Dodge Viper Benjamin had crossed in the parking lot the other day sulked in, wearing creased, over-sized scrubs. Virgil Thibodeaux looked down at his plate and chewed pensively. Joe Rizzo too, seemed unusually quiet, tense. The guy ambled to the buffet table, picked up a slice of corn bread, put it right next to his nose, gave it a loud sniff before tossing it back on the serving platter. He grabbed a chicken breast with his bare hand, chomped out a big mouthful and leaned back on the buffet table.

"Goddamit," he said with his mouth full. "Everything in this damn hospital is second rate."

"Why aren't you in the OR, Krippendorff?" Rizzo asked.

"MAFAT, that's why. Goddam MAFAT," the oaf said.

"Who's that?" Rizzo asked.

"It's not a who, it's a what. Hey old-timer," Krippendorff kicked a back leg of the chair Virgil Thibodeaux was sitting in. "How's your lunch?"

"The price is right," Thibodeaux said, unperturbed.

"I bet it is," Krippendorff said. "They have MAFAT back in the day when you practiced?"

"I still have a full practice," Thibodeaux said.

"You know what I mean," Krippendorff said with a sneer. He turned to Rizzo. "MAFAT. Stands for Mandatory Anesthesia Fuck-Around Time — the bane of my existence."

"Everything's the bane of your existence, Kripp," Rizzo said. "You really got to learn to take it easy and give us all a break."

"Take it easy? Take it *easy*? Let me tell you something, these goddam Ibbidy-Abbidys are killing me." Krippendorff caught a glimpse of Benjamin's perplexed look. "That's how they speak. *Ibbidy abbidy, ibbidy abbidy* — can't understand a damn word they say. I don't know why they even let these foreign grads practice in the first place."

"Screw you, Kripp," Rizzo said.

"No offense, Rizzo. I got nothing against you, personally," Krippendorff said. "But I got this curry-muncher doing my gas, first case this morning, and she hasn't got a clue. Keeps slowing me down, making comments about the patient's heart rate. I know the damn heart rate! I can see it on the goddam monitor! And by the way, the blood pressure is holding up just fine, thank you very much. But she just keeps at it, *ibbidy abbidy, ibbidy abbidy*, until I just want grab her by the neck and press that dot on her head hoping it's a goddam reset button."

"Dr. Agarwala is one of our best anesthesiologists," Rizzo said.

"Yeah, well they're all raghead terrorists to me," Krippendorff said.

Rizzo pushed back in his chair back, fists clenched. Thibodeaux clutched Rizzo's arm, shook his head. At the same time, a wall-mounted phone rang. Krippendorff answered it.

"'Bout fucking time," he said before slamming it back on its cradle and storming out of the lounge.

"I swear I'm going to pop him one day," Rizzo said.

"That would be beneath you," Thibodeaux said.

"Just one good one," Rizzo said.

Thibodeaux chuckled. He picked up his fork and knife and made a fresh incision in the chicken breast.

"Okay, professor," Rizzo said in a calmer tone. "Please illuminate us."

Thibodeaux methodically chewed the mouthful of chicken, swallowed, took a long drag of water and cleared his throat. "Physician arrogance is an all-too-common occurrence: perhaps the greatest threat to the practice of medicine today."

"How do guys like Krippendorff get in the business for starters?" Rizzo asked.

"There are basically two paths to this level of conceit," Thibodeaux said. "On one hand you have those individuals who have been brought up immersed in a life of privilege, and on the other there are those who have suffered dire deprivation. The privileged look down on their fellow man as matter of constitution, whereas those who have suffered hardship view their own success as proof of their superiority. In either case, there is usually an added impetus that leads to such consuming contempt."

"And what's that?" Rizzo asked.

"A truly threatening sense of insecurity," Thibodeaux said.

Rizzo sat back in his chair and stared blankly into space. After a few moments of contemplation he said, "Of course. You're right."

Thibodeaux turned to Benjamin. "You're a man of few words, Dr. Snow."

"I don't know what to say," Benjamin said. "I feel like I'm a stranger in a strange land."

"A strange land it is," Thibodeaux said.

Benjamin thought of every interaction he'd had since arriving to Purgatory. In nearly every instance he was left nonplussed, as though he were always the only one that didn't get the punchline of a joke everyone else was laughing at. His thoughts turned to Jesus Tamez. "Who is *El Chacal?*" he asked.

Rizzo and Thibodeaux looked at each other.

"Did I say it right?" Benjamin asked.

"Some say *El Chacal* is a mythical figure," Thibodeaux said. "Natives swear that the blood of the devil runs through his veins. That he can kill a man just by looking at him."

"He's a drug dealer," Rizzo said. "A ruthless killer, nothing more."

"Which is it?" Benjamin asked.

"Maybe both," Thibodeaux said. "Maybe neither."

"I don't get it. Is he for real?" Benjamin said.

"Who knows!" Rizzo said.

"Yes. He's for real," Thibodeaux said.

"The way it works around here," Rizzo said, "whenever someone gets killed it's always *El Chacal* gets the blame, or the credit, depending on your point of view. And with all the drugs that get smuggled through here from south of the border, there's plenty of killing to go around." Rizzo said. "Why do you ask?"

Benjamin was embarrassed for bringing up the subject. "Never mind. Someone just mentioned the name and I was just wondering."

Rizzo was about to say something but Thibodeaux raised his hand and the ER doc hushed.

"Benjamin, listen very carefully," Thibodeaux said. His voice was frighteningly sober. "I speak as a devoted atheist and unflinching skeptic, and yet I can't deny that there is a pervasive wickedness — some might even call it, evil — right here in Purgatory. And the name of this evil may just as well be, *El Chacal*."

12

Pablo Medina had promised Benjamin the services of his personal real-estate agent to help him find a apartment "suitable for my young partner". In the mean time he suggested boarding at the Twisted Nopal Guest Ranch on Presidio highway heading northwest out of town, where a furnished suite complete with kitchenette could be rented at an extremely reasonable weekly rate with little fuss.

The ranch was a single story L-shaped cinder block building whose only feature which was even remotely ranch-like was a covered, wood-planked porch that skirted its entire front. Off to the side was a kidney-shaped swimming pool, its wooden-deck painted a rusty burgundy that stained the soles of your feet if you dared walk on it barefoot, and just beyond, a separate two-story house which served as office, laundry room, sundry store, and home to Myrtle Beale, the owner and general manager of the property. Myrtle had wispy red hair stacked high as cotton candy. Her left eyebrow seemed permanently propped in a round arc, as though she had become stuck in a state of perpetual skepticism. Though the sun had baked deep grooves in her features, Benjamin could tell that in her youth she must have been nothing short of stunning.

For the most part, the guests at the ranch were long-haul truck drivers waiting for payloads coming from south of the border (the NAFTA boys, Myrtle called them) and middle-management types in shirtsleeves and khakis: men of few words who spent the bulk of their off hours in the air-conditioned shelter of their rooms.

After a few nights at the Twisted Nopal, Benjamin wondered why he should bother moving at all. He liked the idea of his neighbors constantly changing — people who kept to themselves even when they ventured out to sit by the pool sipping low-calorie beer from super-sized cans. It wasn't solitude he was after but the promise of blissful anonymity. When Pablo's agent called and left several messages on his voicemail, Benjamin found he was in no hurry to call her back.

Near the end of the first week, a dark van with tinted windows pulled up, just before dusk, and four garishly dressed young women stepped out. Myrtle dashed out of her office, a bundle of keys in hand, and quickly herded the women into two rooms at the far end of the ranch.

Later that evening, when Benjamin went to pick up a load of freshly-washed clothes from the coin-operated laundry, Myrtle intercepted him on his way out, asked him how he was getting along, and in apologetic tones explained that those young girls that had just come in? "They're circuit dancers. Won't be here but a couple of nights. Still, you better keep your wits about you. They're professionals."

Apparently, the girls did more than dance. And the NAFTA boy in the apartment next to Benjamin's had not done a very good job of keeping his wits about him because at two in the morning Benjamin was awakened by a thumping on the wall behind his head — a thumping highlighted by overblown groans that shed new light on Myrtle's admonition.

Benjamin lay awake listening to the muffled voices, feeling ever the voyeur. Thankfully, the ruckus finished in a matter of minutes. There were some murmurs, the sound of a woman's laugh. Finally, Benjamin heard the sound of a screen door slamming shut and then all was quiet. But by now he was unable to fall back asleep. He lay on his side, looking out the back window onto the parking lot, his eyes fully accustomed to the darkness, and thought of his lack of connections and wondered why his desolation did not provoke more emotion. For his entire young adult life, his professional aspiration had been an obsession that eclipsed all other concerns. The other pieces, he told himself, no matter how naive and inexperienced he was in these matters, would fall into place once he'd reached his objective, once he had truly accomplished something, once his worth as a human being had risen to a tenable value. Until now, he had achieved nothing of consequence: his diplomas meant not a thing — they were just stepping stones that anyone of average intellect could reach with the right motivation. But his quest had been stalled now. He had been placed on an unforeseen hiatus. He wondered if that somehow changed the rules he himself had set, if that might acquit him of a temporary lapse in focus. He closed his eyes and imagined how he would react if, out of the blue, there were a knock on the door from one of the professionals.

The next morning, when Benjamin went to the office to pay for a subsequent week of rent, Myrtle looked worried.

"I hope everything's all right" she said.

"Oh, everything's just fine," Benjamin said.

Looking relieved, Myrtle asked, "Just how long you planning to stay with us?"

"I'm not sure. Do you need some sort of move-out notice?"

"I meant, in Purgatory."

"Oh, one year," Benjamin said.

"And not a day more," Myrtle added as though she had heard it in his voice. "You found yourself a permanent residence yet?"

"Haven't even started looking."

"Well ain't it your lucky day." Myrtle straightened her spine, dabbed her neck with a folded cotton hankie. "I got just the place for you." She slid open a heavy wooden drawer and pulled out a set of keys which she dangled in mid air. "We'll take my truck."

They drove southwest on Presidio highway, about a half mile towards town, turned left on a narrow farm-to-market road that rose and narrowed to a single lane where it crossed an irrigation canal.

"There's catfish in there if you like fishing," Myrtle said. "You like to fish?"

"I don't like catfish," Benjamin said.

Myrtle grinned. "Use the right bait, who knows, you might hook yourself some sushi."

A large field opened on the left side of the road, with evenly spaced rows of green.

“Them’s cabbage,” Myrtle said. “Can hardly smell it ‘cept for the summer, but then you get used to it.”

The truck slowed with a groan of the brakes and pulled into a gravel driveway to the left. To the right of the driveway, which ended right on the edge of the cabbage field, sat a squat white stucco bungalow, a green corrugated plastic carport propped up by flimsy metal poles extending from the back wall.

“It’s cozy. And it’s private,” Myrtle said as she killed the engine.

Benjamin stepped out of the truck. There was a sweet smell wafting through the air, not so heavy to be unpleasant. The outside walls of the home looked as though they had been recently white-washed. The front door had a metal overhang held up by two round metal posts painted in spiraling red and white stripes.

Myrtle stepped up to the door and slipped the key in the lock. “Place was my father-in-law’s, God rest his soul. He called those poles his candy canes.”

“They remind me of old barber poles,” Benjamin said. A breeze picked up, lifting the sweetness from the earth.

Myrtle turned, seemed to study his expression. “I can have them painted over if you want.”

Benjamin said, “No, I like them.”

The house was perfect. The front door opened onto a low-ceilinged but spacious living room with a kitchenette tucked in a corner. The only bedroom had a north-facing wood-framed window that looked onto the cabbage field and, further in the distance, a thin grove of cotton wood marking the border of the farm tract. Throughout the house, the floor was a darkly stained hardwood parquet that seemed to have been recently polished.

"How much are you asking?" Benjamin said.

"Before I tell you, I have to be straight with you about one thing." Myrtle said.

"Bad plumbing?" Benjamin said.

Myrtle smiled wistfully. "Reason I haven't been able to rent out this place, people are a little superstitious around here. You see, Papa died here."

"I'm not superstitious."

"Me neither," Myrtle said. "But still, that expression on your face when we were standing outside? I thought you felt something. It gave me the gooseflesh." She chuckled as he crossed her arms.

"How much did you want?"

Myrtle hesitated. "Five-hundred a month."

"Deal," Benjamin said.

Myrtle handed him the key to the front door. "I never asked what line of work you're in," she said.

"I'm a doctor."

She frowned. "You at El Dorado? That's just a hop and a skip away from here."

"Yeah, I might go there from time to time."

Myrtle shook her head. "Knew I should have asked eight-hundred."

Even with all his possessions moved in, the house looked bare. Benjamin unzipped his back pack and pulled out the check for moving expenses Medina had unexpectedly given him. It was the largest check he had ever received: eighty-five hundred smackers — ten grand in all, if you counted the portion that went to EDPG PAC. He wondered what that was all about, why Medina was evasive when he asked about it, but why should he let it bother him?

What did it matter? He had just been handed a sizable chunk of cash for doing nothing, for just showing up. If this kept up, he'd be able to pay down a good part of his student loans before starting his fellowship. Still, technically speaking, this EDPG PAC took a pretty good chunk of his money (it *was* his money on paper). Again, he thought about asking Medina about what that was all about. But why piss him off? He'd probably let him know soon enough.

Eighty-five hundred. That would take care of two months rent, pay off seven grand on his student loan and he'd still be left with five-hundred bucks. He scanned his apartment. No, he wasn't going to waste any money on furniture. But there was one thing he had wanted for some time.

The mountain bike was a steal at six-hundred bucks. Okay, so he went a little over budget, but he hadn't even received his first real paycheck yet and he was already way ahead of the game.

There were a couple more hours of sunlight left so Benjamin strapped on his helmet, slipped on his Oakley sunglasses and set off on his new wheels. Perhaps it was because he hadn't ridden a bike since college, or maybe he wasn't used to the gear shifter, but as he set off pedaling down the farm-to-market road he felt vulnerable and the thought passed his mind that perhaps he had made a big mistake purchasing the bike. He hadn't done anything to deserve it after all.

He turned north-west on Presidio highway, out of town. The sun was dipping into a haze that sat over the horizon and the sky came ablaze in a bright ochre. It reminded Benjamin of what Joe Rizzo had said about the burning sugar cane making for a hell of a sunset.

Now *there* was a character, Joe Rizzo. Maybe he could ask *him* about the EDPG PAC. Why was he stuck on this? Why was it still bothering him?

He pedaled faster, finally gaining confidence in his saddle. A drainage ditch shouldered the road and now a vast citrus grove spread west-ward: oranges and grapefruit, made red by the blood of innocents according to Dr. Soto-Prinz.

The bike was a great idea. The temporary fog of buyer's remorse had evaporated by now, and with it, that gripping muscular tension which had accumulated over God knows how many years was dissipating from his body. For the first time in a very long time, he felt care-free. So much so that he was oblivious to the pickup truck that pulled a U-turn after passing him from the other direction, and was now approaching at his back, far too slowly.

13

The powder-blue finish of the Ford F-150 had been bleached by the unforgiving Rio Grande Valley sun, giving the portrait of the Virgin of Guadalupe stenciled on its tailgate an eerie glow. Just below the feet of the Madonna, a sticker of a blue and white Dallas Cowboy's star was plastered onto the rusted chrome bumper.

JT and Ruben squatted between the wooden crates in the truck's bed, while Hector sat alone in the cab, one hand on the steering wheel, the other pinching the end of a joint.

Hector coughed up whatever it was that had been rattling in his chest and spat out the open window before taking another drag. "Hey Rube!" he shouted. "The stop sign."

The spindly boy in the truck's bed glanced at JT. JT nodded. Ruben reached into a crate and pulled out a plump yellow onion. "Bo-ring," he murmured, not loud enough for Hector to hear, while he whisked off the outer peel of the onion. The truck slowed to about 30 miles an hour. Ruben stood on the bed and assumed his signature pitching stance.

"Nail the 'O'," JT said. "Fastball."

"What else is there?" Ruben said.

"What are you waiting for, *cabron*?" Hector yelled from the cab. "Hurry the hell up!"

"Let's see what you got, Rube," JT said

Ruben stared at the stop sign in the distance

with those eyes that managed to look sleepy even as they bulged out. JT looked up at him and smiled. If he ever did make it on a pitcher's mound, JT thought, it would be easy to under-estimate the kid with the milky bug-eyes, the knock-kneed gait, the knobby elbows poking out all girly like, and the long black hair tied up over his head, Samurai-style.

His eyes still fixed on the stop sign, Ruben shook his head once. Shook it again. Then nodded. He wound up his southpaw then whipped the arm around in an unconventional way, letting the onion fly. A moment later, the projectile clanged off the stop sign and landed in a nearby ditch.

Before Ruben had a chance to steady himself, the truck screeched to a halt. Ruben tumbled into JT's arms.

Hector laughed, his eyes on the rear-view mirror. He said, "Hey little faggots, no making out in my truck," and laughed again until he coughed, dropping the joint on the crotch of his jeans. "Oh fuck! Look what you made me do."

Ruben sat back on a crate. "How fast was that?" He asked JT.

"Had to be over ninety," JT said.

"No fooling?"

"Yeah. No doubt."

"Damn, cuz. I never got over ninety before. You think I'm ready for the minors?"

The truck started moving again.

"You gotta learn to throw some other stuff first. Sliders, curveballs, changeups, knuckle balls," JT said.

"But I'm all about the fast ball," Ruben said.

Hector called out from the cab, "Ruben! Get ready! Mailbox on the left."

JT looked in the cab, found himself gawking at the back of Hector's buzz-cut head. He could never figure out why Hector's scalp rolled up the way it did, all bunched up like a wrinkled blanket. Ruben once said that maybe the globules of fat couldn't find any other place to settle and had to migrate north onto his head. Made it look like his brain had grown over his skull. Ruben called it "Shar Pei head", but only when Hector wasn't around.

Hector thought himself real tough but JT knew he was just plain mean, and JT had no use for bullies. So he preferred to crouch in the bed of the truck, squatting between onion crates, than to sit in the cab with that prick.

Ruben was palming an onion now, as though it's outer skin was made of cowhide. He said, "Tell me if I hit ninety again."

"I'm looking," JT said.

Ruben took a deep breath. There were fewer theatrics this time before he let the onion rip through the air. Again, the missile found its mark leaving a deep dent in the wall of the aluminum mail box.

"Damn cuz!" Hector hollered. "You nailed it good this time."

Ruben sat back on a crate, wiped his hands on the legs of his jeans, those thyroid eyes sparkling. JT let out a whistle.

Ruben looked down to hide the crooked teeth

behind his goofy smile. He said, "You'll teach me how to throw that knuckle ball?"

"I don't know. Then you'll go up North, pitch in the Minors, and I'll still be stuck in Borderlandia with," he whispered, "Shar Pei head."

"You'll come with me," Ruben said. "I need a manager."

"If I'm your manager, you gotta do what I tell you," JT said.

"Okay," Ruben said. "But I'll still throw fast balls."

JT chuckled. "Yeah. That'll be your signature pitch."

"Like Nolan Ryan."

"Like Nolan Ryan," JT said. He knew what was coming next. Must have heard Ruben say it a million times.

"Hey JT, you know Nolan Ryan?"

"Yeah?" JT played along. He knew Ruben needed this, like some kind of a prayer he had to repeat over and over. "What about him?"

"You know Nolan Ryan? Well, Nolan Ryan, he pitched so fast blind people would come out to the games just to hear him pitch."

"No kidding?"

"Yeah. That's how fast he threw."

The truck bounced over a pothole as it turned south-east onto Presidio highway. A light breeze was blowing from the south. Even with the stench of the onions, JT could smell the smokiness of the air. He patted the breast pocket of his shirt to make sure his inhaler was still there.

"Holy shit!" Hector shouted from the cab. "Hey little faggots! You gotta see this."

Ruben and JT stood to look over the cab. On the other side of the street, coming toward them was a guy on a bicycle, complete with helmet and wrap-around shades.

"Where the hell did this creep come from?" Hector said.

The guy passed by. The truck slowed to a crawl and JT knew that meant trouble.

"Hey Hector, I gotta get home," JT said.

Hector rolled the steering wheel hard counterclockwise. Ruben and JT held on as the truck completed the U-turn.

"Get ready, cuz," Hector said. "You're about to make the major leagues."

"Come on, Hector," JT said. "It ain't worth it."

"Shut the hell up, you little queer. This is my truck. And this is my 'hood. Where the fuck did this *cabron* come from anyway? That's lack of respect, man. Get ready, cuz."

"No way," Ruben said. "Mailboxes yeah, people no."

"You're gonna peg him in the head," Hector said. "Or I'll tell your mom what I caught you looking at on my computer."

"I wasn't looking. They were *your* pictures."

"And it was your boner in your shorts, Junior," Hector said.

"Come on Hector," JT said. "It ain't worth it.

You're on probation."

"Man, you're a real friggin' prick, you know that? What the hell you gotta bring that up for? What's it got to do with anything? You know what? You better shut your mouth or I'll break my probation on your face. Get the onion, cuz."

Ruben glanced at JT. JT nodded. He whispered, "Not the head."

Ruben picked up an onion. The guy on the bike was still about 50 yards away but they were creeping up on him and closing the gap fast.

"Get him good, *entiendes*? Or I'll tell your mother what a filthy little mind you have."

The guy was getting closer. Hector swerved left into the wrong lane of traffic to give Ruben a better angle. They were so close now that JT could see a large stain of perspiration on the guy's back. *Idiot*! What the hell was this guy thinking riding a bike in this heat? Or in any weather, for that matter, in this of all places?

"Do it!" Hector said.

Ruben wound up, whipped that arm around, beaned the guy good just above the elbow. It must have been a hard blow because it made the guy lose his grip on the handlebar. The bike wobbled for a few seconds, then the front wheel went askew and bike and rider plunged into the ditch on the highway's shoulder.

Ruben ducked next to JT as the truck sped away.

"Why'd you throw so damn hard?" JT asked Ruben while Hector wheezed with laughter.

"I only got the fastball," Ruben said.

The truck slowed unexpectedly now. JT and

Ruben were slung to the right as the truck pulled into another U-turn: Hector's victory lap.

JT slouched down against the back panel of the cab, pulled his knees up and tried to make himself small. Hector stuck his arm out the window in the direction of the biker, middle finger outstretched.

The guy was sprawled out on the side of the ditch. There was blood on his face. The wrap-around shades had half fallen off. Even with the helmet tilted down on his brow, JT recognized him. He had to look away.

"Did you see that?" Hector said.

"Why'd you have to throw so hard?" JT whispered.

He was tempted to take another look, just to make sure, but he didn't have to. He knew it was him. Knew it was his doctor. Dr. Snowflake.

14

One afternoon, back in the fifth grade, Benjamin was knocked off his feet by an errant soccer ball that pegged him in the back of the head. As he lay prone on the turf, dazed, still trying to make sense of what had happened, he heard Archie Doyle utter a single word.

Klutz.

Right on cue, Archie's minions burst into howls of laughter. Benjamin didn't move, didn't dare rub away the sting of pain, didn't try to get up. He kept his forehead down in the turf so they couldn't see his face. Just bit down on his lower lip and held his breath to contain his tears.

It wasn't the pain, it wasn't even the fear of standing up to Archie Doyle that kept him pinned down. The force that pushed down on Benjamin, that left him unable to move, frozen in absolute defeat, was the stifling mantle of self-loathing, as though his very state of being had somehow invited that soccer ball to strike him, in retribution no doubt: the exacting cosmic punishment for an unforgotten tort. Sprawled out on the grass, he knew it had to be his own fault that the ball struck him — he should have known to duck. He should have known that he had it coming to him all along.

That same feeling was washing over him again as he lay in the ditch a few feet from his bike. Benjamin tried to replay the sequence of the fall in his mind but his brain was in a fog. He remembered that his left arm had been pushed off the handlebar, as though someone had slugged him above the elbow. That must have caused him to stray off the pavement, onto the dirt shoulder. Almost immediately, the front wheel found a deep rut in the dried mud and jerked to one side, and then… then what?

He recalled going down hard against the stem of the handlebars as the back of the bike came up in a sort of cartwheel. And then he was airborne. But not for long. He must have landed on his left shoulder since he was lying on his side.

And he remembered the sound of a car engine. Had he been hit by a car? He considered this a moment. He couldn't have been. He was already in the ditch when the deep rumble of the engine went by. And he was pretty sure he hadn't been knocked out cold.

There was something warm and sticky on his neck. He rolled on his back and reached up to wipe it. But when he moved his left arm, a searing jolt of pain hit him, as if a white-hot poker had been pressed against his shoulder. He took a few deep breaths, then slowly ran the finger tips of his right hand along the surface of his left collar bone.

He tried to be objective even as his fingers traced the bony hump. *Angular deformity of the medial third of the left clavicle.* Spit began to pool in his mouth. He was going to be sick. He managed to roll over and get to his knees. He retched once, twice. Nothing came up. He took a couple of calming deep breaths, exhaled slowly through pursed lips.

Red splatters were appearing on the dry grass below him. He gazed down to see more spots bloom, stared at them with a mild curiosity. He began to feel detached from his surroundings, as though he were floating, his body growing numb. The sound of an engine growing louder jolted him.

Perhaps someone was stopping to help. He tried looking up in the direction of the highway. Through the sweat that trickled down his brow he could just make out the outline of a blue pick-up truck slowing down. It didn't stop. An arm was sticking out of the driver's window, the hand in an up-turned fist. The middle finger came up slowly. Benjamin heard a cackle of laughter just before the truck sped away.

He was feeling light-headed now. Without even a trickle of a breeze, the air was heavy and stale in the ditch. He wiped his neck with the tips of his fingers and brought them up in front of his eyes. His fingers were covered in blood. *Great. Just great.*

He let his hand fall back to his side. It grazed something hard and round which was sitting on the grass. He grasped the object, looked down to inspect it. It was an onion. He rolled it in his hand. The outer skin stuck to his bloody fingers and peeled off. He released his grasp and let the onion roll onto the ground.

To his relief, the light-headedness was passing. Sooner or later he'd have to get up. He glanced at his bike. The back wheel was still spinning. The front one was still. He could see why. The fork was bent at an angle that made him think of his collar bone.

Once more, he heard the sound of an engine

approaching. He reached for the onion, wild-eyed. Clenched it in his hand. His heart was thumping. He could feel the muscles in his arms engorging and thought he might start shaking from the surge of adrenaline.

But as the sound of the engine grew closer, he realized it couldn't be the pick-up truck this time. It was coming from the wrong direction, and the engine note was completely different: a high-pitched pinging rather than a baritone rumble. The vehicle stopped. The engine shut off.

Through the sparse weeds on the side of the highway, Benjamin could make out a white roof-line and a row of windows along the side of the vehicle. It was some sort of van. No. The sound of that engine was unique. It had to be a VW bus.

There was the patter of footsteps now. He let go of the onion, looked at it roll down a rut in the ditch and wished he had tossed it farther away as though it were incriminating evidence of some kind.

He looked up again. A woman was side-stepping down the dusty bank of the ditch. She wore a floppy large-brimmed sun hat and blue reflective aviators. Some sort of flower-child, Benjamin thought, a wanna-be hippie. Yet she moved with a resolve, an economy of motion that seemed incongruous to her wardrobe. As incongruous as the odd mix of relief and utter embarrassment that now swept through Benjamin.

He looked down, put his right hand on the floor and pushed to try to get to his feet. His first though was to grab the bike, mutter that he was OK, thank you, and ride away, bent fork and all.

"Don't get up," the woman said in a crisp, authoritative tone. A familiar voice. He turned his down-cast eyes to her feet, let his eyes move from her leather sandals, glide up the loose pant legs of her faded jeans, and by the time his gaze had reached her waist he was sure it was her.

"That's quite a gash on your chin."

"My chin?"

"Does anything else hurt?"

There was no hint of recognition in her tone.

"My collar-bone. I think its-"

Claire (he hadn't forgotten her name) pushed on his clavicle before he could finish the sentence. Benjamin let out a scream and grabbed her wrist with his good hand.

"Your left clavicle is fractured."

"You think?"

"Listen, I'm a nurse."

"Good for you. I'm a doctor." He let go of her wrist.

Claire tilted her head down, slid the shades down the bridge of her nose and peered at Benjamin through narrowed eyes. Benjamin imitated her gesture with the Oakley's that were dangling on his face.

She said, "Oh, it's you." She didn't sound too pleased. "I didn't recognize you with the…" She drew a circle in the air with her finger. "And sure as hell didn't expect to run into you in these parts."

"That makes two of us."

"I guess your country club membership hasn't

come through yet." Her voice was saucy now.

Benjamin managed a smirk. "Yeah, well, that was my butler's fault. I had to let him go."

To this she smiled. Most women look far more attractive when they smile. Claire was drop-dead gorgeous even when she scowled, but the smile gave her a wholesome glow that took Benjamin by surprise.

"You're going to need a few stitches," she said. A conciliatory tone this time. "Can you stand up?"

"Sure. I'm fine. Really, if you need to go…"

"Take your shirt off."

"What?"

"We need to put some pressure on that cut to tamp the bleeding before you pass out on me. Can you raise your arms?"

Benjamin nodded. He tried to reach back to pull his t-shirt off but a white-hot jolt of pain reminded him of his broken collar bone. He bit his lower lip until the pain passed.

"Smarts a little. Don't it?" she said.

"Really, I can manage by myself if there's somewhere you need to be."

"Don't be silly," she said. Then in a softer tone, "Let me help you."

She lifted his good arm, dug a fingernail in a seam in the armpit of his shirt, wiggled it until she got her whole finger in, then grabbed the shirt with both hands and gave it a good rip. She managed to tear off a sizable piece of cloth that wasn't completely saturated with sweat. She folded the rag and positioned it on Benjamin's chin.

"Hold pressure."

"That was a good shirt."

She smiled again. "Not really. You think you can walk?"

Benjamin felt wobbly when he stood up. He managed to climb the bank of the ditch but it was when he had to cross the hot black-top that he began to feel disjointed — found himself concentrating on every step, aware of Claire hovering just off to his side. The front fork of the bicycle was so badly bent that she had to lift it up off the pavement and roll the bike on its rear wheel.

"The door's open," she said.

"Need help with the bike?"

"I got it."

She slid the side door of the VW bus open. It came to a stop with a clang.

"Get in. I got this," she said.

Claire lifted the bike with a stiff heave and let it drop in the back compartment of the bus. The bike landed hard and the front fork snapped off.

Claire whispered, "Oops."

"That's a new bike." Benjamin said.

"*Was* a new bike."

Benjamin climbed in the passenger seat without saying a word. As Claire came around the front of the bus and settled in the driver's seat, he just stared straight out the windshield.

She reached for the key in the ignition but then hesitated and glanced at him. "Aw, come on," she said. "With what Pablo's paying you, you can buy a new bike every week."

"Really. You know that?"

"I know a lot more than you think," she said. She turned the engine on. "Let's get you fixed up then. I know someone who can throw a clean stitch faster than you can-"

"You know someone? You're kidding, right? Just drop me off at El Dorado ER."

Claire's laugh was so unexpected Benjamin's body actually jerked. "That's really funny. If you think I'm stepping foot in that cesspool you're either really thick or you bumped your head pretty darn hard."

"Look, it's *my* face, and that's where I want to go, okay?"

"Well it's *my* car and… just shut up and buckle in already."

"You're kidnapping me," he said.

"In your dreams."

She pushed down on the clutch. There was a tooth-jarring grinding of metal as she thrust the gear shifter into first. Her foot came off the clutch too abruptly and the bus lurched a couple of times before steadying on its way.

Benjamin waited a moment and then said, "You have a real soft touch."

"Just not used to driving this thing."

She managed second gear without too much trouble though she forgot to take her foot off the gas and the engine let out a high pitch whine in protest.

"You been driving stick shift very long?" Benjamin asked.

"You been riding bikes very long?" She flashed him a smirk.

"If you wanna know, someone pelted me with an onion. That's how I fell." Benjamin lifted his sleeve to expose the bright-red blotch over his biceps.

She stole a glance. Shook her head. "Dumb thing to do. Riding a bike out here."

"Oh, so it's my fault."

"Just saying, you're going to have to get your bearings around here if you want to make it out of Purgatory in one piece," she said.

"What makes you think I want to leave Purgatory?"

"Oh please!" She rolled her eyes.

Soon they were back in town, crossing strip malls that all looked the same: nail spas, taco joints, cell-phone outlets, dollar stores. And doctor's offices. How could there be so many doctor's offices in one town?

"Wasn't that the turn-off for El Dorado?" Benjamin asked.

"I told you I'm not going there."

"What's so bad about El Dorado?"

She took in a deep breath. "I hope you're dumber than you look. I really, really hope so."

15

Benjamin felt a slight tug on his jaw as Rizzo began to tie the first suture.

"So how'd you twos end up together anyway?" there was a ring in Rizzo's voice that made the query come off like a schoolyard taunt.

"We're not together," Claire said, no annoyance detectable in her voice. "I spotted him in a ditch off Presidio highway. Can you believe it? Out by Sanguinity Point."

"And you stopped?"

"He looked harmless."

"Hell of a place to go for a bike ride." Rizzo said.

"He doesn't know any better," Claire said.

They were carrying on as if he weren't there. Benjamin could only lay still and listen from under the plastic-lined paper drape, trying to relax the muscles of his jaw while Rizzo sunk the curved needle in for the second stitch.

"Funny. I was just thinking the other day of introducing the twos of you to each other."

"That *is* funny," Claire said. "Why would you think such a thing?"

Rizzo chuckled. "Dr. Snow is all right." He raised his voice now. "Benjamin, lift your right hand if you're all right."

Benjamin lifted his hand, relieved his face was covered by a drape, and glad as hell he didn't have to participate in the conversation.

"See," Rizzo said. "I told you he was all right. You know he played soccer in college. At Rutgers no less. Was pretty good too. Made All-American his sophomore year." Again he raised his voice to address Benjamin. "Oh yeah, Benjamin, I took the liberty of trolling you on Google. Hope you don't mind." A little softer now. "Weird thing is, he stopped playing after his junior year."

"Must have got hurt," Claire said.

"Nah, he didn't. You didn't get hurt, did you?" Rizzo nearly shouted, as if Benjamin wouldn't be able to hear him even though he was standing right above him, as though the paper drape on his face had the acoustic qualities of a reinforced concrete. Benjamin wondered why doctors universally developed this tendency to talk as though all their patients were hard of hearing.

Benjamin wagged his index finger at Rizzo.

"No? You quit then." Rizzo said.

Benjamin gave him a thumbs-up.

"A quitter," Claire said. "Just the type of guy I like to meet. Yeah, you should really introduce us some time."

"Hey Benjamin?" Rizzo said. "This is Claire." Benjamin waved. "Claire? Benjamin."

'Enchante', I'm sure."

"Claire speaks French," Rizzo said. "Sharp as a tack. That's why I wanted the two of you to meet. You guys are the two smartest single people I know in Purgatory. You *are* single aren't you, Benjamin? And

Purgatory, well it ain't exactly the kind of place that's easy to meet people."

"Some of us aren't looking," Claire said.

"But that's the very best time to meet someone," Rizzo said, "when you're not looking."

"How are those stitches coming along?" Claire said, in a clear attempt to change the conversation.

"Take a look. Whattaya think?"

Claire said, "Not bad. Not bad at all."

Rizzo chuckled. "She wouldn't let the intern sew you up, Benjamin. You hear me? Comes knocking on my office door, asking if I can do her a personal favor."

Claire said, "That poor intern had this pathetic deer-in-the-headlights look about him. I just didn't want Mr. Know-it-all to blame me for not taking him over to El Dorado. I was gonna just take him over to Pops."

"Oh yeah? Why didn't you?"

"You should have seen him. He made this big fuss. I really don't think he's as smart as you make him out to be. Hmm, that really is looking good, Joe," Claire said.

"I try."

"Pops always said you're a damn good doctor."

"Anything that comes through the door," Rizzo said. "You know what I mean? That's what I love about this job. Anything that comes walking, dragged, pushed or wheeled into my ER, I know I can take care of it. That's the thrill of it. I realize I don't have the book smarts-"

"Don't say that."

"I didn't go to Rutgers and Tufts," Rizzo said.

"That doesn't mean anything in my book," Claire said.

"You want to hear something, Benjamin? I went to med school in the Caribbean. My MCAT scores sucked. So yeah, I'm an FMG: a foreign medical grad, in case you're wondering what the hell I'm doing in Purgatory. But I figure, it's all because I was such a dumb kid. I had so much ground to make up for by the time I got to college."

"I can't believe you were a dumb kid," Claire said.

Rizzo laughed. "I was so dumb as a kid, let me tell you, I was so dumb that when my parents had people come over to visit, I thought, when they stirred their coffee with their little metal spoon, that they did it just to make that pretty clinking noise, like it was some kind of ritual or something, before you drink your coffee. Yeah, that's how dumb I was. Get this, there was a steel foundry out by where my grandparents lived, white smoke coming out the smoke stacks? I thought it was a cloud factory. You know, where all clouds came from."

Claire laughed. "That's not dumb. It's kind of cute."

"The dumbest thing of all? Get this. One day my mom is telling my dad about how a neighbor's kid almost choked on an olive pit. Ambulance had to take him to the hospital and all — he was all right in the end, owns a little dry-cleaning monopoly over in Hackensack now. But it must have left a heck of an impression on me, cause from that day on, every time I heard an ambulance siren, I figured some poor bastard was inside with an olive pit stuck in his throat. Like that was the only thing they used ambulances for."

"That only holds true in parts of New Jersey," Claire said.

"But wait, wait," now Rizzo was laughing. "The worst part, to this day, every time an ambulance pulls up in the ER driveway with the sirens going, first word that pops in my head? That's right. Olive."

"Well, if one day someone does roll in with an olive stuck in his throat, you'll be ready."

"Anything that comes through the door. That's my motto." Rizzo pulled the drape off of Benjamin's face. "But I'm still waiting for that damn olive."

Benjamin squinted under the procedure light, stunned by how vulnerable he felt under its familiar yellow glow. Rizzo reached up and flicked the light switch off. He peeled off his surgical gloves, still inspecting the wound. Then brought his eyes to meet Benjamin's.

Rizzo's gruffness seemed to melt away for a moment. His subtle expression was one of encouragement, of solidarity. No, it was far more. It was an expression of connection: of true caring. Stooping over the gurney, Rizzo gave a slight nod.

Benjamin felt a throb of embarrassment and wondered why he should feel that way. Was it because he had caused so much trouble through his ineptness? Because he wasn't worthy of even the faintest act of compassion? And then he began to wonder what his own patients must see when they looked to him with yearning eyes, and a denseness began to weigh down on his chest.

A stocky nurse in pink scrubs pulled open the drape to the emergency room bay open and said, “Rizzo, you’re needed in Bay 1, STAT.”

“Is it an olive?” Rizzo said.

“An Olive?” The nurse pruned up her face. “I don’t know if the name’s Olive but we got a *señorita* trying to squeeze out a brand new U.S. citizen. Head’s crowning and she’s a damn good pusher.”

“I’ll clean up here,” Claire said.

Rizzo started rushing out, stopped, holding the curtain in his hand. “Everything that walks through the door,” he said, winked and pulled the curtain shut behind him.

Claire stepped by the bedside and seemed to take stock in Benjamin. “You okay?” she said in a tone that was measured but soft around the edges.

Benjamin had been quiet for so long he had to clear his throat. “Sure.”

“You looked a little shaken for a moment.” She pulled the stainless steel table close to her. Poured some saline from a plastic bottle into a shallow tub filled with gauze. “I’ll just clean off some of this antiseptic.”

She picked up a sheet of saturated gauze, wrung it out and began dabbing around the wound.

“Still numb?”

Benjamin nodded.

“You have a good jaw,” Claire said. The comment seemed to startle even Claire. “Some women might find that attractive." The tone had hardened a bit, but her attempt to back-pedal was unconvincing. She tossed the gauze in a metal bucket, got a clean one and resumed cleansing in growing circles, past the perimeter of lidocaine-induced numbness. The wetness was strangely soothing. Benjamin averted his eyes, choosing to stare up at the metal clasps of the curtain that secured their flimsy privacy. Anything to avoid her gaze.

No words were uttered as Claire continued working. Benjamin heard the trickle of another gauze getting wrung out. He closed his eyes. To his surprise he felt the cool wetness of the gauze drawing across his forehead now.

A lump formed in his throat. He breathed slowly, deeply through his nose, squeezed his eyes to keep tears from welling up. Claire passed the gauze over his eyebrows, each stroke slow and measured. And Benjamin marveled at how shallow and empty his life suddenly felt.

Claire said, "I know that house. The one with the candy cane poles?" She down-shifted pretty smoothly and turned north where the irrigation canal drains through a culvert.

"Barber shop poles," Benjamin said.

"So you live in Don Hortencio's old place. That means you met Myrtle."

"How do *you* know the place?"

Claire shrugged. "I used to come here with my dad. House calls. You sure you don't want to stop for something to eat?"

"I just want to get home."

"Got any food in the fridge? I could whip up something in a minute. An omelet. You gotta have some eggs."

"I'm not hungry," Benjamin said. "What I really need is a shower."

"I won't argue with that."

She pulled into the driveway and parked behind Benjamin's SUV.

"Go on in," Claire said. "I'll get the bike."

"What's left of it."

"With what Pablo Medina pays you, you can buy a much nicer one every day this week and two on Sunday."

"You keep saying that. How would *you* know what I earn?"

"You're an El Dorado boy. Aren't you?" Claire said. She slid open the side door of the VW bus.

Benjamin reached in his pocket and fished out his key chain. As he took a few wobbly steps toward the front door, the thought of the signing bonus from the EDPG PAC flitted across his consciousness and he wondered if he really was an El Dorado boy.

"What do you have against El Dorado, anyway?"

Claire dragged the bike out of the cargo bay and let the back wheel bounce onto the gravel. She reached back in and grabbed the severed front wheel.

"Open the door, will you?"

His left arm in a sling, Benjamin fumbled with the lock, pushed the front door open with his foot.

Then he helped Claire lean the mangled bike against the living room wall.

"What do you have against El Dorado?" Benjamin asked her again.

Claire straightened, pivoted on her heels and gazed at the empty walls of his home.

"I love what you did with the place. Your designer must be one of those Scandinavian minimalists. That single chair in the dining area? Now that's a bold statement."

"There's another chair in the bedroom."

"I think I'll skip that part of the tour," Claire said.

"Oh look, I wasn't trying to-"

"You want to know why I don't like El Dorado?" Claire said. "I'll tell you why. When they opened the hospital they had a unique opportunity to do something good for this community. There are needy people in Purgatory, in case you haven't noticed." She shook her head. "But what did they do? They created this massive profit center. A hospital with no soul. They milk every last penny from the Winter Texans that come down from Iowa, Nebraska and Wisconsin, put in new hips, catheterize every coronary they can get their fingers on, scope every open orifice they can find. And the old geezers are happy because they get bottled water and a newspaper delivered to their room every morning, and what do they know? How would they know that the procedure they just had was completely unnecessary? And the locals? Well, the hospital tries to pretend they don't exist, especially if they don't have insurance. Which may be a good thing at the end of the day."

"Wait, you're accusing El Dorado of doing unnecessary surgery?"

"Everybody knows it. One of the Cardiologists was caught red-handed falsifying cath reports. The hospital paid a fine to Medicare, less than a day's take in all likelihood, and the next morning it was business as usual."

"And the Cardiologist?"

"He lost his license," Claire said. "What do they care? There's no short supply of greedy doctors. Are you going to ask me about the nurse?"

"What nurse?"

"The whistle-blower. The one who reported the cardiologist to Medicare when the hospital's administration did nothing. Do you want to know what happened to her?"

Benjamin sighed. "What happened to the nurse?"

"They found her hanging from the terrace of her apartment with an electrical extension cord around her neck."

"She killed herself?" Benjamin asked.

"That's what the sheriff's report concluded anyway." Claire took a few slow steps, turned and leaned against the kitchen counter. "She was a single mom with a three-year old daughter. I knew her."

"Wait a minute, what are you saying?"

"What I'm saying is there are two general categories of doctors at El Dorado: the mercenaries and the useful idiots."

"Wow. That's pretty harsh." Benjamin said. He sat down. He was really starting to feel drained. "So what category is Joe Rizzo in?" Benjamin said.

Claire blinked a few times, as though she were suddenly reminded of a pressing matter. "Joe is the exception. He's in the category that worries me to death."

"What about me, Claire? Do you think I'm a mercenary or an idiot?"

Claire fixed his eyes on Benjamin's in a contemplative gaze.

"What are you doing tomorrow?" she asked.

"I'm not going for a bike ride. That's for sure."

"It's Saturday. Do you have to work?"

"Not this weekend."

Claire nodded. "Okay then. I'll pick you up in the morning." She stood there a moment before crossing the living room and opening the front door. Before shutting the door, she turned and said, "God, I hope you're an idiot."

16

The wind picked up from the west that night and rattled the flimsy windows of Benjamin's tiny house. Every time he dozed off, the noise snatched him awake again. The orange bottle of hydrocodone he had picked up from the pharmacy at Claire's insistence sat untouched on the kitchen counter. He considered getting up to pop one, or maybe two for good measure. That would be sure to help him get some sleep at least. He thought about it some more and decided against it. He hated the way that stuff made him feel. Better to suck it up and bear the pain.

But he knew that part of his refusal to take the medicine was just one more stubborn act of rebellion against Claire. But why? And why couldn't he stop thinking of her?

It wasn't until the early morning hours that he settled into a restless sleep whose calm was rustled by a banal yet vexing dream that kept replaying as if it were on some kind of a loop. By morning he could no longer remember the dream and realized it was the constant gnawing pain, not a nightmare, that spoiled his sleep. Thankfully, it was Saturday so he wouldn't have to go to work. But he'd have to face Claire. She made it clear she was coming — to check on him and to show him something she thought he really needed to see.

He checked the time on his cell phone. It was 6:30. He had no idea at what time Claire would be showing up. He decided he had better shower and get dressed.

When Claire knocked on his front door he was still fumbling with the buttons of a short-sleeve shirt which seemed to be the most reasonable thing to wear while in a sling.

"The door's open," Benjamin said.

She walked in with a paper sack in her hand. Held it up and gave it a shake.

"You like breakfast tacos, don't you? Everyone likes breakfast tacos." She was wearing a beige knitted blouse, navy capri pants and red espadrilles. If there was something consistent in her sense of fashion, it was that she had a penchant for clothes that seemed to be meant for a different era: elegant but anachronous.

She strode to the kitchen counter. Set down the paper sack, picked up the opaque plastic medicine bottle and held it up to the morning light which was streaming in through the window. She shook the bottle close to her ear.

Claire said, "I bet you haven't taken a single one."

"The pain wasn't so bad," Benjamin said.

"You are one really awful liar, you know that?"

She reached in the paper sack, pulled up a small bundle wrapped in aluminum foil and said, "Potatoes and egg?" She tossed the package in Benjamin's direction. Benjamin was still working on getting that last button of his shirt through its stiff little button hole when he saw the taco sailing toward him. He tried to snatch it out of the air with one hand but as he reached for it he twisted his injured collar bone just enough to send needles of pain up his neck. He fumbled the taco and it landed on the floor.

"I'm sorry," Claire said. "I forgot. You were a soccer player weren't you."

And with a wry smile she peeled the foil off of a taco and took a big, satisfying bite.

"Where's your bus?" Benjamin asked from the passenger seat of the car.

Claire was behind the wheel of a sensible gray Toyota sedan this time.

"What, the VW? That's not mine. It belonged to my mom. I finally talked my dad into selling it. I just decided to take it into town yesterday so the buyer wouldn't have to drive all the way out here."

"Your mom passed away?"

"Ovarian cancer. Nine months ago."

"I'm sorry."

Claire kept her eyes fixed on the highway and said nothing. Finally she whispered, "We're almost there."

They took a dirt road off the highway where a painted wooden sign read, "Clinica El Milagro - 2 miles." The dirt road made its way through a neighborhood the likes of which Benjamin had never seen. Tiny unpainted cinder block houses with rebar springing out of concrete columns, and trailers sitting high on brick platforms sat in bare yards bordered by sinking chain-link fences. In every crowded yard, laundry hung stiffly from sagging clothes lines. A hen and her chicks were scratching in the dirt off the side of the road while a tattered dog chained to a tree barked at the car as they passed by. Barefoot boys, no older than four or five, one wearing just Spider Man underwear, waved at them with gleaming smiles.

"What did you say this place is called?" Benjamin asked.

"This is Colonia El Milagro. Where I picked you up yesterday, that was over by Sanguinity Point, which is a kind of no-man's-land."

"Drug trafficking?"

"Drugs and people. Not a good place to stroll through if life expectancy is one of your priorities."

"What about you?" Benjamin said. "Don't you care about your life expectancy?"

"They leave us alone. Besides, we don't really have a choice."

"Us. Whose us?"

"Me and Pops. We run the clinic."

"Your father is a doctor?"

"Are you pulling my leg, Benjamin? Pops told me he met you. Thought the world of you."

It was the first time she had used his name. It sounded nice to hear her say it.

"Wait a minute. I know your father? What's his name?"

She chuckled. "I mean, how many people do you know in Purgatory? No, I'm not telling you. This is too much fun. You'll have to just wait and see."

The road got bumpier. Claire maneuvered around the larger pot holes as if she'd done it a million times. Finally she turned into the dirt courtyard of a one-story building with a covered front porch furnished with two straw and pine rocking chairs. A single vehicle was parked in the lot: a mud-caked Land Rover.

Benjamin said, "Of course. I guess that makes sense."

Virgil Thibodeaux was reclining with his feet crossed atop his desk when Benjamin and Claire stepped in his office.

Claire said, "Hey Pops"

Thibodeaux looked up from the New England Journal of Medicine he was reading. Tossed it on his desk and clasped his hands behind his head.

"You brought a friend. Well, this is truly perplexing."

"Hello Dr. Thibodeaux," Benjamin said.

"What's so perplexing?" Claire asked.

"Well, I just can't figure out if you recruited him to our cause or," Thibodeaux moved his gaze from the gash on Benjamin's face to his sling, "or as a new patient."

"He's here for an education," Claire said.

"Ah. Well you're in the right place for that," Thibodeaux said.

"I'll be glad to help out," Benjamin said.

"He wants to help!" Thibodeaux said, sitting up straight. "I'm sure we have some Pediatric patients coming in today."

"Not so fast. He doesn't lay a finger on a patient. I don't want to give Pablo Medina any ammunition to rip into us," Claire said.

Ammunition. Benjamin thought of the day he first saw Claire, how she had stormed into Pablo's office and let him have it. So this was war between Pablo and Claire.

"But the lad wants to help," Thibodeaux said.

"OK. He can help Paloma make peanut-butter and jelly sandwiches."

"I'm sure we can make better use of his talents than having him spread peanut butter on bread." Thibodeaux said.

"I don't mind," Benjamin said.

Thibodeaux frowned in resignation. "Well, I guess that settles that," he said. Thibodeaux used the arm rests of his chair to push off and get to his feet. He shook Benjamin's hand with a broad smile. "Welcome aboard!"

Claire gave Benjamin what she called, "the grand tour" in a voice dripping with sarcasm. The clinic was clean and orderly though the equipment seemed to be more than one generation out of date. There were six exam rooms lining either side of a corridor which, on one end, led to a laboratory that was scarcely larger than a walk-in closet, and on the other dead-ended into Virgil Thibodeaux's office. The waiting room had an assortment of mismatched chairs that looked as though they had been collected from road-side motels, all pushed neatly against one wall to make room for a couple of plastic fold-out tables set against the opposing wall. A small kitchen was separated from the waiting room by a dutch door, its top half missing. A middle-aged woman with thick round spectacles was setting slices of white bread on a large platter.

"Paloma, this is Dr. Snow," Claire said.

Paloma stopped what she was doing and looked up. "Really? A new doctor?"

"Yes. His specialty is peanut butter and jelly sandwiches," Claire said.

Paloma looked over Benjamin, a slow deliberate scan starting from his shoes all the way up to his hair. Finally her eyes settled on the sling holding his arm and she said, "*Valgame Dios!* And for a second I thought we won the lottery. *Ni modo.* We'll take what we can get, Miss Claire. Beggars can't be choosers."

"We're not beggars yet, Paloma."

"Have you seen the supply cabinet?" Paloma asked.

"I know, I know. But I got a buyer for Momma's bus."

Paloma made the sign of the cross and reached for an over-sized jar of peanut butter. "How much?"

"Enough for a month. Maybe a little more," Claire said.

"Well, Dr. Peanut Butter, the boys will be here soon so you better wash your hands if you're going to help."

As if on cue, two disheveled boys appeared at the kitchen door, bulging back-packs drooping from their shoulders. One of them coughed politely.

Claire said something to them in Spanish and they turned and quietly took a seat next to the far wall. Benjamin thought about those boys he had come across, hiding in the mesquite brush before scuttling away with his french fries the day he drove to Purgatory. He wondered if they too had stopped at the El Milagro Clinic for a peanut butter sandwich before heading north. And he wondered if they would manage to find something to eat today.

Claire glanced at her watch. "We only see the odd walk-in on Saturdays, but we still get a pretty good crowd for the food. We better get moving with those sandwiches."

Spreading peanut butter on a slice of bread without the full use of one hand was more challenging than Benjamin had expected. After Benjamin tore up the first three slices of bread he attempted to spread, Paloma pulled a soup spoon out of a drawer and said, "OK Dr. Peanut Butter, you just scoop the jelly so we don't run out of bread."

Standing at the end of the table, Claire looked on and smiled. She picked up a couple of finished sandwiches and said, "I'm going to check on those boys and then I'm going to check on Pops. You look like you're in good hands, Dr. Peanut Butter."

Pretty soon he got in a good rhythm with Paloma, with Benjamin dropping a glob of jelly on the open sandwiches and Paloma spreading it with a butter knife almost as soon as it landed.

At one point Paloma froze. Without looking at Benjamin she said, "Are you really a doctor?"

"Yes, actually I am," Benjamin said.

"Well then you better do something about that boy bleeding over there."

Benjamin turned towards the kitchen door. A teen-age boy stood leaning onto the door jamb, his lower leg covered in blood which was now pooling on the linoleum floor.

Benjamin snatched a towel from the kitchen counter and quickly kneeled to try to tamp the bleeding. He told Paloma to call Dr. Thibodeaux. He stole a glance at the cut. It was a nasty thing, jagged with deep, sharp borders. The boy said something in Spanish and Paloma replied with unmasked annoyance. She walked towards Thibodeaux's office without bustle — just the efficient gait of someone accustomed to minor emergencies.

Claire wasn't kidding when she said Pops could throw a good clean stitch. Benjamin marveled at how such a complicated laceration came together so nicely after just a couple of well placed mattress sutures. Thibodeaux had asked Benjamin give him a hand and snip the ends of the sutures as he tied the knots, and Benjamin was happy to oblige, but it was clear Virgil Thibodeaux didn't need any help. Perhaps the old man just enjoyed his company. Or maybe he derived a special pleasure in demonstrating his skill. At one point, Thibodeaux tied a one-handed knot on a deep suture which was so flawless Benjamin actually said, "Wow."

Thibodeaux chuckled. "Not too shabby, eh?"

"That's very impressive," Benjamin said.

"Well, I've had a lot of practice." And soon the smile was gone from Thibodeaux's face and he appeared lost in thought.

When Benjamin returned to the kitchen Paloma

wouldn't let him back in.

"I don't need your help no more," she said. Then added, "It's not right. A doctor in the kitchen. It's not natural."

There were about a dozen children in the waiting room by now. All boys. Brown round faces, some bleary-eyed, others with a haunted gaze. The main door to the clinic opened. A woman walked in with a child: a girl, Benjamin surmised from the violet color of the matching jacket and sweat pants she was wearing, thought it was difficult to tell with the floppy fishing cap propped on her head and the dark sunglasses covering half her face. The two walked slowly, the child with a limp, straight toward the exam rooms.

A few minutes later Thibodeaux stepped into the waiting room.

"Dr. Snow, can you assist me for a minute?"

Benjamin followed Thibodeaux to an exam room. The girl with the violet sweat suit was sitting on the exam table. The hat was off as were the glasses. Her chest was exposed. Large swaths of her skin were covered in thick scar tissue, the lower half of her face mercifully spared. She was missing her left eye. There was a single tattered tuft of hair growing from the only part of her scalp that was not gnarled in scar. A bandage with a yellow stain was wrapped over the girl's left shoulder.

The child's mother bowed her head slightly as Benjamin and Thibodeaux approached the exam table.

"This is Isabella, and her mother Lourdes." Neither mother nor child looked up. Thibodeaux said something in Spanish.

The mother managed a weak smile, nodded in Benjamin's direction and said, "*Gracias doctor.*

"I want you to take a look at this wound," Thibodeaux said. "Tell me what you think."

As Thibodeaux donned sterile surgical gloves. The girl puckered her lips and turned towards her mother who murmured something in a reassuring voice.

Thibodeaux said, "Stubborn wound won't heal. He removed the bandage to reveal an ulcer the size of a dime, with a ribbon of iodoform packing sticking out of it." Thibodeaux nodded towards a manila folder sitting on the tiny desk next to the exam table. "Doesn't take a genius to realize that the problem is her nutritional status. Look at her growth chart. She hasn't gained a single pound in at least five months."

Benjamin reached for the manila folder, scanned the tabs along its edge and opened it at the growth chart section. He had been trained in the era of electronic medical records and it took him a moment to get over the fact that the El Milagro Clinic actually used paper records. The feel of the chart in his hands transmitted a winsome appeal. There was something nostalgic about it, as if it were a package wrapped in brown paper and twine.

"She was my wife's patient," Thibodeaux continued. "Jane was a pediatrician. I'm just no good with those nutritional assessments."

After studying the growth curve for a moment Benjamin scanned the rest of the chart. Second and third degree burns on nearly fifty percent of her body sustained over a year ago. Multiple skin grafts. Enucleation of the left eye. Bacterial super-infections and yet more skin grafts.

Thibodeaux grasped the tip of the packing ribbon with a curved Kelly forceps, gave it a slight tug and pulled out a length of ribbon the size of a garter snake. The child didn't even wince.

"What do you think, Dr. Snow? Can you help my little Isabella?"

Benjamin peaked inside the gaping crater. Proud flesh. Clean. No purulence. Thibodeaux was right. There was no sign of infection, just a negative nitrogen balance standing in the way of healing.

"Sure," Benjamin said. He had calculated protein and caloric requirements dozens of times on the wards. "I just need a calculator and a Harriet Lane handbook."

"That's exactly what Jane used to always say," Thibodeaux said. "I bet they're still in her desk drawer."

Thibodeaux was already replacing the packing with a clean strip. His hands worked in a steady efficient pace, like those of an experienced surgeon.

"How did this happen?" Benjamin asked, and was immediately sorry he had opened his mouth. He glanced at the mother and couldn't tell if she had understood.

Thibodeaux started to answer but the child's mother cut him off.

She said, "*El Chacal.*"

"I'm sorry?" Benjamin said.

"*El Chacal,*" she repeated.

Thibodeaux quickly wrapped a gauze bandage roll around the child's extremity and secured it with strips of silk tape. As soon as he pressed down the last strip he said, "Well, let's go look for that calculator then, shall we?".

When they reached the office Benjamin said, "I'm really sorry. I shouldn't have opened my mouth."

Thibodeaux flashed him an avuncular smile. "No harm done." He slid open a desk drawer and peered inside. "Aha! I knew they were here."

"What did she mean, *El Chacal*?"

Thibodeaux placed the calculator and the handbook on top of the desk. He sat down and motioned to Benjamin to do the same.

"As you may have noticed, Lourdes is an attractive woman," Thibodeaux started. "She lived in a *rancho,* a small village, just across the Rio Grande. One day she catches the eye of an uninvited admirer, an outsider. Of course she's happily married, has a young child to boot, so she rebuffs the man's advances. But this admirer is not a regular man. He's an enforcer for one of the Mexican drug cartels. And when she snubs him, well, let's just say he doesn't take it very well. He promises her she is going to suffer like she's never suffered before. So one day, the child is playing just outside their home when Lourdes hears a muffled scream. She rushes out and sees him — let's go ahead and call him *El Chacal* — yanking her little Isabella by the hair. The girl's hair is wet. There's a can of gasoline turned on its side on the dirt, and a large puddle at the child's feet. When the smell of gasoline hits Lourdes, she gets down on her knees and starts pleading. The man says, 'You had your chance,' and pulls out a lighter."

Thibodeaux paused and rubbed his beard. "Isabella was airlifted to the burn unit in Galveston. A week later, her father goes hunting for the man who committed this atrocity. But a machete is no match for a sawed off shotgun, even if the man brandishing the gun has one hand badly burned, still wrapped in bandages. *El Chacal* shoots the father and uses the father's own machete to decapitate his head."

"Did they ever arrest him?" Benjamin asked.

Thibodeaux shook his head. "Mexican authorities never did find him."

"So, who is this *El Chacal*, really?

"You have to understand, Benjamin, the idea of evil incarnate has been around throughout the ages. The story of a human, or a fallen angel perhaps, who is committed to wickedness, is one of the most enduring and intriguing narratives that we have. His name is of little importance. In my parts they call him *Pere Malfait.* Here, he happens to be known as *El Chacal.*"

"So there's actually no one person named, *El Chacal.*"

"Depends who you talk to," Thibodeaux said. "The locals are convinced there is just one *El Chacal* and that he breathes and walks among us right here in Purgatory, that he pulls all the strings and holds everyone's destiny in his hands. They believe that not a bird falls in these parts without his knowing. That he can stop a man's heart just by wishing it and can seduce any woman with just the faintest murmur of his devilish voice."

"He couldn't seduce Isabella's mother."

"Apparently not," Virgil said.

"What do *you* think?" Benjamin asked.

"I believe humans are capable of unspeakable cruelty and one need not resort to supernatural explanations, no matter how comforting they may be."

"Comforting? How is believing in evil incarnate comforting?"

"It reassures us that the monster is not us."

Claire and Virgil Thibodeaux lived in a Texas ranch-style home with a broad sloping roof that extended over a north-facing cedar planked front porch. There was a detached garage on one side, and a tall pecan tree out front whose exposed roots had created havoc with the narrow asphalt driveway.

Claire was in the kitchen preparing a late lunch while Benjamin and Virgil sat in the study. A rustic maple book case spanned the length of the far wall of the room, volumes of dusty books packed tightly on each shelf. The other walls were covered with masks that seemed to come from every corner of the globe. Menacing masks with bug eyes and fangs, wooden masks with impossibly long faces, and decidedly more subdued western masks.

"Jane used to collect them." Thibodeaux said. "She was fascinated, not just by the artistic elements but by the social and cultural aspects. All cultures spanning back millennia have developed their own masks. That has to say something about the human experience."

"That we have to hide who we are?" Benjamin said.

"Not necessarily. Masks allow us to try out a new persona sometimes. They can elicit the paradoxical effect of unmasking our true self."

Benjamin pointed to a red mask with huge bulging eyes. "That one looks like it had a tad too much coffee."

"That's Barong. He's from Bali. And the one to the left of him is his counterpart, Rangda: the queen of death and the devourer of children. Barong and Rangda, good and evil. Oldest story in the world."

Claire called out from the kitchen, "Benjamin knows Rangda. He works for him."

Thibodeaux hollered back, "Rangda is a woman. And Pablo Medina does not devour children."

Claire yelled back, "Oh yeah? Wanna bet?"

Thibodeaux lowered his voice. "She got her keen sense of hearing from her mother's side. Claire's grandmother was a *traiteur*: a sort of Cajun witch doctor."

"Spiritual healer!" Claire shouted.

"I stand corrected," Thibodeaux said. "Anyway, some of that voodoo must have got passed down somehow. You better watch yourself around her."

"I sort of figured that out already," Benjamin whispered.

"I heard that too, Benjamin," Claire shouted.

Thibodeaux raised his eyebrows in an I-don't-know-how-she-does-it way.

"Why doesn't Claire like Pablo Medina?" Benjamin said.

"Pablo worked for us," Thibodeaux said. "Over at El Milagro. He was a fine doctor. Then… well, he developed other priorities and left us in a bit of a tight spot."

"I mean, it's not like I'm going to get involved in all the politics of the medical community down here. I have a one year contract and then I'm off to do my fellowship."

"Critical care, is it?" Thibodeaux said, clasping his hands together.

"That's right."

"And you're sure that's what you want."

"That's what I've always wanted," Benjamin said. "It's the only thing I want."

Thibodeaux shrugged. "Well, you can't argue with that can you?"

"I don't know. It looks like some people want to hold that against me," Benjamin said.

"I want you to try on a mask," Thibodeaux said.

"The good guy or the bad guy?"

"No, no," Thibodeaux said. "Something more suitable for you. Are you familiar with the *Commedia dell'arte*?" Thibodeaux got to his feet and approached one of the walls covered with masks.

"Never heard of it," Benjamin said.

"I'm sure you've heard of Harlequin. That's one of the most famous characters of the *Commedia* — a form of Italian theater dating back to the 16th century.

Oh, here it is."

Thibodeaux carefully removed a black leather mask with a prominent nose from the wall.

"You want me to be Harlequin?"

"Oh no," Thibodeaux said. "This is Pulcinella: a sly character this one, a little on the lazy side, but a real slick son-of-a-gun all in all. He's quite crafty but often pretends to be dim-witted as one of his favorite weapons."

"I don't think that describes me very well at all."

Thibodeaux said, "Try it on."

Thibodeaux handed the mask to Benjamin and Benjamin placed it on his face. It had the unmistakable smell of old tanned leather and it felt harder against his skin than he expected.

"How does it fit?" Thibodeaux asked.

"Not so well. Lots of pressure points."

"Ah, but you see, it's not your mask," Thibodeaux said.

"I told you," Benjamin said.

"It is not *your* mask," Thibodeaux repeated. "This mask belonged to a talented actor. He used it over a career spanning decades. When he first put it on it was uncomfortable, just as it is for you right now. And early in his career he was painfully aware of the presence of the mask on his face. But the wonderful thing about these leather masks is that they gradually mold to the actor's face. Over time, the inside of the mask takes on the actor's features, and eventually the actor dons the mask and he no longer feels it. He is no longer aware of the presence of the mask. He has become the character he is portraying. When that happens, he's no longer aware that he's acting."

Thibodeaux reached for the mask and put it back on the wall. He sat behind the desk again. After a reflective pause he said, "We must pick our masks carefully. Over time, the mask that we end up choosing, even the wrong mask, will conform to our features. Soon, we no longer feel its weight or its rough edges, and then we risk not knowing that we are only acting our way through life, the wrong character in the wrong play."

The two sat quietly for a while. The silence made Benjamin feel awkward. He thought of something to say, something banal even, but could think of nothing. Perhaps sensing Benjamin's growing discomfort Thibodeaux opened his mouth to say something but at just that moment Claire called out from the adjacent dining room that lunch was ready. Benjamin could hear the sound of plates and silverware being laid out on the table.

Thibodeaux said, "I hope you like mac and cheese. Claire makes the very best from scratch."

"Yeah," she replied from the other room. "Because it's pretty much all we can afford."

Thibodeaux smiled. Benjamin grasped the arm of the chair with his good hand to help him get to his feet but stopped when he saw Thibodeaux hold out his hand over the desk. The man had a soft, pained look in his eye.

"I've found, over the years, that the key to being a good doctor is to love your patients."

A fairly general statement, Benjamin thought, not directed at him in particular. He had heard it repeated in various forms over his years of training, usually with the mawkish sentimentality of faculty nearing retirement, but never with the use of the word, "love". There was a sudden silence from the other room. The clatter of dishes had stopped. He had the distinct feeling that Claire was eavesdropping now.

As if she sensed his suspicion she said, "The food's going to get cold."

Her tone had changed. There was an innocence to her voice, but also a subtle tension and just the slightest hint of foreboding.

Thibodeaux continued, "And the only way to do that," a thin smile appeared on his face, "is to allow yourself to fall in love: often, freely, fully."

Benjamin continued holding Thibodeaux's gaze. The thought crossed his mind that the old man was trying to read his reaction but Benjamin quickly dispelled this notion. There was only warmth. Benjamin had to look away. And as he did so he became more aware that it was Claire who was sizing up his reaction from the other room. His gaze roved along the baseboard of the far wall until it settled on something that made him freeze. Jutting out from behind a squat, metal filing cabinet was a framed diploma sitting on its side. The caption was partly obstructed but Benjamin could still make out the name "Virgil Horace Thibodeaux", and an emblem that read, "The Society of Thoracic Surgeons".

"Dr. Thibodeaux," Benjamin said, and pointed

at the diploma. "What is that?"

Thibodeaux swiveled in his chair to take a look and turned back to face Benjamin.

"A relic of ancient history," Thibodeaux said. He chuckled at Benjamin's stunned look. "A mask that didn't quite fit."

17

The drive home from Claire Thibodeaux's house was quiet. After all the badgering of the previous twenty-four hours Claire had become unusually reticent, awkwardly polite. People sometimes behave that way, Benjamin mused, after a private side to them has been exposed. Maybe she hadn't counted on that when she conceived the idea to bring him to the clinic and then to her home. Maybe she already regretted having done so.

She pointed to a narrow road, off to the right which turned into a caliche covered trail some hundred feet off Presidio Parkway. "That's the road to Sanguinity Point," she said. Just a little further, she nodded to the left. "And that's where I found you." It might have been intended as an admonition but the tone she used was too flat to be intimidating. She fell silent again.

Benjamin wasn't very good with small-talk but he thought he'd give it a try.

"That's a nice clinic you have," he said.

She let out a puff of breath and smiled a sardonic smile.

He thought he'd try again. "Really, you're doing a world of good for those kids."

She seemed to be weighing his words, not so much for truthfulness as much as for sincerity.

"Pops gets so busy some days. These boys come up in waves. Some mornings there's a line outside the door before we even get to the clinic."

"How does he manage?" Benjamin said.

"He's pretty level headed. Not like me. He just looks at all the boys and says something like, 'Well Claire, I feel like a mosquito at a nudist colony today. I know what I got to do, just don't know where to start.'"

"But he's a heart surgeon." he said.

She sighed. "Was."

"No wonder he can throw a clean stitch. What happened?"

"You mean, how did he sink so low?" Claire said.

"Oh, no. Not at all." Benjamin said. "I really like your dad. I admire him."

"Why do you admire him?"

"He's a good doctor. I mean, what he's doing... what the two of you do is amazing."

"You really think so," Claire said.

"Definitely."

"If you feel that way, why do you work for someone like Pablo Medina? Oh right. I'm guessing no one else in the state would hire you."

Apparently the politeness was over. Benjamin looked out the side window of the car.

"Benjamin, I'm sorry. I shouldn't have said that."

"It's okay."

"No, it's not okay. It was a really awful thing to say. It's just that Medina and that whole group of doctors-"

"Doctors like me," Benjamin said.

A thin smile dawned on her face. Her eyes were fixed on the road and Benjamin allowed himself a few moments to survey her features. She was back-lit by the low evening sun and a thin halo enveloped her eyelashes, her delicate nose, her full lips stretched in smile; the lips tugging on that tiny scar he had noticed the day they met, a charming blemish that added balance and poise to her features — an absolutely perfect flaw.

Virgil Thibodeaux's words thundered through his consciousness. *Allow yourself to fall in love; often, freely and fully.* With all due respect to Virgil, he couldn't allow that to happen.

"Why are you smiling?" Benjamin asked.

Claire said, "Just the way you said that. It tells me you're not like them at all."

"What is it about Medina that rubs you the wrong way?"

Claire glanced over. "He worked for us, you know? At El Milagro. He was a pretty good doctor."

"And then?"

"And then he hurt us. He hurt us real bad. We never recovered."

"What did he do?"

Claire shook her head. The smile was gone.

They were driving next to the irrigation canal now, behind the cabbage field bordering Benjamin's house. The car slowed as it approached the curve where the road rose over the culvert. She drove the rest of the way in silence. She steered the car into his driveway slowly and kept the engine running even after she came to a stop.

Her gaze was directed towards Benjamin's front

door and he wondered if she wanted to be invited inside.

Perhaps she sensed his uncertainty. She nodded in the direction of the red and white striped poles and said, "Love those candy canes."

"Barber shop poles," Benjamin said. "Want to come in?"

"You know what makes me sad?" she said. "The greatest tragedy, I think, is when someone doesn't live up to their potential."

Benjamin wondered where that statement had come from. In his mind he tried to trace its origin the way a forensic scientist traces back the trajectory of a projectile.

"Look," he said, "I'm just passing through. It's not like I'm going to work with Pablo Medina for good."

"Just passing through," she echoed.

"That's right. And as soon as I get the chance, I'm off to do my critical care fellowship."

"And in the meantime you'll tow the El Dorado line and make yourself a small fortune in the process."

"Claire, I don't know anything about the hospital politics over here and frankly, I don't care. I don't want to get involved. I'm going to stay neutral, like Switzerland."

She laughed. "There's no neutral here. You either stand up for whats right or you get sucked in on the wrong side."

"What do you expect me to do? Leave Medina? The only guy in the state — you said it, and you hit the nail on the head — who offered me a job?"

She gripped the steering wheel with both hands. "Benjamin, listen to me. Sooner or later you will be forced to make a choice, to pick a side. It may happen sooner than you think. I'm worried that you'll make the wrong choice and hurt a lot of good people. Starting with yourself."

Benjamin ran his fingers through his hair. "All I want is to do my fellowship."

Claire rolled her eyes. "The only thing that's perfectly clear, Dr. Snow, is that you have no idea what you want."

"Really. And what do *you* want?"

Claire looked deep in his eyes. "I just want to be ready."

"Ready for what?"

Claire smiled. "For my moment."

"What moment?"

"My defining moment. If we're lucky, at some point in our life fate throws us a moment; what the ancient Greeks called Kairos."

"Never heard of it."

"Kairos is the most opportune time to make a pivotal choice and take action. It's your life's defining moment, a few seconds in which your true character is revealed, where your whole personality is distilled. The Kairos may be our only chance in life to be heroic. Well, when that moment comes for me, I want to be ready."

"I'm not so sure I believe in fate," Benjamin said.

"Then call it what you will."

"Well, I've had lots of moments already. Sometimes things just happen and you don't have much of a choice how to react."

Claire said, "I don't think your defining moment has come, Benjamin. But something tells me, and I have a special instinct when it comes to these things, that when the moment does come, you'll be ready."

18

"You've really gone and done it," Pablo Medina said, an odd queasiness in his voice as he inspected the laceration on Benjamin's jaw."

"It's not as bad as it looks," Benjamin said. "I can manage."

"You'll manage to scare my patients is what you'll manage," Medina said. He turned and waved for Ivan the terrible to come up the hall to join them. "Ivan, I'm relying on you today."

"Yes sir, Dr. Medina," Ivan said, a smug smile on his face.

Medina took one more look at Benjamin, shook his head and walked away.

Benjamin waited until he was out of earshot before turning to Ivan and saying, "Just like any other day."

The medical scribe raised one eyebrow. "Whatever you say, boss."

Despite being a nudnik through and through, Ivan Montero was inarguably gifted. He was quick, efficient and so adept at anticipating Benjamin's needs that it was a little unsettling at times. Still, there was a deliberate swagger in his way, as though the prime motivation for being productive was to upstage Benjamin.

By mid-morning, when his shoulder was gripped by a steady throb, Benjamin stopped caring what Ivan's motivations might be and was genuinely thankful he was around.

When it came to seeing patients (processing patients, as Ivan liked to say) the two just clicked. One by one, patients were examined, forms filled out, prescriptions dispensed with stunning efficiency and exactitude. Perhaps it was true that tension and distrust could be valuable assets for associates. After all, it worked for Sherlock Holmes and Dr. Watson, Fred Astaire and Ginger Rogers, JFK and LBJ. At one point Benjamin detected a knowing gleam in Ivan's eye and he believed that in that moment they communicated a certain shared understanding: that they both relished the fact that they made a good team. Odd collaborators they were, joined only by a common goal.

Medina's clinic wasn't so bad after all. Sure, the number of patients seen was considerable, but the range of pathology was limited to less than a dozen mundane diagnoses, most of which were self-limited conditions. If challenged, Benjamin could unflinchingly defend the quality of care he provided. As for the compensation, despite that unexpected bonus, the salary he was receiving was not really terribly out of the ordinary.

Why was he even entertaining these thoughts? Why did he feel a need to stage this internal debate? It was Claire of course. Claire and her mac and cheese. He had managed to keep his mind busy for the last twenty-four hours, mostly by reading his textbook of Pediatric Critical Care, but today the thoughts of her had been evoked by the most extraneous of triggers: looking in the mirror to inspect the sutures on his jaw, walking past those candy cane poles by his doorway, ordering breakfast tacos at the gas station down the street. Perhaps he was thinking about her much more than he cared to admit.

And now he was feeling guilty. For what? For having a well-stocked medical cabinet? For being able to afford something other than mac and cheese for lunch? For working with Pablo Medina? For counting the days until he could leave this place and get on with his real life?

There was nothing to feel guilty about. The woes of El Milagro clinic were not of his doing. Nor was the political jousting of the local medical community which didn't interest him in the least. He was only a passer-by as far as he was concerned. He had stumbled into Purgatory as a result of regrettable circumstances but he wouldn't stick around long enough to get involved. Not with the local politics. Not with Claire.

The days went flying by. It was Thursday afternoon when Jesus Tamez appeared on Benjamin's schedule as a late walk-in. Again the boy told Ivan to take a walk when the scribe followed Benjamin in the exam room. When Ivan left, with hardly a protest this time, Jesus looked downright giddy.

"Hey Snowflake. I been thinking of you. Been worried sick."

"Worried?" Benjamin said.

"Yeah man, look at you. What happened?"

"I had a fall," Benjamin said. "How are you?"

"All fixed up. That's why I been worried sick about *you*. I was telling my homeboy, 'Man, Snowflake's the best doctor I ever had. Hope nothing bad happens to him, you know?' And just look at you.

"You say you're all fixed up…"

"No more leaky pipes," Jesus said. "The plumbing's all good."

"How about your breathing?"

"Perfect. I been breathing so good I was able to smoke a joint last night."

"OK, I didn't just hear that," Benjamin said, trying to sound unamused.

"Trick, man. I didn't mean that out loud," the boy said. He had a broad smile that was so infectious it was downright virulent. Benjamin had to try his hardest to maintain his stern demeanor.

He pulled the stethoscope out of his lab coat pocket and placed the diaphragm on the boy's chest. Amazing what a short course of steroids can do, Benjamin thought.

"Much better. We'll keep you on the inhaled steroids and I'll see you back in a month. You know which puffer that is?"

"The blue one," Jesus said.

"The blue one. One puff in the morning, one puff at bedtime."

Benjamin stepped over to the sink and started washing his hands. Even the most inane task became onerous with the splint and he started to wonder if he should just ditch the sling and try to just remember to be careful when using his bad arm.

"I told you I was better," Jesus said.

"You told me."

"I'm more worried about you Snowflake. This is Borderlandia. A guy like you can get hurt."

"I noticed," Benjamin said.

"I told you. And you got to be more careful when you go riding that bike."

"Well, the bike's in pieces now." The sound of his own words made Benjamin's heart skip a beat. He felt his face grow warm. A physiologic reaction that preceded the full cognitive processing that made him aware of why he had reacted this way. He turned the faucet off and pulled a couple of paper towels from the dispenser and started drying his hands, slowly, methodically.

"Know what's strange?" Benjamin said.

"What's that?"

Benjamin turned to face the boy. "I never told you I fell off a bike."

"What? Yeah, you did." The boy grinned. "How else would I know?"

"That's a good question. How *did* you know?"

"Dr. Snow, *you* told me. Sure, you told me, remember? You told me when you first walked in."

Benjamin shook his head. "Tell me about the blue pick-up truck."

"What blue pick-up truck?"

"You threw the orange at me?"

"Orange?" the boy said. "OK, you're fucking with me now. I got it."

"Did you throw the orange at me?"

The boy waited. The smile was long gone.

"It was a yellow 1015Y, a Texas Super Sweet

onion. Don't try to make juice with it."

"Why'd you do it?"

"Man, I didn't throw it."

"You're a liar."

"I was in the truck, yeah, but it wasn't me."

"Why should I believe you?"

The boy said nothing. His nostrils were flaring and Benjamin wondered if he had just exacerbated another spell of bronchospasm. No. The little prick was just upset.

"I think you should leave," Benjamin said.

The boy didn't move. He sat there sulking.

Benjamin said, "We're done here." He turned to leave.

The boy jumped to his feet. He trudged towards the door and in a soft voice said, "I didn't know it was you."

Benjamin found himself struggling to concentrate the rest of the afternoon. He attributed this to the gnawing pain over his clavicle which grew by the hour. His thoughts kept coming back to Jesus Tamez. He was still distracted when he drove home at the end of the day, unaware that a powder-blue pickup truck had followed him from a distance, and pulled over on the grassy shoulder by the irrigation canal when Benjamin turned into his driveway.

19

The entrance to the to the El Dorado Emergency Department was located behind the main building, some hundred feet from the delivery loading dock, just past the hospital security kiosk where a green and white SUV with police car flashers was a near-permanent fixture. Dr. Soto-Prinz, who had insisted on this layout, contended that the entrance to the ED was in no way hidden or obstructed from view. And there was no reason to suppose that armed security guards in green uniforms and cowboy hats should discourage law-abiding citizens from seeking emergency medical care if they really needed it.

Unlike Purgatory Regional, Soto-Prinz would point out, El Dorado did not receive federal funds to remunerate for uncompensated care provided to undocumented aliens. Not that he would turn these patients away — that would be illegal. But if those people were more comfortable at Purgatory Regional, what was the harm in dis-incentivising them from stopping in?

Joe Rizzo didn't care much for Soto-Prinz, and he knew that, in return, Soto-Prinz didn't trust him. And people whom Soto-Prinz distrusted did not enjoy longevity at El Dorado. This all made for uncomfortable albeit quiet nights in the emergency department. On more than one occasion Naomi Rizzo had tried to convince her husband that those few shifts each month at El Dorado were not worth the aggravation, that their financial difficulties were not so insurmountable, and there was no need for him to punish himself with the extra work-load. They could do without El Dorado, even if the hospital did pay him nearly twice the hourly rate he received at Regional.

Had it not been Joe Rizzo's own hand to lose years of savings in just a few weeks of bad on-line trades, he might have listened to his wife. Instead, he now sat at the nurses' station, entering orders for yet another winter Texan with chest pain whose cardiologist insisted needed admission, even with normal enzymes and an unremarkable EKG. Rizzo knew better than to argue when he wasn't on his home turf, so he quietly acquiesced with the stupid demands of the staff physicians, particularly those he knew to be investor-partners.

He looked up at the large clock on the wall and let his eyes drift down to the white board he had glanced at at least a half dozen times during his shift: the board with the list of doctors on call. A name he had never seen before was written in blue marker under the heading of Neurosurgery (not good), Krippendorff under general surgery, Soto-Prinz himself under general anesthesia. *Sweet mother of pearl!* He could only hope that his shift remained quiet.

He glanced back at the clock. Just a few more hours to go and he'd have a full thirty-six hours off. Piece of cake. After all, he reminded himself, he could handle anything that walked through the door. That was his trademark.

Soon he'd have breakfast, squeeze in a few

hours sleep, and then maybe they could load up the car and drive down to South Padre Island, walk barefoot in the wet sand, help baby Dylan (Naomi still called him that though he weighed well over 40 pounds) build a castle with his tiny plastic pail and matching shovel, chow down on some fried shrimp at Dirty Al's and still make it on time to Isla Blanca to catch the sunset. Sure, it wasn't Morne Rouge beach in Grenada, but Joe Rizzo knew that an island girl like Naomi needed the sound of the surf, the smell of briny air, the caress of ocean winds to sustain her. He felt he had let her down too many times and these short trips were the least he could do to atone for his sins.

He had barely finished entering the admission orders when a barrel-chested, bleary-eyed male nurse jogged to the nurse's station.

"Dr. Rizzo. Trauma bay 1. We need you now!"

Rizzo reflexively pushed back on his chair and was quickly up on his feet, the adrenaline already gushing through his system as he asked, "What have we got?"

"Blood. Lots of blood. Primip gushing out."

It took a significant hemorrhage to get an ED nurse excited. A torrent to get one huffing and puffing.

"How far along?" Already Rizzo's brain was sorting out the possible reasons for bleeding in a pregnant woman.

"It's a big round belly. Looks like she's close to term."

If the nurse didn't bother to even ask for that much information it was worse than Rizzo had imagined. He felt his heart pounding against his rib cage. *Everything that walks through the door*, Rizzo thought. *I got this.* “OK. Call blood bank. Tell ‘em we need 4 units of O neg STAT and to be ready to keep it coming,” his tone was deliberately calm. The worst thing he could do is convey panic. “And call OB and neonatology on call. And anesthesia. Dr. Soto-Prinz is on call. Sounds like this one’s going to the OR.”

He rounded the counter of the nurse’s station, pulled the stethoscope out of his lab coat pocket so it wouldn’t fall out, and ran towards Trauma bay 1. He stopped cold at the door, surveyed the scene and couldn’t help but mutter under his breath, “Holy mother of Jesus.”

20

The find had been too good to be true. Jesus and Ruben stumbled upon it on a dare from Hector almost a year ago; a dare mixed with a threat, as was always the case with Ruben's cousin. The dare was to go out on Sanguinity Point after midnight on Halloween night with just a flashlight, stay there fifteen minutes and come back without wetting their pants. Hector stayed behind in the pickup truck with a loaded Glock on the dashboard. Just in case.

Sanguinity Point was a peninsula that jutted out where the Rio Grande took a hairpin turn and narrowed to its slenderest span before reaching its delta. Those who thought this an ideal point to wade across would be in for a harrowing surprise. Where the river narrowed, the waters dived deep below the surface creating eddies and currents that could suck even an expert swimmer to its depths. Lifeless bodies would turn up downstream as a regular occurrence.

Not all were victims of drowning. At Sanguinity Point death came by land as often as by water.

The origin of the name was a matter of of some dispute. According to local lore it was a lieutenant in Pancho Villa's army that had first given it the name of "*Playa de Sangre*" when a posse of Anglo settlers, backed by Texas Rangers, cornered a group of unarmed Tejanos on the peninsula and massacred them as reprisal for the killing of a rancher and his son. Blood beach: the latin etymon was translated to its decidedly more pleasant English derivative.

The alternative explanation, paradoxically the one clung to by those who never dared set foot anywhere close to the place, alleged that a small clapboard chapel with this very name (the ruins of which were long ago pillaged, shortly after it had been abandoned)once stood on the grounds.

A place of hope or a beach of death; Jesus Tamez had no interest in onomastics. And it wasn't running into ghosts he was worried about on that Halloween night, but stumbling into the foot soldiers of *El Chacal.* The jackal. He alone controlled the flow of drugs, money, and yes, even people, all the way from Mission to El Paso. He was the most powerful man of Borderlandia — more powerful than the Border Patrol and the DEA combined.

If indeed he was a man. Some said he had supernatural powers, that he could kill a man just by wishing it, though most of his victims were found with various caliber holes in their heads, or with no head at all.

Jesus Tamez did not believe in ghosts or supernatural nonsense. He believed *El Chacal* was of flesh and bone and told Ruben repeatedly that, one day, he would want to meet the man face to face, to stare in those cold eyes without blinking. It wasn't admiration that Jesus felt for *El Chacal* as much as curiosity. He wondered how a man might become a living legend.

Still, when they thought they heard a murmur of voices coming from the beach that night, Jesus and Ruben jumped in the brush behind a curtain of Texas junipers faster than jack rabbits on crystal meth. They waited in the darkness, their ears perked, until their breathing finally slowed to a normal rate.

After some twenty minutes of dead silence, when he finally thought it was safe, Jesus switched on the flashlight. And there it was. It was like winning the Borderlandia lottery, Jesus told Ruben. They sat for a few minutes just to admire it, as if approaching it might make it vanish.

It didn't vanish. It remained planted and constant in all its glory: a thick luscious bush of Cannabis Sativa, just sitting there all by her lonesome. Jesus would not have been more mesmerized if a pink unicorn had suddenly appeared.

In the silence, Jesus tried to conceive how this blessing might have occurred. He figured that, with all the weed coming through these parts, someone must have dropped some seeds. Maybe they got blown into the small concealed clearing and found their way into the rich soil. The same rich soil that gave Ruby Red grapefruit their distinctive color; soil fed by the blood of innocents.

If that were the case, no one could possibly know about this stash. And few would be so crazy to come out here to harvest it even if they did know of its existence.

"We can't tell Hector about this," Jesus told Ruben. "This is ours."

"Finders keepers," Ruben said.

"Damn right."

Ruben wasn't the slickest pebble on the beach

but he always did as he was told, which was both a curse and a blessing.

So for nearly a year Jesus and Ruben made the bike trek to Sanguinity Point, always just after dawn (drug runners are not morning people, Jesus would remind Ruben) and make small withdrawals from the plant they named Connie. They sold most of their small harvests to the few acquaintances they trusted and smoked the rest. *Quality control*, Jesus called it.

This morning, a steady breeze blew from the west and the sun had just scattered the first rays over the hazy landscape. It was one of those perfect days. The weather was as pleasant as it ever got in the summer in these parts. But it wasn't just the weather. Coming to the Point was the only thing that made any sense to Jesus. It had a purpose: an objective with a payoff.

More than that, it was freedom. The only freedom he knew. And the element of danger? Well, that was just the cherry on the *pinche* sundae.

They were almost by the junipers when a rustling in the brush startled Jesus and made him spring sideways. A throaty, raspy sound erupted from the overgrown wild grass. Frozen, Jesus turned his head just enough to face Ruben and put his index finger in front of his puckered lips.

Jesus felt the pounding of his heart. Slowly he reached for his back pocket and felt for his jack knife. Just then a brown form appeared between the tufts of grass. A bird the size of a small pheasant scurried out and plunged into another thicket of bush.

Ruben started laughing.

"Man, you should'a seen yourself," Ruben said. He bent over, holding his mid-section. "You looked like you were gonna piss your pants."

"Whatever."

"You scared of a little chachalaca?" Ruben imitated the call of the chachalaca.

"It's just a bad omen is all."

That made Ruben clam up.

"My grandma says chachalacas are *good* luck," Ruben said. There was an innocent strain in his voice.

Jesus almost felt guilty carrying on. "They're a bad sign."

"But you said you don't believe in things like that," Ruben said.

"I don't. So it can't touch me. But you do, *cavbon*. That means you're the one that gets screwed."

Ruben was quiet the rest of the way. When they got to Connie he told Jesus to hurry up. He wanted to get out of there.

"Relax, Rube. We gotta do some quality control first." Jesus pulled the rolling paper out of the breast pocket of his shirt. He knelt down and was shaping the paper when he heard the rumble of an engine approaching. He reached up, grabbed Ruben by the shirt and pulled him down to the ground.

He whispered, "Shhhhh."

Jesus rolled onto his stomach and did an army crawl to the line of junipers and looked out past their perimeter. He didn't dare raise his head but through the thicket he could just make out a green and white vehicle with flashers on the roof.

Border Patrol. Probably looking for a swimmer. Or just coming to jerk off.

Jesus motioned to Ruben to be quiet and lay low. This wasn't anything as spine-chilling as running into El Chacal's men, who would kill you just as a joke. But a couple of Hispanic kids would have a heck of a lot of 'splainin to do for what were they doing on Sanguinity Point at this hour, and what about that fine bush of Aunt Mary y'all standing next to?

An agent got out of the vehicle, tall and lanky, black, bushy mustache. He moved awkwardly in his hunter green uniform, like it was the wrong size or had too much starch.

A shorter agent got out from the driver's side and came around the front of the vehicle. The tall agent was just standing there, looking out toward the river, and started combing his mustache with his fingers while the shorter agent opened the rear door of the car, reached in and pulled out some poor bastard by the hair. The guy, who was handcuffed behind his back, lost his footing and fell out onto the turf face first. Short agent kicked him once in the ribs and was about to kick him again when the tall one says something, raises his hand and shakes his head.

The tall agent's hand looked weird. It was the color of a pig's snout. And the skin was thick and rough as if plastered in melted cheese.

Jesus felt a tickle inside his nose. In Texas they refer to junipers as Texas cedars and they're known for two things: sucking up all the water from the atmosphere to choke nearby oaks and causing cedar fever — South Texas' version of hay fever. Already, Jesus felt his eyelids scraping against his eyeballs with every blink, as if his tears were turning to glue. He knew better than to rub them. He allowed himself a quiet, cautious sniff.

The short agent stood over the guy on the ground and told him to get up, as if the guy could even if he wanted to. So then he grabbed a handful of hair and pulled him up onto his knees, yanked the guy's head way back. Jesus was able to get a better look at the guy's face now. One eye was purple and swollen shut. Blood trickled from his nose and from the corner of his mouth. Even swollen and deformed, the guy's face looked familiar.

The guy murmured something Jesus couldn't quite make out. His speech was slow, garbled, resigned.

The tall agent turned, fiddled with something on his belt, then walked towards the other two, as if he were taking a casual stroll. When he got closer to the guy on his knees he sped up his pace, and then Jesus noticed a slight jerk of the hand. The lanky guy marched a few more quick steps and barely avoided getting sprayed by the fountain of blood that shot out of the guy's neck.

Holy shit!

The tall agent with the pig-skin hand pulled out a large cloth handkerchief from a trouser pocket and started wiping blood from the blade of the knife he was holding in his other hand, gently, as if he were wiping spit-up milk from a baby's chin.

Jesus could hear Ruben breathing hard and fast. It was a miracle, Jesus thought, that he hadn't started whimpering yet. He reached over and squeezed his shoulder.

That tickle in his nose was getting stronger. He sniffed again, tried to rub the bridge of his nose. Already, he realized it was too late. He began to feel the inevitability of a sneeze coming on like the buildup of a swell approaching a beach, waxing and waning before the final rise and crash.

Jesus opened his mouth, tried to hold his breath, pinched his nose. He could hold out no longer. The sneeze broke through, but Jesus managed to muffle it, turn it into an odd kind of cough.

Right on cue, the lanky agent with the mustache turned in the direction of the boys. He raised the scarred hand in the air as if trying to stop traffic while the shorter agent unclipped his holster and pulled out his service weapon. The lanky one lifted his chin and narrowed his eyes, inhaled deeply before pointing towards the tree line with the point of the knife he had just wiped clean.

Both agents paced forward, the distance between them widening as they searched the area. They were coming in closer to the boys. The shorter one gripped his gun with both hands, moving it in pendulous arcs as though he were hosing down the knee-high wild grass.

Jesus turned his head just enough to glimpse at Ruben. The boy was gawking at the Border Patrol agents, mouth agape. His over-sized Adam's apple lurched once as he swallowed. That tuft of Samurai hair on the top of his hair quivered like a gamecock's feather. Jesus motioned for him to duck lower to the ground.

By now the lanky one was so close Jesus couldn't see above the man's thick lacquered belt without craning his neck. But Jesus had no urge to see the man's face. What captured his eye hung at the level of the agent's thigh: the thin long blade of the knife - no, not a knife; a dagger — a speck of wet blood still clinging to its cross-guard.

He had heard of crooked Border Patrol agents: guys who would coerce their female captors into having sex, who wouldn't think twice about pile driving a detainee head-first into the ground if they didn't like the way the guy looked at them. And Jesus knew that almost any slight can anger some men, but a special rage is unleashed when evil men, placed in unmerited positions of power, think their authority is being challenged. Give a coward a badge, a uniform, a rank or a title, and watch the beastly seed of sadism sprout and grow. But he never expected to witness this.

The agent's steps quickened now. Jesus felt his muscles tighten. He quickly considered his options. Run and hope not to get shot by the guy's partner, or tackle the guy, then run. Run under cover of the cedars, towards the river. Dive in deep, let the currents suck him down to safety. He knew the river. Oh, how he knew the river.

The problem was Ruben. The poor kid would just stay there, frozen, not by fear but by the overwhelming impulse to comply. To obey. To *pinche* follow directions. Survival by servitude. But now it was going to get them both killed.

The agent stopped. He pivoted his feet to the right, changed his grip on the dagger and took one more step towards a thicket of brush. A brown form burst out of the brush with a wild cackle, flew unsteadily just above the level of the tall grass then swooped up and alighted on the crooked branch of a live oak.

The short partner let out something between a gasp and a laugh. "A goddam chachalaca!" the man said. "A goddam chachalaca! Man, you should have seen your face." He tilted back the felt cowboy hat on his head and wiped the sweat from his brow.

The lanky guy said nothing. Shorter guy pulled the hat back over his forehead and started walking towards the other agent, still laughing.

"Hey, I think I got a new nick name for you," short guy just wouldn't let up. "What if from now on we call you, *El Chachacal?*"

The tall guy shifted the dagger to his scarred hand, grasped it by its blade and flung it at his partner. The blade pierced the short guy's cowboy hat and sent it tumbling to the turf as if it were blown off by a gust of wind.

The gun spilled out of the short agent's hand. The guy went pale, stood paralyzed for several seconds, then reached up with both hands and kneaded his balding head.

The lanky agent, in a composed voice, said,

"Bring me my knife, Shorty."

They waited until the green and white SUV was gone. Waited a little longer still.

Ruben whispered, "Hey, JT?"

"What?"

"I don't ever want to come back here."

Jesus stood up, wiped crumbles of dried leaves from his t-shirt. "Get the bike," he said as he ducked beneath the low-hanging branch of a juniper and stepped out of the clearing.

"Where are you going?" Ruben said.

"I got to see something."

"Are you crazy?"

"Get the bike."

Jesus took slow steady steps towards the crumpled body as if he were slogging through ankle-deep mud. There was no need to be scared, he told himself. The guy was dead. The body couldn't possibly jump up at him, slit throat and all, like in those stupid horror movies, so he could stop playing that film over and over again in his head. When he saw the lifeless hand, palm up, he stopped. To his surprise, as he focused on the ashen fingers, his fear evaporated.

He moved in closer, saw the body slumped over on its side. Jesus leaned in and studied the lifeless face. A face he knew. He had no doubt, now. It really was him.

21

Friday morning Pablo Medina called Benjamin into their shared office. He had a disquieting grin on his face. He invited Benjamin to sit with a stiff gesture of his arm and dragged a chair closer so that the two were facing each other, knees almost touching.

"That little truck you drive," Medina said. "Pretty faded and banged up."

"You noticed," Benjamin said.

"Forgive me for saying so, Benjamin," Medina said, "but it's a real piece of shit."

Benjamin shrugged.

"Benjamin, how would you like to get into a brand new BMW? Or maybe a nice SUV if that's more your style? Those new Range Rovers look real sharp, eh?"

Benjamin chuckled. "Pablo, if student debt were quicksand, I'd be in it up to my eyeballs. A new car is nowhere in the foreseeable future for me."

Medina waved his hand. "Purgatory is an MUA: a designated Medically Underserved Area, my friend. The hospital is working on your loan forgiveness paperwork as we speak. And the car, well that's just a metaphor. What I'm getting at is that you're a doctor, Benjamin. A young doctor with enormous potential. A doctor at the right place at the right time. And if you're smart, you can pare down those loans and still have the lifestyle you deserve."

Benjamin said, "Pablo, you've been very

generous but I don't think you understand..."

Medina hushed him with a wave of his hand. "Benjamin, I have great news. The board at El Dorado have invited you to become a partner." Medina reached out and shook Benjamin's hand. "Congratulations *hombre*."

"A partner? What does that even mean?"

"It means that between dividends and bonuses you won't have to worry about money ever again."

"Wait a minute," Benjamin said. "I mean, I just got here, why would they make me a partner?"

"You passed the two key requirements. Number one, you're a physician, number two, Dr. Soto-Prinz doesn't hate you."

"And that's all it takes? Now they're going to just throw cash at me? Why would they do that?"

"The dividends are a return on your investment, of course. It's just that with all the growth and success we've had, let's say the hospital is in an unusually auspicious financial position. The returns are better than you'll get anywhere. Without breaking the law, that is. If you don't let it all go to your head, you can live well on just your monthly dividends."

"Investment?" Benjamin said. "What kind of investment?"

"A hundred grand for starters."

"That's it? A hundred grand? Why didn't you say so at the beginning?" Benjamin said sarcastically. "Pablo, the only money I have to my name is what you already paid me."

Medina stood up, slid open a drawer and pulled

out a large envelope. He handed it to Benjamin and sat down again.

"What's this?" Benjamin said.

"One hundred thousand dollars. You've been pre-approved at a rock bottom rate from Rio Grande Merchant's Bank."

"Pre-approved? Pablo, this makes no sense. Why would they pre-approve me for a loan when my credit sucks?"

"The president of RGMB is the only non-physician partner at El Dorado. He personally approved the loan. You see, he knows it'll be paid off no sweat. The way the contract works, the bank withholds a small amount from your monthly dividend check to cover interest and principal. This way, the bank gets its money back and you won't even feel it."

"Look," Benjamin said. "I appreciate all this. I really do. But I think we're getting ahead of ourselves. You know I have a one year contract with you and then I'm off to do my fellowship."

"You would not be able to keep your shares if you left Purgatory."

"Right, so…"

"But perhaps this would help you change your mind." Medina chuckled to himself. "They say no one leaves Purgatory-"

"Alive?"

"Benjamin, what talk! Look, if you want to leave at the end of the year I'll buy your shares."

"Why would you do that?" Benjamin said.

Medina reached for a leather satchel with his

initials monogrammed above its brass buckle, rummaged through it and pulled out a small rectangular piece of paper. "This is the stub for my portion of last month's distribution. I get one of these every month."

Benjamin studied the paper. It had Pablo Medina's name on it. A column on the far right listed the total distribution for the month as $6,250. Beneath it was a deduction of $937.50 labeled EDPG PAC. The same heading that was on Benjamin's check for moving expenses. Net remittance: $5,312.50.

Pablo Medina said, "Why would I buy the shares from you? Because El Dorado is the best thing that's ever happened to me. And not just me. All the other partners would kill to get more shares."

"Why don't they just buy more shares then?"

"Because we can't. Not directly from El Dorado at least. New shares are for new investors. The only way we're able to get more shares is by buying out other partners. You want to leave one day? You just remember who your buddy is and sell those shares to me, *cabron*!" He gave Benjamin a slap on the knee.

Benjamin was silent.

"What do you say," Medina said.

"What's that EDPG PAC all about?"

Medina leaned back and let out a heavy sigh. "*N'hombre*! Again with this PAC. You come to the partner's meeting tonight. See for yourself."

The room looked more like a wedding banquet hall than a hospital conference room. Chandeliers with plump glass pendants hung from the ceiling on gilded chains, pale tapestries cordoned in red velvet adorned the two side walls, and a buffet table with silver serving platters ran along the back wall. The discordant note was a podium in the front of the room, a sleek acrylic lectern planted in it's center, and a wallpapered partition with the logo of El Dorado Medical Center printed repeatedly along its breadth as a backdrop. It was as if the interior designer anticipated a day there would be a ground-breaking news conference, immediately followed by a reception.

A group of doctors were lingering in the rear, gabbing excitedly while gorging on stuffed mushrooms, scallops, and bacon wrapped asparagus tips. A hush descended as Dr. Soto-Prinz entered the room, walked up the center aisle and stepped behind the lectern.

Benjamin and Pablo Medina were already seated about a third of the way from the front. As Soto-Prinz tapped on the tiny microphone that sprouted from the lectern on a long white stalk that looked like an ultra-modern catheter, Pablo elbowed Benjamin playfully and whispered, "Whatever you do, don't fall asleep."

"I trust you can hear me," Soto-Prinz said. "Good evening!"

The audience replied in near unison.

Soto-Prinz said, "And a good evening it is indeed. And a good month, I might add, as you will see from your distributions. And an excellent start to a new fiscal year." The room broke out in applause. "I must confess that it is becoming a tedious task, month after month, to have to come here and tell you how well your investment is performing. Aren't you growing tired of hearing how rich you're getting?"

The crowd responded with a resounding "No!"

Soto-Prinz chuckled. "I fancy there are some passions that never grow stale. Nonetheless, this evening we will break with convention and not review the financial statements for the prior month. A copy is included in your distribution packet, of course. Tonight, we have something far more important to discuss, but first a short announcement from our vice-president of marketing, Mr. Rangel.

A tall, broad-shouldered, middle-aged man in an over-sized pin-strip suit stepped up to the podium, cleared his voice. "Thank you Dr. Soto-Prinz. I'll be very brief. I just want to let y'all know that our new 3-Tesla magnet MRI is up and working, and as usual, you can schedule tests either on line or by calling our radiology department directly."

Soto-Prinz approached the lectern and Mr. Rangel slinked away. "I don't have to remind you that this new MRI cost a pretty penny but we purchased it because you, the partners, requested it. Now, it's not like me to tell fellow physicians how to practice medicine," Soto-Prinz grinned as the crowd laughed, "but you better damn well be ordering a heck of a lot of MRIs on your patients — when they're medically indicated, of course. As usual, our accountant will be like old Saint Nick: making his list, checking it twice, letting me know who's been naughty and nice."

Benjamin whispered to Pablo Medina, "The hospital's accountant is Santa Claus?"

"Better than Santa Claus," Medina said. "Brings us presents year round."

Soto-Prinz's tone became solemn. His eyes beamed. "Tonight, I have the pleasure of telling you a story. A heart-warming story most of you already know but it bears repeating, with one caveat at the end. It is the story of a young man, bright, handsome, promising, fresh out of law school. A man full of potential but of modest means and few political connections. A diamond in the rough, as they say.

"This young man passes his bar exam, gets a job with the district attorney's office in San Antonio and puts his nose to the grindstone. His talent soon shines through, and before long the flicker of a dream is kindled in his heart. From assistant district attorney he quickly moves up the ranks, forges new alliances, and then he embarks on his dream — a dream that, from mere kindling, has now become a raging bonfire. He decides to serve the people in the Texas House of Representatives."

Soto-Prinz raised his palms. "But alas, the hurdles before him seemed insurmountable. His opposition is a wily incumbent, better connected, better financed, all but entrenched. The odds are stacked against him right from the start. But then, a glimmer of hope appears in the form of a chance meeting on a deer-hunting trip." Soto-Prinz looked wistfully over the seated crowd. "As a young lad, I had the fabulous fortune of attending a speech given by Robert Kennedy. It was electrifying. His charisma bowled me over. I got the same feeling that day, sitting by the fireplace in that hunting lodge with Troy Davenport."

Soto-Prinz straightened. "Troy Davenport was the first political candidate supported by the El Dorado Physician Group Political Action Committee. For this alone he holds a special place in our heart. And he was the first candidate to win a political race, it is not a stretch to say, as a direct result of our support. And now, he is poised to write a new chapter in history."

Soto-Prinz shifted his weight, raised his voice and began thumping his chest rhythmically. "It was through our strength, our unity, our shared sense of purpose that we were able to get a sympathetic ear in Austin, an advocate for physicians, for the plight of independent hospitals, and for a more lucid approach to those border issues that affect us all."

As he listened to the ardent response of the crowd, Benjamin began to wonder if Dr. Soto-Prinz had been a politician himself. Or a preacher perhaps.

"Still," Soto-Prinz said, "there is much work ahead of us. New misguided federal regulations threaten to erode everything we've worked so hard to build. More injunctions to torment us, more edicts to rob us of our autonomy, new decrees to shackle our healing hands. Which is why now more than ever, it is imperative that we once again open our hearts and open our war chest and elect Troy Davenport as the next United States Senator from the great State of Texas!"

The audience rose to their feet in cheers. A chorus of "Troy's our boy! Troy's our boy!" erupted to Dr. Soto-Prinz's delight.

Benjamin watched as Pablo Medina jumped to

his feet with the rest of the crowd, chanting, fist pumping in the air. Benjamin stood up, feeling sheepish, but did not join in the chant.

Soto-Prinz raised his hand, signaled for silence. He waited for the audience to get back in their seats.

"Such enthusiasm! And yet some of you continue to contribute the bare minimum to our PAC. Fifteen percent is a pitiful tithing for all we are about to receive." Soto-Prinz outstretched his arms, palms up, then brought his hands together as if in prayer. "Let us cleanse our hearts of selfishness, brothers and sisters. I solemnly ask… No. No, I shall ask for nothing. But I would like to share with you a vision of a very near future. Look over the deplorable political landscape that has unfolded and consider the unique opportunity for a new breed of political candidate. A man of virtue, a man of vision, a man of indisputable appeal, undeniable ability, absolute integrity. A man of keen intellect matched by profound compassion, who's mind grasps the complex economic challenges of our time and who's heart weighs heavy with the pressing social challenges of time immemorial.

"Friends, gaze over the horizon and try to glimpse the vision that has been seared into my eyes. Behold the golden rays of a new dawn. Imagine, if you will, a banner, glimmering and bold and steadfast, reading: 'Troy Davenport for President of the United States — 2020.'"

The audience jumped to their feet again. The chant of "Troy's our boy!" resumed with synchronous stomping of the feet. Benjamin surveyed the crowd.

The expressions on the faces of all in attendance were rabid, like those of zealots in ecstasy at a tent revival. Medina grasped Benjamin's sleeve, leaned in and shouted, "I don't think you'll be leaving Purgatory anytime soon."

It is a puzzling phenomenon that, once you encounter something for the first time, it suddenly starts appearing all around you, as if a blind spot you never knew existed has suddenly been removed. When Benjamin drove home that evening, he couldn't help but wonder whether the political yard signs on the streets of Purgatory had always been there and escaped his notice, or if they just sprung up like mushrooms after a downpour. Benjamin tried keeping a mental tally and pretty soon convinced himself that the placards in support of Troy Davenport for U.S. Senate just edged out those of his rival, Quincy Vaughn, if that carried any prognostic weight at all.

The investors meeting at El Dorado left him dumbfounded. It was unlike anything he had ever witnessed in the hallowed halls of academia, that sheltering cocoon where young doctors undergo the requisite intellectual metamorphosis unencumbered by the intrusive realities of the outside world. He started to wonder if he was just plain naive. Was this how the real world of hospital politics operated or was El Dorado an aberration?

During his residency, after interacting with senior physicians of all stripes, Benjamin had come to believe that the archetype of the rich doctor was an exaggeration, if not an outright myth, created by soap operas and Hollywood movies. He had accepted the fact that he would never be a wealthy man, not with the status of his student loans and his modest projected income as an employed physician at a University hospital.

Maybe he had been plumb wrong. Just weeks out of residency, he was being handed the opportunity to earn some real cash, pay down his debt before even starting his fellowship. He didn't have to involve himself in the politics. In one year Pablo would buy his shares. No harm, no foul. Maybe, just maybe, he was finally getting a lucky break.

Right on cue the image of Claire floated through his mind, a sneer of disapproval on her face. Why should the mere thought of her dredge up a sense of guilt?

But it wasn't just the money that seemed to be motivating Dr. Soto-Prinz. It was power. If he had his way, El Dorado hospital would have its very own senator. And one day, a friend in the White House.

He pulled into his driveway, killed the engine, unlocked the front door and entered the house. Dropped his bag on the floor next to the sofa and turned the TV on. He stepped into the kitchen and got a beer out of the fridge, walked back in the living area and slumped on the sofa.

The evening news was on. A young field

reporter with a high-pitched, agitated voice was relating the results of a new poll which had Troy Davenport surging, pulling ahead of Quincy Vaughn, the crusty incumbent, even with a five percent margin of error. A video clip showed a man with strawberry blond hair and an athletic build giving a speech from the back of a pickup truck with a bullhorn, shirtsleeves rolled up, a distant gleam in his eye, a strange harmony of resolve and melancholy vibrating in his voice. A small crowd surrounding the truck looked up at him, starstruck.

When the feed cut back to the studio, the two anchors, a gray-haired man and an attractive young woman, were downright giddy. This guy Davenport was a rock star. No doubt about that.

He turned the TV off and got to his feet, started unbuttoning his shirt and ambled in the direction of his bedroom, but froze when he got to the threshold. A chill rippled across the surface of his skin. There was a moment of puzzlement as he tried to pinpoint the origin of his sudden apprehension. He turned around slowly to confirm what he thought he had seen. Or rather, what he had not seen.

The wall by the front door was bare. His bicycle was gone.

He looked around the room. He was quite sure he hadn't moved it. Everything else in the room seemed to be in its place. He tried to concentrate. The door was locked when he got home. He was sure of that much. He distinctly remembered inserting the key in the lock and the tumbler rolling with a solid clunk.

He stepped inside the bedroom. A twenty dollar

bill was on his end table where he remembered leaving it in the morning, right underneath the Swiss Army watch his grandmother had given him as a high school graduation present.

Maybe Myrtle still had an extra key and stopped by. But why would she take his bike? He went to the front door and studied the lock, not quite knowing what he was looking for. There were no marks that suggested forced entry as far as he could tell.

What was he thinking? Who would break in, steal a broken bicycle but leave a television, cash and a watch? It just didn't make sense.

Benjamin's ahead was abuzz as he lay in bed. Nothing made any sense in this place. For once, Benjamin wished he had someone to talk to; not to fend off a sense of loneliness — Benjamin Snow was perfectly comfortable in his solitude — but to ground him. A transient connection was all he needed. To help him get things straight. Again, he thought of Claire and was bothered by the fact that he couldn't quite recreate the entirety of her face in his mind's eye.

It took some doing but the weld on the bicycle fork was a done deal. A little sanding down, a fresh coat of paint and it would look better than new. Jesus Tamez turned off the welder's arc and raised the bulky mask from his face. He blew on the metal callus on the fork. Not a work of art, but it was straight as a pencil and the joint would hold.

He walked across his uncle's workshop to the bench with the polishers and buffers. A small television with a cracked plastic case lay on the bench, just below the poster of an insanely voluptuous calendar girl in a tiny pink thong squatting in front of the grill of a green 1970 Dodge Charger. The volume on the set was turned so high that the broken case vibrated.

Jesus didn't care for the news and if his uncle hadn't been there he'd have turned the damn thing off.

"Can I use the Ingersoll Rand 7 inch?" Jesus called out.

"Long as you put it back when you're done," his uncle replied from under a purple 1997 Buick Regal.

Jesus grabbed the polisher and was about to head back to his work station when a picture flashed on the TV screen stopping him in mid-stride. He stepped up closer to the TV set trying to hear the report over the rattle of the television case.

A somber looking news anchor said, "And tonight, Purgatory police are continuing to investigate the disappearance of a local Emergency Room physician. Dr. Joseph Rizzo finished an overnight shift at El Dorado Medical Center Emergency Room Monday night but never returned home according to his wife, Naomi Rizzo. His car, a black 2015 Chevy Camaro was captured on video as it headed into Mexico at the Falcon Dam border crossing, but the identity of the driver could not be ascertained from computer enhanced still images extracted from that video. Review of security tape taken from the El Dorado parking lot does show Dr. Rizzo getting into his car and leaving the medical center campus at approximately eight-ten am. Foul play has not been ruled out."

Jesus shook his head. "They still haven't found him," he murmured.

"What's that?" His uncle said.

"Nothing *Tio*," Jesus said. Then added, "Listen, I got to go."

Jesus walked out of the shop, shooed away the pit bull that roamed the yard, let himself out of the chain linked gate and headed down the highway, hands tucked in his jean pockets.

Joe Rizzo wasn't missing. He was dead. And he knew who did it too. Damn *migra!* But what he couldn't understand is why the Border Patrol would kill a doctor. Unless he was crooked. He had to be crooked. Likely pushing drugs on the side. Pain pills, maybe a little meth. Border Patrol nailed him because he was horning in on their turf. Everyone knew *those* guys were crooked, more crooked than his grandma's legs.

Of course if he told anyone it might be *his* neck getting slashed. Not to mention that his beautiful stash of Aunt Mary would be found, what with a million cops coming down to Sanguinity Point. But what about the body? It was probably still there, under the stars now, and tomorrow under the sweltering sun. Animals would find it, coyotes and vultures would start gnawing his limbs down to the bone. Forget the stash. He wasn't going to go back down there anyway, not on his life. Not while the ghost of *Chorizo* was still there. He made the sign of the cross as he stepped into the neon glow of a gas station.

Joe Rizzo was Snowflake's friend after all. And Jesus told Snowflake he'd have his back. He felt a growing pang of responsibility. He had to do something.

He headed to the side of the building where he knew there was a pay-phone because he had once graffitied it with a black marker. He would do this for Snowflake. He dropped a quarter in the slot thinking he'd have to be quick. He had seen in the movies how the cops traced calls.

A man's voice answered. "Purgatory Police Department." For some reason he had expected a woman to pick up. It almost threw him off.

"Dr. Joe Rizzo is dead. His body is on Sanguinity Point. The Border Patrol killed him."

He hung up just as the voice on the other end started talking again.

22

"And what is *that* supposed to be?" Claire said. She stared at the twenty dollar bill Benjamin had deposited nonchalantly on the Formica counter top. There was a tautness in her voice, a simmering defensiveness.

Compassion, pity and sympathy, Benjamin had long ago learned, were loaves baked from the same sticky dough. He didn't want to arouse any of these emotions. It was gratitude he wished to express. Simple gratitude with no condescension. Already he was doubting himself.

"My copay," Benjamin said as he extracted the shiny insurance card from his billfold and handed it to her. "You *are* going to bill my insurance for the office visit, aren't you?"

Claire studied the card. Flipped it over. "The problem, you see, is we're out of network. That means your copay is forty dollars."

Benjamin pulled another twenty out of his billfold and flattened it on the counter.

Claire waited a beat. Then she said, "I wonder," she tightened her lips as if to restrain a smile, "have you met your deductible for the year yet?"

"It's the first time I use this card."

"Ahhh, that's just what I suspected. Well, that means you're responsible for the entire office visit then. That'll be sixty-five bucks."

Benjamin pulled out two more twenty dollar

bills and laid them on top of the other notes.

"You don't have the exact amount?" Claire said. "I'm afraid I don't have change. I guess you have two choices: I can give you credit for a future appointment or… what do you guys do at the Medina clinic? Don't you just order an unnecessary test to bump up the difference?"

"I wouldn't know."

"Oh, but *I* know," she said. "Let's see, the only test we have that's fifteen bucks on the nose is a pregnancy test. Benjamin, how would you like a pregnancy test today?"

"I'll take the credit."

"So you plan to come back?"

"The clavicle is still pretty sore," Benjamin said. He judged it unwise to add that he had nowhere else to go for medical care. Nowhere else he wanted to go to.

"You know better than me that the clavicle will heal as long as the two ends of the bone are in the same room. And you could have easily taken those stitches out by yourself, Dr. Snow."

"You know what they say," Benjamin said, "he who treats himself has a quack as a doctor and a fool as a patient."

Claire cocked her head to the side. "Well, I never suspected you of being a quack," she said. The mischievous smile was full bloom now.

"Right," Benjamin said. "Just a fool."

Claire laughed. "I'm sorry. It's really not fair for you to be the constant target of all my slings and arrows."

"It's OK. I'm getting used to it," Benjamin said. "Besides, I've always been a lightning-rod for calamities."

Her smile vanished. "It sure seems that way, doesn't it?" She held Benjamin's gaze with a knowing look that probed him a bit too deeply. He turned his eyes to the stack of bills on the counter.

"Can I schedule a follow-up appointment for next week?" he asked.

"Why don't you come over for supper?" Claire said. She seemed surprised, if not by what she said, by the eagerness with which she uttered the invitation. "One of our patients brought us some home-made tamales. There's more than Pops and I can eat by ourselves." She placed a hand on the counter top, wiped away an imperceptible spot with her index finger. "Pops has really taken a liking to you. Your company seems to lift his spirits."

"I didn't know he-"

"Yeah, I know. He's good at not showing it." She took in a deep breath as if to sigh, shifted her weight and rolled her shoulders. "He just keeps things bottled up. You like tamales?"

"Pork?"

"We got those too."

She told him they would wrap up with patients in thirty minutes, an hour tops, and urged him to go take a peek outside, behind the clinic.

Benjamin sauntered out the front door and headed back to the east side of the building. The sun was low enough that a merciful shadow spread out over a rough patch of grass framed by two mismatched net-less soccer goals, the posts and crossbars made of two-by-fours with bits of gypsum board still nailed on in some spots. A dozen kids were playing, their mouths running more than their feet.

Benjamin sat on the broad stump of a red oak and looked on. The shouts of the kids, even in another language, were all too familiar. It had been the soundtrack of his childhood. What a childhood!

Nostalgia was a stupid emotion, a pernicious form of self-pity: pity for one's former self, encapsulated by that most asinine of laments, "If only I knew then what I know now."

As a rule, Benjamin avoided thinking of his childhood — a time that was neither as unhappy as others imagined it to be (*the poor orphan, no one in the world but his aging grandparents to care for him)* nor as joyful as he had hoped it to be. There had been some joy, to be sure; moments of true happiness: happiness as palpable as the stump he was sitting on. A joy felled in the amount of time it takes a tiny finger to squeeze a stubborn trigger.

A boy in a Barcelona jersey got hold of the ball, a runt of a boy no older than twelve or thirteen. He stopped the ball under foot, made a convincing body fake to the right and sprinted to the left. He moved in sharp, jutting, angles, the sleeves of his jersey billowing out as he moved. He was a flea. Even as he ran, the ball stayed close to his feet as if held there by an invisible rubber band.

A shiver spread down Benjamin's spine. The way

the boy moved, the ease with which he bolted past opposing players reminded him of the best soccer player, hands down, at his middle school. The boy who got Benjamin hooked to the game, who spurred him on to work harder, never give up.

Toby McNulty was the one with all the talent. Benjamin was merely his pupil. A pupil who plowed forward somehow, fumbled his way onto the varsity squad his sophomore year in high school then burst out as the team's top scorer by junior year, district MVP his senior year. The pupil who would win that full ride to Rutgers knowing it rightfully belonged to Toby.

The flea scored. Faked the shot with his right foot, rounded the pudgy goalie and cut the ball just inside the near post with his left. His teammates cheered, arms lifted to the sky. The biggest boy of the bunch, a bruiser with oily hair and an acne pocked face, taunted the goalie. The flea jogged back towards the center of the field, head slightly bowed. He glanced over at Benjamin and winked. Benjamin gave him a thumb's up.

The game resumed.

Out of nowhere, the thought of that cop in Houston popped into Benjamin's mind. Krikorian. Strange name. A good name for a cop, no doubt. The guy seemed to have a morbid interest in Benjamin's affairs. It bothered Benjamin that a connection had been cast in his brain, a synaptic bridge erected, between the memory of Toby McNulty and a new node titled, Detective Glenn Krikorian.

"Maybe next time you can join them." He hadn't

noticed Claire approaching. Her voice startled him.

"I don't want to spoil their fun," Benjamin said. He got to his feet and wiped the seat of his pants with his hand.

"I'm more worried about your collar bone."

"Nothing to worry. I have credit at my doctor's office. For at least one pregnancy test."

Claire smirked. She turned and shouted something at the kids. Benjamin understood *vamonos*, but little else. There was a chorus of groans from the boys. Only the flea was silent. He looked at Benjamin, sizing him up, then lifted the soccer ball with his foot and booted it in a high lob towards Benjamin.

Claire took a step back, lifting an arm over her head. Benjamin followed the arc of the ball, pivoted on his left foot and trapped the ball under his right foot. It was a slick move that drew cheers from the boys.

The flea smiled. Soon, the boys stopped cheering and gathered around Claire, whining. The flea pushed his way passed them and commenced bargaining in a very business-like tone.

"*No, no, no,*" Claire said. "*Mañana.*"

The flea kept at it. He pointed to Benjamin, then to the soccer ball.

Claire glanced over at Benjamin. "Manuel wants to challenge you."

Benjamin pointed at his collar bone. "*No bueno.* Crack!"

"A penalty kick challenge," Claire said. "Best out of three."

"Penalty," the flea repeated.

"*Mañana,*" Benjamin said. "How do you say, another time?"

"Come on, Benjamin," Claire said. "These kids have been through so much. It would mean a lot to them."

Benjamin hung his head in a mock gesture of resignation. "Best of three, then."

The kids cheered. One of them grabbed Benjamin by the wrist and practically dragged him toward one of the goals. The teenager with the oily hair pushed away the pudgy goalie and stepped onto the goal line. He spit in his hands and rubbed them together, pawed his feet on the turf like a bull before a charge.

The flea took the ball from Benjamin. Counted eleven paces from the goal line and made a mark in the turf with his heel. He placed the ball on the turf as carefully as if it were a porcelain vase. He stepped back, took a short running start and rifled the ball into the left lower corner of the goal.

Benjamin clapped.

The goalie kicked the ball out to Benjamin for his turn. Benjamin bounced the ball a couple of times. It was a little overinflated, a bit lopsided. He felt the weight of the ball in his hand before dropping it on the mark in the turf. He looked up at the goalie to make sure he was ready. The goalie nodded. Benjamin struck the ball with the instep of his right foot. It felt right. It was a line drive that was still rising as it plunked hard against the crossbar.

The goalie flinched at the sound of the impact,

but then, after a significant delay, raised his arms in celebration.

"That was so close," Claire said.

"*Uno a zero*," the flea said, and prepared for his second attempt.

This time the flea hit the ball in the upper right hand corner. He made it look easy.

Benjamin lined up for his second shot. The first shot had warmed him up, so he swung at the ball with more power this time. As soon as it left his foot Benjamin knew the ball would go precisely where he had intended. It felt good. He had forgotten how much he loved the game. The ball came off the crossbar with a thud that made the goalie duck. No celebration this time.

"Oh!" Claire said. She looked puzzled.

"What are the chances, right?" Benjamin said. "I guess you won, Manuel."

"*Uno mas*," the flea said.

"You already won. Two to zero," Benjamin said. "I don't have a chance."

"*Uno mas*," the flea repeated. He whistled to call for the ball. He flattened the turf with his heel, placed the ball ever so carefully on the ground, picked it up again, stomped on the grass some more before teeing up his shot. He kicked the ball hard. The ball rattled the cross bar making contact very close to the spot that Benjamin had just nailed.

Clever boy.

Manuel turned, made eye contact with Benjamin. Benjamin winked. The boy smiled, bowed his head in a bashful way.

"This is it," Claire said. "Your last shot."

"My last chance at redemption?" Benjamin said.

"There's no such thing as a last chance at redemption, silly. You always get another chance. But, it *is* your last shot."

Benjamin stepped up for the shot. One of the boys had already positioned the ball. By now the goalie had grown restless. He was arguing with Manuel, pointing at the cross bar. Finally he took his position. Benjamin asked if he was ready. The goalie gave him a thumbs up but remained hunched over, keeping his head low.

This time, when Benjamin struck the ball he got the feeling that he had shifted his weight too far back. He half expected the ball to fly too high, but again the ball sprung off the wood work.

The goalie walked away in a flourish, his strut expressing an ounce of vindication, a ton of relief. The rest of the boys hooped and hollered except for Manuel, the flea. He called out to Benjamin. Gave him a thumb's up. Benjamin returned the gesture.

After dinner, Virgil Thibodeaux and Benjamin sat on faded Adirondacks on the front porch of the house, a bowl of unshelled pecans the size of quail eggs sitting on the table between them.

"You don't need a nut cracker," Thibodeaux said. "Grab two at a time in the same hand and just squeeze them together, like so."

Benjamin picked two pecans with his good hand, was surprised how easily one cracked open in his clenched fist. He picked the wrinkled fruit from the broken shell and dropped it in his mouth.

"Gotta chew 'em slow," Thibodeaux said. "It's a bit like eating tree bark, but there's a pleasant after-taste at the end."

"They're good," Benjamin said.

"From the tree in our front yard," Thibodeaux said. He narrowed his eyes and leaned over. "You know what would really help bring the flavor out?" He whispered, "A thimble-full of single malt scotch."

Claire appeared behind the screen of the front door, a dish towel in her hands. "Don't even start with me, old man."

Thibodeaux leaned back in his chair. "Benjamin, did I ever tell you her grandmother was a witch doctor?"

"You mentioned it," Benjamin said.

Claire pushed the screen open, sat on the armrest of Virgil's Adirondack. She reached over him and scooped up a couple of pecans from the bowl.

The sun was setting and an evening breeze was blowing from the east. There was a smokiness in the air, a scent of burnt mesquite and scorched grass which blended to great effect with the taste of the pecans. The sky seemed to be glowing with distant bonfires.

"That's a beautiful sky," Benjamin said.

"It's our consolation prize," Claire said. She must have noticed the perplexed look on Benjamin's face. "Some people have beaches, some have forests and mountains. The only view we got is the evening sky."

"The kicker is too many people spend most of their life hoping for certain things to happen, awaiting specific events they chose haphazardly as the keys to their happiness to occur. They're looking down the line all the time and they forget to look up," Thibodeaux said. He tossed half a pecan in his mouth, rolled his jaws slowly. "So, Dr. Snow, how are you enjoying your exile?"

Benjamin laughed. "That's a funny way to put it."

"I don't mean it in a bad way," Thibodeaux said. "Going in exile can be a great advantage for a young man."

"How's that?" Benjamin asked.

"Well, being forced to leave behind your home, your family, your friends-"

Benjamin said, "Just my professional career."

Virgil Thibodeaux nodded. "The dream of your professional career, perhaps."

"Dream? I might never get another chance to do that fellowship," Benjamin said. "I'm practically blacklisted."

"It was just a dream you had," Thibodeaux said. "A dream of how your life might have been. But that dream that you created for yourself had little to do with reality. Don't get me wrong, I appreciate how devastating losing a dream can be at your age. When you're young it's easy to conflate your dreams with your identity. When your dream doesn't pan out, it can feel like you lost a part of you."

Benjamin reached for a pecan, looked at it. "Yeah well that dream was pretty much all I had."

"Like I was saying," Thibodeaux said. "Going in exile can be a great advantage for a young man. A wonderful opportunity. Especially if everything is taken from you. It's the only way to see for yourself that your happiness depends on only one thing."

"And what's that?" Benjamin asked.

"Virtue," Thibodeaux said. He chuckled at Benjamin's expression. "In the ancient sense of the word. By which I mean, one's values: what you truly believe in. When you're grounded in your values, when you have a philosophy of life that you are committed to, everything can be taken away from you, Benjamin, without robbing you of your tranquility. Ataraxia, the ancient sages called it, a steadfast, unwavering peace of mind."

There was a prolonged silence. Claire cracked a pecan open, sighed and said, "That really is a beautiful sky."

Virgil Thibodeaux cleared his voice. "Through it all and despite us, it lives and breathes majestic. To wax poetic, if we allow ourselves a moment to be romantic."

"Are you a romantic, Dr. Snow?" Claire said.

"He's one of us," Virgil said. "Aren't you, Benjamin?"

Benjamin said, "I guess I'm sort of pragmatic."

"Pragmatic?" Claire said. "What's that supposed to mean?"

Benjamin hesitated in answering. He didn't want Claire to misinterpret him, to think him cold and calculating. Virgil came to his rescue.

"It simply means he's more concerned about tangible results than trying to understand the system that created them. Isn't that right, my boy? No need to grapple with the idea of a transcendental universal truth. Let others seek the truth; Benjamin will pursue what works best."

Benjamin had never heard his own convictions explained so precisely. He wondered how Virgil Thibodeaux could have come to know him so well in so short a time.

"So you believe nothing," Claire said.

"I really haven't thought about these things as deeply as your father makes it sound," Benjamin said.

"Okay," Claire said. "What *do* you believe?"

"I'm not a philosopher by any stretch," Benjamin said, "but I think the content of our beliefs is defined by our actions."

"That means nothing," Claire said. "It's a tautology. What guides your actions?"

"Like Virgil said, one's actions should be guided by expected results. So you should act in such a way to achieve the best possible result, after a rational examination of the evidence at hand."

"I see," Claire said. "So, when you quit playing soccer in college, did that achieve the best possible result?"

It was just like her to torpedo him when he thought the conversation was navigating in calmer waters.

Virgil Thibodeaux appeared confused. "Soccer?

What does that have to do with anything?"

"He was a hot-shot soccer player on a full scholarship at Rutgers. And then he up and quits," Claire said snapping her fingers. "Just like that."

"We were talking about the sky," Virgil said.

"He's the one who said he was pragmatic, that actions are rational expressions of one's beliefs" Claire said. "I just wonder how pragmatic that decision was."

A sparrow perched on the sinewy branch of an elm at the edge of the yard. It twitched its tail and tweeted sternly. A gust of wind chased it away.

"So why'd you quit?" Claire said.

"I quit because I didn't belong on the team," Benjamin said.

"You were second team all-American. A heck of a player by any standard."

She too had looked him up, apparently. Had taken the time to type his name into a search engine. He was flattered in a shallow way.

"I didn't say I wasn't good enough," Benjamin said. "I said I didn't belong on the team."

Virgil and Claire Thibodeaux seemed to consider this last statement. They exchanged inquiring glances.

Virgil said, "Was it a tough decision?"

"Not really," Benjamin said.

"Was it the right choice?"

"Absolutely."

Virgil smiled at him. "Good," he said, "I guess that's that." He redirected his attention to the bowl of pecans.

"Don't you trust us?" Claire said.

Benjamin chuckled. "Why do you ask?"

"Because I saw that gleam in your eye when you were playing with the boys this afternoon. So I can imagine how much soccer meant to you, and now you say it was such an easy decision. And the two of you are — don't Claire me, Pops — the two of you are closing yourselves off in your cave of manly reticence, as if that's some kind of a virtue. The macho code of silence. Oh, I am *so* impressed."

"I was part of something that I'm wasn't proud of," Benjamin said. Benjamin looked at Virgil Thibodeaux. There was a plain tenderness in the old man's eyes. The eyes of a man accustomed to witnessing sorrow.

Silence fell. The air felt heavier as though the evening heat had caused the air molecules to gel. Inside the house, the phone rang. Claire started to get to her feet but her father grasped her wrist.

"I'll get the phone," Virgil Thibodeaux said.

Claire waited until her father was inside the home. She slinked in the Adirondack and said, "I'm guessing you've never talked about this with anyone before."

"You guessed right," Benjamin said.

"Doesn't it weight on you?"

"Not if I don't think about it."

"Is this an example of what you were talking about? Being a lighting rod for calamities?"

She was digging deeper. She wasn't going to let this one go.

"I made my team lose a playoff game. Missed a penalty kick that would have kept our hopes alive."

"Anyone can miss," Claire said.

Benjamin shook his head. "It was deliberate."

Claire straightened her spine. "Why?"

Hard to believe that game had been the last time Benjamin had played soccer. He still remembered the way number ten of the opposing team moved. The kid was quick, agile, great with his feet — virtually impossible to defend. He was causing all kinds of havoc for the Rutgers defense. He scored one goal at the ten minute mark and kept coming at them. Just after half-time, Benjamin's coach had had enough. He substituted a solid starting winger with Eddie Walker, a clunky midfielder who had the dubious distinction of holding the record for the most yellow cards received in one season in the history of Rutgers soccer. Eddie was not a skillful player. His passes were inevitably either too soft or way too hard as if he had cinder blocks for cleats, which made even the easiest of touches hard to regulate. He had no precision in his shot and he couldn't dribble a ball for the life of him.

What he excelled in was pursuit. He was dogged in marking his man. Using his strength, he was able to keep up with players twice as fast as him by throwing them off stride. His slide tackle was a wrecking ball which could level small buildings. But what made him one of coach's favorites was that he always followed instructions to the tee. Muscle and hustle, coach called him. The rest of the team called him Walker the Stalker.

When Eddie Walker was subbed in at the height

of a divisional semi-final, Benjamin knew it could have been for only one thing. He saw coach taking Eddie aside, far from the bench, to give him his marching orders. When Walker the Stalker stepped on the field, Benjamin had the urge to jog over to number ten to warn him, to tell him to let go of the ball for his own good.

Eddie's first challenge was a body blow that knocked number ten to the ground hard. The kid took that as a challenge rather than a warning, and the next time he got the ball, he dribbled down the side-line Eddie was patrolling, aiming to humiliate him. Walker the Stalker timed his slide tackle perfectly, came in with both feet outstretched leaving number ten no room to escape. The blow was so severe the sound of the impact could be heard in the bleachers. When number ten somehow rolled to a sitting position and lifted his leg with both hands, the angle of his shin just above his ankle, where both tibia and fibula had both been shattered, was so askew that he just looked at it in horror and screamed.

Eddie got a red card. Benjamin's team had to play the rest of the game one player short. But the spirit of the opposing team had been deflated. With five minutes left to play, the referee awarded Rutgers a penalty kick for a dubious hand ball inside the box. Benjamin had not missed a single penalty the entire season. Had he scored, the game would have been tied and, with momentum behind them, Rutgers would have likely gone on to win. But as he teed up his shot, Benjamin couldn't get a picture out of his head: the sight of coach shamelessly patting Walker the Stalker on the butt as the player headed for the locker room. Benjamin made sure the ball sailed well over the crossbar.

After the final whistle, coach jogged up to Benjamin and said, "I know what you just did, Snow."

That night, Benjamin drove to the hospital where they had operated on number ten's leg. He stepped out of his car and paced around the parking lot but couldn't get himself to walk through the main door. It was always the same thing. He simply didn't belong

There was a shuffling of feet by the front door. The door creaked open. Virgil Thibodeaux clung to it, looking unusually frail.

Claire sprung to her feet. "What's the matter, Pops?"

Virgil lowered his head. "Joe Rizzo is dead."

23

He had only just recently met him, but Joe Rizzo had been as much as a friend as anyone he had known through medical school or residency. The news of his death had had a profound effect on him and the following Monday Benjamin found himself slogging through the morning's patients without being able to focus. Ivan the Terrible must have sensed something was amiss and was unusually subdued. At noon Pablo Medina put an arm around Benjamin's neck and said, "Jesus Benjamin, let me take you to lunch."

Benjamin would have been happier spending the lunch hour alone but he had no energy to even attempt to refuse Medina's offer. The two got into Pablo Medina's Mercedes and headed out of the clinic's parking lot. When they stopped at a traffic light Medina asked, "Did you sign your partnership offer?"

Benjamin shook his head. "I haven't had the chance to think about it."

Medina nodded. "This whole thing has everyone on edge. Don't let it trouble you too much."

Medina's comment touched a raw nerve. "I liked Joe Rizzo."

"Of course," Medina said. "I liked him too."

Now Benjamin wished he hadn't accepted the lunch invitation. Ten minutes later, when Medina pulled into the parking lot of El Dorado Medical Center, he was really sorry he had.

"What are we doing here?" Benjamin said.

"Best lunch in Purgatory," Medina said.

The doctor's lounge was relatively quiet. Benjamin and Pablo Medina sat at a table with a radiologist who Medina introduced as a former Vice President of Guatemala.

"El Salvador," the distinguished gentleman corrected.

Benjamin was too drained to care.

Krippendorff ambled into the doctor's lounge, whisked a glass of iced tea from a tray and started slurping it even before plopping into a chair the next table over. A server came by to take his order.

"Two cheeseburgers. Bacon on the side. No lettuce and no damn tomato this time." Everything about Krippendorff was needlessly loud and grating.

The Vice President of El Salvador flashed a decidedly diplomatic smile and turned his attention back to his chicken soup.

"Moral of the story is," Krippendorff said, starting a conversation out of the blue with no one in particular, "doctor know thy patient."

"Moral of what story?" a doctor sitting at Krippendorff's table asked.

"What other story is there? Joe Rizzo."

Pablo Medina looked over and frowned but said nothing.

"Heck of a time to botch a delivery," Krippendorff said.

Medina told Benjamin, "I don't much feel like dessert today. We can leave whenever you're ready."

"What do you know about it?" the guy sitting

next to Krippendorff said.

"What I know is, when the baby was discharged from the hospital," Krippendorff said, "it was picked up by a motorcade of black Chevy Suburbans. A guy over in security ran the plates on one of the vehicles. Guess who it's registered to?" The guy at his table shifted in his seat. "The vehicle was registered to Fernando Ortega." Krippendorff started laughing. "How do you like that?"

Medina turned in his seat and said in a raised voice, "What are you getting at Kripp?"

"The girl that died, that was Fernando Ortega's mistress. The baby is his love child. That's why they offed Rizzo. Joe Rizzo killed Fernando Ortega's freaking mistress."

"You don't know that," Pablo Medina said.

"Get this: they slit his fucking throat," Krippendorff said. "What does that sound like?"

Benjamin said, "Who's Fernando Ortega?"

"Who's Fernando Ortega?" Krippendorff laughed. "New kid in town is pretty clueless."

"He's a local businessman," Medina said.

"Yeah. Except his business is drugs," Krippendorff said. "Mexican marijuana, Colombian cocaine."

"I'd watch what you say," the guy sitting at Krippendorff's table said.

"Come on! Everyone knows it. It's common knowledge," Krippendorff said. "Everyone knows he's *El Chacal*."

The Vice President of El Salvador cleared his

throat. "He can't be *El Chacal*."

"And why's that?" Krippendorff said.

"Because I'm *El Chacal*. At least that's what members of our legislative assembly claimed." The radiologist looked at Benjamin and smiled.

"You can joke all you want. But the guy lives in a damn fortress. Has a motorcade of armored vehicles take him wherever he goes."

The Vice President said, "Looks like you're ready to convict him, counselor. Why haven't the Feds already picked him up?"

Krippendorff said, "The Feds are pussies."

Medina wiped his lips with a paper towel, nodded at Benjamin. He had heard enough. Benjamin nodded back and the two excused themselves from the table.

Back in Medina's car Benjamin said, "You think this guy Ortega killed Joe Rizzo?"

"Leave it be, Benjamin. Leave it be."

"Do you think he's *El Chacal*?"

Medina slammed on the brakes. His knuckles were white on the steering wheel. He said, "Don't ever mention that name in my presence again."

Benjamin wrapped up his afternoon work and left the office at five-thirty. In the parking lot behind the clinic, grackles jeered as they jockeyed for position on the overhead power lines. The sun was still pounding with all of its summer might and Benjamin had to use paper napkins to handle the scorching gear shifter and steering wheel. His truck's air conditioner spewed out hot air.

He rolled down his window and got the car moving. The streets were jammed with edgy drivers getting off work, rushing home to the refuge of their emerald lawns and flat screen TVs. When Benjamin slowed to let a delivery van switch into his lane the car behind him honked.

He was glad when he reached the highway leading out of town and the traffic thinned, comforted by the pungently sweet smell of cabbage rotting in the field behind his home as he drove alongside the irrigation canal. He made the turn over the concrete culvert and slowed as he neared his bungalow. Claire's Toyota was in his driveway. She was sitting on the cement steps between the barber shop poles.

They exchanged subdued, polite greetings and stepped inside. Benjamin grabbed a couple of beers from the fridge. She took a swig from hers, then ran the frosted bottle across her forehead.

"What's the chatter?" she said.

"What do you mean?"

"What are they saying at the hospital, in the lunch room?"

"You mean…"

She nodded.

"Someone said it was retribution. A woman he was attending died in childbirth. Happened to be the mistress of a drug dealer. Fernando Ortega, ever hear of him?"

She squeezed her lips together. "Who said that?"

"A surgeon. A Dr. Krippendorff."

Claire rolled her eyes.

"I guess you know him," Benjamin said.

"Look, there's someone I want you to meet."

The first thought that flashed through his mind was that she was trying to set him up with a date, and for some reason he felt slighted. Almost immediately he realized what a foolish notion that was.

"I'm not really in the mood to talk to anyone," Benjamin said.

"This is not for your sake," she said as she got to her feet and chugged the rest of the beer.

They took her car. His clunky Xterra would stick out like a sore thumb, she said, and it would be best not to catch the notice of the usual rubbernecks.

"The girl that died, did you catch her name?" Claire said.

Benjamin thought about it for a moment. "No. Is this guy Ortega really a drug lord?"

"Some think he is. He's a wealthy businessman. They say he's the richest man in Purgatory. He owns a liquor distributorship that stretches across the Rio Grande Valley. Well, a lot of people think he distributes more than wine and suds."

"What do you think?"

Claire shrugged. "This is Borderlandia. Everything is possible."

"You think he's *El Chacal*?"

Claire glanced at him. "One of them, maybe.

The devil's not as black as he's painted."

Benjamin adjusted the seat belt strap where it stretched tautly over his collar bone. "What's that supposed to mean?"

"It means man created the devil not to explain the universe but to bring order to society. Whenever something vile happens, it's comforting to have a supernatural being to blame. It may sound strange but we'd much rather blame demons than the mere mortals we have to face every day. So there are those who say Fernando Ortega is *El Chacal.* They need to believe that's who he is. In another time and place, they might have called him Lucifer or Beelzebub or Vlad the Impaler. What matters is that people fear him and they revere him. Because placing the blame on him grants us all our bloody absolution."

Benjamin looked at her perplexed. Surprised not just by what she said but how she said it. The placid tone reminded him of Virgil Thibodeaux.

Claire said, "Or maybe he's just a businessman."

They headed east through a part of town Benjamin had not ventured into. They passed by a park with a crushed stone jogging trail that wound through scrawny young oaks, past a metal-roofed elementary school with plate glass windows running high across the soffit, and a vinyl-sided church with an enormous wooden cross on its facade. A tall brick wall ran along the road now, draped in a flowing curtain of purple bougainvilleas.

Claire pulled over to the side of the road. She scanned the rear view mirror.

"What are we doing?" Benjamin said.

"Just checking."

They sat in silence for a couple of minutes, then Claire merged back on the street, proceeded some two hundred yards before pulling into a driveway off to the right, and stopped at the entrance to a gated community.

"Who are we here to see?" Benjamin asked.

"Naomi Rizzo."

The woman who opened the door was an exotic beauty with finely sculpted features in a creamy complexion. She had a lean, athletic body, and long, curled hair that rolled over her shoulders in a windswept look. A breezy white linen dress with a strap that tied around her neck flowed down to her ankles. Not at all what Benjamin had envisioned as the spouse of his friend, but then he reminded himself, Joe Rizzo had studied medicine in the Caribbean.

Moving boxes were stacked in the corner of the living room next to a picture window that opened up to a trim backyard with a sleek rectangular swimming pool. When Claire gazed at the boxes with forlorn eyes, Naomi Rizzo said, "I have nothing to stay here for."

"Are you going back to the islands?" Claire asked.

Naomi shook her head. "New Jersey. Dylan's grandparents live in East Brunswick."

"It's good to have family," Claire said. She clasped Naomi's hand. Naomi nodded, looked down, squeezed her lips together.

They sat on a large white leather sofa. Claire said, "The police?"

Naomi shook her head. "The police have no leads."

"Benjamin, tell Naomi what you told me earlier."

Benjamin was hesitant. He worried about using the wrong words. In hushed tones he recounted what he had overheard in the doctor's lounge. Naomi Rizzo seemed unconvinced.

"You're telling me someone killed my husband as an act of revenge?"

"I… I really don't know," Benjamin said.

"Joe was a good doctor," Naomi said. "No. No. It was that damn hospital."

"El Dorado?" Benjamin said.

"Joe always said something was not right with that place," Naomi said. Claire flashed Benjamin an I-told-you-so look. "The last couple of months he was growing… apprehensive. It was not like Joe to be like that."

"What did he say?" Claire said.

"The usual. He didn't trust that CEO."

"Dr. Soto-Prinz," Claire said.

"That's the one. And he didn't understand how that hospital was rolling in so much cash. They had offered him a partnership and he turned them down. Said the numbers couldn't possibly add up. After that he was a pariah."

Benjamin swallowed so hard he was certain that Claire, sitting next to him, must have heard it. Claire sat with her hands folded on her knees, leaning forward, listening intently.

"There was one more thing," Naomi said.

"What's that?" Claire asked.

"The last few night shifts there, he'd come home and say there's no olive. Something like that. Another ambulance with no olive. He seemed upset. When I'd ask him what was bothering him, he'd try to change the subject."

"No olive?" Claire said. "What does that mean?"

"Don't you remember?" Benjamin said. "He told us the story about the guy choking on the olive pit, and how every time he heard an ambulance siren that's the first thing that went through his head."

"That's right," Naomi Rizzo said, a wistful sparkle in her eyes. "He told me that story too. For some reason, he was expecting an olive at El Dorado, but apparently it never came."

"I still don't get it," Claire said.

Naomi said, "Joe liked to step outside for a breather between patients from time to time. Used to smoke, gave that up, but still liked those few minutes out in the night air. Last few shifts he saw something that didn't make sense to him. He said he'd hear an ambulance siren on its way to the hospital — his olive, right? — but there'd be no call on his pager or cell phone, which, if an arrival was called in on the radio, they should notify him right away. And then, just before the ambulance pulls onto the hospital campus, the siren shuts off. The ambulance goes past the Emergency Room entrance and pulls into the loading dock near the security guard booth."

"No olive," Benjamin said.

"Joe never got his blessed olive," Naomi said.

"What if it was just a carjacking gone bad," Benjamin said as they drove back to his house. "He drove that muscle car which turned heads."

"You ever hear of a carjacking where they slit the victim's throat?" Claire said.

"So what do you make of it?"

"This was something personal. Meant to send a signal," Claire said.

"Or we're dealing with someone really sick."

"I don't see it as an either/or situation."

The sun was low on the horizon, painting the sky in streaks of pink and violet. Benjamin flipped the visor down.

"What about the missing olives?" Benjamin said.

"The ambulances? Use your brain. What are delivery docks used for?"

"Deliveries. But of what?"

"Of something you want to make sure doesn't get stopped in transit. Where the cops don't pull you over for a stupid traffic violation and you won't arouse suspicion if you pull into a hospital."

"So you're convinced El Dorado is behind Joe's death."

"I'm not entirely ruling out the Ortega angle," Claire said. "Krippendorff is an ass and a moron but he's in the inner circle of El Dorado. If something happened in the Emergency Room he'd be one to get the full scoop."

They had reached the road by the cabbage field. A father and son were fishing catfish from the irrigation canal by the side of the road.

Benjamin said, "Why does he hate your dad?"

"What?"

"Why does Krippendorff hate Virgil?"

Claire exhaled through her nose. "A couple of years back Pops is rounding on his patients at Purgatory Regional. A nurse spots him and calls him over. She said a post-op patient of Krippendorff was heading down the tubes and Kripp was nowhere to be found. Not answering his pager, nothing. Pops obliges. Takes a look at the little old man. Sees a bloated belly with a purple discoloration under the navel. The guy's heart rate is through the roof and the blood pressure is steadily dropping.

"They try paging the Kripp again. No reply. They page the surgeon on call. Again, no answer. They even try to overhead page any surgeon in house as they're wheeling the patient to the operating room. The little old man is dying right in front of Pops' eyes. So Pops scrubs in, does an exploratory lap and finds a little bleeder right next to a botched ileo-colic anastomosis. Patches the guy up and saves his life."

"And now Krippendorff hates him?"

"Never forgave him. Got the hospital to suspend my dad's privileges to boot."

"That doesn't make any sense."

"Pops didn't have surgical privileges. He had

only applied for family practice. And there was no time to request emergency privileges when the old man was going down the tubes."

"Wasn't Krippendorff even just a little grateful to him for saving his ass?"

"Grateful?" Claire snorted. "Oh Benjamin, don't you get it? The one thing small men can never forgive is to have their shortcomings exposed."

She pulled into his driveway, shifted to Park but left the engine idling. They sat quietly a moment, then she seemed to read his mind and before he had the chance to speak she said, "I can't stay."

He didn't want to exit the car just yet. He said, "Claire, they offered me partnership at El Dorado."

She turned to him, eyes wide. "Thats great!"

Benjamin detected no sarcasm in her voice. "I thought you wouldn't approve. I thought you'd be upset."

"Upset? Benjamin, don't you see? You're in. You can go to all the meetings now. Listen to what they're saying."

"You want me to spy?"

"Don't you want to find out who killed Joe Rizzo?" Claire said.

"Oh, I see. Well while I'm at it, why don't I look up Fernando Ortega in the phone book and stop by his place for a chat."

"Silly. You're not gonna find the name Fernando Ortega in the phone book. You might try Upper Valley Distributors."

Benjamin said, "I was being facetious!"

"Benjamin, I don't want you to get *hurt.* You don't have to snoop around or anything. Just be there. Keep your ear to the ground."

"And wait for them to say something like, 'Next item on the agenda, on the matter of Joe Rizzo, the guy we murdered.' Why didn't I think of that?"

Claire pressed her lips together and shot him a licentious look. "I bet the money's pretty good."

"I don't care about the money."

She smiled now. "Pops did say you were a romantic."

"I'm just being pragmatic. I'd like to stay alive long enough to start his critical care fellowship."

He stepped out of the car. He could feel her following him with her eyes as he walked onto the front porch and unlocked the front door. She rolled down the windows.

"Hey Benjamin, don't go looking up Upper Valley Distributors in the phone book. I was kidding about that."

Benjamin gave her a two finger salute and she backed out of the driveway. He stepped into the house, let his duffel bag drop to the floor and froze.

There it was. His bicycle was propped up on its kickstand in the middle of the living room, all polished and in one piece.

24

Ivan the Terrible had that insufferable look on his face. He was sitting back in a stiff office chair in the nurse's station fondling his smart phone.

"The first one's all yours," he said without looking up.

"What do you mean all mine?" Benjamin asked.

"It's your little buddy, Jee-zus Tamez."

The bike, Benjamin thought. The little shit came to gloat over his little job with the bike. That had to be it. Benjamin went to the office, tossed his bag onto an empty chair, gingerly pulled a white lab coat over his wrinkled scrubs, mindful of his still-aching collar bone, and headed for the exam room.

Jesus Tamez had a smile that spanned miles across his face. "Hey man, *you* look a lot better."

"Why are you here, Jesus?"

The boy reached into a back pocket and pulled out an inhaler. "Looks like I need a refill. Remember you said I gotta do this one every day?"

The kid was suave in his own stray cat way.

"Last time you were here, I remember something about an onion. What did you call it? A Y-"

"1015Y. Texas Super Sweet. The pride of the valley. My friend Ruben picks them. His parents got this trailer, they go all 'round the valley, county fairs, livestock shows, farmers' markets, you name it. They sell fried onion rings. That's why I call him Gandalf sometimes. Get it? The lord of the rings. Oh yeah. He's real sorry, by the way. He's the one pitched the onion at you but he couldn't help it. All he's got is the fast ball. And he always do what he's told."

Benjamin folded his arms and tried his best to glare at the boy while making sense of what he was saying.

Jesus said, "He's not all there, Rube. You gotta go easy on him sometime."

"And the bike?"

"Oh yeah! How's she running?"

"How'd you break into my house?" Benjamin said.

"I didn't break in." The boy's eyes flitted. "I let myself in."

"Twice."

Jesus couldn't contain his smile. His eyes beamed. "Once you do something the first time, always comes easier the second time."

"How'd you do it?"

Jesus shifted his weight, picked up a dark blue hoodie that lay folded neatly at the head of the exam table and dug in its pocket. He pulled out a pouch. Opened it and took out a lock pick set, held it in the palms of his hands for Benjamin to see. "That lock you got there is pretty flimsy. Might want to get it changed. Meantimes, don't keep nothing valuable in the house."

"Oh thank you very much for the advice," Benjamin said.

"I got your back," Jesus said with a wink as he put the lock pick set away.

Benjamin pulled out his stethoscope. He was

finding it increasingly difficult to conceal his smile. "How are the leaky pipes?"

"I'm cured man. How's your arm?"

"The bruises are fading."

Benjamin had Jesus take in deep breaths as he listened to his chest. He noticed a change in the boy's countenance. Benjamin asked him, "What's the matter?"

"Man, I saw about your friend. On the news you know. Joe Rizzo? Maaan… I'm really sorry."

Benjamin pulled a tongue blade out of a glass jar. Took a peak inside the boy's mouth, checked his ears.

"Jesus, you ever hear the name Fernando Ortega?"

Jesus leaned over, rapped three times on the laminate counter of the built-in desk and made the sign of the cross. "Snowflake, that name is some bad news. Why you ask me that?"

"So you've heard of him."

Jesus said, "Everyone heard of him."

"You think he might be-"

"Don't even say it, man."

The boy was rattled. Benjamin decided to back off.

He finished the exam, printed a prescription for the inhaler with an additional refill. By now, any hostility Benjamin felt towards the boy had vanished.

As they headed out the exam room door, Jesus Tamez nudged him and said, "I changed my mind."

"About what" Benjamin said.

"I don't think I want to work for him no more."

"For whom?"
"You know. Him. *El Chacal*."

25

Pablo Medina had taken the afternoon off to play the back nine at Rancho Viejo Country Club with some compadres. Benjamin couldn't imagine why anyone would want to plod around for hours, weighed down by a bag of golf clubs, with the mercury reading one-hundred in the shade, ocean breeze or not. But it made for a quiet afternoon at the office. Apparently most patients took the afternoon off as well, so Benjamin stretched in Pablo's recliner, heavy-eyed as he tried to read a review on the use of pressors in the post-op care of congenital heart disease surgery.

The office staff started trickling out even before five o'clock with hushed good-byes in the hallway. Ivan Montero entered the doctors' office without knocking, key chain twirling on his finger. "We're all done here boss."

Benjamin wondered if Ivan was asking his permission to leave or just stating a fact.

"Yeah, I'm about to head out too," Benjamin said as he wiped the sleep from his face with the palm of his hand.

Ivan nodded. He seemed to want to say something but then stepped out without another word and shut the door. There was less swagger in his movements, Benjamin thought, something conciliatory in his mien.

Benjamin glanced at his watch. It was already 5 pm. He was in no hurry to go anywhere.

Feeling more alert now, Benjamin tried to finish reading the Conclusion section of the article but found it nearly impossible to focus his attention. He frowned, slapped the journal shut and stuffed it in his duffel bag along with his stethoscope, stopped at the front desk to let the receptionist know he was leaving, and headed for the back exit.

It was hot and bright outside. The glare just beyond the shade of the carport made it hard to see. It wasn't until he was halfway to his truck that he spotted the black Chevy Suburban parked askew.

As soon as he noticed it, the driver's door opened and a man in a dark suit and black sunglasses stepped out. Benjamin wondered how anyone could wear a suit in this weather and as he considered the possibilities his heart beginning to race.

The guy nodded at him without smiling and said, "Dr. Snow?"

Benjamin stopped in his tracks. He didn't answer.

"You Dr. Snow?"

"Who are you?" Benjamin said.

"Don't matter who *I* am. Why don't you step in the vehicle over there, come for a little ride?"

Benjamin looked at the black SUV, then back at the man. He had slick black hair, gelled back to reveal a widow's peak. The knot on his silk tie was large, crooked. The guy widened his stance, standing square now, shoulders splayed out — his tough guy pose. He twirled a ball of neon green chewing gum between his front teeth, his lips curled back like a gnarling dog's flews.

"Look Doctor, I asked you real nice already. I don't like to repeat myself." The man pulled up the hem of his jacket to reveal the black grip of a handgun tucked in his waist.

Benjamin took a step back. He could feel his muscles stiffen, growing more taut with every beat of his heart.

The man looked at him with a sort of puzzled bemusement. Then he shrugged and started moving in close, one hand reaching out as if he were trying to corner a small barn animal, the other hand sliding along his belt until it met the grip of the handgun. He pulled the gun out.

The back door of the SUV opened and on cue the goon with the gun stopped in his tracks, straightened a little, lowered his hands and let the gun dangle next to his thigh nonchalantly. An imposing middle-aged black man stepped out of the vehicle. He was well over 6 feet tall, with a shiny bald head and shoulders that looked like they'd been blasted out of a slab of limestone with dynamite. The only softness in his features was a puffy staleness to his eyes which looked weary and doleful. He wore the same kind of dark suit as the other guy but carried it like he owned it.

"Put it away, Juan," he said. He shook his head as he walked up to Benjamin with a loose stride. "I apologize Dr. Snow. Tact and common sense are implements sorely lacking in Juan's tool box, I'm afraid. The name's Cyril. Cyril Thompson." The man reached out with his hand, left it hanging there until Benjamin finally grasped it. "The thing is, doctor, we've got a real sick child at home, and we'd be much obliged if you could accompany us for a house call." He had a calm, soothing voice.

"The two of you don't look like any parents I've ever met," Benjamin said.

Cyril Thompson chuckled. "It's a friend's child. Extended family you might say."

"If the child is so sick, why don't you take him to the hospital?" Benjamin said.

"It's a she. And, well, it's a heck of a delicate situation. We'd be most grateful if you could help"

"What if I just got in my car and drove off?"

Cyril Thompson rubbed his jaw. "Well, then I'd be forced to appeal to your sense of professionalism with the most cogent argument at my disposal."

Benjamin stared in the man's eyes. Cyril Thompson nodded and said, "We'd be extremely grateful."

Benjamin looked in the direction of the black Suburban, hesitated a moment, then, with his legs feeling like jelly, took lumbering steps toward its open door. After Benjamin climbed inside, Cyril Thompson shut the door and entered the vehicle from the other side.

Juan, who had slipped in the driver's seat, drove slowly and smoothly, constantly looking in his side and rear-view mirrors, the green chewing gum sticking out between his teeth.

Cyril Thompson pulled out a clipboard from the seatback pocket. Handed it to Benjamin along with a pen. He said, "Read this and sign at the bottom, please."

"What's this?" Benjamin asked.

"A non-disclosure agreement. It's pretty standard."

Benjamin scanned it, puzzled. He could never decipher legal mumbo-jumbo. He thought, what the hell, and signed his name at the bottom.

"Next page is a payment services agreement. It just says that you will accept payment in full at the completion of services and make no further attempts to collect or contact my employer in the future."

Benjamin said, "Is this really necessary?"

"Our attorneys are fastidious."

Benjamin signed the form and Cyril Thompson placed the clipboard back in the seatback pocket. They were heading north, toward the city limits. They passed a neighborhood of small bungalows with metal bars on the windows and continued along a highway flanked by small, fenced ranches. The scenery rolled by in a smoky haze through the tinted glass. Benjamin's eyes focused in on the glass. It was only then that he realized that the window could not be opened, that a thick polycarbonate sheet separated him from the outside.

"Who's your employer?" Benjamin asked.

"It doesn't matter," Cyril said. "The child's welfare is your sole concern."

The SUV slowed, Juan glanced at the rear-view mirror again, then swerved onto a cypress lined gravel driveway. They rolled in at a moderate pace, the wheels launching a barrage of pebbles against the metal undercarriage of the vehicle. The path curved past a line of mesquite trees, shielding them from the highway.

Benjamin said, "Why me?"

Cyril smiled. "We do our due diligence. Our intelligence indicated you were our man."

Two other SUVs were parked in the gravel courtyard of the ranch house, an orange stucco hacienda with an oak plank front door studded with iron rivets the size of baseballs. A man with an ear piece spoke in his sleeve and opened the door as they approached the entrance.

They walked down a Talavera tiled hallway to a cozy central living room. A woman sat on an afghan draped couch, rocking a crying infant. As soon as he entered the room, she locked eyes with Benjamin. She was an exotic beauty with arresting, dark Andalusian eyes with facial features that balanced Iberian and Arabic elements. She seemed to size him up, then she redirected her attention to the wailing infant and struggled to sneak a pacifier in the babe's mouth.

Benjamin said, "Hello, I'm Dr. Snow. You must be the baby's mother."

The woman didn't answer. She glanced at Cyril, disapprovingly. Benjamin assumed she didn't understand English. He turned to Cyril and said, "What's the matter with the baby?"

Benjamin was startled to hear the woman speak, "Isn't that what they're paying *you* to find out?"

"I believe the good doctor is inquiring as to the baby's symptoms," Cyril said.

With a testy voice, the woman said, “She’s fussy, she won’t take her milk, and she has a fever.”

“A fever? How old is the baby?”

“Ten days.”

“Ten days old?” This was not good. Benjamin said, “Are you sure? I mean, did you take the temperature with a thermometer?”

The woman said, “No, I used a tire-pressure gauge.” She was glaring at him. “Of course I used a thermometer. What kind of stupid question is that?”

“How high?” Benjamin asked.

“One-o-one point five. Thirty-eight point six degrees Celsius if you prefer.”

“This baby needs to be admitted to the hospital,” Benjamin said.

The woman looked at Cyril Thompson and said, “See, I told you.”

Cyril said, “Aren’t you going to even examine the infant?”

“I will. But it makes no difference. The baby needs a full work-up and IV antibiotics. At her age she’s at risk of sepsis.”

“We can provide you with any equipment you need right here,” Cyril said.

“What I need, what *she* needs, is a hospital,” Benjamin said.

Cyril Thompson ran his hand back across the smooth dome of his head and began palming the nape of his neck. He looked at the infant with his heavy, mournful eyes.

Benjamin pulled the stethoscope out of his

duffel bag and kneeled in front of the couch. He asked the woman, "What's the baby's name?"

"Fatima." With a glower, she added, "We haven't picked a last name yet."

"Mom, what's your name?" Benjamin said.

"Veronica Sandoval, but I'm not your mother."

"I meant, as in the baby's mother."

"I'm not the baby's mother either," Veronica said. "I'm the aunt. The mother died in childbirth."

Somehow, Benjamin had known it all along. How could he not have? Who but a drug boss would send for a doctor with armed thugs in a bullet-proof car? He began to wonder who had acted as Joe Rizzo's executioner, greasy Juan or smooth Cyril Thompson, with his overdone eloquence? He steadied his hands to skim through his exam — to inspect, auscultate, palpate, head to toe, system by system — knowing it was unlikely to reveal the source of the fever, that, regardless of what he might come across, the baby needed a full sepsis evaluation, the likes he had performed dozens of times as an intern but never at gunpoint; never under penalty of death.

His exam complete, Benjamin stood up and spoke in a definitive tone, as though his findings were unambiguous and corroborated his initial impression. "The baby has a life-threatening infection. She needs a full evaluation including blood work, urine culture and a spinal tap. She needs immediate intra-venous antibiotics and any delay will put her life at risk."

"What kind of infection?" Cyril asked.

"I don't know yet."

"Then how can you tell it's life-threatening?"

"Because every infection is life-threatening at this age," Benjamin said.

Veronica shifted the baby to her shoulder and got to her feet. She gave Cyril an annoyed look. "Didn't I tell you? What hospital are we taking her to?"

Benjamin hadn't even thought that far ahead. Now he found himself vacillating. His lips moved before he could think it through. "El Dorado."

A voice behind Benjamin said, "Not a chance." A man stepped into the doorway from an adjoining room. He was tall and lean and fierce looking. He was wearing a pale gray hand-tailored suit, a lilac silk tie and spit-polished black leather boots. He scanned the room, then began to circle Benjamin with a steady pace. "The baby's not going back there."

As soon as the man stepped into the room, Cyril Thompson quickly moved to the doorway the man had just come out of, leaned inside and nodded to someone out of view before positioning himself in a military at-ease posture on the threshold.

Veronica said, "Fernando, we don't have time to argue."

So this was Fernando Ortega, Benjamin thought, this was *El Chacal.*

Fernando Ortega said, "She's going to Purgatory Regional."

"Fine," Benjamin said. "I just have to call bed control. And I'll need the baby's date of birth. And a last name."

Fernando Ortega regarded Benjamin. Benjamin

tried to keep cool and looked back at him, as though any show of fear might get him mauled. The man had a long thin nose, narrow, deep set eyes and the slightest of lips, as though his entire face was designed for an austere efficiency. The effect was cold and striking.

"Her last name is Sandoval," he said. "Just like her mother."

"If the mother is deceased," Benjamin said, "who will be signing consent for treatment?"

"Her aunt Veronica has temporary custody," Ortega said, no sign of impatience in his voice. "You don't need to bother with such trifles."

Veronica grabbed a large purse and said, "What are we waiting for? Let's go."

Cyril signaled for Benjamin to follow her.

"Dr. Snow, just one thing," Fernando Ortega called out. "This child means a lot to me. She is in your hands now. See that you don't disappoint us."

The flower of the sepsis workup, Joel Shapiro liked to tell his residents, is the lumbar puncture. And a rose of a spinal tap is one free of contaminating blood. The key to extracting clean spinal fluid, he would stress, was to put just enough pressure to pierce through that tough mother of a ligamentum flavum without letting the momentum drive the needle so deep as to skewer the internal vertebral venous plexus. Do that and you've got red Kool-Aid.

Dr. Shapiro upheld the tradition, common

among Pediatric educators, of rewarding a champagne tap (one with zero red blood cells reported by the lab) with a bottle of bubbly. In his three years as a pediatric resident, Benjamin Snow had received more bottles of champagne this way than any resident in the history of Houston Children's Hospital. Still, his hands were unsteady as he donned the sterile surgical gloves and peeled the cover off of the infant lumbar puncture tray, his back turned to the supervising glare of Veronica Sandoval, who insisted on being present in the cramped procedure room. Juan, the goon/chauffeur, stood just outside the closed door, his piece stuffed in his belt, barrel pointed at his ass-crack, all too eager, no doubt, to pop a couple of rounds in an uppity young doctor if the situation called for it.

Benjamin unfolded the paper drape with care and started setting the four clear plastic tubes upright in the molded plastic wells of the tray, which is when his hands really started shaking. They shook worse as he twisted off their plastic caps. He removed the sheath from the spinal needle, checked to make sure the stylet separated easily from the needle's lumen and at this point his hands jerked and the needle twirled to the floor.

"I need another twenty-two gauge, one-and-a-half inch spinal needle," Benjamin said trying to sound unruffled.

"Yes, doctor," a young Filipino nurse said as she scooted around the instrument tray. She opened a cupboard, sorted through a plastic tub, finally turned, and carefully opened the small package, letting the needle drop onto the sterile field without contaminating it.

She shuffled back to the procedure table, grasped the infant with one hand on the nape of the neck, the other behind the pelvis and balled her up until she cried. Benjamin cleansed the baby's back with a brush dipped in antiseptic solution, starting from a central spot, proceeding in ever widening circles. He always thought this part of the procedure had a calming, Zen-like quality to it: one of the comforting rituals of medicine. He tossed the used brush in a trash bin and repeated the procedure twice more, taking in slow deep breaths through the surgical mask.

Now, Benjamin carefully positioned the drape over the baby's back. He knew that just hanging it slightly crooked was enough to mess with your orientation. He felt for the usual landmarks: the iliac crest of the pelvis, the tiny vertebral processes. He placed his left thumb over L4 and realized how uncomfortable this was going to be with the limited mobility of his broken clavicle. He hunched to his side to reach for the spinal needle, and finally leaned forward over the procedure table.

He could feel the probing eyes of Veronica and of the nurse, knew they could see the quiver of his fingers. He was sweating inside his gloves so much that he had to adjust the position of his hands. He tried bringing them together, letting them touch in order to mitigate the shaking. He rotated the needle between thumb and index finger to get it bevel up and inserted it in the baby's spine.

The baby let out a yelp and then her cries turned to short, regular screams.

"Jesus!" Veronica said.

"This is normal," the Filipino nurse said. "Do you prefer to wait outside?"

"No, I don't want to wait outside."

"He's almost done," the nurse said.

It was all a matter of feel now, muscle memory guiding how deep to go in case that sweet little pop of poking through to the sub-arachnoid space wasn't felt. But there it was. He was sure he felt it.

He removed the stylet and glacier clear spinal fluid swelled into the hub of the needle. Benjamin reached for the first tube and caught the first drop just as it started to fall. The sight of the spinal fluid dripping out in metronomic ticks was the most beautiful, pure vision Benjamin could ever remember seeing.

"You got it doctor," the nurse said, with excessive relief. Then she added, with absolute sincerity, "Good tap, sir."

Benjamin said, "Good hold."

And as Benjamin had so often witnessed at these moments, the baby's cries diminished to a whimper. And then the infant dozed off into a halcyon sleep.

26

Later that evening, the cerebro spinal fluid microscopy report read zero red blood cells, zero white blood cells. A champagne tap. But the urinalysis was a horror show. Infection fighting white blood cells were seen clumped together like seeds on a raspberry in every microscopic field.

After reviewing the results on his laptop at home, Benjamin decided that professional diligence required him to take a look at the baby's medical record from her stay in the newborn nursery at El Dorado hospital. He accessed the hospital's physician portal and typed in the baby's name and date of birth. Benjamin knew that retrieving an infant's medical record could be tricky. Often the last name changed, or the first name was listed simply as Baby Boy or Baby Girl. In this case, he found the record on the first try, but he got a message that read, "ACCESS DENIED. Confidential record — restricted access. Your attempt to gain access to this record has been logged and forwarded to the medical records department. Further attempts may result in disciplinary action."

He had never encountered a message like that before. He read it a couple of times, thought about it. He recalled that once at Houston Children's (after several nurses and doctors were caught snooping) that access to a child's medical record was restricted because his father was a star wide receiver for the Houston Texans. He guessed they took the same approach for all children of celebrities, even when the father was a famous drug lord.

He returned to the search menu and typed in the name, Sofia Sandoval. He didn't know her date of birth but he knew the date of service: it was Fatima's birth date. He clicked on the "search" tab and again, the "ACCESS DENIED" message flashed across the screen.

Benjamin considered calling the medical records department to request access, but it was late in the evening. Chances were the request would have to be cleared by administration, and the odds of that happening at this hour were slim. He powered off his computer and told himself that next time he went to El Dorado, he'd have to stop by the medical records department.

A urinary tract infection can be devastating to an infant and when Benjamin arrived at the hospital the next morning baby Fatima was flush with a temperature of 102. Still, this was known territory for Benjamin, nothing more than a layup for someone with his level of training. He began to feel he would survive the hospitalization if Fernando Ortega had any sense of fairness.

It was Veronica Sandoval who looked worse for wear, looking exhausted on her feet, clutching the metal bars of the hospital crib, gaping at the baby, bleary-eyed.

"She's getting the right combination of antibiotics," Benjamin said. "She'll start feeling better soon."

"Do you think God listens to prayers from

someone like me, Dr. Snow?" Veronica said.

"I don't know you. Or anything about God's plans," Benjamin said.

"Neither do I," she said. "None of this should have happened."

Benjamin had prepared to talk to her about lab results and treatment plans. He wasn't ready to paddle through the turbid waters of spiritual conversation.

"She's going to get better," he said.

"Yes. Of course she will."

Pablo Medina must have spied him through the one way mirror because as Benjamin reached for the door handle to the office the door swung open. Medina pulled him in and shut the door right away. Pablo Medina was acting like he had gulped down way too much coffee.

"Jesus, Benjamin, what are you trying to do?" Medina said.

For a moment, Benjamin suspected Medina had caught drift of his encounter with Fernando Ortega somehow. But how could he have? Medina interrupted him before he had a chance to ask what he was talking about.

"I got a call from Dr. Soto-Prinz this morning. This is bad, Benjamin. This is very bad."

"I have no idea what you're talking about," Benjamin said.

"He offered you partnership."

"Yeah."

"And you go and slap him in the face."

"What?"

Medina said, "Did you admit a baby at Purgatory Regional last night?" Benjamin was shocked that Soto-Prinz would know about it. Or care.

"So?"

"So, that baby was born at El Dorado" Medina said.

"Does it really matter that much?"

"Benjamin, make no mistake. This clinic is… aligned with El Dorado. We keep privileges at Purgatory as a formality, so no one thinks we play favorites."

"But we do play favorites," Benjamin said.

"Of course we play favorites. Soto-Prinz can cut our life-line in a heart beat. El Dorado funded me when I opened my practice and no bank in town would give me the time of day. We still get regular cash flow from the hospital. How the hell do you think I can afford to pay you?"

"I guess he'll have second thoughts about offering me that partnership," Benjamin said. This was a buoyant thought. It would relieve him of having to actually consider the offer, and it would derail the silly scheme Claire had concocted before it could even get started.

"Are you kidding? You've *got* to sign that offer now. You have no choice. He needs to see a sign of loyalty. You got to show him who's side your on."

"I don't really want to be on anyone's side," Benjamin said.

"You don't sign that partnership then *I'm* the one has to show him who's side I'm on. You're forcing my hand. *Lo entiendes, cabron*?"

Benjamin let his duffel bag fall to the floor. He said, "The dad didn't want to go to El Dorado."

"Who cares? I mean, Benjamin, it's all how you present it to them. You got to be smooth. Parents don't know any better."

"Oh, I think this father knew something all right," Benjamin said.

"*N'hombre!* You're the doctor. You lay down the law. You can't be scared."

"Actually, I was pretty scared, Pablo. Pretty damn scared."

Medina furrowed his brow. "What's the name?"

"The baby?" Benjamin said. "Fatima Sandoval."

"Mmm." Pablo Medina shook his head. "Doesn't ring a bell."

"Her father's name is Fernando Ortega."

Medina went pale. "*Chingado!*" He took a couple of steps back. Brought a fist to his mouth. "No wonder Soto-Prinz…" He stepped in close again. "You know who that is, Benjamin?"

"*El Chacal*?"

Medina reached up as though he were going to smother Benjamin's mouth but ended the movement by bringing his extended index finger to his own lips. "Shhh. Don't ever use that name. Ortega is no drug-dealer. He's an esteemed member of the business community. He's on the board of Rio Grande Merchant Bank, the bank that's giving you your loan. He might as well be on the board of El Dorado."

"Does he ever come to the partner meetings?"

Benjamin said.

"Are you fucking kidding me?"

Pablo Medina looked so flustered that Benjamin almost started feeling sorry for him. If he hadn't been so preoccupied with his own situation he may very well have felt more than a glimmer of compassion.

Like a good intensivist, he began to catalog his active problems. For starters, he had become persona non grata with the CEO of the hospital which was paying his salary. Now he had to choose between signing a contract for something far too big for him to wrap his brain around or risk losing his job. One of his only acquaintances in town had been killed and another was pushing him to investigate the murder, which, were he to acquiesce, would very likely get him killed and probably get him fired. And of course he was doctoring a sick child who could suffer unanticipated complications, which would definitely get him killed and possibly get him fired. To sum up, he estimated the prognosis for keeping his job for the rest of the year was poor at best, and for keeping his life, as guarded.

Every time they crossed paths that day, Medina's face would contort into an ache-in-the-gut look at the sight of Benjamin. By four o'clock he could take it no more and he told Benjamin to leave early and "go do your hospital rounds."

The Filipino nurse from the night before was on service again. She brought Benjamin a print-out. The urine culture had a preliminary report of Lactose fermenting Gram negative rods.

"Probably E. Coli," Benjamin said.

"The blood culture and spinal fluid are no growth so far," the nurse said.

"Let's hope it stays that way."

"The baby looks good," she said with spartan poise. Of course she couldn't know that the guy in the suit standing in the hallway, the one blowing a neon green bubble with his chewing gum, was carrying a loaded gun and looking for just half a reason to use it. "No fever since ten a.m."

"That *is* good news," Benjamin said.

Benjamin walked up the hallway, nodded at Juan the chauffeur, and was about to knock on the hospital room's closed door when Juan raised a palm and said, "Wait a minute."

For a second Benjamin thought Juan was going to frisk him. Instead he rapped on the door twice with the knuckle of his middle finger as if it was some secret code. There was a "Come in," and Juan nodded, stepped aside and let Benjamin step through.

The ceiling lights of the hospital room were off and the blinds were partly pulled, casting a fence of light across the linoleum floor. Benjamin walked down the entry hall, past the bathroom alcove, and entered the hospital room with a meek "Hello?"

Veronica Sandoval replied with a cheerful, "Hello again."

At first he didn't catch sight of her in the play of light and shadow. Then he spotted her, sitting on a recliner, her shoulders stooped. Her blouse was unbuttoned revealing a bare, smooth, supple breast. The other breast was obstructed by baby Fatima, suckling frantically.

Benjamin stuttered but managed to say, "Oh, I'm sorry. I can-"

"Don't be silly," Veronica said. "Have a seat, I think she's almost done."

Benjamin dragged a padded wooden chair from against the wall and sat down. He tried not to gawk but found himself getting another eyeful of the bare breast.

"Do you find this unnatural?" Veronica asked.

"Not at all," Benjamin said. "It's perfectly natural."

"It's the strangest thing. After the spinal tap last night I noted a little moisture in my bra. By this morning, every time she cried I felt, you know, like a fullness. At noon, I was giving her a bottle and I noticed I was gushing, so I thought, what the heck? You probably find it strange."

"Before there was infant formula, many babies were fed by wet nurses. It's all part of a neural reflex. You can stimulate lactation just by regular suckling," Benjamin said.

"I was close to my sister, Dr. Snow. Very close. I have a special connection to Fatima."

"No doubt," Benjamin said. "That has to be it."

Veronica nudged the baby off her breast. "My nipples are getting sore already."

"You don't want her latching onto the nipple," Benjamin said. "Have her get a mouthful of your breast."

"How?"

"Position her so that she's facing you directly, and when she opens her mouth wide, pull her to you until her nose is squished against your breast."

Veronica said, "How do they breathe?"

"Through their neck. They still have gills at this age. I'm kidding."

Veronica flashed him a smile. Amazing how quickly attitudes change when a sick child shows signs of improvement.

"Well don't just sit there," she said. "Show me."

Benjamin hesitated. "Just turn her a little."

"Show me, doctor. It's not like Fernando's going to kill you just for touching my boobs."

Benjamin slowly got to his feet, went to a dispenser on the wall and stretched some disposable gloves onto his hands. He bent down and cradled the baby's crown with his good hand. "Lift your breast a little. That's the way." He avoided touching her breast at all costs. "You got it now. All the way in."

The baby started suckling again. Benjamin removed the gloves, tossed them in a bin and and retreated to his seat.

Veronica frowned. "You married?" Benjamin shook his head. "Girlfriend?"

"No."

"Well, I can't say I'm surprised."

Benjamin tried to ignore the comment. He cleared his throat, went into a meandering briefing of lab results, pending studies and treatment plans. He used the usual cliches but didn't repeat himself more than once.

When Veronica sensed he was finished, she asked, "Was he a friend of yours?"

"Who?"

"That doctor. The one that let my sister Sofia die."

Benjamin paused. "Dr. Rizzo was a good doctor. Yeah, he was a friend."

"Such a tragedy." Her voice was flat. "He didn't deserve to die that way."

"Tell that to Mr. Ortega," Benjamin said.

Veronica looked up, "What makes you think Fernando had anything to do with it?"

"For starters, your sister Sofia was his mistress."

Veronica pulled baby Fatima off her breast, tugged at her blouse to cover her chest. "Get out of here! Well? What are you waiting for? Scram! I told you to leave!"

27

Two kids were playing catch in the cabbage field behind his house. One kid lobbing the baseball to his mate underhand, the other firing it back at the first with some serious heat. Only one mitt between the two of them. Benjamin first caught sight of them as he crossed over the irrigation canal. It wasn't until he turned in his driveway and the kids started jogging toward him that he recognized one of them as Jesus Tamez. The usual broad grin was plastered on his sweat soaked face. The other kid, dressed in a ratty short-sleeved plaid shirt and frayed, cut-at-the-knees jeans, had an out-of-place tuft of hair that stuck out from the top of his head.

"Where you been? Seems hours we been waiting for you," Jesus said. "Man, your backyard smells like farts. Good thing I went nose blind."

Benjamin looked on as they pounded their feet at the end of the driveway, bits of gravel getting stuck to the black dirt on their shoes.

"Let me guess. You just happened to be in the neighborhood," Benjamin said.

"No man," Jesus said. "We made a special trip for *you*."

"I'm surprised you didn't let yourselves in."

"Oh we did," Jesus said looking mortified. "Ruben had to use the bathroom. I told him to go commando out in the field, but it was a number two, so… But we took our shoes off. And we locked up again after he was done."

"If my house smells like cabbage now, I'll know why," Benjamin said.

Jesus cracked up laughing. "Good one! No, but seriously, the reason we're here, Ruben has something to tell you." Jesus thumped his friend's shoulder with a sideways fist as if he were trying to get the picture steadied on an old TV set.

Ruben took a step forward. "I want to say, I'm sorry."

Benjamin said, "I was only kidding about you using the bathroom."

Jesus said, "Say the whole thing like I told you."

"I want to say, I'm sorry I threw the onion at you so hard," Ruben said. He added (and this sounded unrehearsed) "But the fast ball's all I got."

"He's sorry," Jesus said. "But it ain't one hundred percent his fault. You see, Gandalf always do what he's told. You tell him to jump in that canal right now, I swear he'll do it. Got expelled from school once 'cause this guy Frankie Ramos tells him to get a feel of Aracely Aguilar's titties. And what does he do? He walks over and cops a feel right in front of the assistant principal. Yeah, but that was worth it. Wasn't it, Rube?"

"Nuh, uh," Ruben said. "She slapped me hard."

Jesus laughed, quickly regained his composure. "It was his cousin told him to peg you. He's bad news. Thinks he's a gangsta. But his momma still irons the crease in his pants."

Benjamin looked at the odd kid with the funny hairdo. Everything about him was gawky or mismatched.

"But he got a hell of an arm, don't he?" Jesus said. "He learns to throw a slider, a changeup, maybe learn to catch a ball once in a while, he got a real chance in the minors."

"The fast ball's all I got," Ruben said.

"You ready told him," Jesus said.

"You know Nolan Ryan?" Ruben said.

"Here we go," Jesus said. "He'll tell you this story a million times, you let him. Go ahead, tell him, just one time, though, okay?"

Ruben started again. "You know Nolan Ryan? Nolan Ryan pitched so fast blind people would come to hear him pitch."

"Is that a fact?" Benjamin said.

"Yeah. That's how fast he pitched. Get it?"

Benjamin glanced at Jesus. There was no trace of embarrassment in his features, just the gentle glow of brotherly solidarity. There was simply no way to hold a grudge against this pair.

Jesus said, "Next time he sees you he'll tell you the same story again. I promise."

"You guys want to come in for some cold water?" Benjamin said.

"Sure," said Jesus. "Or one of those nice *cervecitas* in your fridge would be good too."

Benjamin said, "Not a chance."

Benjamin unlocked the front door as the boys took their sneakers off. Let the boys in. Jesus couldn't suppress a smile when he saw Benjamin's bike propped up near the far wall. The coolness of the home seemed to make the kids sweat even more. Benjamin took a jug of water from the fridge and poured two glasses.

"Sure don't look like no doctor's house," Jesus said. "'Course I never seen a doctor's house in real life. But it don't look like I imagined."

They chugged the water, saying nothing between sips.

Finally, Jesus wiped his mouth with the back of his hand and whispered, "Sure feel bad about your doctor friend."

Benjamin said, "Tell me again. How'd you know about Dr. Rizzo?"

Jesus said, "Man, his face was all over on TV." He took a long draw from his glass of water. "They caught the guys yet?"

Benjamin shook his head. "Last I heard, the police had no leads."

"No leads?" Jesus said. "You hear that Gandalf? No leads, *la chingada!*"

Benjamin said, "Why do you say that?"

"It's getting late," Jesus said as he propped the baseball mitt on his head. "We gotta go."

Ruben stuffed the baseball in his back pocket and nodded. The boys stepped out the front door. Jesus walked up to Benjamin's Xterra and pointed at the driver's door and said, "Just one thing, doc. What's with the duct tape?"

"A deep gash," Benjamin said. "Don't want it to rust."

"With duct tape? Man, bring it to my uncle's garage, Nacho Tamez on Walnut Avenue. I'll buff it out, paint it, it'll look even better than your bike."

"I'll think about it," Benjamin said.

"I'll only charge you the paint. No labor."

They mounted a black BMX bicycle that had been leaning against one of the barber shop poles, Jesus on the seat, Ruben standing on chrome pegs protruding from the back wheel axle.

"Don't trust no one Dr. Snow," Jesus yelled out as he pedaled away. "Not the cops. And sure as well not the Border Patrol!"

Benjamin looked at the bike zig zag down the street. Thought they would topple over a couple of times, Ruben grasping Jesus' shoulders for dear life. Only after they rose over the culvert and dipped out of sight did Benjamin re-enter the house and slump on the couch. Strange visit. Strange kids. And a strange thing for Jesus to say as he left. *Forget it.* There were already plenty of things to worry about than to start analyzing a visit from a couple of screwy kids.

28

It was still pitch black when his phone rang. The display read 5:45 am. He didn't recognize the number on the caller ID.

He cleared his voice before answering. Half-way through his first month of residency he developed the quirk of never wanting to sound like he had been awakened, no matter what hour of the night it was.

"This is Dr. Snow."

"Dr. Snow, Jack Ryan, El Dorado ER. Looks like your group's on call for Pediatrics?"

"I … I wasn't aware of that."

"Yeah, well I just got off the horn with your partner, Dr. Medina? He told me to call you."

"Oh, okay. What's up?"

Dr. Ryan apologized for dumping this on him, but they had a patient, a train wreck of a kid who they needed to ship out from the ED. The kid had cerebral palsy, malnutrition, uncontrolled seizures, you name it — he had never seen anything like it. Kid's father decides to make the trek from somewhere in the Mexican jungle and shows up on the door step of El Dorado ER, smack in the middle of his shift, of course. What he needed was a Pediatrician to certify that the kid needed a higher level of care and sign off on the transfer. Ground transport to San Antonio was already being arranged.

"Oh, and the other thing? The father needs a letter of medical necessity to let him through the

Border Patrol check point at Falfurrias. The guy still smells like the river."

Benjamin didn't bother to shower. He'd go sign the papers, still have time to come back home and get ready for work. He pulled on some scrubs and was on his way. There were no cars on the road and, even without speeding, Benjamin was coasting onto the hospital grounds just a few minutes later. The doctor's lot had just a few cars parked in the row closest to the hospital.

As he walked past the security guard kiosk a guy in a hunter green uniform stepped out. Benjamin flashed him his hospital ID card before the guy had a chance to say anything. He kept walking, looked past the ED entrance, found himself staring at the metal rolling door to the loading dock and thought of Naomi Rizzo packing her boxes.

Jack Ryan was a bear of a man, probably around forty but looked older in his black rimmed glasses and prematurely gray hair. "Soon as you're ready," he said, "I just need a couple of autographs." He went back to slurping coffee from a tall mug stenciled with a likeness of Elvis Presley while Benjamin reviewed the child's vital signs from a computer screen.

A tall security guard, sinewy, trim mustache, emerged from around a corner and strode across the emergency room. Benjamin noticed he was wearing leather driving gloves and had the sleeves of his shirt pulled down over his wrists.

Jack Ryan looked up and said, "Hey Tito! Looks like your boys let one get through last night."

The security guard stopped. Paced over to the counter. "Say again?"

Jack Ryan said, "Just saying, you'll have some 'splaining to do with the boss."

The security guard took the mug from Jack Ryan's hand, studied the picture of Elvis Presley for a moment, brought the mug up under his nose and gave it a whiff. Finally, he took a sip, sloshed the liquid around in his mouth and spit it back in the mug. He handed the mug back to Jack Ryan and said, "You have yourself a nice day, doctor." He ambled away.

Jack Ryan waited until the man turned the corner before murmuring, "Asshole."

At this point Benjamin just wanted to get away. He asked Ryan, "Will I need a translator?"

"You mean interpreter," Ryan said in a bitter tone. "Interpreter is the preferred term when it's oral communication. Miss Fuentes is on her way." He turned his back on Benjamin and directed his attention to a computer monitor.

Miss Fuentes happened to be a blonde with a Houston twang. She swaggered through the emergency department wearing a fuzzy pink cardigan, all fastened up except for the top button. Reading glasses dangled from a beaded chain that hung around her milk-white neck which sported a small tattoo of a bumble bee peeking out just above her sweater's collar.

She had a peculiar way of translating, adding far more emotion and flair to the flat enunciation of the child's father. It was almost theatrical: her standing like an actor on stage, the father, sitting below her, feeding her lines from an invisible prompt box.

Benjamin gazed at the child in the gurney. He had never seen anything nearly as disquieting in his entire Pediatric residency. The boy looked like a giant pretzel slouched stiffly on the mattress, his arms and legs were tangled twigs, their joints frozen in place like rusted hinges. His skin, dark and flaky, pulled on his spindly ribs like the taut leather pelt of an indigenous drum. The boy's fissured lips jutted out in a silent, persistent groan. His father, a compact, husky man with sparkling eyes, dabbed at the spittle that collected at the corners of his son's mouth with a folded cotton cloth and, every so often, murmured what sounded like words of encouragement.

"He was perfectly healthy until he was fifteen months old," Miss Fuentes said. The father spoke in guttural tones, pausing every so often to allow Miss Fuentes to translate. "He talked, he walked… he ran. He was a strong boy." Miss Fuentes flexed her biceps and scrunched up her face. The father smiled, exposing a mouth-full of silver-capped teeth. "Then one day he started crying with a strange cry – like cats do sometimes at night – and then the fever started. The village doctor gave him medicine but the fever was too strong. That night, in his sleep, he let out a squeal and his body started to shake. It was like an earthquake that went on and on. When it stopped, the body was limp. I thought he was dead. I couldn't wake him up but still he was breathing. I jumped on my bicycle, rushed into town. I found a doctor who had a car. He drove to our home and said Ikal had the meningitis and there was nothing anyone could do. To light a candle and pray. That not even the doctors in Merida could help him now."

Benjamin said, "Merida. That's in the Yucatan peninsula."

"Yucatan, *si,"* the father said with a smile.

"How did they get all the way up here?"

Miss Fuentes turned to the father and spoke to him in Spanish. Benjamin couldn't understand the words but the intonation sounded very formal, proper.

As the man started to speak, Miss Fuentes resumed her soliloquy. "We rode on the back of a chicken truck all the way to Campeche. There we were able to stow away on a freight train with all the other boys."

"What other boys?" Benjamin said.

"So many boys. From Guatemala, El Salvador, Nicaragua. We slept in a pile of straw, switched trains in Matehuala and again in Monterrey and made it all the way to Reinosa. There we met some not-so-good people. *Coyotes*. They said they would help us cross but there was poison spilling from their eyes. So we headed west. Walked a few kilometers on a dusty road — Ikal is not so heavy. A car pulled over. It was a Catholic priest. He brought us to his home in Ciudad Mier, fed me black bean soup and read out loud from the gospel of Luke until I fell asleep in his armchair."

"How does he manage to feed the boy?" Benjamin asked.

The father listened to the translation, then smiled apologetically. "He clenches his teeth so tight,"

Miss Fuentes said, "It's very hard. I dip a wash cloth in milk and squeeze the drops over his lips. I know it's not enough but it's the only way."

"How did they cross the border?"

"A neighbor of the priest had a patched-up inner tube. I tied a burlap sack over the top of it to hold Ikal, and we paddled across, praise God. I drank so much water I thought my insides would come out." The father chuckled when he finished.

Benjamin started cataloging a problem list in his mind. Post-infectious static encephalopathy; seizure disorder, uncontrolled; malnutrition, severe; dysphagia, severe; moderate dehyrdration; likely electrolyte abnormalities; multiple contractures; risk of re-feeding syndrome, and that was just for starters. A few months ago he'd have been chomping at the bit to fix this kid. Now he just wanted to avoid getting into more trouble than he was already in.

"Tell the father," Benjamin said, "that his son, Ikal, did I say that right? Ikal needs very specialized care. We will transfer him to a hospital in San Antonio with experts. Real experts that can give him the very best care."

The father listened to Miss Fuentes then whispered with an embarrassed expression, "*Mi nan takin.*"

"What did he say?" Benjamin asked.

"I have no idea," Miss Fuentes said.

The man said, "*No tengo mucho dinero.*"

"That's not a problem," Benjamin said, happy he was able to understand one of the few Spanish phrases he knew. "Tell him not to worry about that. Nobody can afford hospitals in this country. But they will take care of Ikal. I promise."

The man spoke again. Miss Fuentes turned to Benjamin and rolled her eyes. "I knew from the moment I saw you that you were a great doctor, a great man. That you would help my Ikal."

Benjamin felt a flush of guilt sweep over him. Doctors had a word for unloading a patient to another service: "dump". Here he was, complicit in the dump of the century, and this innocent man was actually thanking him. Benjamin nodded, turned to leave. The father called out, "*Jach Dyos b'o'otik.*"

Benjamin froze. He felt a tingle spread down his spine. There was no doubt. They were the same words the father of little Anselmo uttered right before he blew his brains out. He turned.

"What did he say?"

Miss Fuentes said, "Beats me. That's not Spanish."

"Ask him what it means," Benjamin said.

There was a little back and forth between the man and Miss Fuentes. Finally she said, "It's a Mayan language. Literally it means, 'Very much God pays you.' It's somewhere between a thank-you and God bless you."

Benjamin stepped up to the bedside again, surveyed the emaciated boy, and for the first time he could see him, in his mind's eye, as a toddler, taking his first steps, smiling, saying his first words. He could see him, wrapped in a rough blanket in his father's arms in the crowded bed of a freight-train car, his father wringing a wet washcloth onto his lips, whispering to him all the while through silver-capped teeth. He pictured the crossing of the Rio Grande, the father clinging to the inner-tube that cradled his child, struggling to paddle through the murky eddies and currents.

He gazed at the father now. The features on the man's face emitted a familiar aura: the look of relief after an exhausting race, of welcomed sacrifice, of unfathomable love. A vision of little Anselmo's father came to mind: his black braided hair, the stony features of his face. It was as though the lighting had shifted in the picture of his memory, a filter had been lifted and he could finally see the man's face as it really was in that last moment. He recognized the same expression of tranquility, the same resolve.

Benjamin's collar bone began to throb. A heaviness spread across his chest and he found it increasingly hard to breathe. The air of the emergency room was stagnant, stifling, unbreathable. A metallic taste welled up in his mouth and he knew he was going to be sick. He shuffled away, then jogged down the corridor, turned a corner and ran the last few steps until he had to double over, gagging and retching into a large rubber trash can.

He took deep breaths, spit into the trash can trying to rid himself of the rancid taste in his mouth and slunk into a bathroom, locked the door behind him. Benjamin plodded to the large ceramic sink, tried patting some cold water on his face, cupped his hand to take a mouthful, swished it around and let it spill back out into the sink. The nausea was passing. There, he could breathe again. He gazed up at the mirror and his reflection startled him. He looked like shit. He stared down at the sink again. Retched out another mouthful of bile.

"I guess I'm going to be late for work this morning," he whispered to himself. He rinsed his mouth with tap water once more, used his wet fingers to comb back his hair, straightened his back and re-tied the belt of his scrub pants before heading out into the emergency department. The queasiness was gone but he felt horribly self-conscious, as though he were walking across the main dining room of a fancy restaurant after having a couple of drinks too many. He swayed his arms to keep his balance, to steady his stride.

Dr. Jack Ryan was still sitting in the same spot, looking oblivious. When he saw Benjamin marching toward him he said, "You ready to sign some paperwork, bud?"

Benjamin said, "I'm keeping him."

"Say what?"

"I'm admitting the boy to my service."

Jack Ryan cocked his head. "You sure about this?" He studied Benjamin's face for a few seconds. "Well, I hope to hell you know what you're doing."

"I know what I'm doing," he said. "I'm a doctor." He said the words not with the intention of being rude to the ER doctor but as a way of admonishing himself. Benjamin felt like the phrase carried with it a new sense of gravity: it had consequence; it really stood for something.

Jack Ryan studied him. "I don't mean medically. I have no doubt you're competent. I mean, you know… this is your decision. I'm off the hook either way."

Benjamin looked at him. "I didn't know there was a hook."

Jack Ryan left to attend a middle school assistant-principal with chest pain. Benjamin finished entering his admission orders in the computer. He was about to get up to leave when he decided to try something. He navigated to the medical record search menu, entered Sofia Sandoval's name and the requisite date of service and clicked on the search tab.

As he expected, the message he had previously encountered popped up: "ACCESS DENIED. Confidential record — restricted access. Your attempt to gain access to this record has been logged and forwarded to the medical records department. Further attempts may result in disciplinary action."

It didn't matter. He got what he wanted. On the top right of the screen, under Sofia Sandoval's name was her date of birth and medical record number. He picked up a hospital phone, dialed for the operator and asked to be transferred to Medical Records.

A very polite woman answered.

"This is Dr. Snow from Pediatrics," Benjamin said. "I'm trying to review the medical record of a mother of one of my patients, and I keep getting a message that says, access denied."

"I'm so sorry," the lady said. "Let me see if I can help you. Do you have an MR number?"

Benjamin read the medical record number off the screen.

"And the patient's name?" the woman asked.

"Sofia Sandoval," Benjamin said. As he said the name, a stocky male nurse that was standing in the hallway in front of him turned and accosted the desk where he was sitting. He loitered a few feet away, barely concealing the fact that he was eavesdropping.

"Mmm. Let me see. Well, that's odd," the woman from medical records said. "Can you repeat the MR number, just to be sure."

Benjamin read the number out loud. "And the name is Sofia Sandoval. Do you need the date of service?"

"What did you say your name is?"

"Dr. Benjamin Snow, Pediatrics."

"I'm sorry Dr. Snow, but access to that medical record is restricted."

"Why is it restricted?"

"Usually that means there is the potential for litigation or the patient specifically requested confidentiality."

"I'm taking care of the patient's daughter over at Purgatory, and Sofia Sandoval is deceased. So how do I get access to the record?"

"Let me check something," the woman said. "OK, the restriction was ordered by Dr. Soto-Prinz. You'd have to talk to him about it."

Benjamin thanked the clerk and hung up the phone. He was deep in thought when the stocky male nurse bent down and whispered, “We have to talk,” and passed him a small slip of paper.

Benjamin waited until the nurse walked away to turn the paper over. On it was scribbled, “Pole Position - 8 pm.”

29

With the new admission at El Dorado, the morning turned into a bustle. Benjamin had ordered a panel of labs, an EEG, and a CT of the brain on his newest charge. He helped get an IV started in the wispiest of veins, snaked down an NG tube to start drip feedings, reminding himself he'd have to keep a close watch on the phosphorus and potassium levels in case the refeeding syndrome decided to rear its ugly head. He ordered consults from Neurology and Physical Therapy — the Gastroenterology consult for the insertion of a gastric tube button could wait a day or two.

To add to his strain, in another hospital across town, he had yet another inpatient to tend to — the one with armed hit-men pacing the hallway outside her hospital room. He called the office and told Ivan the terrible he'd be running late today.

He was able to wrap things up at El Dorado by 9 o'clock and drove directly to Purgatory Regional. Veronica Sandoval had kicked him out of the room the day before and now he was dreading having to face her again.

To his relief, on entering the room he found a transformed woman. Veronica was simply glowing in a floral print summer dress. Her hair was smartly coiffed. A sunny smile lit up her face. Benjamin knew that the appearance of parents and caretakers, as much as their demeanor, was a reliable barometer for their child's condition and, upon seeing her, Benjamin hardly had to ask how baby Fatima was doing.

"I have to apologize for yesterday," Veronica said. "My behavior was deplorable."

"Don't worry about it," Benjamin said, placing the ear buds of his stethoscope in his ears. As long as his ears were covered he wouldn't have to listen to a word she said. It was a brief respite.

"My grandmother had a saying she would always tell us as we were growing up," Veronica said. "The more powerful the man, the larger his appetite." She picked up a cell phone from a bedside table. "You didn't know my sister. Sofia was beautiful." She drew a finger across the glass screen, handed the phone to Benjamin.

Benjamin looked at the picture on the screen. "She looks just like you."

"She was prettier than me. And not such a bitch."

Benjamin handed the phone back to Veronica, who took another doleful glimpse at the picture on the screen before turning the phone off.

"Veronica was better than me. She was fresh and pure. I didn't want her to… I didn't want her to be like me. When she told me she was pregnant, even after she started to show, she refused to tell me who the father was. She told me she simply couldn't tell me, asked me to trust her, that she'd tell me when the time was right and then I'd understand." Veronica shook her head. "I should have known then. Maybe I did know but I just didn't want to believe it.

"After you left yesterday, I started thinking of Fernando's wife. How every time I'm with him I'm stealing from her. I called her up on the phone, thinking I would tell her everything. Tell her I'm sorry and ask her if she could possibly forgive me. When she picked up, I didn't say a word. I didn't have the guts. The truth is, I have no intention of leaving Fernando."

"I'm sorry, I thought *you* were his wife."

She shook her head. "I'm his mistress." She put a hand on her forehead. "What a word! Anyway, I'm sure Sofia and I aren't the only ones. I really should have listened to my *abuelita*."

As soon as Benjamin set foot in the clinic, Pablo Medina pulled him into their shared office.

"What are you trying to do, kill me here?" Medina said.

"I'm sorry I'm late," Benjamin said.

Medina waved it away. "It's not that, Benjamin. I get a call from Dr. Soto-Prinz this morning, didn't sound too happy. Did you admit that kid from the ER at El Dorado?" Benjamin nodded. "Are you out of your mind?"

"Earlier this week you were pissed I admitted a kid at another hospital."

Medina said, "That other kid was the child of a VIP. This kid is a… an indigent, for crying out loud. This is the kind of kid you *don't* admit to El Dorado."

Benjamin was surprised to notice he felt a perverse joy in Medina's frustration. "It's all kind of hard to keep up with. Does Dr. Soto-Prinz have written guidelines on all this so I won't mess up again?"

Medina's tone turned dark. "Don't fuck around, Benjamin. You don't know who you're dealing with. To start with, only partners can admit patients to the hospital."

Benjamin pulled a large manila envelope out of his duffel bag and handed it to Pablo Medina. "I signed the contract. I guess that makes me a partner."

Medina's voice lightened. "That's good. No, that's real good. I was starting to worry about you. Now, there's a couple of things you can do to redeem yourself with Dr. Soto-Prinz. For starters, he's having a reception at his house for Troy Davenport, the guy running for Senate. A fund-raiser, ten-thousand dollars a plate. You're expected to attend."

Benjamin laughed. "Even if I had ten-thousand dollars…"

Pablo Medina stepped away, pulled a stuffed envelope out of a drawer, tossed it at Benjamin. "Deposit only nine-thousand in your bank account so the IRS doesn't ask any questions. Keep the other thousand in cash and enjoy yourself for crying out loud. Write a check from your personal bank account for ten grand to the El Dorado Physician's PAC, put it in an envelope and bring it to the reception."

Benjamin opened the envelope. It was full of hundred dollar bills. "Is this even legal?"

"Sure," Medina said. "It's all legal. More or less. Benjamin. Benjamin! Stick with me and we're going to get out of this mess without a hitch."

Benjamin gauged the weight of the envelope in

his hand. There was nothing to think about now. He had already reached a turning-point, already traversed that fateful point of no return. He had done so when he signed his name to the admission orders for an emaciated boy by the name of Ikal. He stuffed the envelope in his duffel bag and pulled the zipper shut.

"*Que bueno*, Benjamin. One more thing," Medina said. "Soto-Prinz would like regular updates on the Ortega baby. Now you can manage that, can't you?"

30

When he first read the note that the nurse at El Dorado emergency room had slipped him, he couldn't make out the meaning. He figured Pole Position had to be a meeting place of some kind. But what kind of place?

As evening approached, Benjamin typed the name in his computer's search engine. He got a list of sites pertaining to automobile racing. He tried typing in, "Pole Position Purgatory Texas." This time the top entry was for "the premiere gentleman's club in South Texas." He looked up the address and mapped out the location. It was only seven pm. There was no reason to drive out there on an empty stomach so he headed for a burger joint, sat inside, downed a cheeseburger and stuck around drinking coffee until quarter to eight.

The Pole Position Gentleman's Club was a two-story building off highway 83 on the eastern outskirts of town. A nine-foot wooden fence surrounded the parking lot to provide a modicum of discretion for its patrons. There were about a dozen vehicles in the lot, mostly pick-up trucks, a couple of later model sedans, and one service van from Doctor Flush, Commercial and Home Plumbing. As he got out of his SUV and started walking for the front entrance, Benjamin was thankful for the nine-foot fence.

The inside of the club was dark, with a neon-purple hue. Techno music was blaring with enough bass to rattle Benjamin's rib cage. A balding man with bluish bags under his eyes stood behind a counter working on a cross-word puzzle. He looked up at Benjamin and said, "Ten dollar cover, two-drink minimum. You pay for the drinks now. That'll be thirty dollars."

Benjamin handed him two twenties. The man took the bills, opened a cash box, and gave Benjamin one five, five ones and two plastic tokens. He redirected his attention to the cross-word puzzle, managing to not show excessive annoyance for the interruption.

Benjamin walked into the main lounge and looked around for the nurse. There were purple button-upholstered booths lining the walls. Small round tables circled around two center stages where topless dancers slithered around poles. A glass-bottomed cage protruded from the second floor where two dancers in matching thongs groped each other and kissed with an excessive exchange of tongue. In the corner of the room was a bar with a brass foot-rail and, to the side of it, a swinging padded door with a sign on the top that read, "V.I.P.".

Benjamin tried not to look too prying as he scanned the faces of the men seated in the darkness of the booths. After a couple of minutes he was quite sure the ER nurse wasn't there, so he scooted into a booth with an unobstructed view of the front door.

As soon as he sat down, a redhead in a see-through blouse leaned over his table, shook her breasts and said, "Buy me a drink?"

Benjamin looked up at her face. He recognized her. She was one of the girls who had stayed at Myrtle's ranch. He wondered if she was the one who kept him awake that night with the truck driver next door.

"I'm waiting for someone, but get yourself a drink." He handed her one of his tokens.

She rubbed her leg against his thigh. "What do you say I come back later, give you the lap dance of your life?"

"Maybe later."

"Hey, you look familiar. Where do I know you from?"

"From here," Benjamin said. "I come here sometimes."

"You're not a good liar, honey. This is your first time, ain't it? Otherwise you'd know tokens are for patrons only. You want to buy me a drink it'll be ten bucks."

Benjamin reached into his wallet, pulled out two fives and handed them to her.

"So what're we drinking?" she said.

"Bring me a gin and tonic, but wait about ten minutes, won't you?"

She bent down, rubbed her breast against his arm and whispered, "I don't know that I can wait that long, darling. But I'll sure try." She walked away clumsily in her high heels, turned to blow Benjamin a kiss.

As soon as she was gone, the ER nurse sat down on the other side of the booth. He was wearing a black turtle-neck and had a baseball cap with the visor pulled down over his eyes.

Benjamin said, "Could have picked a better place to meet."

"There's nowhere more private," the nurse said.

"My name's Felix, and after I walk out of here today, I don't know you and you don't know me. Only reason I'm talking to you is 'cause you were Dr. Rizzo's friend."

"How'd you know that?" Benjamin said.

"I saw the two of you together over at Purgatory Regional a couple times."

"So, what did you want to talk about?"

"You're trying to get a look at Sofia Sandoval's medical record. How come?"

Benjamin thought about how best to answer. To say he was trying to get information for the care of Sofia's daughter would be too banal. From the look on Felix's eyes he could tell that the nurse expected something more. Something he would gauge to decide if Benjamin was worthy of his consideration. He decided it would be best to go with a more ambiguous answer.

"I want to know the truth," Benjamin said.

Felix's eyes gleamed. "What I'm gonna tell you, you didn't hear from me, OK?"

"I never met you," Benjamin said.

"I'll tell you the truth," Felix said. "That lady's death? It wasn't Rizzo's fault. What really happened? Rizzo ordered blood, lots of it, right from the start cause she was bleeding so bad. Then Soto-Prinz gets on the phone with blood bank and cancels the order without even telling him. Dr. Rizzo was a good doctor. The lady could have made it through. Soto-Prinz is the one that killed her."

"Why would he do such a thing?" Benjamin said.

"Cause he thought she was a wet-back. Standard operating procedure for the old douche-bag."

"So, who do you think murdered Joe Rizzo?" Benjamin said.

"Holy shit, man. Don't make me say it." Felix said.

"I'm just trying to get to the truth."

"The lady, Sofia? She was Fernando Ortega's mistress. You know who that is, don't you?"

Benjamin nodded. "How do you know that?"

"I was there, man. Right before she died, she tells Rizzo that she has to tell him who the father of her baby is. And she tells him."

"You heard her say Fernando Ortega's name?"

"I couldn't hear what she said from where I was standing. She kinda whispered it to him and there was so much noise in the room. But Soto-Prinz sure heard it. His face looked like someone kicked him in the nuts. All of a sudden he's doing everything he can to save the baby, but it's too late for poor Sofia." Felix rubbed his hands together. "Man, Rizzo didn't have to die. It was Soto-Prinz killed the girl.

"You know, maybe this is evil, but every night I say the same prayer. I say, God, have mercy on Dr. Rizzo's soul, and let Fernando Ortega know it was that bastard Soto-Prinz that killed his girl. Just let him know and God have mercy on all of us." Felix made the sign of the cross.

"Who else did you tell this to?"

"Nobody, man. I don't even know why I told you, except that you're Rizzo's friend and you look like a straight shooter."

"How about the police?"

"You haven't been in these parts very long, have you? The law don't apply to people like Ortega and Soto-Prinz."

"What do you expect me to do?" Benjamin said.

"You said you wanted to know the truth. So there you go. I don't know, I hope you do the right thing."

Felix got up, reached in his pocket, dropped his two plastic tokens on the table and walked out without saying a word. Benjamin waited, not wanting to follow him out.

He caught sight of the red-headed stripper, plodding toward him with a cocktail glass in each hand. She had removed her see-through blouse and her bare breasts jiggled with every clunky step. Benjamin slid out of the booth.

"Hey cowboy!" she called out. "I got our drinks." She placed the glasses on the table and put a hand on Benjamin's waist. "What is it? You don't like me?"

"I gotta go. Something's come up."

"Sneaky little fibber," she said. She pressed up against Benjamin and whispered in his ear. "You sit your tight little butt back on that couch and I'll make sure something comes up."

Benjamin nudged her away. "Not tonight."

31

Things were coming together in the care of little Ikal on the glitzy pediatric ward of El Dorado hospital, despite the repeated efforts of clinical managers to hinder and withhold essential treatments nearly every step of the way. A young physical therapist whispered an apology to Benjamin for her department's refusal of the consult, and then devoted over an hour of her personal time to teaching Celestino, the boy's father, the correct technique for passive stretching exercises.

The pediatric neurologist, a tall, stooping man with a pleasant musical accent, who walked with a bouncy, ambling gait as though he were timing his steps to the rhythm of a tune playing in his head, had initially ordered an anti-epileptic which cost over two-hundred dollars a month. Benjamin asked him to recommend a much more affordable alternative, preferably one which didn't require frequent blood-level monitoring, and was readily available in Mexico.

"Are you a priest?" the neurologist asked Benjamin.

"No. Why do you ask?"

"Nothing. It's just that I'm from Lima, Peru. I did part of my internship in a region by the name of Chanchamayo, over on the eastern slope of the Andes, right where the rain forest begins. There was a missionary physician there, a Jesuit who trained at Loyola — that's in Chicago, no? You remind me of him, the way you fight for your patient. OK, my friend, we'll go old school. Just like in the jungle, but with no giant flying cockroaches, thanks God."

The only hitch came with the gastric tube insertion. The only pediatric gastroenterologist on staff, upon discovering the child was self-pay, refused to perform so much as an initial evaluation without a two-thousand five-hundred dollar deposit, up front.

That would have to wait. Meantime, Ikal was tolerating the feedings through the naso-gastric tube without any complication and was already gaining weight.

Benjamin enjoyed talking with Celestino, resorting to pantomime when an interpreter was not available. The man possessed an imperturbable temperament and a native wisdom which he was able to express with just a few words and a well-delivered gesture.

That evening, Benjamin lingered in the hospital room well after he had been done examining the boy and reviewing his laboratory results.

"What does Ikal mean?" Benjamin asked Celestino.

"Ikal, *en Maya, significa espiritu.*"

"Spirit," Benjamin said. "*Y su mama?*"

"*Tuvo un susto,*" Celestino said. He tilted his head and narrowed his eyes in a mournful way. "*Esta triste. Muy, muy triste.*"

"*Ah, si. Entiendo,*" Benjamin said.

A nurse came into the room to take vital signs. She greeted Celestino in Spanish. He got to his feet to reply to her. Sat down again.

"*Y usted, doctor? No tiene mujer?*"

The nurse said, "He's asking if you have a wife or a girlfriend."

"*Oh, no. Nada, nada*," Benjamin said.

"*Nadie? Seguro?*" Celestino said something Benjamin couldn't make out.

"He says he can see in your eyes that there is a woman in your heart," the nurse said.

"Oh, no. Not really. Well, there's a woman I met, but, well, I've been told she's something of a demon."

The nurse laughed and translated what Benjamin said into Spanish.

Celestino did not laugh. He seemed to consider the matter seriously. He spoke to the nurse.

"He wants to know, is she beautiful?" the nurse said.

"Yes, she is," Benjamin said.

"With beautiful long hair?"

"Yes."

"Does she sit at the base of the Ceiba tree, the sacred tree of life that sends its roots down to the underworld?"

"I've never seen her do that."

"And does she comb her hair with the spiny needles of the Tzacam cactus?"

"No. She doesn't"

"Then she can't be X'tabay, the ensnaring goddess. She's probably just a beautiful woman."

Benjamin said, "Tell him he's a very wise man, and he's probably right."

"He wants to know if her spirit, her personality

is like yours."

"I think we're complete opposites," Benjamin said.

"*Ah, que bueno!*" Celestino said on hearing the nurse's translation. He talked with animated gestures now, waving both hands.

The nurse was aglow. She was clearly getting into it.

"He says you are like the hero twins: day and night; sun and moon; sky and earth; life and death." She paused as he continued speaking. "May your union be blessed."

"Oh, tell him there's really no union to speak of," Benjamin said.

"*El doctor dice que no estan juntos,*" the nurse said.

Celestino shook his head. "*Doctor, todos estamos juntos.*"

When Benjamin got home that evening, he felt restless. He glossed over the online version of the New England Journal of Medicine but couldn't focus and found himself reading the same sentence over and over again. He closed his laptop, went to the fridge, got himself a beer, and went outside to sit on the concrete step of his front porch.

The sun was low on the horizon, its fading light painting the wispy clouds overhead in violet and pink. A lone whooping crane drifted over the cabbage field, yawed unsteadily, then swooped down into the sycamore grove at the edge of the property.

His plan had been to come to Purgatory to work, to study, and to remain detached. To keep a low profile until he could get his career back on track. That was impossible now. He had made a conscious decision to change course. And yet he felt no regret, no angst or dread, just a sense of nervous anticipation. And he felt lonely now. He had savored the first few nibbles of a new way of being and it only whet his appetite for more.

When he caught the gleam of the sun's light reflecting on the windshield of a car coming over the culvert, he found himself holding his breath, hoping it would be her. The car approached slowly, the sound of its engine lowering in pitch as though it were hesitating to come forth. It slowed to the point that it seemed as though it would come to a stop on the street, far short of his driveway. Then it picked up a little speed.

He could make out the color now, the model. It was a Toyota Camry. It had to be her. The turn signal started blinking and the car turned in his driveway. Benjamin got to his feet, leaned on one of the barber poles.

Claire got out of the car. She held up a small book.

"Pops wanted me to drop off a book for you," she said, as though she had to justify her intrusion.

"Want a beer?" Benjamin said.

"Only if we drink inside. I don't want to feed the mosquitoes."

Claire traipsed around the living room while Benjamin retrieved the beer from the fridge. She ran a finger along the edge of the small dining table, changed direction and settled on the sofa.

"How have you been?" she said.

Benjamin paused. "Purgatory is a really interesting place, you know?"

"Tell me about it."

Benjamin twisted the cap off the beer bottle, handed it to her and plopped down on the couch next to her. He took a swig from his beer to legitimize his sitting next to her.

She took a sip from her beer, then balanced the small book on his knee.

"I think you'll like it," she said.

Benjamin picked up the book. "The Art of Living," he read aloud.

"Epictetus. One of Pop's favorites."

"I'm going to read it."

"You really should." She took another very short sip of beer. "I'm sorry, I didn't want to make it sound like you need special help in figuring out your life."

"Maybe I do need help."

Their eyes locked. Benjamin wondered, as she studied his expression, if he had truly changed somehow and, if the change was noticeable, whether she might detect it just by looking into his eyes. He wished for her to see it.

"Well, I think a good place to start is to figure out what you really want," she said. "What do you want, Benjamin?"

"Out of life?" Benjamin said. Her gaze was steady. She wasn't going to fall for such a transparent stall tactic. "Well, I want to do pediatric critical care medicine one day."

"Why?"

"It's been my goal since the start of medical school."

"Why?

Benjamin took a deep breath, jutted out his bottom lip. "Because I want to have absolute proficiency in the care of critically ill children."

"Why?"

Benjamin laughed. "How many times are you going to ask me why?"

"Five," Claire said. "It takes five whys to get to a tiny kernel of truth. Why do you want to have absolute proficiency in caring for sick kids?"

"Critically ill children," Benjamin corrected. Claire waited for his answer, a patient resolve in her poise which told Benjamin he was cornered.

"Because I want to save the lives of children who would otherwise face certain death."

"Why?"

"It's just what I have to do. I feel I have to make amends."

Her expression softened, she leaned closer as though she were getting ready to catch something that was about to spill out towards her. "Why?"

Without thinking about it twice, Benjamin said, "Because I saw my best friend die and I felt so helpless."

Claire bowed her head over her knees, pressed her lips together, and let the silence linger. Finally, she looked up and said, "What happened, Benjamin?"

In all these years, he had told no one what had

transpired that afternoon. Not the truth, anyway. He had never intended to talk about the subject but something inside him had changed. A latch had come unfastened, a glint of candor had already escaped from its dank lair. So, after clearing his voice, he began the narration of the events without further urging, with neither a feeling of release nor the heaviness of shame.

He told her how Toby had insisted on showing Benjamin the 9 millimeter Luger pistol his grandfather had brought home from the war, the one his father kept in the bottom drawer of his bedside table. Toby had chided him when Benjamin said he didn't really care to see it, called him a sissy.

No one was home that day, Toby's father still at work at the hardware store, his mother running errands in town. Toby slipped in his parents' bedroom while Benjamin waited by the doorway, slipped that bottom drawer open and removed a bundle wrapped in a gray striped handkerchief.

They went to Toby's room, down the hallway, sat on pillows on the floor. Toby removed the magazine from the pistol's grip, set it on the parquet floor. He grasped the gun by its barrel, held it out towards Benjamin.

"Wanna give it a try?" Toby said.

"That's OK." Benjamin said.

"Don't be such a wuss. I took the magazine out."

"We should put it back in the drawer."

"What are you so damn scared of?"

"I'm not scared," Benjamin said. "You said you

were gonna show me the gun. Well, you showed me. That's all."

"You're such a chicken," Toby said. He started flapping his arms and squawking.

"Well if you're so tough, pull the trigger then," Benjamin said. He didn't want him to do it really. He just wanted the taunting to stop. The best way was to turn the tables.

"I shot this gun before. My dad taught me how. Besides, I already told you, I took the magazine out."

"So do it. What are you waiting for? Pull the trigger. Or are *you* chicken?"

Toby crossed his eyes and stuck out his tongue sideways. It was his nothing-to-it expression, the same look he flashed Benjamin after he dribbled past two defenders and slid the ball between the goalie's legs in their come-from-behind win against the Crusaders.

He grasped the gun, rested his finger on the trigger.

"What're you waiting for?" Benjamin said.

Neither boy knew there was a round in the chamber. And Benjamin hadn't expected Toby to press the tip of the barrel against his temple before pulling the trigger.

The sound of the blast still rang in Benjamin's ears as he ran through the hallway, down the stairs, out the door, and across the yard to his grandparent's house. It still echoed in his ears ten minutes later when he finally dialed 911 from the kitchen phone.

Claire clasped Benjamin's hand. "Benjamin, it wasn't your fault."

"I was a coward. I goaded him into doing it to deflect from my own cowardice."

"You couldn't have known. You were just a couple of kids that didn't know better."

"That's the thing. I did know better. And then I lied about it. I've lied about it ever since. I've never taken responsibility."

"Oh, but you have," Claire said. "In your heart, you've taken responsibility. You've run your whole life based on this moment, do you even realize that? How much longer are you going to carry this weight?"

"I don't know that I have any other choice."

"You really think Toby would want this for you? If you want to honor his memory, let go, start living your life on your terms. Now *that* takes real courage."

Benjamin wiped away a solitary tear that trickled down his cheek. He gazed into Claire's eyes.

She said, "Toby lives within you. His memory is alive in your heart. Now make him proud."

Benjamin pictured Toby's face, his goofy smile. He knew what Toby would want him to do at this very moment. He didn't need him to tell him twice. Benjamin leaned forward and kissed Claire's lips.

It was unlike any kiss Benjamin had ever experienced, free of concealed passions, of veiled desires, of lingering cravings. It was complete and pure and cleansing. The moment had the transcendent quality of a quiet, gentle, sweeping communion.

Their lips met but once, remained pressed together for several seconds before reluctantly coming apart.

A moment later, Claire squeezed Benjamin's hand then let go of it. She said, "I better go."

"Why?"

"I have to think things through."

"Why?"

"I just want to be sure."

"Why?"

Claire pinched his forearm. "You little snake!"

"We're only on the third why."

Claire sighed. "I'm just scared we'll both get hurt."

"Why?"

"Because I always end up getting hurt and I've had my fill of heart-ache."

"Why do you think you'll get hurt this time?"

Claire got to her feet, walked to the front door and grasped the door knob. Without turning to face him she said, "You're the one who's aching to leave. Your plans don't include Purgatory or me. I accept that. Don't make it worse than it has to be."

32

There was a line of cars crawling towards Dr. Soto-Prinz's mansion, mostly late model European and Japanese luxury sedans. Benjamin worried his Nissan Xterra wasn't just out of place; there was a real risk the engine would overheat driving at such a slow pace in the evening heat. So he kept turning the ignition off when he came to a dead stop, and back on when it was time to roll forward a few more feet.

Just in front of him, Krippendorff's Dodge Viper came to a full stop and valets wearing black bow-ties and burgundy vests opened both doors. Krippendorff squeezed out of his car wearing a black tuxedo, immediately adjusting the gray cumberbun stretched across his paunch when he got to his feet. The voluptuous woman that was helped out of the passenger side, presumably his wife, moved with the nervous delight of an adolescent, wearing a dress that looked like something inspired by a Bavarian dirndl. Benjamin thought the only way to soften the couple's lack of fashion balance would have been for the Kripp to change into lederhosen.

Still, something about seeing the two of them together made Benjamin regret not having invited Claire to the affair, just so she could see the spectacle and have a laugh, but then he remembered the entry ticket was a cool ten grand a head.

A valet jogged up to Benjamin's truck, opened the door and greeted him with a politeness that bordered on reverence. He handed Benjamin a ticket without so much as a smirk.

Benjamin meandered toward the front door of the mansion, past a cantera fountain, purposefully lagging, trying to widen the space between him and the Kripp. He could feel his back moistening in the evening heat.

The house was a huge thing made of stucco with rough stones framing the windows and doors. The roof was topped by multiple blue-tiled cupolas with clerestory windows. Wooden beams protruded from a side wall. Benjamin wondered what one might call this architectural style. If it were up to him, he'd propose the name, *Monastic chic.*

The tall front door was open. Soto-Prinz's assistant, Giselle, was standing at the threshold next to a table holding a mahogany box with a slit on its top.

She smiled at Benjamin. "Good evening, Dr. Snow. So glad you could make it."

From the breast pocket of his sport coat, Benjamin pulled out the envelope with the check for ten-thousand dollars he had drafted earlier that evening. It felt so light in his hand now. "I guess I'm supposed to give this to you."

"If you can be so kind as to drop it in the ballot box," Giselle said.

Benjamin slipped the thin envelope in the box. "What are we voting for?" he said.

"Success of course," Giselle said. "Representative Davenport is eager to meet you."

"To meet *me*? He doesn't even know who I am."

"Oh. Well he must know of you," she said. "A few minutes ago he pulled me aside to ask which of the guests was you. I told him you hadn't arrived yet."

"That can't be right," Benjamin said. "Are you sure?"

Giselle made a comical face and shrugged. She took a step to the side. "The reception is in the ballroom, down that corridor and to the right. You might want to start making your way over there."

Benjamin started moving toward the front door.

"Hold on a minute." Giselle said.

Benjamin stopped and turned to face her. She reached up and adjusted the collar of his jacket.

"That's a little better," she said. She winked and whispered, "Relax. You look nice."

Medina waved at him as soon as Benjamin stepped in the ballroom, hailed him to an empty chair at the round table he was sitting at. The man looked tense, sipping on a rum and coke, an empty glass with a bent swizzle stick on the table in front of him. He was sitting alone while the other guests chatted and mingled.

"I was worried for a second you weren't going to show up," Medina said. "I thought maybe you'd just run off with…" He laughed. "Never mind. We need to cue up in the receiving line. Kiss *el jefe's* ring and meet the future President of the United States."

"You mean senator," Benjamin said.

"If you say so. I guess we'll have to wait and see. Need a drink?"

"I'm fine."

"Good. Don't drink. Try to stay sharp." Medina

downed the dregs of his cocktail, slammed the glass on the table and murmured, "Troy's our boy."

There must have been a couple hundred people crowded together, not counting the wait staff and the surprisingly large security detail: professional looking guys in suits with the coiled cords of ear pieces snaking in their collars, pacing next to tapestries hanging from the mahogany paneled walls of the ballroom which was the size of a regulation basketball court. Benjamin recognized a few of the doctors' faces from the partner's meeting. They looked like kids at a Halloween party, finding it hard to contain their excitement, their giddiness only subdued by the uncertainty of how they should behave in their costumes.

Soto-Prinz, on the other hand, was as comfortable and steadfast as a veteran diplomat. Had he worn a medallion hung from a fat ribbon around his neck, no one would have batted an eye. He was introducing the guests in the receiving line to Troy Davenport in polished style, as though he had rehearsed every word.

Troy Davenport looked like he had just stepped out of one of those classic black and white movies Benjamin's grandmother used to watch late at night. Had he been born a few decades earlier, he might have been a leading man in an age when all men wore hats and ate supper in a jacket even in their own home. He was taller than Benjamin had expected, and quite a bit younger looking. Maybe it was just his tan. Whatever it was, he exuded an aura of salubrity that seemed beyond the reach of mere mortals.

The couple in front of Pablo and Benjamin stepped away and Pablo nudged Benjamin smack in front of Dr. Soto-Prinz. Soto-Prinz looked exuberant. He grasped Benjamin's hand firmly as if he were glad to see an old friend.

"Well good evening," he said. "Mr. Davenport, I'd like to introduce you to our newest partner, Dr. Benjamin Snow, and to his sponsor, Dr. Pablo Medina."

Troy Davenport gave no sign of recognizing Benjamin's name. Giselle must have been mistaken.

Davenport shook Benjamin's hand, reached over for Medina's hand. "Thank you both so much for coming. I appreciate your support," he said.

"Dr. Snow and Dr. Medina are two of our esteemed pediatricians," Soto-Prinz said.

"Is that so?" Davenport said. "Well, I can't tell you how much respect I have for you for what you do. I know the special challenges you face practicing here on the border in the midst of this humanitarian crisis."

"Our pleasure," Medina said. His voice was starting to sound slurred.

Davenport put a hand on Benjamin's shoulder, looked him square in the eye. "Thank you so much, for all you do. For all the children you care for so selflessly."

The remark didn't sound corny or polished. Not with that look in his eye. There was a deep sincerity to the politician's voice that was, not just plausible, but warm and moving.

Soto-Prinz clenched a fist. He politely gestured with his other hand that it was time for them to move on. "Thank you doctors."

Davenport shook Benjamin's hand again. He said, "It was nice to meet you, Dr. Snow. I look forward to chatting with you again some day."

Medina and Benjamin walked away. They were well out of ear shot when Medina said, in a childish voice, "Nice to meet you, Dr. Snow. So nice we're both white men, isn't it?"

"Where did that come from?" Benjamin said.

"He hardly even looks at me. You, I thought he was going to hug you for a second."

"Come on."

"Don't even try to argue with me, Benji," Medina said. "Shut up and walk me to the bathroom."

Medina and Benjamin went out the ballroom, back down the marble corridor to an atrium that opened onto a lavish back yard bordered in its entirety by a ten foot brick wall. Benjamin waited in the atrium, looking out in the garden as Pablo Medina shuffled into the bathroom.

He waited there a few minutes, then stepped down a shorter corridor adorned by art work. One relic caught his eye. There was a glass dome mounted on a granite pedestal against the wall. Benjamin stepped closer to inspect it. Under the dome, on a red velvet base, lay an antique dagger and its silver scabbard with inlaid green onyx. It was identical to the one Soto-Prinz was handling the first time they met on that private jet.

"If your wondering, that's the original."

Benjamin turned to the voice. Dr. Soto-Prinz was standing behind him. He was holding the brown, leather-bound notebook Benjamin had caught eye of during his interview. As if feeling Benjamin's gaze, Soto-Prinz hid the notebook from Benjamin's view by casually bringing his hands together behind his back. For the second time, Benjamin got the odd sense that Soto-Prinz was particularly sensitive about his gazing at that little book.

Soto-Prinz continued unperturbed, "It's a family heirloom. It belonged to Don Sebastian Gonzalo Garcia-Fernandez, one of Hernan Cortez' top lieutenants and my most illustrious ancestor. It's been handed down to the first born males in our family for generations. A line never unbroken. One can only wonder how many throats that blade has slit. But alas, I'm saddened to say, this is one family tradition which has come to an end. You see, I was blessed with only daughters."

"I'm sure one day they'll enjoy it as much as you have," Benjamin said.

Soto-Prinz laughed. "You're a mischievous one, aren't you, Dr. Snow. If I didn't know better I'd say that you take pleasure in needling me. For instance, this crippled child you admitted to my hospital the other day; do you know how much money we will lose in unreimbursable services? But that's quite all right. All in all, you're doing a fine job. And you handled yourself nicely with Mr. Davenport so far tonight. Looks like you know when to keep your ears open and give your lips a rest."

Benjamin knew Soto-Prinz wanted an update on baby Fatima, the Ortega baby, as Pablo Medina had called her. He started thinking how to respond should the topic come up. Even if the father was a drug dealer, Benjamin was bound to the sacred obligation of patient confidentiality.

"And it looks like when it comes to brass tacks, you're a very practical man," Soto-Prinz said. "You were very wise to sign that partnership contract."

Benjamin heard the sound of footsteps coming from the atrium. It was Medina, stumbling out of the restroom. He was still zipping up his fly when he looked up and caught sight of Soto-Prinz. The expression on Soto-Prinz' face hardened.

Medina bowed in an apish way. "Dr. Soto-Prinz, did Benjamin tell you all about the cute little baby? Come on Benjamin, tell him about baby Ortega."

Soto-Prinz said, "Dr. Medina, you had better sober up. And if you can't do that, see to it that you keep your mouth shut." He turned and marched back towards the ballroom.

Medina turned to Benjamin and said, "Come with me Benjamin, I need a drink."

When they re-entered the ballroom, the other guests had taken their seats. Medina lifted two tall rum and cokes from a waiter's tray and headed for the table he had been seated at earlier. Benjamin sat next to him. In just seconds, Medina downed one of the glasses.

The high-pitched whistle of amplifier feedback directed Benjamin's attention to a small podium where Dr. Soto-Prinz stood, beaming a proud smile. The doctor tapped the microphone a couple of times and, as if on cue, Medina knocked the second drink over making a mess of the tablecloth. Benjamin quickly pulled up the hanging flap of the tablecloth in an attempt to mitigate the damage.

Soto-Prinz was in the midst of introducing Troy Davenport but, as much as he wanted to listen in, Benjamin was too busy to focus as he tried to scoop ice cubes from the table top and plop them back in the overturned glass, dabbing at the saturated tablecloth with his and Medina's cloth napkins. By the time things were under control and Benjamin was able to redirect his attention, Troy Davenport was standing on the podium, microphone in hand.

"Coming to Purgatory," Davenport said, "is like coming home for me. And being welcomed this way by you, members of the El Dorado Physician's Group, is like being embraced by old friends."

The audience erupted in applause.

"I've had the opportunity to travel all over our great state in the last year, met many good people in every county and every town I passed through, but I can attest with no hesitation that my heart," he placed a hand over his chest, turned his head and seemed to be looking directly at Benjamin, "will forever stay in Purgatory."

Davenport looked moved as he uttered the words, to the point that it stirred a sense of sympathy in Benjamin, not for the words that were uttered but by the genuine sentiment that they carried.

"Next week I will have the opportunity to debate… I was going to say my opponent, but I have to tell you, that's a word I hesitate to use. Quincy Vaughn is a decent and honorable man who has served our great state and our country with dignity and distinction, and I am reluctant to refer to anyone with that sort of billing as my opponent."

The audience was shifting in their seats.

"Now, now. That is the truth, my friends. Listen doctors, our country is suffering from a pernicious ailment; an ailment that has enfeebled our sense of civility, stifled polite conversation, and pitted neighbor against neighbor. That ailment is righteous indignation. An ailment borne of moral certitude which propels us, not just to disagreement, but to pass moral judgment on those with whom we disagree. We can do better than that. We must do better. We must find a way to elevate our discourse to a higher plane — to a plateau of comity and respect.

"Next week, I will not confront Quincy Vaughn as an opponent. I will simply make the case that our movement has better ideas for a better government: a government that does not hamstring the natural talents and creativity of its citizens, a government that shuns petty legalism, a government based on justice and not patronage, a government that celebrates the accomplishments of its most successful members while never neglecting the needs its most needy brothers and sisters."

Medina put his elbows on the table and leaned forward to rest his face in his hands. There was a tap on Benjamin's shoulder. It was Giselle.

She whispered in his ear, "Dr. Snow, won't you be a darling and drive Dr. Medina home? He seems a little indisposed."

"Now?"

"The valet already pulled your car up to the front door."

Benjamin grabbed Medina's arm, half lifted him out of his chair and the two managed to slink out of the ballroom without attracting too much attention. Benjamin could hear repeated bursts of applause and cheers echoing down the marble corridor as they neared the front door to the mansion. By now he had to grab hold of Pablo Medina's elbow to buoy his equilibrium. A valet came to Benjamin's aid and, between the two of them, they managed to push Medina into the passenger seat of Benjamin's truck.

Benjamin went round the front of the vehicle and was about to get in the driver's seat when something caught his eye. Some fifty feet away, standing next to a line of black sedans, Cyril Thompson was engaged in conversation with members of Troy Davenport's security detail.

Benjamin got in the car. He asked Medina for directions to his house. Medina pointed vaguely out the driveway and said, "That way." He tried a different tack. He managed to get Medina to recite his street address, entered it in his phone's GPS and drove off.

Medina drifted off during the drive, his head bent down with his chin resting on his chest, a light snore emanating from somewhere in the back of his throat. Every so often the man's head seemed to drift forward to some critical nadir and jerk back up, never quite waking him. Benjamin was grateful Medina was asleep. He wanted to be spared the uneasiness of witnessing his plastered boss gushing. Or even worse, to hear him say something that would make them both embarrassed once he sobered up.

Ten minutes later, they pulled into the driveway of a surprisingly tasteful modern single story home. Benjamin went around the front of the truck, opened the passenger door and woke Medina with a brusque shake of the arm. He helped him out of the vehicle and the two started walking to the front door, Medina leaning into Benjamin with his arm dangling around Benjamin's neck, resting on his still-sore clavicle.

When they got to the front door, Medina rang the doorbell. He turned and gave Benjamin a look of mock perplexity. "Nobody's home." He laughed, started fumbling with the keys, dropping them on the floor.

Benjamin picked them up, "Which key is it?"

"The one Jessica left behind," Medina said. "I was married once, Benjamin. Honest to God."

"Oh yeah? What happened." Benjamin tried a couple of keys until he found one that slipped in the lock.

"She changed. When we first married, she only criticized me for things I did. But as time passed, she only criticized me for who I am." They stepped inside. Medina leaned on Benjamin's shoulder. Benjamin pushed the door shut with his foot. "One day I ask her, Jessica, do you still love me? She looks at me and says, 'Do I love you? I don't even like you.'"

"That's cold."

Medina pointed in the direction of his bedroom. "She left me for a plumber. You hear that?

Not a urologist, mind you, but this *gringo pendejo* (no offense) that came to unplug our toilet. Poor bastard is still dealing with her shit." Medina let out a cackle of laughter.

Benjamin steadied him onto the bed. Helped him take his jacket off, loosened his tie and pulled it off with one clean jerk.

"But it hurt real bad Benjamin. There were days driving home from work, I swear I was one bad song on the radio away from swerving head-on into the grill of an eighteen-wheeler."

Benjamin knelt down to untie the laces of Medina's shoes. Medina plopped backwards on the bed, lifted one foot to allow Benjamin to slip off the first shoe. It was a bit of a struggle. Medina wasn't wearing socks, and the perspiration made his feet cling to the insoles.

"I'm sorry, Benjamin."

"Don't sweat it. I got it," Benjamin said as he dropped the first shoe on the floor and began tugging on the other one.

"I should have never brought you down here. Fine mess I got you in."

Benjamin dropped the other shoe on the floor, got up and wiped his hands on the side of his pants. "What are you talking about?"

Medina put his finger on his lips and said, "Shhhhh! Just remember, in Purgatory you can't trust anyone. Not even me." At this he laughed softly.

Benjamin stared him down.

Medina closed his eyes. "Don't worry

Benjamin," he said, "we'll get out of this mess somehow, dead or alive."

33

One-point-six million. Not a bad take for a banquet of chicken breast and over-cooked vegetables. “Not bad at all,” Fermin Soto-Prinz muttered under his breath as he entered the figure in his leather bound notebook. The smooth feel of the pen’s lacquer, the weight of the notebook’s parchment, heightened the pleasure of scrawling the figure with his distinctly European penmanship.

Fermin Soto-Prinz was an obstinate traditionalist. He still listened to opera on vinyl records, shaved every morning with a Dovo straight razor after lathering up with a silvertip badger hair brush, and always carried a cotton handkerchief in his trouser’s pocket like any self-respecting man should.

But there was a more practical aspect to using the notebook for his most sensitive record-keeping: computer spread sheets inevitably left a ghostly imprint on hard-drives even after the files were deleted — faint traces that clever agents could sniff out and retrieve with sophisticated algorithms. It was a risk he wasn’t willing to take.

He scanned the prior entries on the page. With the two-point-three million dollars already tendered by the PAC, El Dorado hospital had now contributed nearly four million dollars to Troy Davenport’s campaign coffers, a campaign that was surging with the implacable momentum of a tidal wave.

And yet, Davenport had looked distant tonight,

even preoccupied. It was understandable. Perhaps, he was feeling worn in this last stage of the race. And surely that other meddlesome matter weighed heavily on his mind. Soto-Prinz could see it in his eyes. If only the two of them had been granted a private moment, far from the constant surveillance of the security detail, Soto-Prinz might have been able to reassure him that his secret was safe, the right steps had been taken, and Soto-Prinz would personally see to it that Davenport's reputation remained untarnished. There was nothing to worry about, Soto-Prinz told himself. Except for Pablo Medina.

His drinking was getting out of control. He wasn't concerned about Medina's insistence on pursuing the thorny path of self-destruction — that was his business. But a drunken mind speaks a sober heart, and Medina knew too much.

The man's history proved he was a mule, still engaging in reckless over-billing after already having been disciplined by the state's government insurance commission. The fool acted like a miser, stooping to pick up tarnished pennies whilst in a gold mine. His indiscretions had already brought him shame and caused the ruin of one clinic. Suddenly jobless, he had resorted to seeing patients in a cash-and-carry clinic tucked in the back of a pharmacy on the outskirts of town, scraping by until an old high school chum came to see him with a curious proposition.

Fernando Ortega had wanted Medina to act as a middle-man between himself and the CEO of an upstart surgical center on El Dorado highway to discuss a one-of-a-kind business opportunity. Ortega had a peculiar problem: an excess of cash. Cash that needed to be invested with particular delicacy and tact. He had devised a plan by which the money could be funneled to the clinic, to be used for capital expenditures and to attract further investment from other physicians. The money, a fungible resource, would thus be mixed with clinic revenues and other liquid assets before being re-distributed among investors, including an agent acting on behalf of Ortega. Ortega preferred not to have his name on any documents for personal reasons. Mix, cycle, distribute. Ablution by dilution, Soto-Prinz had called it.

With the massive infusion of capital, the surgical center grew rapidly. It soon morphed into a full service hospital. Physicians chomped at the bit to become investors. And then the juiciest of cherries was plopped on the very tip of the sundae: a political action committee was created. Ortega and Soto-Prinz could now handpick political candidates and contribute generously to their war chests in a completely legal way. Perhaps that had been Ortega's intention all along. It was true genius. A master stroke. Not even the most cynical voter would believe that the most admired candidate for the United States Senate in a generation was being bankrolled by a Mexican drug cartel.

There was a knock at the door.

"Come in, Tito," Soto-Prinz said.

A man walked in, removed his black felt Stetson and sat down across the desk from Soto-Prinz. Tito Melgar looked less out of place in his street clothes than he did in his hospital security uniform, still he moved as though his western snap shirt had been accidentally over-starched. Thank goodness he was wearing his black leather driving gloves; Soto-Prinz couldn't stand the sight of his scarred hand.

"So?" Soto-Prinz said.

Tito Melgar leaned back and crossed his legs, placed his Stetson on his knee.

"They went straight to Medina's. The boy had to practically carry him inside the house."

"Pablo Medina was unconscious?"

"Not unconscious but not all there either," Melgar said.

"Hmmm. You think they talked long?" That was the underlying concern. Until now neither of the two knew enough individually to fathom the situation, but if they started exchanging information, even by accident in idle talk, one or the other might start to make sense of it all.

Melgar adjusted the collar of his shirt. "The boy was out of the house in five minutes. I followed him to his home. He lives in a bungalow next to a cabbage field, not two miles away from here. I took down the address." He plucked a folded piece of paper from his breast pocket and placed it on Soto-Prinz's desk.

"Well done," Soto-Prinz said. "Tito, there is another task I need you to attend to tonight. I hate to keep encroaching on your free time, but I promise to make it worth your while."

"It ain't work when you love what you do," Melgar said.

"Pablo Medina has become too much of a liability," Soto-Prinz said.

"I can go back there right now and torch his house. He's so sauced he won't even wake up."

Melgar's obsession with fire was a nasty fetish, one deeply rooted in his pscyhe, no doubt. Soto-Prinz mused that, as a child, Tito Melgar was cruel to animals and regularly wet his bed well into adolescence to complete Macdonald's dreadful triad. Even the all-too-recent incident with that little girl which left his hand permanently disfigured couldn't quench his vile thirst. Nonetheless, it was Melgar's complete lack of empathy that made him so useful to the organization.

"I was thinking of something a tad more graceful," Soto-Prinz said. He slid open a drawer and pulled out a syringe filled with a straw-colored liquid. "Make it look like an accidental overdose."

Tito Melgar grabbed the syringe, held it up to the light and looked through the fluid.

"What about the boy?" Melgar asked.

"All along, the plan was to have Dr. Snow replace Medina."

"Yeah, but things changed."

Soto-Prinz could see that Melgar was particularly hungry tonight. Killing Medina would only rouse his murderous appetite. Soto-Prinz drummed his fingers on the desk top. Having both men gone would certainly mitigate much of his anxiety, at the risk of arousing undue suspicion, but he felt an unanticipated reluctance in ordering the hit on Benjamin Snow. It was not out of a sense of fondness for the lad, but the fruit of a tickling curiosity.

Here was an ambitious young man, highly analytical, not so gifted in the sensitivity dimension, ostracized at the start of his professional career as a result of an incident that could not be considered entirely his fault. Benjamin reminded Soto-Prinz of a younger version of himself. The question that vexed Soto-Prinz was whether Dr. Snow would process these life events with the necessary objective detachment and embrace the same philosophy of life that he had. Perhaps he had not been looking for an immediate replacement for Pablo Medina — what he had caught a glimpse of during that interview on the Gulf Stream jet was a potential apprentice: a possible future replacement for himself.

"I have other plans for Dr. Snow," Soto-Prinz said.

"What if he becomes a problem?"

"Then we make him disappear."

Tito Melgar slipped the syringe in the breast pocket of his shirt, put his Stetson back on and got up. He headed towards the door.

Soto-Prinz said, "What about the man who was with you when you took care of the late Dr. Rizzo?"

Tito Melgar smiled. "No one will ever find him. And just between you and me," he chuckled, "I wouldn't eat the chorizo from my cousin's meat market for a little while."

34

It's amazing how careless people can be, Tito Melgar thought when he pushed down on the handle with his gloved hand and the front door of Pablo Medina's home popped open. It was enough to take all the fun out of his job when it was this easy.

He slipped inside, slowly shut the door behind him. He stepped into the living room, scanned the room to get a feel for the house's floor plan. He went through the kitchen, found the door to the garage, opened it. The garage was empty except for some cardboard moving boxes, a few buckets of paint, a practically never-used lawn mower, and a red plastic gasoline can. No car. Medina's car was still on the street outside of Soto-Prinz's complex where the valet had parked it. So no one else was home.

Melgar paced back through the living room, slid with his back against the wall, moved up the hall leading to the bedrooms. One of the two doors was open. Melgar peered inside.

Pablo Medina was passed out on the bed wearing his trousers and dress shirt. Melgar's muscles relaxed. He ambled into the room, put his hands on his hips and looked down on Medina with disdain. Too damn easy.

Maybe he could still find a way to have a little fun. He wasn't at all worried about the El Dorado security truck parked outside. It was partly hidden by a drooping Magnolia. Not that it mattered. The color scheme of the vehicle was so close to that used by the Border Patrol it made the truck practically invisible: people didn't bother to look twice when he drove by. It was a stroke of genius on Soto-Prinz's part, to appropriate all but the agency's insignia, a choice designed to keep the *mojados* away from the hospital. But it wasn't just the illegals that fell for the deception; all but the most careful observer was fooled at first glance. The only drawback was those damn uniforms with their stiff cloth and mis-placed stitching that always made his shirt bunch up.

Tito walked back to the garage. There was something there that had caught his eye. He lifted the gas can off the stained concrete slab, gave it a shake. It was darn near full. He twisted the cap off, took a whiff. He loved that smell. He screwed the cap back on. He wasn't planning to disobey the boss, but damn if he wasn't going to have just a little fun.

Soto-Prinz would never understand: it wasn't just the fire that thrilled him, the acrid smell of burning fuel, the warmth of the lapping flames, the purity of the light they radiated. There was this unceasing wonder that intrigued him, of the power of fire to evoke that deep-seated unbridled fear, that innate terror shared by all living beings, be it a kitten dipped in tar or a crooked cop dowsed in kerosene. Tito Melgar relished the moment, announced by a brilliance of the eyes, when a soul discerned the inevitability of imminent death, saw the beast of oblivion poised to make its pitiless, savage plunge. For many people, that moment would be the only honest instant of their entire shallow lives. It was an honor, for Melgar, to tease it out of them. It left him with a fleeting sense of inner peace.

He hurried back to the bedroom, lay the gas can on the floor, pulled a lighter out of his pocket. He flicked on the lighter, turned the regulator until he got a tall blue plume and kneeled. He waved the flame under Medina's foot, calculating the distance so that the heat's focus would just kiss the skin.

Pablo Medina awoke with a whole-body jerk and a sort of squeal. Tito Melgar burst out laughing. Medina propped himself up on the bed.

"Good morning, sunshine," Melgar said. "You don't look too happy to see me. And now you're wondering how the hell I got in. Looks like your little friend left the front door unlocked." He clucked and shook his head.

Medina wiped perspiration from his forehead.

Melgar said, "You don't look so good, Pablo. Room spinning?"

"Tell Soto-Prinz the kid doesn't know a thing."

"That's good. Real good. But, you see, things have changed. You remember those little tape players, you know, the ones you carried around, played cassettes."

"Walk-mans."

"That's it, Sony Walk-Man. Well, you're my little Sony Walk-man, see. Till now I been pushing that little play button, listening to the music. But you only got that one tune you keep singing over and over. It's getting old. Looks like it's time to press the delete button."

"Walk-mans didn't have a delete button,"

Medina said.

"You know what? You're right about that. Know what I used to do to when I really got tired of a song? I'd bash the damn thing in with a hammer."

"I've done everything you wanted."

"You done enough. That's just the thing. The boss don't need you no more."

Medina pulled himself back in bed, clutched the bedspread.

"Relax!" Melgar said. "The good doctor is a grateful man. He's even giving you a choice."

"What kind of choice?"

Melgar unbuttoned the breast pocket of his shirt. Pulled out the syringe and held it up. "You can choose this," he said, "or this." He lifted the gas can off the floor, shook it and put it back down."

And there it was, that first flash of primal fear.

"No!" Medina shouted, and lunged at Melgar. Tito timed his right hook just so, caught him near the nose.

Dr. Soto-Prinz had taught him that the most efficient way at knocking someone out was by inducing sudden torque on the brain-stem. Didn't require as much brute force as landing a jab on the forehead to produce contrecoup. Along with locating the precise position of the carotid artery merely by identifying the external landmarks of the neck, it was some of the most useful medical advice Soto-Prinz had shared with him.

Medina was out cold. Tito rolled up Medina's shirt sleeve and was about to tie the rubber tourniquet to the arm when he realized he didn't know whether Pablo Medina was right or left-handed. Soto-Prinz had urged him to make it look like an accident. It was attention to details like this that was the mark of a true professional. Make a careless error and pretty soon someone gets suspicion and fouls up the works. If Medina was right-handed, and chances favored this, he would need to inject him in the left arm.

He rolled up the other shirt sleeve, tightened the tourniquet. A pipeline of a vein swelled in the soft of the elbow. Melgar eased the needle in, bevel up, advanced it cautiously and tugged gently on the plunger. He feasted his eyes on the beautiful red swirl which emerged, as graciously as a butterfly emerging from its cocoon, and mixed with the straw colored liquid in the barrel of the syringe. He released the tourniquet and pushed steadily on the plunger all the way down to the hub, left the whole thing in place, sticking out of the arm.

He didn't need to stick around. There was no doubt that a veteran anesthesiologist as capable as Dr. Soto-Prinz would not err in calculating the lethal dose of heroin. He picked up the gas can, brought it back to the garage, left the front door the way he found it and slowly drove out of the neighborhood, without neglecting to admire the elegant flower gardens and manicured lawns.

35

Medina was late for work the next morning. Benjamin wasn't terribly surprised. The way he looked last night, Pablo was probably in the grips of a massive hangover. Benjamin's own schedule was light so he started seeing his partner's patients as well. By ten am, Pablo Medina had yet to show up.

Cristela, his nurse, was besides herself. "He's not even picking up the phone, Dr. Snow."

"He's probably not feeling all that well," Benjamin said. "Don't worry. He'll show up."

"How do you know? You didn't take him drinking last night."

"The only place I took him was back home."

"*Dios mio*, with that man. After his wife left, the only thing he has lips for is the bottle."

"Give him a couple of hours," Benjamin said.

Lunch time came and Pablo Medina was still AWOL. Cristela came back, clutched onto Benjamin's coat sleeve and started sobbing.

"I'll take care of him," Benjamin said. "Don't worry. I'll douse him in coffee and drag him back if I have to. He thinks I'm seeing all his patients today he's got another thing coming."

It wasn't how he hoped to spend his lunch hour but in truth, he was starting to get a little worried himself.

There was no answer when he rang the doorbell to his home. He tried calling him on his cell phone. No reply. He walked around to the back of the house in case he was out in his backyard. There was a sliding glass door in the back of the house off of a hexagonal wooden deck. Benjamin climbed up on the deck, tried pushing on the door. It was locked. Then he realized he hadn't tried opening the front door. He went back around, pushed down on the door handle. It clicked open.

"Pablo!" Benjamin shouted. "Hey, Pablo, you coming to work today?"

There was no answer. Benjamin pushed the door open, stepped inside.

"I sure hope you have some clothes on."

He walked through the living room down a hall to Medina's bedroom. He stepped in the doorway, looked at the body sprawled out on the bed and immediately knew Pablo Medina was dead.

Benjamin knew better than to touch anything as he waited for the police to arrive. Medina was still wearing his pants and the dress shirt from the night before. But the sleeves of the shirt were rolled up now. A rubber tourniquet lay under Medina's left arm, the one that had a syringe still buried in the antecubital fossa.

Don't touch, but look, Benjamin told himself.

Benjamin had had his fair share of encounters with users in his medical school days and had learned to recognize track marks. There were none on Medina's arms. And the median cubital vein was always one of the first one's to blow on an addict, because it was inevitably the first choice while it lasted. Medina must have been a naive user. But why were both sleeves rolled up then? That almost suggested he'd been looking for a decent vein on both arms.

There was some dried blood in Medina's nostrils, a patch of ecchymosis extending from the left nasolabial fold to the vermilion border of the upper lip. The poor fool must have taken a bad fall, probably when he got up to get his stash. Benjamin looked around the room. There was no overturned furniture. The drawers of the bedside table and dresser were all shut.

He went back to the front door, inspected the lock. It had a latch to lock the door from the inside. Medina hadn't been able to see him out the night before, which explained why the door was still unlocked when he arrived.

The police were taking their sweet time getting there. Benjamin called the clinic to tell them to reschedule all patients this afternoon. He didn't plan to tell them anything more, not over the phone. But Ivan the terrible was the one who picked up, and on hearing Benjamin's voice he said, "Holy mother! The son-of-a-bitch is dead, ain't he?"

"Dammit, Ivan. Keep your mouth shut."

"Relax, Snow. I'm in your office. It's cool."

Benjamin asked him if Medina ever used drugs, as far as he knew."

"He'd ask me to get him a little Acapulco Gold once in a whiles." Ivan said. "But he was more of a drinker — not a very good one."

"Did he ever mainline?"

"You kidding me? Pablo Medina was scared of needles. Whole time I worked here, he never got a flu shot he was so chicken."

A Purgatory PD squad car pulled into the driveway followed by a van from the morgue. Benjamin hung up and put the phone in his back pocket. The officers did a perfunctory inspection of the death scene. They asked Benjamin a few questions, got his contact information and told him a detective might call him, "Case we have any further questions, but I don't think so. Looks pretty cut and dry."

Benjamin started driving back to the clinic. It was hard to believe he had only been in Purgatory just a few short weeks, and already two of his colleagues had died. Maybe it was true. Nobody ever left Purgatory. Not alive.

36

The agar plates incubating Fatima Sandoval's blood and spinal fluid showed no bacterial growth even after three days. The urinary tract infection responded promptly to the antibiotic cocktail which Benjamin had started empirically the night of admission and the infant now showed no sign of distress.

Benjamin was pleased that the time to discharge his first inpatient in Purgatory had arrived. The only question remaining in his mind was how the follow-up care would be arranged.

"You're his doctor," Veronica Sandoval stated matter-of-factly, "and that's settled."

Benjamin said, "I'm not sure when the clinic's going to re-open."

"Sorry about your partner," she said. She tore a corner off a page of the discharge instructions and scribbled the address of the hacienda that Benjamin had been taken to when they first met.

"Put that in your GPS," she said. "I'm sure you don't need goons in suits to baby sit you."

The first follow-up visit was three days later. Benjamin pulled into the driveway of the hacienda and approached the house slowly, to give the guards time to consider the necessity of discharging their weapons on a run down Nissan Xterra before actually doing so. There were fewer vehicles parked in the courtyard this time. Benjamin came to a stop, leaving the truck parked at an odd angle, and got out.

A man Benjamin did not recognize started to frisk him before he even got to the front door, until Juan the chauffeur told him not to bother. Cyril Thompson was nowhere to be seen.

Juan escorted him to the same room where he had examined baby Fatima the first time.

Veronica greeted him with a smile and an eager, "You made it!"

Benjamin pulled his stethoscope out, asked Veronica the usual questions, and examined the baby head to toe. The baby was a beautiful creature, dressed in pink with a yellow bow on her hair. Poor thing. It wasn't her fault her father was a drug boss.

When Benjamin put his stethoscope away, Veronica said, "Fernando would like a word with you before you leave. He's always anxious to settle his accounts. It's part of his nature."

The hair stood up on the back of Benjamin's neck.

Veronica saw the look of dread on his face and said, "Don't be silly, Dr. Snow. You have nothing to fear. Fernando Ortega is a just man. Ask anyone. Besides, he admires how you handled yourself through all this." Veronica nodded in the direction of a closed door. "Go ahead and knock. He's expecting you."

Fernando Ortega's office had bare walls, no artwork, no portraits or knick knacks on the desk. It looked as though the sparse furniture had been installed as mere props. But what surprised Benjamin the most when he stepped into the room was that Ortega was not alone.

Ortega leaned over the desk to shake Benjamin's hand and said, "Dr. Snow, allow me to introduce you to Mr. Charles Moss, president and CEO of Rio Grande Merchant's Bank."

Benjamin shook hands with Mr. Moss and said, "Pleased to meet you." And he truly was pleased. Not even Ortega would kill him with a bank CEO as a witness. He sat down when Mr. Moss and Ortega settled back into their chairs.

Charles Moss said nothing. He looked to be in his early sixties. He had a narrow, tall head with wavy gray hair. He wore thick black-rimmed spectacles and his pale, thin eyes seemed to blink excessively, as though he were constantly staring into a spotlight.

Ortega said, "You're probably aware that Mr. Moss is the only investor at El Dorado hospital who is not a physician." Turning to face Moss, Ortega said, "Dr. Snow is a new partner."

Benjamin wondered how Fernando Ortega could possibly know that.

"I was aware of that," Mr. Moss said. "I personally signed off on his loan."

And there was his answer. Benjamin thought of what Jesus Tamez had told him: in Borderlandia, nothing is as it seems. The exchange between Ortega and Mr.Moss smacked of poorly rehearsed play-acting.

"I asked Mr. Moss to meet me here so I could express my profound concern over the death of Sofia Sandoval at his facility," Ortega said.

"We are all deeply disturbed by this incident," Moss said. "A truly unfortunate sentinel event."

"Having occurred within twenty-four hours of admission, the death required an autopsy by the county medical examiner and the usual review by the hospital's quality assurance department. According to the death certificate, the mechanism of death was extreme blood loss. But, as you well know, Dr. Snow, there's a difference between the mechanism of death and the cause of death. Mr. Moss has just given me his assurance that the full truth will come out."

The two men stared at Benjamin. They waited so long that Benjamin felt compelled to say something.

"That's great," Benjamin said. "I mean, I can appreciate your efforts."

"I thought you would," Ortega said, "seeing as you've already undertaken your own investigation."

"My own investigation?"

"Mr. Moss tells me you tried to gain access to Sofia's medical record and were denied."

Benjamin wondered how Mr. Moss would have known this. Maybe he had traced Benjamin's attempts to gain access on the computer portal, or maybe the polite clerk from medical records he had talked to reported directly to him. Or was it Felix the nurse? Did his prayers travel on the wind right into Ortega's ear? "I was just trying to get some background information to help me care for Fatima," Benjamin said.

"And you've been spending a lot more time at El Dorado lately," Ortega said.

"I have a patient there, on the pediatric ward."

"You met with the widow, Mrs. Rizzo. Did you not? Oh, come now, Dr. Snow, don't look at me that way. If you want to find out the truth about your friend's death you'll have to set aside the silly notion that I had anything to do with it."

Benjamin recalled the words of Virgil Thibodeaux: not a bird falls in Purgatory without *El Chacal* knowing. "I met her once. Gave her my condolences."

"Do you know who refused to grant you access to Sofia's medical record?" Ortega said.

"I believe it was Dr. Soto-Prinz," Benjamin said.

"And did you know that Dr. Soto-Prinz was the anesthesiologist attending Sofia's delivery?" Ortega leaned back, tapped his index fingers together. "I see. You already knew that. You're further along in your investigation than I had hoped."

Benjamin wondered if Ortega knew that Soto-Prinz had canceled the blood transfusions that would have saved the life of his mistress. If he did know, why was he needling Benjamin? If he didn't know, disclosing this fact was tantamount to signing a death sentence for Dr. Soto-Prinz.

Mr. Moss leaned forward and rested his elbows on his knees bringing his hands together. He said, "We're very concerned about Dr. Soto-Prinz's conduct. His behavior has become erratic of late, and we suspect he may be involved in… nefarious activities."

Moss leaned back, turned in his chair and crossed his legs. He looked at Ortega as if waiting for confirmation that he had delivered his line correctly.

Benjamin was stunned. A bank president was telling him how worried he was about a doctor's behavior while sitting in the office of a drug dealer. Benjamin couldn't think of an appropriate reply.

"Hand me your phone, please," Ortega said after a prolonged pause. Benjamin complied, thinking that Ortega wanted to check his call log.

Ortega took less than thirty seconds to type something on the touch screen, then returned the cell phone to Benjamin.

"Now you have a direct number where you can reach me anytime," Ortega said. "I simply ask that you keep your eyes and ears open, and if you hear something, anything at all, that you call me first."

Benjamin looked at the screen of his phone. The number had been entered under the heading: *El Chacal.*

'That's who you think I am," Ortega said, "so suit yourself. After all, it's preferable to having my name on your phone. Think of it as our little inside joke."

Benjamin slipped his phone in his shirt's breast pocket.

Ortega said, "And now it's time to settle our account. You made two house calls and provided hospital care for four days. I trust two-thousand dollars is reasonable and customary compensation?"

It was Mr. Moss who retrieved a check book from inside his suit coat.

"I can't take your money," Benjamin said.

"You're a man of strange sensibilities, Dr. Snow," Ortega said. "But we all have our idiosyncrasies and one of mine is that I never leave an account unsettled. Give your money to charity if you have any qualms, as absurd as they may be, but I insist on paying my debts."

Ortega had given Benjamin an idea. He hated to think of Ikal as a charity case, but it was time to be pragmatic. He recalled the amount requested by the gastroenterologist for that G-tube.

Benjamin said, "In that case, you better make it for two-thousand five-hundred."

37

When he went to make his rounds on Ikal that evening, walking the halls of El Dorado hospital, Benjamin felt like an intruder. Keep your eyes and ears open, Ortega had told him. Benjamin hadn't agreed to anything, and yet he had a new entry in the contacts folder of his phone which he hadn't deleted — hadn't as much as edited. It still read, *El Chacal.* He started to wonder, if he did notice anything unusual, would he actually dial that number?

He was still on the first floor, turned a corner from the hallway where the doctor's lounge was located, and entered a corridor that held potted lady palms at either end. A door swung open mid-way down the hall. Dr. Soto-Prinz stepped out, seemingly engrossed in thought, not noticing Benjamin's presence, and locked the door to his office. He turned abruptly and almost bumped into Benjamin. The older man was so startled, the leather bound notebook he was holding flipped out of his hand and dropped to the floor. Benjamin stooped to pick it up.

Soto-Prinz snatched it out of his hand. Then he smiled, abashedly. "Oh, it's you." He brought the notebook to his chest, almost shielding it from view, slipping a corner inside the lapel of his lab coat. He patted Benjamin's cheek with the other hand. "I'm so glad to see you. You have a minute to chat? Let's step into my office a moment."

Benjamin didn't care to speak to Soto-Prinz but

wasn't assertive enough to invent a reasonable excuse to slip away. But as Soto-Prinz inserted the key in the door's lock, Benjamin thought this might be a worthwhile meeting after all.

The office was not as garish as Benjamin had imagined it would be. It was decorated in Swedish inspired office furniture, the only discordant note a large maple banker's desk planted in front of a large window. The window looked out onto a small courtyard that led to the physician parking lot. Soto-Prinz's Rolls Royce was parked just outside, presumably so he could keep an adoring eye on it.

"Please, have a seat," Soto-Prinz said. He sat behind the desk, slipped his notebook in the center drawer. "What did you think of that little fund-raiser we had?"

"I didn't get to see much, really."

"Of course. Poor Pablo. What a dreadful affair that was," Soto-Prinz said, his face suddenly morose. "Dr. Medina had been struggling with substance abuse for some time. Few people knew. Please forgive me for not mentioning that fact at our first meeting but I was bound to uphold the duty of confidentiality required of my office. And I confess I'm guilty, as is usually the case in these situations, to have been deluded by a sense of hope in believing Dr. Medina might overcome his vice."

"His staff told me Pablo Medina had never touched hard drugs. Alcohol yes, the occasional joint, but not anything like this," Benjamin said.

"It's simply remarkable how well he hid it. He had us all fooled for the longest time. But these things always have a way of catching up with you."

Benjamin said nothing.

"Poor lad," Soto-Prinz said, "you must be terribly worried. But as long as you uphold the necessary requirements, your position at the clinic, and with El Dorado hospital, is secure. El Dorado will take over management of the clinic and open it under a new name. The Snow Clinic has a pleasant ring to it."

"What are the necessary requirements?"

Soto-Prinz tapped the side of his nose with his index finger. "That infant, the Sandoval baby, you discharged her from Purgatory Regional, yes?"

"She's doing fine."

"Well done, Benjamin. I confess that I would have preferred if you had admitted her here. After all, no one can match our facilities, and I was so keen to provide you with any assistance at my disposal. But you did a fine job, I'm told. The family must be very happy with you."

"They're relieved," Benjamin said.

"What are they like?"

"Who?"

"The baby's family?"

"I don't know. Mostly I spoke to the aunt."

"I see," Soto-Prinz said. He paused as if he were considering his next question. "Did you meet the father, per chance?"

"I did."

Soto-Prinz straightened. "You did? What's *he* like?"

"You don't know Fernando Ortega?"

The expression on the face of Dr. Soto-Prinz was a mix of relief and embarrassment. "Ortega… I've heard the name. Don't believe I ever met the man."

"That's strange," Benjamin said. "I got the impression he knew you personally."

Soto-Prinz looked at his wristwatch. "Heavens, it's already half past seven." He slipped open the center drawer of his desk, retrieved the leather bound notebook and got to his feet. Coming around the desk he said, "Benjamin, I'm so glad we had an opportunity to talk. We must do this again. Perhaps you'll come over for dinner one of these evenings. Mrs. Soto-Prinz will be happy to prepare you a home cooked meal. I vaguely remember that the life of a bachelor, despite all its perks, is one dismally lacking in the area of balanced nutrition. Do you like French cuisine?"

They walked out of the office together, Soto-Prinz keeping a herding arm on Benjamin's back all the way down the hallway until Benjamin stepped on an elevator with Soto-Prinz nodding a good-bye from the corridor.

Upstairs, Celestino was barefoot, washing a pair of blue polyester socks in the bathroom sink when Benjamin stepped in the room with the nurse who would serve as his interpreter.

"*Buenas tardes, doctor,*" Celestino said.

"*Buenas tardes,*" Benjamin replied.

"*Ah, muy bien! Su Espanol esta mejorando.*"

Benjamin chuckled. "*No, no. No hablo, no hablo.*" He pulled the stethoscope off his neck. "How is he?" he asked.

Celestino said, "*Convulsion? Nada!*"

"Nada?"

"*Ni una convulsion.*"

"That's great," Benjamin said. "*Muy bien. Muy bien.*"

Even though Benjamin was trying to smile, Celestino had clearly detected some sort of turmoil in the young doctor's spirit.

"*El niño esta muy, muy bien, doctor,*" Celestino said, as if to comfort him.

Benjamin examined the child. When a nurse walked in, he told her, "Please explain to him that we'll be able to get that gastric tube button, but we'll need his consent to proceed.

When the nurse finished translating, Celestino said, "*Si Dios quiere, doctor.*"

Benjamin was in no mood to chat with Celestino tonight. After writing his progress note and entering the necessary orders in the computer, he headed downstairs. He decided not to take the elevator, to avoid running into anyone who might try to engage him in conversation, opting instead for a stairwell in the corner of the ward. His steps echoed on the metal stairs as he hopped his way down, two steps at a time.

At the bottom of the stairwell there were two fire doors: one led inside the hospital; the other was an exit. Benjamin took the exit, not knowing were it would lead him. He found himself on a sidewalk, half-way between the Emergency Room entrance and the loading dock. He stood there a moment, looking at the dock door when it started rolling open, revealing a metal ramp in its interior. From the opposite direction, he heard the sound of a siren growing louder. He turned his head to look in the direction of the Emergency Room. Blue and red lights were circling on the sidewalk and on the corner of the building. Then an ambulance came into sight on the street.

It turned into the driveway of the Emergency Room and turned off its siren and lights as it came off the public street. Not terribly unusual Benjamin thought. But then the ambulance bypassed the Emergency Room, steered straight for the loading dock and went up the ramp. Immediately, the metal door started rolling down, but not fast enough. Benjamin just caught sight of Soto-Prinz appearing on the ramp by the ambulance's back door.

"There's no loitering," a voice behind him said.

Benjamin turned. The security guard who had spit in Jack Ryan's coffee the night he admitted Ikal was standing behind him.

"I'm a doctor," Benjamin said.

"Pardon *me*," the guard said, "I meant to say, there's no loitering here, doctor." He flashed Benjamin a smirk. "What are you doing out here?"

Benjamin patted his breast pocket. "Looks like I forgot my smokes."

The security guard eyed him suspiciously. Then he reached in a pocket, retrieved a pack of Newport's, tapped out a cigarette and offered it to Benjamin. "Strange habit for a doctor."

"Got a light?" Benjamin said, as he placed the cigarette between his lips.

The guard put the cigarettes away, pulled a lighter out of a different pocket and flicked it on. Only then did Benjamin notice he was wearing black leather gloves. The sight of the lighter in gloved hands sent an inexplicable chill down Benjamin's spine. "Just the kind of habit that'll kill you," the guard said. "You better move along."

Benjamin took a drag, exhaled and said, "Thanks." He walked away in the direction of the doctor's parking lot, erupting in a coughing fit within just a few steps.

38

The clinic remained closed the next day. Benjamin stuck around the office with a skeleton crew that remained to answer phone calls and turn away patients that insisted on knocking on the locked front door. Before noon, a sedate Ivan the Terrible advised him not to come back after lunch: his presence was only adding to the staff's anguish. Nothing personal.

Benjamin headed out to El Dorado to round on Ikal. The gastric tube button had been successfully inserted and the ward's clinical manager was dropping not-so-subtle hints that it was time to discharge the patient from the hospital.

"One more day," Benjamin said. "To make sure he's tolerating his feeds through the button."

"Tomorrow morning, then," the manager said.

He explained to Celestino that the child would be going home. The interpreter told Benjamin that, in that case, Celestino and Ikal would prepare their final farewells. He planned to start his journey to the Yucatan immediately.

Benjamin explained that wouldn't be safe. He'd prefer they stay in Purgatory a little longer.

"He says he has nowhere to stay," the nurse said.

Benjamin said, "Tell him not to worry. I think there's someone who can help us."

After finishing his work, while still seated at the nurse's station, Benjamin dialed the hospital operator. He felt a little ridiculous, the way his heart was pounding when he asked her who was on call for anesthesia tonight.

"Let's see," the operator said. "That would be Dr. Soto-Prinz. Would you like me to page him."

"No. Thanks." Benjamin hung up right away.

When he got home, Jesus and Ruben were playing catch in the cabbage field behind his house again. They stopped playing and jogged to the driveway as soon as they caught sight of Benjamin's truck. As soon as Benjamin stepped out of the vehicle, Jesus greeted him with a mischievous grin.

"Hey doc, you like pizza?"

"Sure I like pizza."

"So do we. Don't we Rube? Hey, I know! Why don't you order up a couple of pizzas. Look!" Jesus reached into his pocket and pulled out a crumpled piece of paper. "I got a coupon."

"You think of everything, don't you?" Benjamin said.

Ruben seemed distracted. As Benjamin and Jesus talked, the boy wandered up to Benjamin's truck, grabbed hold of a corner of the duct tape that had come unglued and, before Benjamin could stop him, ripped the patch off the door in one clean jerk.

Jesus stepped up to the side of the car, read the words etched in clean through the paint down into the metal. *Baby killer.* He couldn't get his eyes off it but didn't say anything.

Ruben tried to press the tape back onto the door but it wouldn't stick.

"Snowflake, you gotta bring your car down to

my uncle's shop. Told you, I can buff that out, paint over it so's it looks like new. Heck, we can paint the whole damn truck. How's a sweet candy rootbeer sound? Man, it would look *chingon*."

"Never mind that," Benjamin said. "Let's go inside. What kind of pizzas do you want?" Benjamin was about to slip his house key in the lock. He stopped. "Say, Jesus. You happen to have that lock pick set with you?"

"We didn't go inside this time," Jesus said. "Honest."

"You think you can teach me?" Benjamin said.

Jesus regarded him suspiciously. "Now why you want to learn to pick locks?"

"Never know. Case I forget my keys."

Jesus walked up to his bike, unfastened a pouch that was tied to the bottom of the seat and pulled out a piece of metal that looked like a tiny, flat corkscrew, along with a thin wrench. He walked up to Benjamin's front door and motioned for Benjamin to pay attention.

"This is called a Bogota. Easy to use. You slip in the tension tool first. Then rake with the wrench." Jesus gave it a couple of yanks, turned the lock and opened the door.

"That looked too easy," Benjamin said.

"Told you you had a flimsy lock."

Benjamin gave it a try. It took him twice as long but he was finally able to unlock the door. "Does this work on any lock?" he asked. Jesus flashed him a wily smile. "In case I get locked out of my office," Benjamin said.

"Then you're talking a commercial lock. That's six pins. Most residential locks only have five. Yeah, a Bogota can work, sometimes. Course when you rake inside the tumbler you leave scratches on the pins. If someone gets wise they can tell you broke in. You know what kind of lock your office has?"

"No idea."

"Of course if it's a lock with security pins, something like a Primus, a Medeco biaxle, or a Shlage Everest, you can try a hook pick, but that takes skill, and you still might not get it."

"Show me."

Jesus pulled out some other wrenches, demonstrated how to push up one pin at a time, then quickly turn the tumbler with the torsion wrench. Benjamin gave it a try. Couldn't do it.

"Don't worry," Jesus said. "Takes time, takes practice."

"I don't have time to practice. I have to do it tonight." Tomorrow morning he would discharge his only patient from El Dorado hospital. His mere presence there would be difficult to explain. Besides, he was getting antsy. It was time to get to the truth. And with Soto-Prinz being on call, he could be sure he would be at the hospital.

Jesus looked at him. "Rube is getting hungry. How 'bout we order that pizza and talk about it some more."

"Who's office are you gonna break into?" Jesus asked, as he grabbed a slice of pizza out of the box.

"I'd rather not tell you," Benjamin said.

"If you want my help I have to know what kind of lock you'll be up against."

"It's in a hospital."

"A hospital?" Jesus frowned. "This is about your friend, Dr. Rizzo, right?"

"I think I can find out who killed him," Benjamin said.

"Border Patrol killed him," Ruben said. Up until now he had hardly said a word. Now he made the utterance matter-of-factly.

Benjamin looked at him, stunned. "What did you say?"

"We saw it, right JT? It was the Border Patrol."

"Jeez, Snowflake," Jesus said. "I was gonna tell you sooner or later, but I didn't know how." Jesus went on to tell him about their stash of marijuana at Sanguinity Point, how they happened to be harvesting it when a Border Patrol vehicle pulled up, and how the agents killed Rizzo and left his body behind. He told him he phoned the cops anonymously, not that he expected Purgatory PD to solve the crime, but because poor Dr. Rizzo would have still been out there if he hadn't called.

"It doesn't make sense," Benjamin said.

"I'm just telling you what we saw," Jesus said.

"I've gotta get a hold of this little leather notebook," Benjamin said.

"What's in the notebook?" Jesus said.

"I'm not sure. An answer, I hope."

"I'll help you," Jesus said.

"No way. I can't let you get involved."

"Man, I was there. I'm already involved."

"I don't want to put you in any danger," Benjamin said.

"Danger's my middle name," Jesus said. "Besides, there's no way you're gonna open a commercial lock. You need me."

Benjamin slapped down the slice of pizza he was eating. "I don't know."

"Check this out. We walk in the hospital, you're a doctor, so no one thinks nothing about it. We slip in the office, get your little notebook and we're out in five minutes."

"Show me how to use that lock pick again."

"Dude, listen to me. You won't get it. You'll be stuck."

Benjamin knew Jesus was right.

"Okay, how's this," Jesus said. "Rube comes too. We bring the bike. Rube waits outside with the bike, in a bush or something — he's good at that. I go in with you, pick the lock and leave. Me and Rube come back here on the bike. You get your little notebook and we meet here. Take a little look-see together."

"I have to do this after eight, after visiting hours end and the hospital thins out. But I don't want the two of you riding your bike on the street in the dark."

"It ain't gonna get dark," Ruben said. "The harvest moon comes out tonight."

"You see. It ain't gonna get dark," Jesus said.

"Ruben knows."

Benjamin thought about it. "You think you can pick that lock?"

"I know *you* can't." Jesus figured out it wasn't the answer Benjamin was looking for. He changed his expression into one of cool confidence and said, "Sure I can pick it. Piece of cake."

"Eat your pizza," Benjamin said. "Let's sit tight and wait."

They loaded the bike in Benjamin's Xterra, drove all together to the edge of the patient lot where they dropped off Ruben and the bike in an area bordered by short cypresses. Benjamin and Jesus would enter through the Emergency Room. They could only hope it was a busy enough night to slip by unnoticed.

Benjamin parked in the doctor's lot, got into his white lab coat and the two headed towards the ER. Soto-Prinz's Rolls Royce was parked in the usual spot. Benjamin peered through the small courtyard and could see the lights were on in Soto-Prinz's office. He could just make out the back of the man's head, jutting above the chair's back rest. So far, so good.

The glass doors of the Emergency room slid open and Benjamin was already stepping through the threshold when Jesus stopped. Benjamin turned.

"What's the matter?"

Jesus whispered, "That wasn't no Border Patrol killed your friend."

Benjamin followed his gaze. Jesus was staring at

the hospital security kiosk where a green and white SUV was parked.

Benjamin could have kicked himself for not having made the connection. It was a mistake to bring thc boys. He knew it all along.

"We can turn back," Benjamin said.

"Not a chance," Jesus said. "Let's go."

The ER waiting room was nuts. They sailed through it without saying a word. Benjamin swiped his hospital ID card on a reader and they headed up a hallway towards the wing housing the office of Soto-Prinz. They stopped in a small waiting area.

Benjamin picked up a house phone and dialed for the operator.

"How can I direct your call?" the woman at the other end said.

Benjamin said, "Can you page anesthesia on call to the Emergency Department please? We need to take a patient to the OR stat."

"That's Dr. Soto-Prinz. You want me to try to put you through to his office?"

"There's no time. Have him come to bay five STAT."

"The patient's name?"

"Ortega," Benjamin said. "Fernando Ortega."

Benjamin and Jesus slouched in a padded sofa just behind a decorative wall. Not two minutes later, Dr. Soto-Prinz trotted by in the direction of the ER. They wouldn't have much time now.

Benjamin and Jesus sprinted up the hall, turned the corner into the corridor with the lady palms at either end. Jesus kneeled outside Soto-Prinz's door, opened his pouch of wrenches and started working on the lock.

After ten seconds Benjamin asked him, "How's it going?"

"I think I got the first pin."

"You *think* you got it?"

"Wait. No, I don't got it," Jesus said.

"I hate to rush you but…"

"Screw this," Jesus said. He pulled the tools out of the lock, dropped them in the pouch. He pulled out a silver key with rounded even cuts, a rubber ring at the shoulder.

"What's that?" Benjamin said.

"A bump key for a six cylinder lock. You got a hammer or a screw driver by any chance?"

"I have a reflex hammer," Benjamin said.

"That'll work."

Benjamin handed Jesus the reflex hammer. Jesus slipped the key in the lock, tapped the key's head with the reflex hammer and quickly turned the key. The lock opened.

"How come you didn't show me how to do *that*?" Benjamin said.

"Cause then you wouldn't have brought me. I told you, didn't I? I got your back."

The boy said the words with such earnestness, it melted Benjamin's heart. "Go get Ruben. Head on over to my place. But be careful."

"You sure you don't want me to stick around?" Jesus said.

"I got it from here," Benjamin said. "Now get the hell out of here."

Benjamin had calculated that Soto-Prinz would have the leather-bound notebook with him, but wouldn't risk bringing it to the Emergency Department when he might end up having to go to the OR. If he was right, the notebook, and its secrets, would be in that central drawer of the desk.

The lights were still on in the office. Benjamin went behind the desk but didn't dare sit in the chair. He slid open the drawer. And there it was.

He leafed through it. It was a ledger of some kind. Page after page of columns, the headers reading, arrivals and departures. Each row had a date, and a two or three digit number in the columns. Benjamin scrolled through the pages. He checked the date for the last entry. It was yesterday's date, the night he witnessed the ambulance rolling into the loading dock of the hospital.

He flipped to the back of the book. There was a list of phone numbers. He didn't recognize many of the names, but there were numbers for Fernando Ortega, Charles Moss, and — this one took Benjamin by surprise — Cyril Thompson.

Benjamin was still considering this when he heard the sound of a key grating inside the lock of the office.

39

There was no way Jesus was going to leave Snowflake alone to fend for himself. He had been on the street long enough to know that, when breaking and entering, you always need a lookout. He stood at the far end of the corridor, behind a potted palm.

What the hell was taking him so long? He should have got the notebook and got out right away. Maybe he couldn't find the notebook. Or the notebook had nothing and now he was looking for something else. Whatever he was doing in there, the man was taking way too long.

Jesus was about to go back to the office and knock on the door when he saw the old doctor turn the corner at the other end of the corridor. He looked pissed. Guess he didn't appreciate the little joke they played on him. More than pissed, he looked pissed and scared. A dangerous combination.

The guy pulled out a set of keys and was ready to slip one in the lock of his office. Jesus knew he had to do something fast.

He didn't have many options so he went with the first thing that popped in his head. He pulled his pants down to his knees, got into a spread-foot stance and started pissing on the potted lady palm. He called out, "Hey, old man! You work here?"

Soto-Prinz turned to look at him. The old man looked discombobulated, like he might have a heart attack right there on the spot.

Jesus said, "Who the hell is putting plants in my pots? Last time I almost sat on a cactus."

Soto-Prinz managed to mutter, "What on earth?"

Jesus started whistling a tune, swaying up and down. He splashed a trickle of urine on the wall. "Oops. My bad."

He could see Soto-Prinz was pacing toward him. It was time to zip up. Two more steps, then Soto-Prinz started running toward him screaming, "You little Mexican bastard!"

Jesus let him get closer. The key to baiting was to stay just far enough ahead that the pursuer doesn't abandon the chase. He needed to take the old man as far away from Snowflake as possible.

Jesus started walking away, turned the corner, still walked a few steps, then broke out into a comfortable jog when the old man turned the corner. Finally he started running — the old dude was really pissed now, shouting at him to stop. *Yeah whatever, old man.*

He turned just enough to flash him a mocking grin. More bait. But then something caught him hard on the shin. He tripped and flew head first onto the marble floor. Jesus felt someone grab his wrist and pull his arm hard against his back.

He heard the old guy say, "Tito, thank God. This little prick-"

"Is with your doctor," the guy putting a knee on his back said. "I got something to show you."

"Let's go to my office," the old man said.

The guy pulled Jesus up by the scruff of his neck, pulled out a knife and said, "You give me any trouble, I'll cut you up." Jesus recognized him. He was the dude that stabbed Joe Rizzo in the neck on Sanguinity Point.

They headed back toward Soto-Prinz's office. Maybe Snowflake was still there, hiding, ready to bash the security guy's head in as they walked through the door. Then they'd get away, go to the cops this time, get them arrested.

But the office was empty. At least Snowflake got away. But now he was really screwed. The security guard got a length of nylon rope and tied Jesus to a chair. The two men went behind the desk and the guard started fiddling around with a computer.

"The time stamp is eight-o-five pm," the guard said. "Camera number twelve, ER entrance." Jesus didn't have to see the screen to know they were watching Snowflake and him walking into the hospital.

"Who are you?" the old man asked.

"I'm yo' mama's pimp," Jesus said.

The security guard came around the desk and punched him hard in the gut.

"Don't get smart, little shit," the guard said. "You're in way above your head."

In an overly patient voice, the old man said, "Now let's try again, little boy. Who are you and what are you doing with Dr. Snow?" The blow had knocked the wind out of him and Jesus was having a hard time breathing, never mind talking. The guard was about to hit him again when the old man said, "Give him time.

I'd like to hear what he has to say before you knock every tooth out of his mouth." He walked around the desk, bent down near Jesus' ear and, in a grating fatherly voice said, "Just tell me who you are and what you're doing with Dr. Snow and we'll let you go back to your little shack on the river."

"Speak up," the guard said.

"What were you doing with Dr. Snow?"

"He's my doctor," Jesus said. "No lie. At the Medina clinic."

"And what were the two of you doing here tonight?"

"He wanted to run some tests on me," Jesus said.

"What kind of tests?"

Jesus said the first thing that came to his mind, "For leaky pipes."

"For what?" the old doctor said.

"You know, when you pee and it feels like needles. That's why I had to piss so bad, man. Couldn't make it to the toilet."

The old man looked at the security guard. The guard said, "He's lying."

The old man looked out the window pensively. His eyes widened. He shouted, "Blast!"

"What's the matter," the guard said.

"My window screen is missing," the old man said.

The guard hurried to the window, looked outside. "It's down here. Frame's all bent like someone knocked it out."

"Bloody hell!" The old man stumbled behind his desk, pulled open a drawer. "It's gone! My agenda is gone!"

Melgar smiled, "Looks like we're going to make a house call on Dr. Snow tonight."

When Benjamin heard the sound of the key slipping in the lock, he knew he was trapped. There would be no way to explain himself out of the situation. One option was to barrel straight into Soto-Prinz as he walked in the door. But he wanted some time to work things out, before Soto-Prinz could know for certain that it was Benjamin who stole the notebook.

He put the notebook in the side pocket of his lab coat, turned and slid open the window. But then the damn window screen wouldn't come off. He gave it a good kick. The flimsy aluminum frame bent but it was still stuck in place. Benjamin leaned into it with all his weight and it finally popped out. Before stepping out the window, he looked back at the door and couldn't believe Soto-Prinz hadn't walked through yet. He climbed over the ledge, slid the window shut, and ran out across the courtyard into the doctor's parking lot.

That was damn close! He still couldn't believe his luck as he drove out of the lot.

40

The harvest moon spilled a yellow glare across the landscape, blunting the shadows of trees and road signs, as though the shadows themselves were being drawn into the earth by a hungry, mysterious force. Benjamin's head was swimming as he drove home.

There was so much to think about, to analyze, to reconsider. One thing was clear: everything was connected; like a disease with myriad symptoms, each symptom connected to the other either through a cascade of biochemical events or as a result of anatomic determinism. The difference was that here the web had been spun with the sticky substrate of human emotions: greed, fear, conceit, vanity, ambition. And like a systemic disease, there would be no cure, no elixir that could possibly restore homeostatic balance. The best he could hope for, at this point, was to find a way to get through the current crisis, survive the golden hour. And the highest priority was to find the boys.

He was relieved to see the reflector of the bike as he came over the culvert of the irrigation canal. He flashed his brights a couple of times and only then realized there was only one boy on the bike. It was Ruben, pedaling furiously.

Benjamin slowed as he approached the bike, lowered the passenger side window. Ruben looked over his left shoulder, his eyes bulging. He stopped pedaling and hopped onto the pavement, letting the bike roll into the ditch on the side of the road. The boy lunged towards the SUV, but instead of opening the passenger door, he mounted the running board with the vehicle still moving and shouted to Benjamin, "Don't stop! Don't stop!"

Benjamin let the vehicle roll without accelerating.

"Where's Jesus?" Benjamin asked.

Ruben shook his head. "He got him. He's gonna kill him."

"What? Who got him?"

By now they were approaching Benjamin's driveway. He turned and let the front of the car roll just onto the driveway and stopped, letting the engine run.

"We gotta go back," Ruben said.

"Tell me what happened,"

"The Border Patrol got him," Ruben said. "I saw it. Same guy that killed your friend."

"We've got to call the police."

"You crazy, man? He *is* the police."

"Listen to me, Ruben. That guy's not Border Patrol."

He was reaching for his phone when he heard a car approaching. Saw it just as it crossed the irrigation canal.

"Ruben, get down. Get under the truck, don't make a sound."

He could already make out the distinctive front grill of the car. It was Soto-Prinz's Rolls Royce. It stopped some twenty feet short of Benjamin's driveway. Soto-Prinz emerged from the driver's door, the lanky security guard from the passenger side, pointing a gun at

Benjamin.

"Step out of the vehicle, Dr. Snow."

Benjamin dropped his phone on the passenger seat, on top of Soto-Prinz's leather-bound notebook. He got out of the truck.

"Good evening, Benjamin," Soto-Prinz said. "For a moment I was worried we wouldn't find you at home. Forgive us if we can't stay too long. Now, it seems you have something in your possession that doesn't belong to you."

"Where's the boy?" Benjamin said.

"Dear heavens, what boy?" There was a thumping sound coming from the rear of the Rolls Royce. "Oh. *That* boy. He's quite comfortable, I assure you. These cars have very spacious trunks."

"I have what you want. I'll trade you for the boy."

"Were it that simple, Dr. Snow. I wish we could negotiate. I truly do, but by now I surmise you've seen the contents of the agenda. It pains me, the way you've betrayed my trust. Was I not generous with you? Didn't I provide you with a golden opportunity? Compensated you handsomely? Now, see how you've gone and spoiled it all."

"Then take me. Let the boy go."

"Well come along, then. Bring the agenda."

"The boy goes free."

The security guard racked the slide of the gun.

Soto-Prinz said, "It appears your negotiating position is feeble at best. Tito, can you escort Dr. Snow to the back seat of the car. If he resists, shoot him."

Tito said, "If I have to come all the way over there, you'll be sorry."

Benjamin stared at the gun. He could almost feel the weight of it as though it were in his own hand. He imagined the cold fullness of the grip against his palm, the stiffness of the trigger on his index finger, and was surprised to find that he felt no apprehension.

"You know about Nolan Ryan?" Benjamin said. He said it loud enough to make sure Ruben was listening from his hiding spot." Soto-Prinz exchanged a confused look with Tito. "He was a baseball pitcher."

"I bloody well know who he is," Soto-Prinz said.

"Well did you know how fast he pitched? Why, he could throw a ball so fast," he paused, hoping Ruben was paying attention, "blind people would come to hear him pitch."

Soto-Prinz said, "What in heavens name are you gibbering about?"

"Honest to God," Benjamin continued with a chuckle. "That's how fast he could throw. So fast *deaf* people would come out to hear him pitch.'

"He's gone mad," Soto-Prinz said.

"I thought it appropriate to bring up because, right now, all we got is the fastball." Benjamin was sure Ruben could hear him. If he could only get through to him. Let him understand what he needed to do. "All we got, Ruben, is the freaking fastball!"

There was a hollow thunk and Tito's head whipped back. A baseball bounced off his forehead and his body crumbled onto the pavement. The gun fell to the floor and skidded a couple of feet away. Benjamin sprinted towards it.

Soto-Prinz was still trying to make out what had happened. He seemed paralyzed for a moment, but when Benjamin reached down for the gun, the old doctor jumped in his car. For a moment Benjamin thought he'd try to run him over, but the Rolls Royce took off in reverse, made a sloppy maneuver to turn around and sped off in the direction of the irrigation canal.

Ruben jogged next to Benjamin. He said, "What do we do?"

At Benjamin's feet, Tito was starting to come to.

"Give me a hand, Rube."

They grabbed Tito by the legs, dragged him down the street, onto Benjamin's driveway and plopped him with his back leaning on one of the barber poles. Benjamin found a set of handcuffs on Tito's belt and used them to secure the man's hands behind his back onto the pole.

"I have to go after them," Benjamin said.

"Sanguinity Point. They're going to Sanguinity Point," Ruben said.

Benjamin ran to his truck. Got his phone, tossed it to Ruben. "You stay here, call the police."

"But I don't trust the police!" Ruben said.

"Call them!"

Benjamin pushed the gear shifter into four-wheel drive. Soto-Prinz had a head start but maybe he could make up for lost time. He sped forward, to the end of his driveway and onto the cabbage field. He knew the other side of the field bordered the highway to Myrtle's guest ranch. From there it was a straight shot to Presidio highway and to Sanguinity Point.

The truck lurched as its wheels went in and out of plow lines. He could hardly hear over the sound of cabbages bouncing off the undercarriage with the force of bowling balls. As he neared the end of the field, he accelerated to plow through a cedar post and barbed wire fence and screeched to the left when the wheels finally gripped pavement.

He turned onto Presidio highway and could just make out the rear lights of a single vehicle. It had to be Soto-Prinz's Rolls. He kept the gas pedal pressed to the floor. Even so, he was losing ground. A couple of miles later, he saw the Rolls Royce veering left onto the caliche path to Sanguinity Point.

Benjamin did his best to keep pace but there was so much dust kicked up he could only see a few feet in front of him. There was a fork in the road where the path met a tree line. Benjamin pressed down on the brake and the SUV slid to a halt. He could no longer see the tail lights. He turned the wheel counterclockwise and pushed on. Just around a bend, the path dead-ended onto a berm off the river bank.

He braked, thrust the shifter in reverse and drove backwards as fast as he could. Back at the fork in the road he skidded to the right and accelerated down the other path. It led onto a grassy field. He could see the the Rolls Royce, the lights still on. Standing next to the open trunk, Fermin Soto-Prinz was clutching Jesus by the hair, his other hand pressing the tip of a dagger's blade against the boy's throat. Even with his hands bound behind his back, the boy looked as defiant as ever.

Benjamin came to a stop. He grabbed the notebook and Tito's handgun from the passenger seat and stepped out of the car. He started walking toward Soto-Prinz, pointing the gun in a one-handed grip, his finger off the trigger.

"Let him go!" Benjamin shouted.

"Have you ever actually shot a firearm in your entire life, Dr. Snow?" Soto-Prinz said.

Benjamin pointed the gun in the air and let off a round. He was surprised. He had expected there to be more recoil. Mostly he was surprised at how easy it had been to pull the trigger. He brought the gun down again and pointed it at Soto-Prinz.

Soto-Prinz laughed. "I am very impressed. Of course, if you intend to shoot me, you had better aim very carefully indeed, or you might hit your little friend."

"Shoot the old fart!" Jesus yelled out.

Benjamin kept pacing toward them until Soto-Prinz said, "That's close enough. I'm quite handy with this dagger and I know the anatomy of the neck well enough to find the carotid artery in a jiff."

"I have your agenda," Benjamin said, holding the notebook up over his head. "Just let him go."

"I can't tell you how disappointed I am, Benjamin. I had such big plans for you. I was planning to groom you for a splendid career."

"You killed Joe Rizzo," Benjamin said.

"That was an extremely difficult decision I was forced to make. He was not trustworthy. He knew things that might have put our whole operation at risk."

"He knew the truth about the baby. Knew who her father is. That's why you had him killed."

Soto-Prinz seemed to loosen his grip on Jesus' hair. "I couldn't take a chance. We've come so bloody close now. Rizzo was an incalculable entity. Far too volatile to be able to discern his intentions."

"Well, I'm very practical. You have nothing to worry about," Benjamin said. "I want to protect Fatima too. Here's the notebook. I'll toss it to you."

"I'm sorry about Dr. Rizzo," Soto-Prinz said, "He left me no choice."

Benjamin said, "Let's make a deal." He lobbed the agenda. It landed at Soto-Prinz's feet.

"Now toss me the gun and I'll let the boy go," Soto-Prinz said.

Benjamin hesitated.

"Don't do it!" Jesus yelled out.

Benjamin turned the gun around in his hand, held it by its barrel. He brought his arm back, ready to lob it. He knew he had only one chance to get this right. He swung his arm and let go of the gun. The gun flew in a soft arc and landed a little closer to Soto-Prinz than Benjamin would have liked.

Now it was Soto-Prinz who was thinking things through. Benjamin could read his mind, was following along the calculations going through the old man's head. It was going to go down soon. He was waiting for the moment, his muscles already taut to spring into action, like a runner waiting for the sound of the starting gun. And then it happened. Soto-Prinz pushed Jesus face first into the turf and darted towards the gun.

Benjamin was ready. He sprinted in the direction of the gun, planning the length of his strides, timing his steps. He thought of Dennis Walker, Walker the Stalker. One last time, in his mind's eye he replayed the Stalker's movements. The key was to slide in with both feet, then bring them up, be sure to lock in square on the supporting leg.

Soto-Prinz was already leaning down, his hand about to grasp the gun.

Benjamin hoped he wouldn't land short. He began his slide. He felt his left foot make contact first, at the level of Soto-Prinz's ankle. His right foot slammed in at the middle of the shin, tore through with the momentum of a battering ram. He felt the snap of brittle bones, heard a wail of agony.

Benjamin rolled out of the slide tackle and onto to his feet. Soto-Prinz was on his back, sobbing and screaming. Benjamin picked up the gun, popped out the magazine and put it in his pocket, flipped the safety on and slipped the gun in his belt. He had done all the shooting he cared to do for one night. He walked over to Jesus Tamez who had managed to get to his knees, picked up Soto-Prinz's dagger from the turf and cut Jesus free of his binds.

"You okay, buddy?" Benjamin said.

Jesus said, "You the man, Snowflake. You the man."

Benjamin and Jesus walked over to Soto-Prinz who was still wailing. Benjamin was about to kneel to take a look at that leg but there was a flash of headlights that made him stop and turn. Several vehicles made their way onto the field and encircled Benjamin and Jesus. They were not police vehicles.

Juan, Ortega's chauffeur, got out of one vehicle and walked over to Soto-Prinz, his gun drawn. Ruben jumped out of the back seat of another SUV, ran up to Jesus and hugged him. Fernando Ortega followed him out, ambled towards Benjamin.

"I thought I told you to call the police," Benjamin told Ruben.

"I told you, I don't never trust the cops," Ruben said. "But you had the phone number of *El Chacal* on your phone, and I thought, if he's a friend of the doctor, he can help us. No one's stronger than *El Chacal*."

"Smart kid," Ortega said. "We picked him up at your house, along with that scum bag you shackled to your porch. He already confessed to murdering your friend, Joe Rizzo."

Benjamin turned to see Soto-Prinz getting loaded by Juan and another goon into the back bay of an SUV.

"What's going to happen to them?" Benjamin asked.

Ortega shrugged. "A poet once said, 'Justice does not descend from its own pinnacle.' It's not up to me. My guess, they're not coming back."

Benjamin stooped down. Picked up Soto-Prinz's leather bound notebook and handed it to Ortega. Ortega flipped through the pages, looked up at Benjamin and said, "Come, let's talk."

They sat alone, in the back seat of a bullet-proof Suburban.

"I don't know how much you've been able to piece together," Ortega said.

"I don't want the kids to get hurt. They know nothing," Benjamin said.

"You still think I'm a drug dealer. I've never sold so much as a joint in my whole life. What I am is an interceder. I'm a highly specialized accountant working for a private interest. I move money, make it jump through hoops, and still keep track of every penny. I'm well compensated because I'm fastidious with my accounts."

"The ambulances at the loading dock."

"That was Soto-Prinz's idea. Load an ambulance with bundles of cash, turn on the sirens. No cop's gonna ever pull it over."

"So El Dorado's just a huge money-laundering operation," Benjamin said.

"Not at all. El Dorado's been a boon to the community. Elevated the quality of medical care in these parts more than you can imagine. Purgatory needs El Dorado."

"But it wasn't good enough for baby Fatima."

"That was a different matter."

The two men sat in silence for a couple of minutes.

"I want to meet with him," Benjamin said.

"Who?"

"Come on, Mr. Ortega. You don't think I'm *that* naive."

41

The limo driver was a thin black man with a gray goatee and penetrating hazel eyes. He wore a black suit, white shirt, and a jade bolo tie.

"Did you have a nice flight, Dr. Snow?" he said as he pulled away from the curb at Austin-Bergstrom International airport.

"Nice and short," Benjamin said. It was slow going up highway 183. "Is it rush hour already?"

The driver chuckled. "It's always rush hour in Austin. Don't worry. We don't have too far to go."

Fifteen minutes later the limo exited the highway and turned left on East 7th Street. They were moving along steadily now, catching one green light after another.

Benjamin leaned his head back and closed his eyes. It wasn't time to rest. Not yet. In his mind, he rehearsed the key points he wanted to make. He recalled his first encounter with Dr. Soto-Prinz, how the man had forced him to eat a slice of ham to fulfill his hideous requirement. This time it was Benjamin who needed some assurances, who would set the agenda for the meeting.

He opened his eyes when he felt the limo turning right. There, down Congress Avenue, stood the Texas Capitol. It was a sprawling building, imposing to the point of provocation. How appropriate, Benjamin thought.

The limo pulled over in the middle of the next

block, in front of a twenty story glass office building. Cyril Thompson was standing at the curb. He opened the limousine's door from the outside. Benjamin thanked the driver and stepped out.

Cyril and Benjamin walked through the marble lobby of the office building to a bank of elevators. Cyril pushed the button for the 14th floor, took a look at his watch and settled in a military at-ease pose.

"He's eager to see you," Cyril said.

Benjamin nodded.

As they were passing the tenth floor, Cyril said, "Doctor, if I can say something, at the risk of sounding impertinent, you're really something. You know that?"

They walked down a brightly lit hallway whose walls were decorated with photographs of Texas wildlife. Cyril stopped in front of a door on which hung a heavy bronze plaque engraved with a Texas star. He knocked on the door.

A voice inside said, "Come on in."

Cyril shook Benjamin's hand and said, "I'll be standing out here, in case you need anything."

Benjamin stepped inside the office and Cyril shut the door behind him. Troy Davenport walked around his desk, greeted Benjamin with a two-handed shake, and led him to a chair, his hand lingering on Benjamin's shoulder. Davenport sat on the corner of his desk.

"I'm so glad you decided to come to Austin, Dr. Snow. I've been wanting to talk to you for some time, but circumstances didn't allow it. First, I want to thank you for-"

"Taking care of your daughter?" Benjamin said. "Or keeping my mouth shut about it?"

Davenport leaned back, crossed his arms.

"I want you to know, Fatima means the world to me. We are creatures of free-will, Dr. Snow, and yet we are tossed and tumbled about in the currents of the river of life like so much flotsam and jetsam."

"Ain't that the truth," Benjamin said.

Davenport got to his feet, paced towards a window facing the Capitol. "I met Fernando Ortega at Texas A&M. We were both undergrads. He was studying business; I was a political science major. We lived in the same dorm but I didn't know him until one night, I was coming back home late from the library and a vagrant tried to mug me with a knife. Fernando came to my rescue. That was it. We were friends for the next four years, played tennis together, went drinking together, typical college buddies. After graduation we went our separate ways, ran into each other a few times at functions and fundraisers but really didn't keep in touch.

"Then one day, a week after I announced my bid for the Texas House, he calls me out of the blue. He tells me he wants to contribute to my campaign. Great, I say. And then he tells me there's a whole PAC interested in supporting me, but the members want to meet me first, kick the tires, so to speak."

"So you went to Purgatory," Benjamin said.

"The first of many trips."

"And you met Sofia."

"Not on that first trip. One evening, after a

fund-raiser, we went to Fernando's hacienda for dinner. He invited Veronica, whom he already had been seeing for some time, and she brought along her kid sister, Sofia. Sofia was… well, she was unlike anyone I had ever met. She was dignified and pure. I knew that night, I had found my soul-mate."

"And your wife?"

Davenport put his hands in his pockets. "She knows nothing. I'd like to keep it that way. No reason for her to suffer for my sins. But I'm not ashamed of my love for Sofia. And I pray every night that Fatima turns out more like her mother than her father. So if you were to walk out this door, walk straight down Congress Avenue to the local newspaper and tell them what you know, I would deny nothing."

"Even if I were to tell them everything," Benjamin said, "you wouldn't stop me?"

"That's right."

It's what Benjamin needed to hear. Davenport knew nothing of the killings; nothing of the murder of Joe Rizzo, of the death of Pablo Medina, of the mysterious disappearance of Fermin Soto-Prinz. Just like on that night in College Station, Fernando Ortega was still protecting him — shielding him from the darker impulses of tawdry men.

"What would I gain by doing that?" Benjamin said.

"What would you lose?"

"An opportunity. I'm not here to black mail you, Mr. Davenport."

Davenport took his hands out of his pocket,

took a few steps in Benjamin's direction and rested his hand on his desk. "I'm listening."

"Are you a pragmatist, Mr. Davenport?"

"Depends on what you mean by the word."

"Well, I am. I believe in creating the greatest possible good for the largest number of people, by analyzing contingencies and weighing outcomes."

Davenport smiled. "Looks like you got it all figured out."

"I do," Benjamin said. "You better get Fernando Ortega on the phone."

42

Benjamin was driving past the turn-off to Sanguinity Point, listening to his Spanish lesson on CD, repeating elementary phrases at the prompts, when his cell phone rang. A familiar voice greeted him when he answered.

"Hey, Snowflake, where you been?"

"What's up, JT?" Benjamin said.

"Dude, your truck's ready. Better than new. The undercarriage is still banged up but you can't see that 'less you look. Got a new front fender from the junkyard and, man! We gave her a sick new paint job! The color? Now that's my surprise for you."

"You're scaring me now."

Jesus Tamez laughed. "When you gonna come pick her up? We gotta go cruisin' baby!"

"Forget cruising for a minute," Benjamin said. "How'd you do on your first math quiz?"

"Smoked it! Got a seventy-six."

"Not bad," Benjamin said. "There's room for improvement. How about Ruben?"

"I'll let him tell you. The *cabron* is standing right here."

"Hello?" Ruben's voice twanged with a nasal pitch over the phone.

"Hey, Rube," Benjamin said.

Before Benjamin could get another word in, Ruben blurted out, "Eighty-two."

"You got an eighty-two?"

"Eighty-two. Like a fast-ball."

"That's awesome. Did you know you were good at math?"

"No. Because high school sucked. I like GED better."

"I'm proud of you, Gandalf."

Ruben never heard the words. Jesus was back on the line. "When we going cruisin'?"

"Soon, JT. Real soon."

In the Autumn morning sunlight, the dirt road to El Milagro clinic reflected a new palette of colors. The tones were softer, as if the land were projecting a cautious optimism.

A bungalow set on cinder blocks had a fresh coat of paint. Benjamin was glad to see it; happy to realize that he had become familiar enough with the landscape to have noticed the change. A little boy wearing nothing but tiny boxers, yellow galoshes and a straw cowboy hat waved to him bashfully from the front porch of another home. Benjamin lowered the car window to wave back at him.

Virgil Thibodeaux's Land Rover was the only vehicle parked outside the clinic. Benjamin pulled up next to it, killed the engine, reached over to grab a box wrapped in brown paper from the passenger's seat, and got out of the car.

He was half-way across the lot when Claire burst out of the front door, took a couple more steps and stopped on the edge of the front porch.

"New wheels?" she asked as Benjamin

approached her.

"It's a rental," Benjamin said.

"What's in the box?"

"A little present for Virgil."

Claire smiled. "Haven't seen you around for a while. Guess your clavicle is all healed."

"I had to go out of town, take care of a few things."

Claire nodded. "For a moment, I thought you left for good without saying good-bye," she said.

"I didn't."

"I know, Myrtle told me you hadn't moved out yet. Pops said you'd be back."

"So you've been snooping on me," Benjamin said.

"Just checking on you. It's horrible what happened to Pablo Medina. I heard you resigned from El Dorado. You know Soto-Prinz is still missing. Guess who they selected as interim CEO?"

"Krippendorff."

Claire let out a little snort. She looked off in the distance. Her eyes were flitting, as though she were having difficulty deciding what to focus on. "I guess now you'll really be looking for that critical care fellowship."

"Didn't even have to look. The director of a program in Chicago called me up. One of their first-years dropped out. Asked for my resume. He's willing to take me start January."

"Well, there you go," Claire said, matter-of-factly.

"How's the clinic?" Benjamin said.

Claire was scanning him with a suspicious eye, trying to decipher that mischievous smile Benjamin could no longer contain.

"Well you're not going to believe this," she said, finally unable to curb her enthusiasm. "The president of Rio Grande Merchant Bank calls Pops last week, invites us to come meet with him at his office, doesn't bother to say what it's all about. We get there and he has us sit down in these alligator skin chairs and hands Virgil a check for a hundred and fifty thousand dollars. Says it's from a philanthropist he represents who admires our work but prefers to remain anonymous. Tells us this is only the first installment, that this guy wants to fund us over the long term. Only proviso is part of the money has to be used to recruit another physician."

"Well, that's great!" Benjamin said, trying to sound surprised. The only surprise was that Fernando Ortega had apparently decided to grant fifty-thousand dollars more than what Benjamin had asked of him.

"You looking for a job?" Claire asked, playfully.

"I already have a new gig," Benjamin replied.

Claire looked down. "Yeah, I was just kidding."

"But you would hire me?"

Claire looked up at him, brushed a strand of hair behind her ear. "Yeah, I'd hire you. I think you're trainable. And Virgil was kinda getting used to having you around."

Benjamin waited, feeling a bit underhanded, to see if there was more she might divulge, but then the clinic's door opened and Virgil Thibodeaux stepped out.

"Good morning, pilgrim," Virgil said.

"How are you, Virgil?"

"Swell, my boy. Just dandy." He popped a pecan in his mouth and started chewing. "What's in the box?"

"A little something for you," Benjamin said.

"A present? I love presents. Can I open it now?"

"Be my guest."

Benjamin handed him the package. Virgil tore off the brown paper wrapping unceremoniously, letting it fall on the floor. He lifted the top flaps of the box and peered inside. His face lit up.

"Won't you look at that!" Virgil said. "Well, hello gorgeous!"

He reached inside the box and pulled out a mask, held it up and turned it to admire it. The mask was carved of basswood, stained a coffee brown. It had large white eyes pierced by tiny round eye holes, a long aquiline nose and broad twisted lips

Benjamin said. "It's a Fake Face mask, native American. It was used for healing diseases and changing bad behavior."

Virgil grunted in approval.

Benjamin said, "The Iroquois knew they couldn't kill bad spirits — they didn't have that sort of power. But with the right mask they could at least keep them at bay."

"Did you try it on?"

"I wore it for a little while," Benjamin said.

"Did it fit?"

"Surprisingly well."

Virgil chuckled. "I guess you found your alter ego." Virgil eyed Benjamin with a mock stern expression. "If I didn't know better I'd surmise you're trying to butter me up, bringing me a present and all."

"Perhaps I am, Dr. Thibodeaux," Benjamin said. "Perhaps I am."

"Either way," Virgil extended his hand to Benjamin, "welcome aboard!"

Benjamin got to his feet, shook Virgil's hand. He was about to release his grip when Virgil pulled him in for a bear hug and whispered, "Welcome home, son."

"Can someone tell me what the hell is going on here?" Claire said.

"I forgot to tell you. Dr. Snow is our new pediatrician," Virgil said. "I offered him the position and he happily accepted. I hope you don't mind I didn't consult you on this one but I was pretty sure you wouldn't object."

"I thought you said you were doing a fellowship in Chicago," Claire said.

"I only said there was an opening there," Benjamin said. "I turned them down."

"But you just told me you had a new gig."

"This *is* my new gig."

Claire crossed her arms in mock exasperation. "I don't know if I'll be able to deal with the both of you day in, day out." She stepped up to Benjamin and extended her hand. "Welcome to El Milagro. I hope we're not over-paying you."

"I think he's going to easily cover his salary," Virgil said. "He's got two new patients scheduled this morning already. Your fame precedes you, Dr. Snow."

A black Chevy Suburban with darkly tinted windows rolled into the dirt lot and parked in the spot nearest to the clinic's entrance.

Virgil said, "I imagine that's them right there."

Veronica Sandoval stepped out of the driver's seat of the SUV, waved at Benjamin and opened the rear door. She struggled a moment before extracting an infant's car seat. Meantime, Celestino hopped out of the passenger side, and with a broad smile called out, "*Buenos dias Doctor. Como amanecio'?*

"Muy bien, Señor Celestino," Benjamin replied. "*Gracias.*"

"Someone's practicing their Spanish," Claire said, leaning into Benjamin.

"I figured I better start learning, seeing as I'm staying."

Celestino pulled a folded wheelchair from the back of the Suburban, quickly opened it, and in no time was transferring Ikal into the padded seat from the back of the Suburban.

"*Ya se sta ponendo gordo,*" Celestino said.

"Help me with that one," Benjamin whispered to Claire.

"He said the boy's getting fat already."

Veronica approached the front porch, Celestino and Ikal just behind her.

"Welcome to El Milagro clinic," Benjamin said.

"Thank you," Veronica said. "Thank you for everything."

"I'm the one who should thank you," Benjamin

said. He glanced momentarily at Celestino.

"Are you kidding? He's the best handy man we've ever had. And he sure knows his way around a garden with a rake and a machete."

Virgil stepped up, took the car seat holding baby Fatima from Veronica and shook her hand. He said, "I'm Virgil Thibodeaux. So glad to have you here. Allow me give you the grand tour."

Virgil escorted the visitors inside the clinic leaving Benjamin and Claire alone again.

"Are you sure about this?" Claire said.

"Yeah, I'm sure."

"You're giving up a lot."

"Am I?"

Claire studied his expression.

"All along," she said, "even when I first met you, something told me you'd be ready."

"Ready for what?"

"For your defining moment. You did well, I can tell."

Benjamin said nothing. Had he really done so well? He had once told Claire and Virgil that he was a pragmatist. True to his word, he had found a way to be brutally pragmatic. He had managed to contrive a scheme whose sole purpose was to achieve the best possible results, unaffected by the superfluous romantic urge to consider the virtue of the methods employed.

"You did well," Claire repeated. "It's time to rest your weary heart."

An autumn breeze rustled from the south. It carried the now familiar scents of this strange land. A gust picked up — a warm cleansing wind. Claire and Benjamin huddled together, they grasped each other in a tentative embrace.

Benjamin closed his eyes and savored the moment. He didn't know what else the future had in store for him. Didn't know what challenges tomorrow would bring or if he'd be up to the task. It didn't matter. There was one thing he was sure of. Somehow, he had found the place where he belonged.

A WORD FROM THE AUTHOR

Thank you for reading Sanguinity Point. I truly hope you enjoyed my novel. If you did, won't you please leave a short review on Amazon and GoodReads? Independent authors such as myself do not have a huge advertising budget and every honest reader review helps. And since writing is a lonely process, it's nice to get feedback from our readers from time to time.

Also, please be sure to download my first novel, The Art of Forgetting, winner of the 2014 North Texas Book Festival.

Good reading!

Peter Palmieri
New Braunfels
December 12, 2017

Made in the USA
Middletown, DE
30 December 2017